# Praise for

'Donald has taken the legendary berserkers, those frothing-at-the-mouth shield-biters, and made them human, which once again proves that Donald is a writer not only at the top of *his* game, but of *the* game ... It is a wonderful, rich and violent brew. A tale worthy of the skalds'

Giles Kristian, author of the Raven series

'With *The Last Berserker*, Donald has given us the first cut of some serious Dark Age beef. By turns heart-racing, intriguing and touching, this is not a book for the faint-hearted – I can't wait for more'

Theodore Brun, author of *A Burning Sea*

'*The Last Berserker* strikes with the thundering power of Thor's hammer. The tale of young Bjarki Bloodhand finding his calling as a fabled berserker is rich with the earthy depth, historical detail, intrigue, violence and adventure that we expect from Donald. But it is the likeable duo at the heart of the novel, Bjarki and Tor, that makes *The Last Berserker* stand out. Donald's masterful creations will live on in the imagination long after the final page'

Matthew Harffy, author of the Bernicia Chronicles

'A wonderful, blood-soaked tale of redemption and revenge, set amidst the eighth century clash of civilisations between Pagan Vikings and Christian Franks, by a master of the genre'

Saul David, author of *Zulu Hart*

'Well researched detail and stunning battle scenes make *The Last Berserker* a white knuckle ride. A thrilling, up-all-night read'

C. R. May, author of *The Day of the Wolf*

# Blood of the Bear

Angus Donald is the author of the bestselling Outlaw Chronicles, a series of ten novels set in the 12th/13th centuries and featuring a gangster-ish Robin Hood. Angus has also published the Holcroft Blood trilogy about a mildly autistic 17th-century English artillery officer, son of notorious Crown Jewels thief Colonel Thomas Blood. Before becoming an author, Angus worked as a fruit-picker in Greece, a waiter in New York City and as an anthropologist studying magic and witchcraft in Indonesia. For fifteen years he was a journalist working in Hong Kong, India, Afghanistan and London. He now writes full time from a medieval farmhouse in Kent.

www.angusdonaldbooks.com

# Also by Angus Donald

## Fire Born

# BLOOD OF THE BEAR

## ANGUS DONALD

🔟 CANELO

First published in the United Kingdom in 2024 by

Canelo
Unit 9, 5th Floor
Cargo Works, 1-2 Hatfields
London SE1 9PG
United Kingdom

A CIP catalogue record for this book is available from the British Library.

Print ISBN 978 1 80436 235 8
Ebook ISBN 978 1 80436 234 1

Cover design by kid-ethic

Cover images © Shutterstock

Look for more great books at www.canelo.co

Printed and bound in Great Britain by Clays Ltd, Elcograf S.p.A.

1

# Prologue

## A bargain struck in darkness

The hooded man paused outside the entrance of the low, reed-built hut and shivered. But not from the cold, damp climate of this northern marsh. It was fear. Pure and simple. Fear of this place; terror of the powerful one who lurked inside this dwelling.

A pair of otter skulls on short ash poles guarded the entrance, set up on either side of a greasy leather flap that served as a door. The huge nasal cavities of these long-dead animals seemed to yawn like extra mouths, the two long canines extending down from the upper jaw appeared as a pair of monstrous fangs, and the bone itself had been stained brown with sacrificial blood.

The hooded man made the sign of the holy cross, his right finger moving from crown to chest, then left shoulder over to right. But, even as he made it, he doubted the protection this habitual gesture would offer him. Strong magic was here. He could smell it. He was breathing in its stench. Foul magic, the essence of sin – *seithr*, they called it – and the hooded man knew its author, the individual who could summon the demonic powers, they said, and shape them to his malign will.

They called him the Crow, and this was his nest. This reed-walled hut with tendrils of smoke seeping from the roof. Evil lurked within.

The hooded man was no coward, yet coming so close to this damp dwelling in southern Jutland unmanned him, it filled his guts with an icy chill. His immortal soul was at peril. He felt far away from God, and from his only son Jesus Christ. Far away from his own home and all that he knew. Yet this dark deed must be done. He did it to further the glory of the Lord of Hosts. And so it was surely God's will. A marsh bird shrieked in the distance, the sound like a girlish scream, and the hooded man started violently. He cursed himself for a foolish child, afraid of strange noises in the dark.

'Christ, protect me in this place,' he whispered.

It was deep dusk, the witching hour, and a light rain was beginning to fall.

He stepped forwards and entered the foetid interior. He called out a greeting in a voice full of false boldness, but there was no reply. Yet, crouched over a few embers in the sunken hearth, he could easily make out a small figure in the darkness. The hooded man heard the exhalation of breath and saw the embers glow brighter, and a cloud of some kind of dark powder falling upon the glowing coals…

A bright flash of light, searing to the eyes, and the impression of a short, stooped figure, in a dark, hairy cloak, the garment bedecked with seaweed, bones and shells, his face painted fantastically with red, black and white whorls… Then the image was gone, back to the darkness. The hooded man's eyes burned.

'You came alone?' the Crow said.

'I did,' replied the hooded man. 'As you instructed me to.'

'You were not followed?'

The hooded man shook his head.

'And you are fully prepared to go through with our arrangement?'

'I would not be here otherwise.' The hooded man tried to sound confident.

The Crow made a hissing noise.

The stench in the hovel was almost overwhelming – rotten meat and decay, overlaid with a mouldy spiciness, the smell of clogged ditches. And something else, a fruity odour, like perfume a fine lady might dab at her bosom. The man felt lightheaded. The Crow threw a few sticks on to the fire and the flames licked upwards.

By this new light, the Crow seemed less terrifying. He rooted around in the mound of rubbish behind him, a mass of ancient bones, filth and rags. The sorcerer found what he was looking for, and held it over the flame for an instant to see it more clearly. It was an iron knife – short, wide-bladed, encrusted with old dirt.

'I need blood,' he said. 'Give me your hand, Chrissstian.'

The hooded man hesitated.

The Crow smiled at him. His black-lipped mouth revealed teeth filed into sharp points, like some savage animal. The hooded man felt his fear begin to rise again.

'There mussst be trusst between usss,' the Crow hissed. 'Your hand.'

The hooded man paused a little longer then slowly extended his left hand.

The Crow took it in his own stick-like claw, and made one quick incision into the meat below his thumb. The hooded man felt the burn of it, and more pain as the Crow squeezed the flesh until the hot blood began to run freely.

The sorcerer tossed aside the knife and reached into the bosom of his robe. He brought out a small leather pouch, a dark shapeless thing. He undid the leather thong securing the bag with his pointed teeth, and pulled it open. It seemed to be filled only with a wad of thick, blond hair. The pain in his hand flared again, the sorcerer was squeezing it so that some drops of running blood slid over his palm to drip into the interior, darkening the yellow strands.

'Christian blood isss bessst for *ssseithr*,' the Crow said, conversationally.

The hooded man said nothing. He bit his lip. When the Crow released his hand, he took it and cradled it in the other. He looked reproachfully at the Crow.

'A very sssmall price for the gloriousss prize you crave,' said the sorcerer. 'You have made an exsssellent bargain thisss night.'

The hooded man just licked at the angry, bloody cut on his left palm, tasting the salty iron tang of his own gore.

The Crow loosely re-tied the thong on the pouch. 'Now, go, wait for me outside,' he said. 'I mussst be alone to work the *ssseithr*. It will not take long.'

The man rose and stumbled quickly outside into the rain and the darkness. He felt relieved to be away from the sorcerer's dank stench.

He looked up at the blanket of dark cloud above, feeling the cool drops spattering on his face. He could hear the Crow chanting inside the hovel, low and menacing, the words unintelligible, half-mumbled, half-sung deep in the throat.

There was more grey smoke coming from the eves of the reed house, and strange, sweet smells, too. He sat on the damp ground, holding his cut hand and looked out over the cold, empty marsh – not a light to be seen in any direction. This was no land for Christian men; this was

4

no place for good men at all. It was a place for frogs, rats and eels – and all your darkest terrors. It was just the place to make a bargain with the Devil at the risk of your own soul. One day, perhaps, he would build a fine new church here and cleanse this whole place of its infernal stain. One day. He thought about what he meant to do with the *seithr* the Crow was preparing, and what godly things he hoped to achieve with it.

It *was* an excellent bargain, he thought. But not without a heavy price. He would commit a sin, a grave sin, a mortal sin for which he must seek absolution – only after it was done. But a fine bargain, no less. And for the greatest cause of them all.

The leather flap of the door cracked open and the Crow emerged. He was a little taller than the hooded man remembered from their previous meetings in daylight, much leaner too. It was as if this fell place had changed his body somehow. Yet the same foul stink came off him. And the whorls of red and black paint on his face were smudged, as if by a careless hand wiping his sweat.

The hooded man scrambled hurriedly to his feet.

'Take thisss,' said the Crow. He pushed a soft, squashy leather object into the hooded man's hand. It was warm and wet. 'You mussst keep it ssssafe.'

'What must I do?'

'Place it high, near the place where he sssleepsss. Hidden. The magic works bessst when mind and body are at ressst. Raftersss are good, or in thatch.'

'When will he come here?'

'He will come at Yule. You must lodge it near hisss sssleeping place then.'

'At Christmas,' said the hooded man and turned to go. 'It shall be done.'

'Wait.' The Crow seized him by his jerkin and pulled him close. He looked into his frightened eyes. 'I ssshall know if you fail to do your part,' he hissed.

The hooded man could not meet the sorcerer's gaze; he flinched away.

'I ssshall know if you play me falssse,' the Crow whispered, 'and you will sssuffer agoniesss; sssuch pains in your sssoul. But if you do as I sssay, I will use my power to grant your heart'sss desire. But only if you sssucceed in the tassssk. Do thisss and I will reward you… but only when Bjarki Bloodhand has lost hisss Fire Born ssstrength, and the Rekkr isss dead… or hasss run mad!'

# Chapter One

## *The dragon's prey*

A face. A ferocious face. Mouth wide, red tongue lolling. The long, white-painted teeth seeming to shine with malice. The bulging eyes dyed blood-red, and with pure jet where the pupils might be. The creature's long snout was covered with green scales; a high gold ruff, or comb, jutted proudly from the back of its serpentine neck.

This terrifying face emerged from the curtain of thick grey sea-mist, and the rest of the long, lean dragon ship slipped on through behind it. Just below the fierce painted wooden dragon's head, at the blade of the longship – the curve where it sliced through the grey waters of the estuary – a pretty young woman stood with her right arm curled around the prow-post. Her fine, elfin face – all hard angles and scars, strong and yet beautiful nonetheless – was dotted with beads of spray.

She was lean and short with a thick mane of bright red hair, shaved at the sides to reveal whirling tattoos above both her ears. She wore a mail coat that covered her torso to her elbows and fell to her knees. It was belted with thick leather, and a long straight sword was hanging by her left side. A foot-long seax with an ivory handle hung across her loins. A leather strap diagonally across her chest supported a round lime-wood shield slung over her back.

She was bareheaded but she cradled a plain, dull, steel helm in the crook of her left arm. Both her wiry forearms were thickly tattooed with stick-like runes and delicate images of birds, animals and flowers.

She turned to look back along the line of the ship, along the double line of the rowers at their oars, all heaving in unison, driving the vessel into the bloody sun, a half orb on the western horizon. 'One point to larboard, Kynwulf!' she called, her voice low, pitched just loudly enough to reach the man at the tiller, sixty feet behind her. He was an old man, grizzled like a badger and much battered by war.

'Then you keep her nice and straight and steady on the approach,' she said.

The tiller-man did not reply; he grunted derisively but he shifted the ash pole he held clamped between his right arm and ribs and the ship's course changed subtly.

From the prow of *Fafnir*, Torfinna Hildarsdottir watched the slowly oncoming land, a low, black mass on the eastern horizon. Perhaps only half a mile away now. There were several hundred buildings, workshops and warehouses, that she could see. Ship-building yards, too. And a scattering of dwellings. The tallest building in the town was a long white church, a golden cross on the eastern end, flashing in the dying sunlight. A high, square-built stone tower sat at its west end, a fortress, which cast a thick shadow over the streets and houses. The church was on the eastern side of the town, near its palisade, at the extreme end of this settlement, fifty yards back from the long, curving shore. It had its own jetty for the loading and unloading of goods.

There were about two dozen craft hauled up on the shore before the main part of town, their bare masts also casting a corresponding forest of lengthening shadows. A few stick figures were quietly pacing the muddy strand, clearly very deep in thought, for they apparently paid the approaching dragon ship no mind at all. Here and there, she could see the wink of cooking fires in the close-packed houses beyond the shore, as hearths were stoked and replenished with wood for cooking the evening meals.

Tor had never laid eyes on this town before, but she had had it described in great detail by several experienced old sailors, Sea-Danes who knew all these shallow waters as well as they knew their own salt-gnarled fingers. Dorestad, the town was named. A port in the land called Frisia, a sprawling settlement grown rich by its trade.

This was the gateway to Austrasia, a northern province of Francia and, indeed, the entrance and exit to much of the King of the Franks' enormous realm. Ships came sailing into Dorestad from all over the Frankish lands, bringing grain from Neustria, wines and dried grapes from Aquitaine. And valuable commodities from other nearby lesser realms came through the busy port, too, huge barrels of dried, smoked shellfish from the rocky coast of Brittany, fat bales of wool from England, across the sea, and tin from Cornwall, razor-keen swords and knives from smithies in the Dane-Mark.

These goods were transported into Francia through Dorestad, some of them destined for the King Karolus's palace in Aachen, a mere hundred miles inland, some for the border fortresses of Xanten, Cologne and Coblenz, and a host of other towns, for the mighty rivers Rhenus and Meuse both entered the sea at Dorestad, and a flood of goods flowed back and forth along them. The merchants of Dorestad had grown fat. They were so rich, Tor knew, they'd earned the right to mint their own silver coin.

She could make out the soldiers, now, a pair of red-cloaked spearmen standing and idly chatting at the side of a workshop where another fellow hammered away at something. She could hear the tinny sounds carried across the water to the *Fafnir*. Not long now, she thought, not long till their ship was driven up on to the beach…

Yet Dorestad clearly had no fear of them, and this fact puzzled Tor greatly.

The two Red Cloaks on the beach had not even glanced over at the strange, beast-headed pirate vessel coming straight towards them out of the sinking sun. She and her three fine dragon ships had been raiding along the northern coast of Francia all summer long, relentlessly targeting fishing ports and the rich coastal towns, coming in with the dusk, attacking their churches and warehouses, then making away with their booty before the local noble could muster his men and come out to fight.

She had already sent two ships of the original three raiders home to Ymirsfjord, crammed full of assorted Frankish booty and manned by those of her own brave people who had been wounded, or injured, or had had enough of the hard *vikingr* life.

The *Fafnir* was the last sailing vessel under her command, and for it she had saved the plumpest prize of all. Dorestad. Dorestad, so rich it minted its own coin. Dorestad which, astonishingly, didn't seem to fear her at all.

*Had they not heard tell of their brutal summer-long depreda-tions along this very northern coast? Were they blind? Were these wealthy merchants particularly stupid?*

None of these things seemed likely, so… *Could it be a trap?*

Some ancient fear prickled at the back of her shaven neck. She turned again to signal to the helmsman. 'Kynwulf! Forget the beach. Turn to steerboard. Make straight for the jetty by the church, to the east, over yonder!' She released the post and pointed. 'We still have enough time to hit the plumpest target in this place. Stay sharp, all of you. Something in this well-fed pleasure-hole may not be what it seems.'

They were now three hundred yards from the shore, the movement of Kynwulf's tiller angling the ship in a smooth curve towards the church jetty east of the beach.

The two chatty red-cloaked Frankish soldiers had now utterly disappeared.

A bell began to toll, an insistent clanging from the tall church. The alarm.

'Heave, Fafnirs, heave those oars!' shouted Tor. There was no point in stealth any more. The enemy was alert to them. 'We must be in and out, quick as the wind.'

The longship surged forwards, the sweating drummer increasing the speed of his booming beat. A hundred paces to the jetty. Men were emerging from between the houses of the town, spearmen, the glint of steel in the last of the sun. And torches.

The *Fafnir* raced forwards, fifty paces now. As she buckled the straps on her helm, and threaded her left arm through the loops of her shield and gripped the iron tang of the hollow boss in its centre, Tor could see men now forming up in the strand, a hundred yards from the jetty. Trained soldiers, by their briskness.

Small army units were forming between the beached trading ships, too. Red Cloaks, and some others, as well. Swordsmen in furs, helms and iron mail. Officers shouting, shoving their men into position. Soldiers of Karolus, King of the Franks.

For a single moment, just one tiny moment, Tor considered ducking this coming fight. It was clear that the Franks had been expecting them all along, anticipating their arrival, if not this day, then another. It was clear they had made preparations.

Tor knew she could give the order to turn the ship, to row away, back out to sea. To flee from their ready opponents. No, not opponents. These were her enemies.

The Franks were her enemies. And she would not willingly flee from them. Karolus had imprisoned her and her big brother, not once but twice, in a stinking cell below the city of Aachen. They had been humiliated, starved, beaten, and forced to fight for their lives for the amusement of jeering Frankish crowds. Karolus's armies had invaded those northern lands that still followed the old gods and had destroyed a sacred place of worship she held very dear. Many of her friends and comrades had been slaughtered by Karolus's ruthless spearmen. His Christian ministers had sent paid spies to betray them, and soldiers to kill them more times than she could count.

These were her *enemies*. She hated them from the very pit of her belly, from the marrow of her northern bones. She desired all they possessed, including their lives.

The Franks doubtless thought that they had set a cunning trap for these *vikingir*. They would very soon discover what they had snared in their cleverly spread nets.

A mighty dragon. A beast of feral fury and terrifying skill.

'Odiiiin!' yelled Tor from beside the prow-beast. 'Odin, witness our deeds!'

The sharp bow of the dragon ship crunched against the wood of the jetty, and Tor threw herself from the prow on to the slimy wooden planking, skidding a full yard before recovering her balance. Others were leaping, too, pouring on to the land.

'Kynwulf,' Tor turned her head and yelled behind her, 'keep six crew with you and get *Fafnir* safe off-shore! Stand you ready for a swift extraction.' She seized a passing man by the shoulder. 'Mogils, take two dozen shields and be prepared to aid our departure. It will be nip and tuck.' The young warrior nodded obediently at her and trotted briskly away, westwards. Then, to the rest of her crewmates: 'Forwards! To the church, and run like deer! There is not a moment to waste!'

She drew her sword and began to sprint towards the looming square tower a hundred yards distant. She was aware of a mass of Red Cloaks advancing in a block upon her left flank – but still sixty paces away – so she ignored them. Her shipmates were all around her, forty men, give or take, and a few women, each one a seasoned warrior, a proven fighter, the victor of many a bloody sea fight – and they all ran too.

Towards the church.

A line of resistance had formed directly in front of this white Christian temple, across the street between two houses, a double row of warriors – not Red Cloaks or other regular Frankish troops, but local men, about fifty barely trained levies in rough leather and fur, armed with shields, swords and spears, summoning up their courage.

Too few, and too loosely formed.

Tor did not hesitate. She yelled 'Odinnn!' once more and charged straight at the centre of the terrified, quavering line of levies. A score of bellowing Ymirsfjord vikings ran along beside her. One big fellow called Olaf, who wielded a long-handled hammer, was shouting the name of Thor as he surged ahead of the main pack. Behind her, the ship's archers were loosing, their shafts arcing overhead to fall on the enemy.

She crashed into the centre of the line, her sword flicking out to steal a life, taking a frightened man in the pit of his throat, and slashing his neck away.

Her round shield smashed into his falling body and the wall was breached. The dying man clutched at his neighbour and fell away, dragging the next man with him. The warrior in the second row flinched away and, as her weight hit him, shield to shield, he was knocked a step backwards. Tor burst through the line and into space on the other side. Olaf was smashing at the Frankish levies with his hammer, felling lesser men left and right, and the rest of the Ymirsfjord crew were in among them too, killing, hacking them down. In moments the line of foes had dissolved. A dozen men were down bleeding in the mud, the rest were running for their lives back into the warren of Dorestad's narrow streets, crying for their God and Jesus to deliver them.

'The church, the church!' shouted Tor.

It lay before her, she saw, now only twenty paces away. A long, low building with a red-tiled roof, built of wattle and daub, and whitewashed to a brilliant shine that reflected the last rays of the dying sun. The door was in the centre of the southern wall – and open! – and a figure was kneeling there under the high wooden arch. It was a young man, sweaty and fat, wearing a brown robe of rough homespun woollen cloth. His head was shaved to resemble that of a much older man, his pate as pink as a mouse's nose, his glossy chestnut hair forming a ring around the skull above his large ears. He was shakily holding up a large wooden cross, their talisman against evil, as Tor knew perfectly well, and he was mumbling a long prayer or incantation.

Something landed beside her left boot. A javelin, quivering upright in the mud. She looked up – and flinched aside just in time as another lethal missile streaked down from the tower. She caught a glimpse of scarlet and the shine of a polished iron helm. There were armed men up there. Frankish soldiers. The second black javelin slammed into the earth just two yards away. Arrows were hissing down too, pattering in the mud of the street. She heard a man curse the gods: it was Ingmar One-eye.

She looked back at the monk. His kneeling body blocked the door. A *Fafnir* crew member, a nimble little fellow known as Black Ivar, sprinted up, and without hesitation chopped his hand axe on the monk's pink head, splitting his skull open.

The monk gave a weird cry and toppled to one side, and Black Ivar leapt straight over him and disappeared inside the church. Tor was right on his heels; she jumped over the sprawled, bloodied monk, and found herself inside the church beside Ivar. Other Ymirsfjord men were barging in now, some sporting arrows in their mail or stuck in their furs. Ingmar One-eye had a shaft jutting up from his right shoulder, but his scarred hands still held the long Dane axe. Tor knew it was his favourite weapon.

It was bright in the church after the shadowy dusk of the street. Two dozen yellow candles were burning and there was the sound of voices, too – they were singing, of all things! Tor looked right and saw a circle of monks, near the altar, all holding hands tightly and just standing there singing one of their slow Christian dirges. A psalm, she thought. It was an unnerving sight. Half a dozen grown men, all with half-shaven heads, making no attempt at all to defend themselves, standing there singing and waiting for death. One of her younger vikings, a dark, handsome fellow called Joralf, a skilled swordsman, flew at the circle of monks and immediately killed one, with a sword lunge that drove his long blade through the man's right kidney.

Others among her crew joined in the joyous monk-slaughter, hacking the Christians down amid fountains of fresh blood. Black Ivar sank his axe into the spine of one poor fellow, who screamed like a little girl. A skinny, much older monk fell to his knees, amid the carnage and horror, and said loudly – 'God have mercy on you all!' The words were perfectly understandable, but with some strange foreign accent.

And the monk's face was instantly familiar to Tor.

Joralf stood over him, sword raised. 'Wait!' shouted Tor. 'Not him. Leave him be. To me, Joralf – to me, all of you!'

Tor led all the men inside the church to the western end, the end furthest from the altar. There was a little wooden door set in the lime-washed wall. She tried the handle. Locked from the inside. She threw all her weight against it, and bounced off.

'Get that open, now,' Tor ordered. 'Where is Olaf the Hammer?'

More and more of the vikings were bursting into the church, a score of them now inside. Olaf the Hammer was found and put to work on the oak door. Others joined him with their long-handled axes, hacking into the wood and levering out long white splinters. Olaf pounded it with his big hammer. The whole church echoed with their blows. In short order, the door was kindling. An arrow whizzed out from inside, taking Ingmar in the belly – he dropped, cursing his own bad luck.

Tor was the first through the wrecked door, her shield high, sword lancing out to take the kneeling archer full in the face. He screamed and fell back, his face all lacerated, and Tor whirled and clashed blades with a Red Cloak spearman. Her people were all around her, jostling in the small space, stabbing, hacking wildly at half a dozen frightened Frankish soldiers, cutting them all down in moments. Yet Tor was already climbing the wooden stairs that led up into the very heart of the tower.

More arrows, thudding into her big, round shield. But some of the Ymirsfjord archers were just behind her and, as they loosed their wicked shafts up the steps, clearing the way, she surged on forwards and engaged two Red Cloaks at the top on the first floor. She dropped one with a feint and lunge and Black Ivar, at her shield side, hacked the other man down.

Suddenly the upstairs room was full of her shipmates. Five of the Red Cloaks lay dead or dying, bleeding on the floor, and there seemed to be no living enemies at all. Tor could hear the sound of heavy military boots clumping back and forth on the floorboards above. Looking in the far corner of the square room, at the ceiling, she could see a trap door. Bolted, no doubt. And a slender hazel-wood ladder lying on the floor by the sprawled corpse of a Red Cloak.

'Up, mistress? Shall we go up, and take them?' said Black Ivar, standing by her side, looking into her face. He had a broad stripe of fresh blood across his forehead.

'No need, Ivar. That there is what we came for!' said Tor, pointing to the other corner of the chamber. There was a wooden bench with a wide scatter of discarded iron tools, stamps and hammers and a pair of heavy iron shears. Beside the bench was a stool and an iron anvil. Beyond that – where Tor was pointing – was a small pyramid of cube-shaped iron chests. Three of them, one on top of the other two. Tor strode over to the top box, an ugly thing secured with a strong hasp and heavy iron padlock.

'Olaf, get this thing open for me, will you?' she said. 'Quick as you like.'

The hammer-man came forwards, his long weapon held in one of his ham-like fists. He stepped in and swung. With a single mighty blow of the hammer, the padlock disintegrated. Tor reached forwards and flipped open the lid of the box. Every warrior in the room immediately craned forwards to see the box's contents – a sea of shimmering silver. Hundreds of coins, thousands, maybe. Minted in Dorestad.

'All we need to do now,' said Tor, grinning like a madwoman, 'is get out of here alive.'

# Chapter Two

### The Golden Viking

Bjarki Bloodhand, the Rekkr of Ymirsfjord, a *berserkr* of high renown, said to be possessed by the spirits of not one but two wild bears, a known killer and victor of a dozen bloody battles, picked up the tiny girl by the waist and, with a terrifying growl of almost demonic fury, hurled her far up into the blue sky.

She screamed: a long, girlish shriek of mingled fear... and delight. And, as she began to fall, Bjarki caught her, spun her up and around and set her on his shoulders, her pudgy legs and feet dangling either side of his blond beard.

'Forwards, pony!' the girl cried, drumming her heels against his broad chest.

So Bjarki let out a reasonable imitation of a whinny, and began to stump up the zig-zagging slope away from the village and towards the north ridge, with the girl bouncing on his neck and gripping two fat plaits of his hair like a pair of reins.

'Don't get Lili too excited!' said Edith. She was standing by the gate of the kitchen garden, a five-month-old baby cradled in her arms. 'And don't give her too much of it to eat. Or I'll never get her to go quietly to her cot tonight and to sleep.'

'As you command, my love,' said Bjarki, giving his wife a smile.

'And be back before nightfall. There are wolves in the woods: Trudi says she heard their eldritch singing only last week when she was gathering blackberries.'

'Do not fret, dearest. We will be home before dusk with all our sweet loot!'

'And… and don't let her get stung…' Edith's words trailed after Bjarki but he was no longer listening to his lovely Saxon wife. He was striding away up the path that cut up the side of the valley, heading north-east, with his three-year-old daughter Lili bouncing on his neck, urging him to go faster… *faster!*

Eventually, Bjarki was forced to pause and catch his breath, about halfway up the steep slope. He took his daughter off his shoulders, begging for mercy. While he breathed deeply, drinking in the mountain air, they stood side by side, her tiny hand held in his paw, and looked down the valley towards the settlement of Ymirsfjord.

The fjord was about four miles long, with high, sheer cliffs on either side, and Bjarki's hall and the many accompanying outbuildings stood on a flat piece of land at its eastern end, beside a gently winding river. It had been a *vikingir*'s pirate lair before Bjarki and his followers had taken possession of Ymirsfjord four springs earlier, and its location had been chosen by its previous owners – who were now all dead at Bjarki's hand – for its very remoteness and awkward inaccessibility. Any ships that approached the settlement up the long, narrow fjord could be spotted by a keen-eyed lookout hours before they were close, which would allow Ymirsfjord to make its preparations – either to fight or to run for the mountains.

The original hall and its courtyard were surrounded by a high palisade of sharpened stakes and formed the keep, stronghold and place of last refuge for the much-expanded village. For over the past four years there had been a large influx of people to the settlement from across the North – folk from Frisia to the Finn-Mark – including old friends, those who had marched and fought beside Bjarki or Tor, young adventurers, exiles, even a few on the run from feuds or a great king's wrath.

All had been welcomed to Ymirsfjord, so long as they understood and accepted Bjarki's absolute authority as the chieftain – or *hersir* – of the settlement, and swore to make no trouble of any kind. The penalty for even the smallest transgression against the community was expulsion. For the greater transgressions, it was death.

The dwellings that the hundreds of incomers had constructed for themselves sprawled up behind the hall and its walls, extending a quarter of a mile into the narrow valley, and climbing the slopes on both sides. There was still a large kitchen garden directly behind the palisade where Edith and the other women of Ymirsfjord grew onions, leeks, beans, turnips and cabbages, and had built wooden pens for the pigs, chickens and goats, but this ordinary farmyard was now surrounded by half a dozen timber longhouses, as well as a larger number of huts, built with wattle and daub, and roofed with straw from the barley and oat fields, lands which Bjarki had painstakingly cleared, ploughed and sown in the first few weeks after their arrival in Rogaland, as this territory on the edge of the North-Way was commonly known.

In truth, they did not *need* to grow all their own food; Bjarki had amassed a considerable store of moveable wealth, in both treasure and goods, in three seasons of raiding along the coast of Francia, and further afield, and he could, if he chose, have purchased almost anything he needed for this much-expanded *vikingr* community.

They called him the Golden Viking – for his blond hair and beard and for the abundance of gold that men claimed that he had stored in his coffers. But some innate sense of caution, or perhaps just simple prudence, caused Bjarki to order his people to plant the fields ever year, to weed them, tend them carefully, and bring in the harvest. But on this day, while his sister Tor and half the warriors of Ymirsfjord were off raiding, Bjarki was going in search of another kind of golden treasure.

'Come on, Little Hare,' he said to Lili, 'time to mount up. Not far now.'

He scooped his daughter up on to his shoulders and began to plod up the steep hill once more. Bjarki was a strong man, an active man, but the uphill walk was tiring him more than usual. He felt all of his twenty-nine years in the Middle-Realm this brisk autumn morning – and hard, bloody years they had been too. He had been fighting wars for a full decade and that day his burnt, battered, much-scarred body seemed determined to remind him of every wound, cut and bruise he had received.

For the first time this year, in the spring, he had allowed his half-sister Tor to go raiding without him. And while he was a little envious of all the bloody adventures she must surely be enjoying, a part of him was also deeply relishing his role as doting father and firmly rooted husbandman. Edith had been near her time with his baby son, Hildar, when the raiding season had begun in the month of Einmánuthur, at the tail end of the winter, and he had also twisted his left ankle on a loose stone on the mountainside, and was limping a little. So he made his feeble excuses to Tor.

It was no great injury, and indeed soon healed, but he found himself overcome by a dark weariness at the idea of sailing off to go a-*vikingr*. Even the thought of the vast riches of the ill-defended Frankish towns along the coast did not inspire him.

'Are you ill?' Tor had asked. Bjarki denied it. He was not sick. But there was a lassitude that had come over him, a kind of exhaustion, a heavy, bone-deep tiredness that, despite a long, lazy winter, in which he had rarely strayed from his hall, refused to lift. The two *gandir* who lived in his heart – the spirits of two bears, the mother Mochta and her son Garm – had many times given him a terrible animal-like ferocity in battle. But perhaps they had now exhausted him, for each time he called on them for help, they filled his limbs with their strength but afterwards left him ever more sickly and weak. They still spoke to him, from time to time, inside his heart, but he was increasingly reluctant to tap into their power. Indeed, a part of him hoped he would never have to call on them again.

'You just need a good, bloody fight to stir up your blood,' Tor had said. Bjarki sighed. This was the very opposite of what he needed. But he could never articulate his deepest thoughts very well, even to his beloved sister. And so he simply shook his head and muttered something about wanting to watch over Edith at the birth of their child, and hoping to get Ymirsfjord into proper order for the new arrival. There was so much to do here, he said, so much to mend, and no time to waste...

So Tor had merely shrugged and gone off raiding without him, taking more than two hundred of his finest warriors with her and three fast dragon ships.

'May the Bear guard you,' he shouted to Tor, as he waved her off on the beach. And then he had immediately busied himself in her absence with small tasks that were more suited to a miserable thrall than a lord of war: he forged a new iron latch on the gate to the pig-pen, and fixed it in its place; he rebuilt the main hearth in the hall, laying flagstones he quarried from the mountains; he replaced all the wooden shingles of the roof on the little temple dedicated to Odin by the main gate. He did the back-breaking work of a thrall not because he did not own any, for he did. There were a dozen of these wretches living in the settlement – mostly Franks or Wends, not honest men of the North, not his own people, but folk who had been captured in raids, and were now forced to labour, to do the ploughing, the hard harvest work of reaping and stacking the sheaves of grain, and picking the fruit from the orchards.

Bjarki did these apparently menial tasks because it pleased him to do so, but also perhaps because he felt a sliver of shame that he was leaving others to do the bloody labour on the raids, the hard, brutal sword-work that brought Ymirsfjord its wealth.

They were nearing the ridge, with nothing beyond but clear blue sky, and Lili began squeaking with excitement, shouting, 'Bees, Daddy, bees! I want the honey.'

She was pointing to a row of two dozen bell-shaped objects, nestled into a fold on the hillside under a sloping brushwood roof. A small hut built of planks and turf stood at the end of the row of skeps, as these bee 'houses' were locally called.

Bjarki set Lili down beside the store hut, crouched down next to her and said: 'Stay clear of the skeps, Little Hare, and remember, if a bee lands on you, then gently –

just very gently – brush it off. He won't sting unless you frighten him.'

Lili gazed up at Bjarki with her enormous blue eyes and said: 'Honey, Daddy! I want some honey!' He poked his tongue at her. And she, laughing, ran towards the nearest skep. Bjarki caught her after a couple of paces, whirled her up on his shoulders again, muttering, 'Well, I tried.' Then, with Lili on his shoulders, he went to the store hut, opened the door and removed two capacious leather shoulder-bags.

He pulled a flask from his belt, set his daughter down and began to rub ointment on Lili's face, arms and neck, followed by a liberal application to his own skin.

'This is wild mallow juice, Little Hare – and the bees don't like it at all. Now, my sweet, you must promise me you will keep a good distance while I do my work.'

When they were both thoroughly smeared with mallow juice, he rummaged in the back of the hut and produced a long, dry lozenge-shaped item about the size of his seax, which he lit, using steel and flint, until it was smouldering well at one end and producing a pungent smoke with more than a whiff of old cow manure.

'I beg you to stay back, Lili,' he said. 'Stay back or you will surely be stung.'

Shouldering the two leather bags, he approached the first skep, and held the slowly burning lozenge to the small hole in the front, which was the bees' entrance. As the smoke trickled inside, Bjarki looked over his shoulder and was very glad to see Lili keeping ten paces away – but she was hopping from one little foot to the other, as if she urgently needed to relieve herself.

'The smoke makes them very sleepy, Little Hare,' he said. 'Then they don't mind so much if we steal a little part of their precious treasure.'

He gently tipped up the skep, a sort of upside-down wicker basket covered in dried mud, and peered inside. A swarm of drowsy bees erupted around him, but the smoke and the mallow juice seemed to be having their deterrent effect.

Using his seax, he cut a big chunk of dripping honey-comb from the walls inside the skep and dropped it into the first leather bag. Then, very carefully, he put the skep back in its original position.

'You must only ever take one third part of the honey-comb, Little Hare,' he said without looking behind him, 'otherwise the bees will have nothing to eat all winter.'

He looked down and saw a tiny pudgy hand reaching between his legs, delving into the leather bag, to emerge with a sticky handful of runny golden goodness.

'All right, my darling, you may have some,' he said, 'but go and eat it over there, will you?'

He cut his daughter a large piece of dripping honey-comb, set it on a large leaf and allowed her to sit conten-tedly by the hut, wallowing in its explosive sweetness.

He licked his own sticky fingers clean. Then he prop-erly set to work.

Bjarki had just finished going along the line of skeps and filling the leather bags with honeycomb, when he heard a long, low booming sound reverberating through the still mountain air. He hauled the two heavy bags back to the hut and scrambled up on to the plank and turf roof, idly scratching at a bee sting on his neck.

The noise sounded again, a mournful, elongated call. Bjarki shaded his eyes against the sun and looked down the length of the glittering blue fjord.

One of the first things he had done, when he arrived at Ymirsfjord, was to build a little watch-point at the end of the promontory on the southern side of the narrow mouth of the fjord. A simple structure, no more than an open-sided box, thatched with gorse brush, with enough room – just – to shelter two lookouts.

It also housed the Great Horn of Ymirsfjord. An instrument as long as a man's arm and as wide at the mouth as his head, taken from some enormous, long-dead bull. When the Great Horn sounded, it meant that a strange ship – or perhaps fleet of ships – was approaching the settlement by sea. Every man who heard the Great Horn knew that his duty was to take up arms, make himself ready for the defence of their homes.

It was now long after noon, Bjarki judged by the height of the sun, and looking down the channel of water almost directly into its yellowish glare he could just make out the ship – a wide-bellied *knarr* – as it entered the mouth of the fjord. It was an unfamiliar vessel. Could be a Svear trading ship – wide, capacious craft such as these ferried goods across the whole of the North – but Bjarki could also see the round shapes of shields hung on the outside of the craft, and he thought he caught a glint of steel spear-points, or perhaps even sword blades. An armed trader, perhaps? It was wise to be armed, and did not necessarily indicate evil intent, because men who carried valuable goods across the North lands would often need protection against... well, folk like Bjarki and his *vikingr* crews.

He licked a finger and held it in the air. The soft south-westerly wind would waft the strange ship up the fjord but at a slow pace – it would surely be the best part of an hour before the ship reached the village. He had time to meet it.

'We need to go home now, Lili,' said Bjarki. 'We have visitors.'

He looked at his daughter, who was singing and playing with a twig and a tiny ant hole, letting the ants crawl up the stick. She heard his words and glanced up lovingly at him. Her face was a sticky mass of snot, wax, mud and honey. But she seemed more than content. She sang a few more words and returned to her game.

Bjarki was not overly worried by these newcomers. If it was a single ship – and it looked like a fifty-footer, with a beam of fifteen-foot – there could be no more than two dozen warriors on board if the craft was carrying cargo. Oddvin and Rask, members of his *Felaki* bodyguard, were both down in the hall today, and there were another hundred men within hailing distance. The Great Horn had been sounded and they would be mustering, arming themselves and making ready to receive the strange ship at the jetty in front of the village.

There was probably nothing to worry about. It was a ship full of Svear traders who wished to sell luxuries to the Golden Viking. No great matter. Indeed, it might be very useful. He slung the bags of honey, one on each shoulder, and herding Lili before him, the girl gambolling like a goat, he set off down the path to Ymirsfjord.

–

Bjarki Bloodhand greeted the newcomers in his hall. He had washed and changed his clothes, donning a clean linen shirt, a pair of heavy woollen trews and a rich, moss-green robe trimmed with jet-black mink fur. He belted a long sword around his waist and added a fine circlet of gold around his brow to remind everyone he had once been the King of Vastergotland, if only for a few short months, before his voluntary exile to this inaccessible pirate fortress in the remote wilds of the North-Way.

He sat upon an oak throne at the end of the hall with two *Felaki* bodyguards, one at each shoulder, and stared coldly down at these interlopers.

The old man who was now standing before his throne knew Bjarki well enough. He was a trader and a wanderer, a meddler in other people's business, a drunkard and often something of a nuisance to Bjarki. He was also a friend: Valtyr Far-Traveller.

'Bjarki Bloodhand, I bring greetings from the King of the Danes,' he said.

Bjarki stared at Valtyr, noticing his ill-looking, pallid skin and the bruised ring under his one remaining eye. He saw that a tall boy, of perhaps ten or eleven years, stood beside him, a child with straw-coloured hair, hard brown eyes and the wary expression of someone who has been beaten brutally and often. A thrall, perhaps.

'You bring me greetings, do you?' Bjarki said. 'Greetings from King Siegfried of the Dane-Mark, the king who declared me outlaw four years ago, who put a price in silver on my head. Is that the same King of Danes that you refer to?'

'Are you going to pretend, Bjarki, that you do not know him?'

'I know him. What does he want?'

'Siegfried sent me to you to say that...'

'Hold hard just a moment, old man,' said Bjarki, 'what is *he* doing here?'

The Rekkr pointed at Valtyr's other companion, at his right shoulder, a tall and handsome warrior in an exquisite bright crimson cloak, who was smiling up at Bjarki as if he found his host's whole 'Lord of Ymirsfjord' performance most amusing.

'I've come to talk about my bride price,' said Widukind, Duke of Saxony.

'Your what?'

'You ran off with my sister Edith – you abducted her, some might say – although I suspect she was willing enough. And I have heard that you live with her as your wedded wife, out here in the back of beyond. Therefore, according to the ancient laws and customs of the North, as her only living male relative, I am owed a bride price. You can afford it: the Golden Viking is the name you now use, or so I hear.'

'You hear a lot of things in Saxony. I'd have thought you would have far more urgent things on your mind, duke, than my private doings up here in Rogaland.'

'I no longer live in Saxony,' said Widukind. 'The Christian Franks have fully overrun my homeland. It all belongs to King Karolus now, every river and hill, the whole First Forest, all of it, all except little Nordalbia, that small, poor marshy part up beyond the Elbe, which I'm sure you remember perfectly well from… No, I'm a resident of the Danish king's court, which is at Ribe these days. Old Siegfried has generously appointed me his King's Counsellor. He's given me a small company of his best spearmen to command, too – not that he has very many of *them* left, not after… well, *you* know, you were at Norrkoping.'

Norrkoping – the battle to end all battles. Yes, Bjarki and his half-sister Tor had been there. They had both fought and bled and nearly died in that great and pointless struggle between Harald Wartooth, high commander – or *Armathr* – of the mighty Danish spear-host and the hard men and heroes of King Sigurd Hring of Svealand. Dane had fought Svear without mercy until the steam of their wounds rose in clouds above the battlefield. Thousands had died that day, the Wartooth had also fallen, and Sigurd Hring had triumphed over the Danes.

The King of the Svear had won the right on that bloody field to call himself King of the North, overlord of all free men in the northern lands – including King Siegfried of the Dane-Mark. And after that battle, Bjarki had fled, with Tor and his surviving men, and he had taken the beautiful Edith along with him to Ymirsfjord. He had indeed stolen Widukind's sister away from Siegfried's court, where she had been promised to another man, which had resulted in Bjarki being declared an outlaw.

'Do you think you can come here, to my hall, to demand that I pay you a bride price?' Bjarki stood up; he could feel a black rage slowly stirring in his belly, a sluggish heat, a pulse of hatred. 'Did you honestly think I would pay it to you?'

For a moment, he actually considered killing this duke, this silver-tongued popinjay who liked to call himself the Saxon Wolf. He felt his two *gandir* stir from their sleep inside his heart. Not that he would need their ursine ferocity. The hall was packed with Bjarki's warriors, all ready to obey his commands – and Valtyr and Widukind had only a half dozen Danes round them. If he gave the order, Bjarki knew his guests would be corpses in moments. He *could* kill them – but should he?

'I don't want your money,' said Widukind calmly. 'I just want to remind you of the debt you owe me. I want it to be acknowledged before many witnesses.'

Bjarki glared at him. He was still considering this irritating nobleman's murder.

'Why don't we sit down and discuss this,' said Valtyr. 'We have come a long way by sea and have not had so much as a drop to drink yet. How about a jug of ale, or a drop of mead, if you have it.' Valtyr licked his lips. 'And I'll explain it all.'

As Bjarki gave instructions to his servants to bring ale, bread and cheese, and ushered his guests to the nearest long table, his beautiful wife came into the hall.

Edith gave a cry of delight and rushed towards her brother. They embraced for a long time and Bjarki, watching them, knew then that he could never kill this man, this so-called Duke of Saxony – no matter what the provocation – while Edith still lived. He smiled tightly at his unwelcome guests, and gestured for the thrall to pour the ale.

On his return from the mountain, Edith had immediately taken charge of Lili and, somehow forbearing to scold Bjarki, she washed the encrusted honey, snot and mud off her daughter and gave her bread and milk and, after a fierce struggle, had got her to lie in her little cot until exhaustion overtook her tiny body.

She gazed at her handsome brother, and noted the extra lines of care on Widukind's face. Was that a first line of silver in his fair hair? Hair which also now seemed a little thinner than when she had last seen him more than four years ago. She had heard about the expulsion of the last rebel Saxon troops from their homeland – Ymirsfjord might be a quiet and lonely backwater, but passing ships did bring news of the outside world from time to time. She also knew that Widukind had taken up a fat sinecure with the old Danish king, who had long been his staunch ally. She wondered what the purpose of his visit to Ymirsfjord could really be.

'Good ale, this,' said Valtyr, holding out his empty cup to be refilled.

Bjarki filled up the old man's cup himself. 'You said you had a message for me, old man, from the King of the Dane-Mark. What is it?'

Valtyr took a swallow of his ale before smacking his lips and replying.

'I do,' he said. 'Siegfried asks you to come to his court in Ribe. He invites you to spend Yule with him, as his honoured guest. He would speak with you.'

'No,' said Bjarki. 'Even I can see this is a trap. That old fool has outlawed me, put a price on my head. I'd be walking into a wolves' den. The answer must be no.'

'The king thought you might say that,' said Valtyr. 'Which is why he sent me. He knows you fully trust me and revere me as a beloved relative, almost as a father.'

Bjarki made a harsh noise in the back of his throat that might have been a grunt of assent or a scoff at the absurdity of the notion that he might fully trust Valtyr.

'As for the price on your head, it was only for a very small pouch of silver. A mere handful of coins. You must have a hundred times that amount in your own bulging coffers, O Golden One, perhaps a thousand times. This is what men say, anyway. You must understand that Siegfried was forced to outlaw you and set this most insignificant bounty on your head. You kidnapped his guest – a woman under his personal protection. You took her from under his nose. The sister of his ally.'

Valtyr flapped a hand towards Widukind, who winked at Bjarki, irritatingly.

'The king was obliged to outlaw you. What else could he do? You made him look very foolish. And your humiliation came on top of his defeat by Sigurd Hring.'

'Nobody was stolen,' said Edith. 'Nobody was kidnapped. Bjarki asked me to go with him and I said yes. If there is any question of punishment, I am as much to blame as Bjarki. I broke my oath to marry Abbio. This is all my fault.'

'Nobody's going to be punished,' said Bjarki. 'If the King of the Dane-Mark wants to come against me, if he wants to fight, by Odin, he knows where I am. Let him sail to Ymirsfjord. Let him come! And, if it is true that he only wishes to speak with me, let him also come here. I am not subject to his Danish laws or royal decrees. I am not to be commanded like some lowly thrall. If he truly wants to speak with me he can rescind my decree of outlawry – cancel the price on my head at the same time. Then – *perhaps* – then I shall consider talking to him.'

'You were not always this high and mighty, Bjarki,' said Valtyr. 'Living out here on your own has considerably swelled your already fat head. Besides, the king has *already* lifted the decree of outlawry and cancelled the pittance in silver on your head. He had it proclaimed last month in his great hall. Siegfried is a very old man – he has lived four score years already. And he would never survive the journey out here to Rogaland, to the storm-tossed wilds of the North-Way. Out of simple courtesy, Bjarki, you should go to him – it is the only decent and honourable thing to do.'

Bjarki stared at Valtyr. 'If I were to be so foolish as to stick my head into that snake pit, if I were so rash as to sail to Ribe and feast with the King of the Danes at Yuletide. What would Siegfried then say to me? What does he want?'

'He wants to adopt you,' said Valtyr. 'He wants to make you his royal heir. He wants you, Bjarki Bloodhand, you fat-headed oaf, to be the next King of the Danes.'

# Chapter Three

### Renewing an old acquaintance

They hauled the three heavy iron boxes down into the church, two men carrying each one, and piled them in the centre of the tiled floor. Tor poked her head out of the door, and saw that a loose wall of Red Cloaks was forming about fifty yards away, scores of them, a barrier across the street that led back to the waterfront. Their leaders were forcing their young troopers into a tight formation, shoving men hard up against their neighbours. The line was thickening fast, alarmingly fast, with more Frankish warriors running in from all directions to add their numbers to the wall. This was a primarily defensive formation, not an attacking one. She still had a little time. She licked a finger, held it up, tested the wind. It was westerly. Tor smiled, a look of satisfaction.

Tor glanced back inside the church. The monk whose life she had spared was kneeling by the altar, sunk deep in prayer. The other Christians in the church were all dead. Beyond him a pair of vikings were stripping the altar of anything shiny – golden candlesticks, silver bowls and plates. She called to one of them, Sambor the Polans, and the huge bald man trotted obediently over to her side, gripping a long-handled Dane axe in one meaty paw, making it look like a kindling-chopper.

'Find another axeman and make me a big hole in that back wall, over there!' Tor pointed to the rear of the church beyond the stripped-clean altar. There was a large mural painted on the lime whitewash, a man with a kindly face and big golden circle around his head talking to some adoring sheep and goats. White doves were flying around his head, and chubby babies with white wings looked on from the eves.

Sambor nodded and went away.

The church walls were mostly made of wattle, a thin, double lattice-work of hazel wands and covered with a mixture of dung, straw and mud, which was then smoothed, dried and whitewashed. It wouldn't take much to knock a big hole in it.

'Joralf – to me,' she called. The dark young swordsman came to her side.

'I want that mint tower ablaze, soon as you can. Find some clothes to burn. The monks' robes should do. Make them all wet. Piss on them, if you have to.'

'The Franks are there,' said Joralf. 'In the chamber above the mint room.'

'So?' said Tor. 'Get a fire kindled. I want smoke. Lots and lots of smoke.'

She went back to the doorway and looked out again. The Frankish shield wall was now formed. The officers were shouting at men, putting heart into them. Exhorting them to fight hard. In a little while, when they had screwed their bravery to the highest notch, they would attack. Behind her she could hear the crack, crumble and smash of axes against the painted wall behind the altar. She turned back to the church interior: 'Archers!' she called. 'Sven, Einar, Harald, Ivar, get up here!'

She placed the archers by the door with orders to drop as many in the shield wall as possible, pointing out officers with red plumes on their helms as targets.

'Make them uncomfortable,' she said. 'If they begin to advance, sing out.'

Now she could smell smoke. Joralf stood with the doorway to the mint tower behind him; she could see red flames dancing, black tendrils of smoke wafting past the young man, drifting towards the open door, towards the four archers, who were now methodically loosing shafts, dropping Franks in the wall. Ingmar One-eye was sitting on the floor by the back wall in a pool of blood, eyes wide open. An arrow protruded from his shoulder, another from his belly. He had left the Middle-Realm.

'Till we meet again in Valhalla, brother,' she said, slapping his shoulder, then she turned away. She stalked over to the praying monk, and stopped beside him.

'I know your face, Christian,' Tor said frowning down at him. 'We have met before somewhere – I know it – but I cannot place you. What is your name?'

The skinny monk looked up at her. He seemed unafraid of this blood-spattered shield-maiden standing over him, her hands on her hips. He looked round at the bodies of his fellow monks, scattered loose across the church floor, then back at Tor.

'The last time we met,' he said, anger glinting in his eyes, 'you were in a gaol cell. Captives of Karolus in Aachen. You and your brother. You had been treated shamefully by Bishop Livinus, and I protested at your imprisonment. The Franks said you were barbarians, butchers of men, little better than savage animals, and I objected and said you should be treated with all due honour and respect. But now I wonder if perhaps my hosts were indeed correct in their assessment of your barbarous kind.'

'Father Alwin,' said Tor, grinning at the kneeling man. 'Priest of the Auxilla! The Angelcynn holy man. I thought you'd be back in your home across the West Sea, now the Auxilla has been disbanded. What brings you to this church in Dorestad?'

'Misfortune,' said the priest. 'In truth, a whole series of foul misfortunes.'

One of the archers in the doorway shouted, 'They're getting ready to charge.'

Tor looked at the priest a moment longer. 'You can write, Alwin, yes? You know the secrets of all the Christian letters; you can make these letters, read them too?'

Father Alwin said: 'Of course. I studied for years at the cathedral in York.'

The archer shouted, 'Tor! They are all starting to move. They are coming.'

Tor ran to the door and looked out. It was true the Franks were moving forwards, all at the same time, shields linked, a slow forward tramp. The first rank of the Red Cloaks were now only thirty paces away. They had lit torches, a dozen men standing behind the lines with burning pinewood brands. But the wafts and tendrils of their black smoke were now drifting across the space between them, obscuring their view.

'One more arrow each, lads,' she said, 'then let's get this door shut on them.'

The four archers loosed one last time while Tor took a grip on the dead monk's robe and hauled him out of the door frame into the body of the church. She left a trail of brains and blood as she dragged the sagging corpse. The four archers helped her to close the huge door quickly on the enemy and, once it was securely bolted, Tor found she could already feel the growing heat from the fire inside the church's mint tower.

The air inside that space was now thick with choking black fumes. Tor coughed, and looked east towards the altar. The three axemen had broken through at last and she could see the darkness outside through the small ragged opening and the corner of a small house, thatched with reeds. No Red Cloaks visible there.

Father Alwin was praying once more. 'You're coming with us,' she said to the priest, slapping him hard on the shoulder. 'It's that – or be roasted to death in here.'

The axemen were still busy, widening the hole in the church's back wall.

'I'm in God's loving hands, as always,' Alwin said. 'Only He knows my fate.'

'You are in *my* hands,' said Tor, 'in fact… Joralf! You've got this priest. He is your prisoner, your responsibility. Bring him with us and make sure he is quiet.'

She could hear the Franks at the door, battering, roaring, the scrape and thud of weapons against the oak. 'Nithi,' she called to an immensely strong warrior with a hedge of black beard, 'you are on the coin boxes. Pick two men and guard them well. Lose even one coin and I'll have your hairy balls on an iron skewer!'

The axemen were still chopping, hazel splinters and whitewashed daub flying.

The big warrior nodded and went over to the nearest box; he effortlessly hefted the iron casket filled with silver coin, the muscles of his forearms, which were thickly tattooed with images of ships and boats, writhing under his skin like a nest of over-wintering snakes. Nithi called two of his crew-mates to grab hold of the others.

'Here we go!' shouted Tor, drawing her sword. And she ran towards the now gaping hole in the east end of the church. 'Everybody out! Out! Quickly now.'

The crew of the *Fafnir* burst out of the church in a tight, swift-running pack, shouldering aside the splinters of wattle and clumps of dried mud and plaster. They erupted out on the dark street, and ran south, some forty warriors, with the three coin chests in the centre of the pack along with the Angelcynn priest Father Alwin, who was being alternately pushed and dragged along by young Joralf. Tor led the way. A lone Frank warrior challenged her, no Red Cloak, just a local fellow in furs, and she batted him out of her path with a wide, almost casual swipe of her sword. Sambor, who was lumbering along just behind her, surged forwards as he stumbled away from her blow and crushed the man's right shoulder joint with a plunging blow of his axe.

Tor glanced right, as the man staggered away, his mouth gaping wide in shock and pain, and saw that the mass of Red Cloaks was still outside the closed church door – they had found a long log, or perhaps a cut-down tree trunk, to use as a battering ram, and a dozen men were swinging it enthusiastically at the bolted oak door. They were partially enveloped in a thickening cloud of drifting darkness from the burning tower, the shifting banks of smoke strangely red in the light of their torches. The high walls of the church were starting to catch too, with yellow flames licking up under the eaves. Yet an unobscured view of the battering Red Cloaks came and went with the billows of grey and black. For a brief moment the smoke bank cleared entirely, a strong eddy of the westerly wind, and one of their plumed officers, looking east simply by chance, gave a loud cry and stabbed a finger at the swift-running *Fafnir* crew. Tor cursed. She had hoped for longer, but their trick was blown.

A few moments later and all the Franks had abandoned the locked church door and scores of them were now in full pursuit of the running Fafnirs – shouting in their excitement, sprinting after the fleeing vikings, the Franks' scarlet cloaks billowing out behind them. More than a hundred of their enemies joined in the chase, Tor guessed, in a strung-out pack, hallooing like excited huntsmen. Yes, it had been a trap all right – she knew that for certain. Why else would so many Red Cloaks be posted to one small port? How else had they mustered so quickly? She had been raiding all summer along the coast; it would not take much wisdom to guess Dorestad was next.

She urged her people on to greater speed, as they splashed along through the dark, muddy streets towards the harbour. Changing direction, turning corners into new streets, dodging down alleys, but always heading back towards the jetty.

Tor came to a crossroads. She hesitated a beat – left or right? – and saw the red-clad vanguard of her enemies bearing down on her fast. 'This way,' she yelled, stabbing out her index finger at random. *No time to get lost, you idiot*, she thought.

They pelted down a narrow street. The Franks were right behind them by now, some even pausing to throw their javelins. An arrow hissed evilly past her shoulder. She heard cries of pain behind her. Her people were now strung out over a full fifty yards, panting, stumbling, the three strong men with the heavy coin chests falling ever more behind. It was no good, she would have to do something to discourage their pursuers. To give the rest of her people a chance to reach the *Fafnir* in time.

'Steerboard watch, to me. Halt. *Skjald-borg!* Right here. Archers at the rear.'

About half the running men stopped abruptly, turned and formed up beside Tor in a double line, twenty men in a short chain across the narrow street, shields held up.

It was a raggedy shield wall and far too thin – in another time and place, Tor would have been furious at its sloppiness – but this was real battle, not practice. It would have to do. She could hear the men panting from the run, their chests heaving.

A dozen of her archers now were lining up behind the wall, nocking shafts to their bows. The rest of her crew were running on south – by Odin, she hoped south.

'Brace, now, brace!' Tor bellowed, as the first of the running Red Cloaks crashed into the thin wall of her people. Behind her the archers were steadily loosing at the oncoming Franks, dropping one, two, three men. One Red Cloak, a dark, heavy man ahead of the pack, charged straight on to her upheld shield and it took all of Tor's strength not to take a step back; he was grunting, snarling, shoving at her, shield to shield, his breath foul from sour wine and garlic, huffing it right into her face.

She yelled out: 'Kill them, Fafnirs! Put them all down now!'

She felt the man directly behind her, Black Ivar, shove her whole body forwards, his shield pressed tight into the small of her back. She found her right arm suddenly free and the sword in her fist slipped round the edge of her shield and drove hard into her enemy's left side, jabbing into his ribs. He screamed, recoiled a little, battered at her helm with his own long sword. But she could tell he had been mortally struck.

She heaved him off her shield, using all her strength, and he staggered back and away and dropped to the mud of the street. Tor looked swiftly left, then right. The wall was holding – just. She saw Sambor growling, swiping at a pair of terrified Red Cloaks with his long axe. Olaf the Hammer was striking at the enemy from the second rank, his weapon looping out to crack shields, crush bones and shatter skulls.

Many Franks were hanging back – it takes a great deal of raw courage to throw yourself directly on to the enemies' blades when they're formed in a half-decent wall.

An officer with a nodding red plume was slapping at a young man's face, pointing at the wall, ordering him to attack. He shook his head, arguing and afraid.

She listened to her heartbeats, shield high, counting to one hundred. A lone young Red Cloak screamed a battle cry and ran madly at the wall – but he was swiftly cut down, half a dozen viking blades lancing out to steal his life. A clear gap had formed now between the two masses of warriors, but the Red Cloaks on one side, seemingly more of them than ever, were getting ready for a full-on frontal assault, summoning their courage for an over-whelming attack. In a few moments they would charge and Tor and her folk would be swept away. The officer was shouting, pointing at the wall.

Tor shouted: 'Now run, all of you – flee. To the harbour. Run for your lives!'

She felt the shield wall instantly dissolve all around her and, stealing a last glimpse backwards at the astonished line of Franks, she too turned and pelted away.

*Practice*, she thought. *Practice and repetition – that is what wins battles.* They had performed this exact battle manoeuvre over and over again during the long, idle winter months: the sudden stop in full flight, then the swift making of a shield wall, with the archers lined up at the back; resisting the first deadly clash, then a sudden, unexpected flight once more at her word of command. She had practised this time and again with her reluctant, awkward, sluggish men, big fellows who believed that, because they were rough-tough outlaws living on the edge of the world, they had no need for the smack of proper discipline. They were wrong. She had made that plain. She had bullied and beaten them, shouted at them and shoved them, until even the surly ones with the worst hangovers had mastered this and several other complicated manoeuvres until they were heartily sick of the formations, the movements, the drills, of her hectoring voice and of all their lumbering, ox-dull comrades. Yet today it had repaid them with their lives. No one had made a false move, her commands had been obeyed. The foe had been held off, and very few of her *vikingr* comrades had been lost.

*Practice and repetition.*

Not far to go. The jetty was only a few dozen paces away now – she could see the rest of her crew already waiting at the water's edge. There was Joralf with the skinny priest. Nithi standing over the little pyramid of square iron coin boxes, his long sword drawn. And behind them the wide expanse of muddy harbour water stretching out towards the German sea and their escape, behind them was… nothing.

There was no sign of the *Fafnir*. A few bare-masted moored vessels out in the dark, shallow water, a couple of skiffs bobbing slowly at anchor – where in the name of Odin was Kynwulf and the men he needed to manoeuvre the ship? Could the old man have been captured? Not Kynwulf. Could he have betrayed them? No, never.

She skidded to a halt on the slimy jetty, and turned to look back at the dark town. The church was like a giant torch illuminating the whole of Dorestad, and many other houses were burning too, over to the west of the town, individual homes ablaze, but too far away to have been ignited by wind-blown sparks from the church.

Then the first signs of the Franks – coming on cautiously now, edging forwards, clumps of men emerging furtively from the side streets and from behind houses, and then some of them grinning to see their *vikingr* foes now trapped by the water's edge.

'Boar's Snout!' bellowed Tor, taking two paces towards the Franks, sheathing her sword and drawing her wicked seax. It was as good a formation as any. If they could not go backwards into the sea, then they would have to go forwards – right through the Franks. They might even manage it, too. Who knew till it was attempted?

Her whole crew formed up around her, she and Black Ivar formed the flat face of the pig's snout, with the other warriors crushing in behind her in a tight wedge shape. Shields on the left, ranks of spears and swords on the right. In the centre, towards the rear, was Joralf and the thin priest, and Nithi and his precious coin chests. And the Franks were forming up too – a shield wall, and taking their time about it.

Tor yelled out: 'Who are we?'

And the mass of warriors at her back, shouted back: 'Ymirsfjord!'

'I cannot hear you,' said Tor. 'I said: Who are we?'

'Y… mirs… fjord!' the crowd of people responded, louder this time.

46

'Don't be shy. These Christian *nithings* really need to know this. Who are we?'

'Y... MIRS... FJORD!' came the bellowed reply from forty, hoarse throats.

'That's right. That's who we are. Now, let us prove it... Forwards!' and Tor and Black Ivar leapt towards the ill-formed Frankish lines. They ran full pelt. And the wedge of warriors came after them, a fierce, bristling Boar's Snout, hurtling forwards.

They drove straight into the Frankish wall, and Tor found herself shoving at the line of enemy shields, struggling to use her seax in the crush. Behind her, the spears of her comrades lanced out, slicing into clean-shaven Frankish faces below their helmet rims, causing the enemy to dodge and duck away. She felt ringing blows on her own helm but the sheer momentum of the tight-packed wedge propelled Tor forwards into the midst of the enemy host... which to her surprise somehow seemed to be melting before her.

She called out, 'Who are we?' one last time, and received the response, and found it echoed by a more distant call of 'Ymirsfjord! Ymirsfjord!' coming, astonishingly, from directly to her front – from *behind* the ranks of the enemy line.

A name popped into her head: *Mogils*.

A space opened up in front of her and she hacked at an older Frank with her seax, an officer, making him flinch back, then shoved the blade point into the neck of another man beside him. She barged her shield hard into another fellow's shield and sent him reeling, too, and then at last she could clearly see.

There was the wonderful, the heroic, the magnificent Captain Mogils, with his two dozen seasoned Ymirsfjord warriors, driving a wedge into the rearmost men of the Frankish shield wall. The enemy, now confused, and frightened by this double assault, by the unexpected attack on their unguarded rear, were cowering, stepping back, turning round to look – some were already running away into the streets of the town, seeking safety. The rest soon followed their example. The Boar's Snout had burst through their lines now and the harbourfront was theirs. Mogils was smiling at her, mail blood-spattered and black with soot. He pointed behind her with his sword.

Tor whipped round and saw what Mogils saw – the *Fafnir*, twenty paces from the jetty and coming on smoothly to scrape against the wooden platform, six men at the oars, and Kynwulf, manning the tiller at the back. He was grinning at her, too.

'Back!' she shouted. 'To the ship!' But the warriors of the Boar's Snout needed no urging: they, too, had seen the arrival of their sea-borne rescuer, and were all now streaming back towards the *Fafnir*. Tor took one final glance at the harbourfront; there were still several knots of Red Cloaks there, a handful of them just standing there on the cobbles, swords drooping, shields low, staring in shock as the dragon ship bumped gently against the wooden pier. The vikings clattered down the jetty, shouting with triumph, and scrambled aboard.

There were dozens of dead and wounded lying on the blood-streaked mud of the harbour, the gory puddles illuminated by the flames of burning town. Tor recognised some of her own folk among them, but not too many. The Frankish officers were still trying to get their shattered men to form up to attack the *vikingr* marauders one last time. But the Christians were beaten. And they all knew it. Some Frank nearby was blowing a trumpet. A mournful howling blast, echoing out again and again. A young man lying on the ground screamed in pain, another knelt beside him, whispering.

Captain Mogils tapped Tor on the shoulder. They were the last two on the jetty.

A new group of Red Cloaks came trotting round the street corner – another company of fifty men, smart, clean, marching in unison, their trumpets sounding.

'Come, Tor, we must get away,' he said. 'We cannot hope to kill them all!'

# Chapter Four

*'What is in the king's mind?'*

'Are you mad?' said Bjarki. He was staring at Valtyr. 'Siegfried outlawed me – he made it lawful for any man to slay me. And now he wants me as his son?'

'He has always liked you, Bjarki. If you look into your heart you will know it to be true. Did Siegfried not choose you to be King of Vastergotland?'

'He only did that so I would raise fighting men for his army!' said Bjarki.

'You were so much more than his recruiting officer,' said Valtyr. 'He honoured you above the rest. He was kind to you when you had been wronged.'

'We guarantee your safety – if you fear for your life,' said the Saxon Wolf.

Bjarki glared at him. 'I can guarantee my own safety. By staying right here.'

'I'm saying, if you're fearful of a trap, my men and I will be with you.'

'I trust you, Saxon, even less than I do King Siegfried. I watched you at Norrkoping. You and your men hardly fought, and fled quickly from the field.'

'What are you saying?' Widukind shot to his feet, his face darkening.

'I am saying your actions at Norrkoping speak of your true character.'

Widukind put his hand on his hilt. A hilt Bjarki knew well. A blue jewel adorned the pommel of this ancient blade, a royal sword once wielded by a god.

'Do you call me a coward?' snarled Widukind. 'Be careful how you chose your next words, Rekkr! If you think I fear your god-given madness, I do not.'

'No!' the word was bellowed across the table. Valtyr, who was pouring himself another cup, started and spilled a slick of ale on the wooden surface.

'No,' said Edith again, more softly this time. 'I will not have the two men I love most in the Middle-Realm fighting each other over a few ill-chosen words.'

Bjarki and Widukind had been on their feet staring at each other, just a yard of table between them. All about them fifty warriors were poised for action.

Edith came over and linked arms with her husband. She stood on her toes and kissed his bearded cheek. 'Apologise to my brother, Bjarki. You insulted him just a little.'

'He started it! He said I was afraid to go to Ribe and meet that old goat.'

'I did not intend my words that way,' said Widukind. 'It was not at all my intention to anger you, Rekkr.'

'Hrrumph,' muttered Bjarki.

'Therefore, I humbly beg your pardon, brother,' said Widukind. 'I spoke rashly. I know that you fear naught in the Middle-Realm, not even death itself.'

Bjarki squinted at the Saxon duke – was he being mocked by him? Edith nudged him in the ribs, and then nudged him again. Quite hard.

'Forgive me, duke,' said Bjarki tightly. 'I spoke hastily and I regret it.'

'Sit down both of you, and have another drink,' said Valtyr. His face was flushed and his eyes unfocused. 'Let me tell you what is in the king's mind.'

The two men resumed their seats, and Valtyr began to draw circles in the ale puddle on the table. For a while he said nothing, then cleared his throat. 'Siegfried's last legitimate son, Eyvindr, was killed at Norrkoping. You knew that, Bjarki?'

'I did not even know he had a son.'

'He was only fourteen summers and although his old father forbade him to fight, the boy ran off and joined Jarl Lars Crookback's retinue as an ordinary spearman. He was killed in the first assault on the Kolmarden. A sad waste. And Siegfried has no other legitimate children. He lost the older son years ago to fever and his daughter Geva, who was married to Widukind for years, was kicked by a horse in the head. She, most unfortunately, had no children with our Saxon friend.'

'I am sorry to hear that,' said Bjarki nodding at Widukind, who shrugged.

'What about bastards?' said Edith. 'He has been king a very long time, and he cannot have been short of willing young women to warm his royal bed.'

'There is one that we know of – a fellow called Halfdan – whom the king got by a Frisian serving girl. He is living with his mother near the sea but...'

'But what?' said Edith.

'Siegfried does not recognise him. He is no warrior. He's a Frisian peasant, not a man of blood and iron. He grows cabbages. He is not fit to be a King of the Danes.'

'So Siegfried does not want a cabbage-grower as his heir. I can understand that. But why me?' said Bjarki. 'I'm not his kin. I'm no relation to him at all.'

'Told you,' said Valtyr, 'he likes you. You are a famous Sword-Dane. He thinks you're strong; he thinks you are an honourable man. He says you made a good King of Vastergotland. He says you would fight to protect his folk against all their foes.'

'Foes?' said Bjarki. 'Is the King of the North threatening his kingdom?'

'No, Sigurd Hring has his hands full with all the Goths. He is at present campaigning in Ostergotland, fighting the last remaining Wulfings, who have now decided they do not like his direct rule after all. No, not Sigurd Hring. The King of the North is content, at present, to leave the Dane-Mark to mind its own affairs.'

'So which enemies threaten the Danes?' said Bjarki.

There was a silence. Valtyr looked at Widukind, who merely shrugged again.

'No,' said Bjarki. 'No. I know what that look means. I know what you two have been plotting. The answer is no. Most emphatically no. Never. No, no, no.'

'What can you possibly mean?' said Valtyr, striving for an innocent smile.

'You want to drag me back into the wars in Saxony. You want me to fight King Karolus and his Franks and, against impossible odds, reclaim Saxony for you, duke.'

'Why would you think that?' said Widukind, who now looked even less sincere than Valtyr. 'I only want you to return to the Dane-Mark to wait on the old king.'

'All we want is for you to come to Ribe,' said Valtyr. 'To visit a sweet old man who loves you, and for you to be reconciled with him again, forgive him, and let him make

53

you his heir. Do you not wish to be a king again, Bjarki? Ruler of a kingdom?'

–

Later than night Bjarki lay beside his lovely Saxon wife in their marriage bed in the curtained-off room at the far end of the hall of Ymirsfjord. They had just finished making love, yet it had been a perfunctory coupling with neither fully engaged.

'You think I have to go to Ribe?' said Bjarki.

'I do,' said Edith.

'Even if I don't want to? Even though I have no desire to be King of the Dane-Mark or anywhere else – except to be *hersir* in Ymirsfjord? Is that it?'

'Yes.'

Bjarki was silent for a while. 'I must say, my love, I am surprised that your brother is pushing me to be Siegfried's heir. I always thought that he secretly had his eye on the Danish throne. If he could not get Saxony back, that is. Perhaps I was wrong. But anyway... I don't want to go to Ribe. I want to stay here with you and my children. I want to be here where I am my own master. I must still go to Ribe?'

'I think you must.'

'Why?'

'I love you. I love our life together here. But Siegfried has always been good to me, and also kind to you. I know that he outlawed you, and set a price on your head, but he never sent his ships of war against you, or against Ymirsfjord. And all the gods know he might well have done so. The Dane-Mark is far stronger than we are. Yet he forbore to attack us here. He left us in peace, did he

54

not? He left us alone to let the dust settle. He calmed my brother's wrath, too. And that of his man, Abbio the Crow, to whom I was betrothed. We owe Siegfried a debt. I think we may trust his word.'

Bjarki said nothing beyond a grunt. He rolled over on to his side and gazed at his wife's beautiful face, framed with her dark-gold hair. He could hear the sounds of merriment drifting through from the hall, although it was past midnight. He could hear Valtyr telling some hoary old story to the groans and cheers of his listeners.

'Truly and honestly, do you not wish to be King of the Danes one day, Bjarki, when old Siegfried is gone to Valhalla? Would you not wish to direct the lives and fortunes of the Danish people? Your people? What greater work could there be than to stand as a guardian over a nation, and protect them from the evils of the world?'

'I direct the fortunes of the people of Ymirsfjord, and protect *them* from all evil,' said Bjarki, half-heartedly. But he was now thinking of Edith and her narrow-channelled existence here. It was not a hard life, by his lights, yet it was not the life she was born into. She milked the goats each morning, and fed the chickens and tended to the kitchen gardens, and her children's daily needs. She had a servant – Trudi – who helped in her tasks, and she had never once complained of her lot. But she had been raised a great lady, the daughter of a duke, and now the sister of a duke, with many maid servants and fine clothes, and a life of ease and comfort. He took one of her hands and gently lifted it towards his face, to kiss. As he did so, he saw the reddening of the skin around the knuckles and felt the roughness of the thick callouses on the pads of her fingers. He kissed it lovingly anyway.

'When I fell in love with you,' said Edith, 'it was not because you were King of Vastergotland, nor because you were the bold and terrible Rekkr, feared by all men. It was because I knew you were a kind man inside your secret heart – despite all the *berserkr* fury of your reputation – and because I could see a seed of greatness in you. You were a man unlike any other, I recognised that. You had it within you to be a great man – not just a viking lord of war, in hiding out here on the very edge of the world, but a man who had it within him to make a deep mark on the Middle-Realm, a great man who would be long remembered after his death. That is why I love you.'

'I love you, too, Edith. And I hate the thought of being parted from you.'

'It would not be for long, my love. A few months, perhaps. And, if nothing more comes of it, we can still have what we have here, with Lili and Hildar at Ymirsfjord. But if you turn your face away from this royal invitation, then we shall never know what the future might hold for us, and for our children. If you did become king, think of the inheritance our baby son might gain. He might even one day be King Hildar!'

'I will sleep on it,' said Bjarki. 'My head will be clearer in the morning.'

Yet sleep eluded him. He lay there thinking, aware that Edith was also awake beside him. Eventually, he said: 'Who was that boy standing beside Valtyr?'

'I wondered, too. I thought it might be his son, but Valtyr said no. Just his servant. He said that he was merely a lost waif that he had collected on his travels.'

Bjarki suddenly felt a chill. 'Did Valtyr say where he collected this waif?'

'On one of the Danish islands. He said he thought the boy had potential.'

Bjarki laughed. Once he, too, had been one of Valtyr's waifs. A half-grown boy with 'potential' whom the one-eyed old trader had picked up on Bago, the tiny island a few miles off the coast of Jutland, the place where Bjarki had grown up.

Valtyr had taken him and Tor south to Saxony, to a sacred place where the mighty One Tree, the Irminsul, had grown atop a plateau that thrust out from the Diemal Valley – the Groves of Eresburg, that special place was called. Until its destruction by Karolus and his Frankish legions, it had been the holiest place of all in the North, the place where Bjarki had trained to become a Rekkr. *Was this to be the boy's fate?* It seemed unlikely, because the Groves of Eresburg had been destroyed.

With that in his mind, Bjarki Bloodhand, the Rekkr of Ymirsfjord, fell asleep.

–

The Great Horn on the headland boomed out the next morning an hour after dawn, and Bjarki, who had been in the forge with the Ymirsfjord blacksmith, helping him to cast a dozen new axe blades, immediately came rushing out into the courtyard.

He bounded to the stairs, taking them two at a time until he reached the wooden walkway that ran inside the palisade of sharpened pine trunks. He went over to the gatehouse and briefly acknowledging the guards, he shaded his eyes and stared out west along the deep blue fjord. A ship, just one, but a large one, was approaching. A ship of war holding perhaps eighty warriors – he could see the shields hung along the sides. Its woollen sail was made of dyed red and white strips of cloth, sewn together, a familiar pattern, used by many northern sailors, some of whom were also *vikingr*. As he watched, a small object was run up the single mast, and broke out, unfurling in the stiff breeze: a bright yellow flag with the image of an upright brown bear.

And he could make out the prow-beast now. A fearsome carved dragon, painted in green and gold, with a sliver of red tongue. So there was no doubt in his mind.

It was Tor. His sister was returning home to Ymirsfjord in *Fafnir* at long last.

# Chapter Five

*A fitting gift for a fine lady*

The journey home had been largely uneventful, even a little dull, Tor reflected, from her usual position standing at the dragon's head prow, looking out at the rolling waves in front of her. The only happening of note was that Hrolf the Fat had died of his wounds on the second day after the *Fafnir* had left Dorestad. Tor, to her shame, had not even known Hrolf was badly wounded until he showed all his crew-mates the small bloody hole in his belly from a spear thrust, a surprisingly neat puncture.

He died quietly at his oar on the morning of the second day and they beached the ship on the north-western coast of Jutland, on a long empty stretch of grey and windswept sand, and buried him in a shallow grave above in the grassy dunes.

Tor had said a few words of praise over his body but they had not lingered. Tor did not know what local Danish jarl currently ruled here but she did not relish another battle so soon after the last – her men were exhausted, some wounded, although no one as badly as Hrolf. But they were *vikingir*, after all, and outlaws, according to the Danish king. And any liegeman of Siegfried would be unlikely to let them continue on their way without an attempt to detain and question them.

They had beached the *Fafnir* once again at Oddernes, where the local petty king had welcomed them with enthusiasm, and set his people to help pull the dragon ship up on to the strand, and had thrown them a modest feast the same night.

Ole Karlsson was a king in name only. His tiny kingdom held fewer than three score folk, most of whom were men fleeing from something or someone, and he scratched a living from the sea and the land as best he could with the help of his four lazy and doltish sons. The king was an ally of Bjarki's and was charged with keeping a watch on these western waters between the North-Way and the Jutland peninsula; he was supposed to be keeping an eye out for Bjarki's enemies, and had promised to send a fast skiff round the coast or a runner over the mountains to give him warning.

So far, Ole had never given warning of anything. But Bjarki still gave him a few piglets each year and a dozen sacks of barley for this watching 'service'. It was simply a bribe to keep the old bastard sweet, Tor reckoned. The price of his friendship.

They spent the night with Ole Karlsson in his hall and ate reasonably well. This was because Tor provided all the food and wine from her ship's stores – they had a few Frankish wine casks left from their plundering that summer – and some sacks of dried herring which was turned into a salty stew with oats, and they slept warm.

Then two days later, they turned the steerboard-side into the jaws of the fjord and, with a brisk north-westerly filling the striped sail and rifling Tor's red hair, they began the passage east towards the settlement of Ymirsfjord. Tor heard the booming of the Great Horn from up on the headland as they passed, and smiled. At least Bjarki had kept a watch while she was away. It could not all have gone to ruin in her absence.

–

'He wants you to be *what*?' said Tor. She was standing on the Ymirsfjord beach looking out to sea, with Bjarki looming at her shoulder. A humpbacked whale was blowing a watery spume out in the fjord, the sunlight shining off its glossy hide.

'To be his heir. Siegfried wants me to inherit the Danish throne as well as his lands, goods and chattels when he is dead, which Valtyr says may be soon.'

'I cannot understand, brother, why people are always so eager to make you their king. Everywhere we go, we come across another bunch of cheerful fools who take one look at you and think, "Ah yes, this lumbering ox ought to be in charge of it all. Let's make him our king." I find it mystifying. But it seems to be your chief talent.'

Tor delivered this sally with a grin to take the sting out of her words, but Bjarki frowned anyway. 'Siegfried said I made a very good king, if only for a short while.'

'I'm sure Kynwulf and the rest of the *Felaki* think you were a fine monarch too. Maybe it's just me who finds it odd. No one has ever asked me to be their queen.'

'That is probably because no one likes you.' As soon as Bjarki said this, he regretted it. He glanced at Tor's face and saw her staring back at him bleakly.

'I'm sorry. I did not mean that. All our folk think you are magnificent.'

'I don't care if people don't like me. Or if they love me. I don't care if they hate me, as long as they do their duty, obey orders and don't ask stupid questions.'

Brother and sister looked at each other a while, both feeling bruised by their exchange. The whale gave a final blast of watery air and sank below the waves.

Eventually Tor said: 'So, will you go to Ribe? Will you go and see the king?'

'The truth is I don't want to leave Edith and the children,' said Bjarki, and braced himself for a crack from Tor about his lack of manliness, a comment about how he was tethered by his wife's apron strings, or something of that nature.

'Take her with you,' said Tor. 'Edith would enjoy it. She finds the life here a bit crude for her tastes. Take her to the royal court. I'm fairly sure it would be safe.'

'Will you come too?'

'I'll come – and we will bring along a strong escort, just in case. Say fifty of our fittest shield-men, all fully armed and armoured and ready to fight. We can go there in the *Fafnir*, which can outrun most ships on these seas. I think we will be safe at Ribe but there is no point being overly rash. Siegfried can feed and house us all at his own expense over the Yuletide period, and I'm sure our Ymirsfjord lot will make the most of his generous hospitality. He may well come to regret his invitation in time.'

'I just hope *I* don't regret taking up his invitation.'

Tor smiled at him. 'Hey, cheer up, brother – it might even be fun!'

–

Tor stood in the doorway of the one-room house in the Ymirsfjord compound which Edith had designated the nursery. The day was warm, a last blast of golden autumn before storm season began. Tor watched Bjarki's wife on her knees playing with Lili and her dolls, pretending they were attending a feast.

In a basket slung from the rafters by the back wall, the baby Hildar was gurgling happily and playing with a large polished piece of deer's antler. Tor watched them all silently and felt a huge surge of protective warmth for all three.

The shaft of pain ignited by Bjarki's comment still glowed in her memory. It was true, there were very few people who actively sought out her company, unless they were obliged to do so. But you could not just command people to like you. She had always pushed others away, priding herself on her fierce independence and her refusal to suffer fools. But somehow her bruised spirit felt wonderfully soothed by this sweet, familial scene. It was like a balm to her: she loved her niece Lili and, now she had seen him, her baby nephew Hildar, too, almost as much as if they were her own. And while Edith and she were as unlike each other in temperament as it was possible for two women to be, they had built a kind of friendship between them over the past four years based on strong mutual respect, even if there was little mutual comprehension. The bond they shared, and what united them at a deep level, was love for Bjarki, which was enough to make them firm allies.

'Perhaps the Lady Torfinna would graciously join us at the royal feast,' said Edith, turning to smile at Tor, and making a hand gesture inviting her to sit.

Tor came in and sat down cross-legged on the floor between Edith and Lili. 'Drink some wine, Tor,' said Lili. 'It's the best wine, the king's very best wine.'

The child passed her a clay cup that contained, on closer inspection, a little muddy water. Tor pretended to take a gulp, smacking her lips enthusiastically.

'You are too kind, your royal highness,' Tor said. 'It is fine wine indeed.'

'I'm not the king,' said Lili. 'That would be silly. Helga is the king!' The child pointed to a doll made from a pine cone and a few old woollen rags. Tor saw that the doll had a tiny circlet of golden straw balanced on its kernel head.

'My apologies, highness,' said Tor, bowing to the doll. 'I beg your pardon.'

Then Hildar began to grizzle, and Edith got up and went to the hanging basket to soothe him. She picked him out of the basket and came to stand by Tor.

'Would you like to hold the baby for a little while?' she said.

Tor jumped to her feet. 'Gods, no – I'm sure I would drop him or something.'

'You won't drop him. Just support his head and hold him tight to your chest.'

'No, no, I would rather not.' The proximity of the baby was making Tor feel strange: something ached between her breasts, she felt suddenly breathless, almost ill. She found she could not stop looking at his sweet little pink face and wide blue eyes.

'As you wish,' said Edith, but there was a touch of coldness in her voice.

'Do you want roasted venison, Tor?' said Lili. 'It is the king's fanciest meat. Only the king is allowed to eat this special meat but you can have some if you like.'

'No, thank you, Lili. I can't stay,' said Tor. 'I have to go and see Kynwulf about the ship. We're leaving tomorrow, and I have to… anyway, I need to see Kynwulf.'

Tor suddenly felt horribly awkward in that company. It was so alien, so wrong, so sweet and comfortable, that she felt the urge to smash something. Kill someone.

'Thank you for coming to see us, Tor,' said Edith. 'We have all missed you.'

'Oh, I forgot. I have this for you, Lili,' said Tor. 'A present. I saw it when we were fighting in a big church in Francia and I thought you might like to have it.'

Tor rummaged in her pouch and came out with a round silver box, about the size of Lili's fist, with an image of a kindly man in a blue robe on the top.

'It had little slices of bread inside, which the Franks eat in church, but they were stale so I threw them away. I thought you could keep nice things inside it.'

Lili was entranced. She took the shiny box and turned it over in her hand.

'That is kind of you, Tor,' said Edith. 'I thank you – Lili thanks you too.'

'I have something for you, too, sister.'

'That is not necessary – just having you home safely is enough for me.'

'We spoke in the spring before I left about books and writing,' said Tor. 'Do you remember? You said that you hoped Lili and the baby would one day learn to read and write, like educated Christians, so they could record their lives in books and communicate with other people far away, and perhaps even after they were dead.'

'Did I say that?' said Edith. 'Yes, I remember – we talked about writing.'

'I thought about bringing you a book – we picked up some bibles, which is their holy book, in Francia – but what use is a book if you cannot read it?'

'What use indeed?'

'So I brought you a gift, Edith. Wait here a moment and I will fetch it.'

A few moments later, Tor returned, leading a man on a leash tied around his bound hands. It was Father Alwin, the Angelcynn priest, looking dazed and dirty.

'I captured him in the raid in Dorestad,' said Tor. 'He is my thrall. And now I give him to you. All the fine ladies in Francia have a priest to attend them. So I thought it fitting. He can read and write – he learned at a cathedral, a grand church, in his land. I thought he could teach you – and Lili and even Hildar – to make letters.'

–

Tor walked back towards the longhouse with her insides in turmoil. There was something cloying about the nursery that had made her feel vulnerable – and lonely, too. Nobody likes you, Bjarki had said. And it was true. She had no one close but her brother and Edith. She felt oddly empty inside, as if nothing in her life had any meaning. She did indeed wish to see Kynwulf about readying the *Fafnir* for the three-day voyage to the Dane-Mark, on which they would embark the next day, but that could surely wait an hour or so. There was someone else she needed to see first.

She was determined not to think about what she meant to do. Not think at all. Thinking was overrated, that was her firm opinion this morning; thinking was for cowards and fools, for people who were too scared or indecisive to take the course they desired. She would act. She would do the deed – and fuck the consequences.

She strode into the longhouse, looked left and then right, searching. There were a dozen men moving around the space, a few women in headscarves too, and some of them thralls. There was no sign of Bjarki – and then she remembered that he was busy dealing with the new rigging this morning. Valtyr was lying on one of the benches by the far wall, eyes closed, mouth open, snoring gently.

She had seen him in the same position earlier that same day.

And there he was, over by the curtain that separated Bjarki's private chamber and the rest of the long hall. There was the big, blond, arrogant prick. Seated at one of the long tables and playing at *tafl* with one of his spearmen, both men hunched over the board, studying the pieces. Both totally absorbed in their game.

Tor strode directly over to him.

'You, get up now and follow me,' she said.

Widukind, Duke of Saxony, turned to see who was addressing him so rudely.

'Tor,' he said. 'Greetings. What can I do for you this fine morning?'

'You can get your arse up off that bench and follow me,' she said. 'Now.'

The spearman opposite rose, growled and began reaching for his seax.

'Peace, Sigfinn, peace. Tor is an old friend. I'm sure she means me no harm.'

Tor glared at him. 'I am told that your wife Geva is dead,' she said.

'That is the case, sadly. She died last summer. Kicked in the head by a horse.'

'Good. Now come with me.'

Widukind frowned at her; he was on the edge of real anger. 'Why?'

'Just come with me, will you?'

Widukind rose from the bench, adjusted his clothing, and followed Tor out of the hall. They walked across the compound towards the main gate but stopped before it and Tor unbarred and entered the temple at its right-hand side. It was cold and dark in there. The only light coming in through chinks in the log walls.

Tor shut the door behind Widukind and came to stand close to him. Over the musty, meaty odours of the temple, she could clearly smell his long-remembered scent – the spice of sweat and old leather – as she reached up and pulled his head down towards hers, and kissed him, long and deep. Tentatively at first and then with a genuine eagerness, even a hunger, he returned her kiss.

'Don't say anything,' she whispered. 'You'll ruin it. I just want to fuck.'

# Chapter Six

## *A leap of faith*

The rain hissed on the surface of the sea in the harbour Ribehaven, the port that served the town of Ribe, which was two miles inland. Bjarki, soaked to the skin, stepped from the deck of the *Fafnir* on to the slippery wood of the jetty. Kynwulf reached forwards a helpful, steadying hand but Bjarki slapped it away.

'I don't need help getting out of my own ship, War Chief,' he snapped. He stamped his booted feet on the jetty planks as if to demonstrate his steadiness.

In truth, it had been a long, cold, difficult voyage: almost immediately after they had left Ymirsfjord waters, a black storm had come driving in from the west with icy rain and mountainous seas, and the *Fafnir* – as well as her consort, the *Wave Elk*, the ship that carried Widukind, Valtyr and the rest of their party – had been forced to take shelter at Oddernes in the hall of King Ole for nine days, while the wind howled and shrieked, the rain fell like iron spears and Thor split the sky with his thunderbolts.

Ole had feasted them all, given them shelter, providing as well as he was able – and he lavished praise upon Bjarki, particularly when he became aware, no doubt alerted by some spearmen's gossip, that his neighbour might soon become the heir to the Danish throne. But Bjarki felt a growing sense of frustration being cooped up in Ole's dilapidated hall, day after day, while the rain seeped through the king's thatch and dripped on the benches. If he had to sit and do nothing, he would rather be at home. Each dawn he stomped out, looked up at the dark sky and came inside cursing.

It had stopped raining on the ninth day and they had been able to launch their ships in weak sunshine and set sails to briskly travel south across the Skagerrak and down the west cost of Jutland, but it seemed that the gods had been playing a trick on the Ymirsfjord folk, for the rain had resumed later on the same day harder than ever, soaking them all in their open ships. Bjarki had decided to press on to Ribe rather than beach again on the coast of Jutland and delay the royal visit even longer.

Bjarki sneezed. A great trumpet blast of sound, which caused one of his *Felaki* bodyguards, a wiry, little man called Rask, to jump a few inches in the air.

'Our arrival has been noted,' Kynwulf murmured to Bjarki, who was busily blowing copious amounts of snot into a scrap of linen. The grizzled *Felaki* pointed to a small group of a dozen men armed with spears and shields, who were approaching the jetty along the muddy road that followed the river all the way up to Ribe.

'The *Wave Elk* must have rowed all the way to the town,' said Bjarki. 'They are slender enough to pass. So Valtyr and his folk will surely have heralded our arrival.'

This seemed likely. There was no sign of the *Wave Elk*, which had become separated from the *Fafnir* in the storm that afternoon. It was a much narrower ship.

The well-dressed man who led the welcoming party was a nervous-looking elderly fellow called Mundi, whom Bjarki knew as the king's efficient steward.

'His highness, Siegfried, King of the Dane-Mark, welcomes you, Bjarki Bloodhand, Rekkr of Ymirsfjord, to his realm,' said Mundi, in a deep, rich speaking voice that belied his meagre stature, balding head and thinning, grey beard.

'If you and your men would be kind enough to follow us,' the steward continued, 'we will take you to your accommodation. I trust you will find it sufficient to your needs. There is plenty of room for you all to be comfortable there.'

Mundi did not lie. An hour later Bjarki and Tor found themselves in a whole compound of their own, a grouping of huts and small houses inside a high wall, to the south of the town of Ribe, which was a spear-toss away on the far side of a water-filled ditch and rampart. There was indeed plenty of room for all Bjarki's entourage.

'Siegfried doesn't want us inside his walls,' said Tor, eyeing the fortification that divided them from Ribe. 'He doesn't trust us not to try to hasten his demise.'

'A reasonable precaution,' said Bjarki. He gestured to the crowd of his armed men, *vikingir* and outlaws, who were unloading their belongings inside the compound – Bjarki's *hird*, including five *Felaki*, and the fifty warriors that Tor had suggested.

At that moment, Valtyr Far-Traveller came wandering in through the open gates of the compound, with the boy trailing after him, carrying a heavy bag. Bjarki's old friend looked horribly grey, his lean face drawn with tiredness, but he had, it seemed, changed out of the wet sailing clothes he had arrived in and now sported a fine black woollen cloak, trimmed with white fox fur.

'Widukind kicked me out,' said Valtyr. 'He told me to stay with you, since you have all this space. He says he wants to be alone in his chambers at night. If I didn't know better, I'd think he had a girl. He has not been this cheerful since Geva died.'

Tor made an odd little noise in the back of her throat.

'You can roost with the *Felaki*,' said Bjarki. 'In that big, square house there, the one beside the kitchens. But don't keep them up all night, drinking all their ale and telling them your old stories – or Kynwulf will sling you out on your skinny arse.'

'You are most gracious, O Bjarki the Erfingi,' said Valtyr with a tight smile. 'So generous, too, with the king's accommodation. And speaking of drinking ale...'

'There is a barrel already open in the kitchens. Help yourself. And don't call me Bjarki the Heir, old man,' said his new host. 'Not yet. It's very unlucky. Not until I've spoken with the king, at least. Do you know when he will grant us audience?'

'Not today, that's for sure. He's in his bed. A mild chill, they say, a tickle in his throat. He'll be better in a day or so. Meantime, make yourself comfortable here...'

There was no royal summons the next day, nor the day after that. And since the weather was fine for once, Bjarki went out to explore the town of Ribe, which he had never seen before. He was admitted to the town with no difficulty, the spearmen on the gate greeting him by name, and with smiles, and he found the town a pleasant place, with several busy streets and a bustling marketplace selling fresh herring and oysters. He stayed well clear of the royal hall, not wanting to seem importunate before he was summoned, and spent a few happy hours watching the smiths hard at work, wreathed in smoke, in the armourers' quarter. The king would surely call for him soon enough. But Siegfried did not. His chill had moved from his throat to his chest, and a famous healer was summoned from Viby in the north, a wise old crone, and so Bjarki was forced to kick his heels in the compound all the next day, as well.

He came into the hall around noon to find Father Alwin, Edith and Lili engaged in a lesson. Alwin had set up a large piece of smooth slate about the size of a shield against the wall and was making symbols on it with a piece of chalk. He would invite Lili or Edith to come up to the slate and copy his marks.

'Would you care to join us, Bjarki,' asked Alwin, 'in learning our letters?'

'No,' said the Rekkr of Ymirsfjord. 'Not today, I think. Some other time.'

In truth, he found the Christian priest a strange and rather unsettling character. He was perhaps the oddest thrall he had ever known. They had first met seven years ago, in Aachen, capital of the Frankish empire, when Alwin had been the chaplain to the Auxilla, a mixed force of mercenaries, Saxons, Danes, Svear and Frisians, who were in Karolus's service. Bjarki believed that Father Alwin was a kind and decent man – although he was a Christian and therefore an enemy – for he had remon-strated at great personal risk with Bishop Livinus when Bjarki and Tor had been imprisoned there by Karolus's queen.

If Father Alwin was a decent man, Bishop Livinus was, in Bjarki's eyes, the opposite. Livinus was Francia's most powerful prelate – chaplain and chancellor to the King of the Franks. Karolus's right-hand man. He also called himself Archbishop of Saxony – a claim that had once seemed preposterous for a land that followed the old gods but which now seemed to be no more than plain truth.

Saxony was overrun by the Franks, Widukind had told him. And Livinus was their spiritual overlord.

Bishop Livinus was an unusually brutal man, cruel and tyrannical, as Bjarki knew very well, but what made Father Alwin unusual, in Bjarki's opinion, was his perpetually cheerful disposition. He was a thrall, a miserable slave. Tor had captured him in Dorestad. She owned him. Yet the man always seemed to be smiling and Bjarki had never once heard him complain, even when he was put on bailing duty in the ship for hours, doing the backbreaking work of scooping up the sea water from the bilges and tossing it overboard.

He seemed to be impervious to discomfort, and was never less than sunny in his outlook. Now he was happily teaching Edith and Lili to make their letters.

Bjarki had never met a thrall who could write before. It made him uneasy.

So he brusquely refused Father Alwin's offer and spent the rest of that day walking moodily along the shore, kicking shells and looking out at the grey sea, as the rolling waves came in endlessly. But, in the evening, after supper, he sought out Father Alwin and made him sit down across the table from him with a cup of ale in the guest hall. The priest thanked him for the great honour he was being shown.

'It has been a while, Father, since we sat and drank together,' said Bjarki.

'I remember it, lord,' said Alwin. 'We shared a jug of ale in the Auxilla compound in Aachen and, if I recall, the weather was just as bad as in recent days.'

'What happened to you? The last I remember, you were shouting at Bishop Livinus and protesting our imprisonment. You called his behaviour outrageous.'

74

Father Alwin sucked in air through his teeth. 'I was a little rash, I admit it, even foolish, but you had been unfairly treated. You had come to us in good faith, under a flag of truce, and were thrown in gaol for no good reason. I had to protest. But, sadly, Bishop Livinus never forgave me for that unruly outburst.'

'So what happened after? Where have you been? In Aachen all this time?'

A servant came over and refilled their ale cups, a man Bjarki did not know, one of half a dozen men and women provided by Siegfried for their comfort.

'I had to do penance, of course, as is right and proper, for my insolence to a superior in the Church,' said Father Alwin. 'It was a very severe penance. I was imprisoned myself for many months on bread and water, and then upon my release I was sent to the east, to the wild lands beyond the Oker, to the territory of the pagan East-phalians. I was ordered by Bishop Livinus himself to spread the Word of God out there. You see, lord, these eastern Saxon folk had knelt before Karolus a few years before and been baptised but, since then, many of them had sadly sunk back into pagan darkness and were mired in their sins. Worshipping false gods, human sacrifice… Even their jarl, a brute of a man called Hessi, went back to practising the old pagan ways. And Karolus had made him a count! I ministered to these folk, preaching the Gospel to any who would listen. Trying to guide them in the path of Jesus Christ.'

'How did the Eastphalians take the Gospel? Did they change their ways?'

'A few did, certainly, mostly poor, destitute women and their children. And with their help, after a year or so, we finally managed to construct a small wooden church in the deep woods near Schöningen. But the attendance there was very sparse. Some Sundays I had no more than six people in my congregation. Jarl Hessi offered me no help at all. When I asked him to invite all his people to attend Mass for the good of their souls every Sunday, he simply laughed at me. And I am afraid I employed some choice, unwise language to him in return. I was rash again. I believe I called him a callous, disloyal, idol-worshipping heathen and a God-damned backsliding barbarian.'

'I knew Hessi,' said Bjarki. 'He was always touchy about insults.'

'He still is,' said Father Alwin. 'I do not know whether Jarl Hessi ordered this or not, though I strongly suspect he did, but not long after my outburst a dozen armed Eastphalian men, hooded and masked like robbers, came out to our little church in the woods and set fire to it. The congregation were driven terrified into the endless forest and one old woman was killed. I was myself badly beaten by these men and anything of value we had accumulated was taken, not that there was much to steal.

'When I appealed to Jarl Hessi afterwards, he said he could do nothing to help me, and suggested that perhaps I had made myself unpopular by berating his folk about their own affairs. He told me to return to Aachen and never come to Eastphalia again. So I went miserably back to Francia to throw myself on Bishop Livinus's mercy.'

'The words "mercy" and "Livinus" are not ones that nestle comfortably together in my mind,' said Bjarki, with a wry smile at his companion.

'Perhaps you are right, lord. In any case, back in Aachen the good bishop gave me a thorough scolding. He said I had failed in my mission in Eastphalia, failed to spread the Word, and I had failed him, too. He said I should go home to Angleland and trouble him no more with my stupidity. Francia, he said, had no need of me.'

'So how was it that Tor found you in Dorestad?'

'I truly meant to go home; I still mean to, one day. But I took the notion that since I was already in north Francia, and near to Saxony, I should visit the land of my forefathers. They were Saxons, originally, coming from a little place called Brema on the river Weser, many generations ago. At least, that was the family legend that my grandparents told me. I thought, since I was here, that I would go to Brema and see if I could find any relatives. Or perhaps just to say I had seen the earth from which my Saxon ancestors sprang. I went to Dorestad first, travelling up the river Rhenus from Aachen, and I looked for a bed and a meal at the church there. I was there as a guest – a pilgrim, if you like – resting a few hours by their kind charity before travelling on towards Brema. That was where I was when Tor and her men burst through the door waving swords, and killed my hosts and took me prisoner.'

'And here you are, in Ribe, west Jutland. Teaching my wife and children their letters. Do you sometimes curse your God for the misfortune you have suffered?'

'No. Never. God has a plan for me. I am sure of that. I do not know what it is, or where He requires me to go to do His good work. But I think perhaps He wants me to be with you and your sister again. I am not unhappy here. But wherever He sends me in the world, I can only strive to live a good Christian life with a cheerful heart.'

'Do you plan to teach the Christian faith to me – and to my family?' said Bjarki, suddenly feeling alarmed. He had, in fact, been baptised already but he had forgotten almost all the confusing nonsense he had been told about Jesus.

'Not unless you ask me. I am your servant – I shall do your bidding, lord. But I shall not hide my faith. And if any man asks me about Christ I will not lie.'

'If I were to release you from thraldom, would you leave us and go back south to Brema – or would you go straight home to Angleland?'

Father Alwin thought for a few moments. 'I tell you in all truth, Bjarki, as my master and, I hope, as my friend. I would *not* leave you, if you freed me. I would stay with you and Edith, and the children. I doubt if there are any who remember my family in Brema, after such a goodly length of time, and I have found a purpose here in your household. If you released me from thraldom, I would not leave but would gladly continue my labours here. But, to free me, you would have to make what we Christians call a leap of faith. For as a free man, I would have the right to do and go wherever I chose. Whenever I chose.'

'Very well,' said Bjarki. 'A man such as you should not be treated like a slave. I will make your leap, and speak to Tor about it. You may consider yourself free.'

'Thank you, Bjarki. I hope you never have cause to regret your decision.'

'I doubt I shall. I hope you do not regret your decision to remain with us.'

'I will not,' said Father Alwin, smiling, 'but if I do, I shall surely tell you.'

–

The days and weeks passed and autumn turned to frosty winter and still there was no summons from the king. They were snug in their compound with a good fire in the hearth of the hall, and ample meat and ale provided by Siegfried's servants. Yet Bjarki was becoming uneasy in his mind. He slept badly, almost every night, and he was plagued with horrifying dreams of battle and slaughter.

In his dreams he saw the faces of all the folk he had ever killed, and they accused him, their shouting voices overlapping with each other so he could not understand exactly what they said, nor what they wanted from him. They screamed in pain and begged for mercy, over and over. And he awoke almost every morning drenched in sweat. Yet this was not the only cause of his uneasiness. His unspoken fear was that, during this period of waiting, Siegfried would die of his never-ending chill – he was, after all, a very old man – and he would never have his audience with the king, and never be declared his heir. It was then that the Rekkr of Ymirsfjord realised that, despite all his previous protests to friends and family, he did indeed deeply desire to one day rule the Dane-Mark. It was only when this rich prize was dangled in front of him, then cruelly snatched away, that he understood how much he truly wanted it.

He saw little of Tor during those interminable weeks of waiting. She seemed occupied most of the time with errands in the town of Ribe itself or on trips to hunt game or take exercise in the surrounding countryside. He found her one night alone, eating a bowl of hot venison stew in the hall, and went over to join her.

She looked up from her steaming meal with a scowl at his greeting, and did not reply, and Bjarki wondered if he had offended her in some way and she was no longer speaking to him. It would explain why she now seemed to avoid him.

He made remarks about the weather – they had seen the first flakes of snow the day before. She grunted replies. But they *were* replies – she *was* speaking to him.

So he went straight to the heart of the matter that was troubling him.

'I wonder a great deal at this long delay, Tor,' he said, 'with the summons to see the king, I mean. I wonder sometimes if Siegfried has changed his mind and does not, after all, wish to make me the heir to his kingdom.'

Tor said nothing but only spooned in another mouthful of the stew.

Bjarki ploughed on: 'At other times, I wonder if he has died of his illness and no one has yet thought to tell us. We are well out of the main run of things here.'

'He's not dead,' said Tor, and took another spoonful of stew.

'How do you know that?' asked Bjarki, delighted to have engaged her.

'Widukind saw him yesterday,' she said. 'He's feeling better. A lot better.'

'Oh, indeed? Widukind – a Saxon, a foreigner – *he* has been in the king's presence, but Siegfried keeps *me* kicking my heels here for more than a month?'

'Widukind is King's Counsellor, one of his high officials, not to mention his former son-in-law, husband to his dead daughter. Also, he is leaving the Dane-Mark at dawn and he wished to bid the king farewell. You are not going anywhere.'

'Wait!' Bjarki said. 'You say Widukind is leaving us? Where is he going?'

'Keep your voice down, oaf, don't shout it out to the whole hall.'

'Where is Widukind going?' asked Bjarki in a slightly quieter voice.

'He is off to Saxony, just him and that creature of his, Abbio. He didn't say why but I gathered he was going to meet a few Saxon jarls and some prominent *hersirs*.'

'What? He is going into Frank-occupied Saxony? Creeping into his homeland under the noses of Karolus's men? Why? Is he on some kind of scouting trip?'

'Something like that,' said Tor. 'He told me he was just testing the waters.'

'And how come *you* know so much about Widukind's movements?'

Tor hailed a passing servant. 'Bring a bowl of this excellent stew for my brother, here, will you,' she said to the man. 'He is hungry. Fetch some fresh ale too.'

She turned to Bjarki and said: 'I have other news for you as well, brother,' she said. 'The king will likely summon us tomorrow or the next day – so you had best be ready. There is to be a ceremony of reconciliation, which has to happen before he can declare you as his heir. Valtyr knows all the protocols, what you have to say, and so on. But I am tired, oaf, and I'm off to my bed.'

As Bjarki watched his sister walk away, he realised she had not answered his last question.

# Chapter Seven

*An astonishing turn of events*

It was a sickness, Tor thought. Something entirely beyond her control. She craved the touch of his fingers, she dreamed about his musky scent. On her arrival at Ribe, she had sworn she would stay away from him henceforth. It had been a one-off thing, a pleasant afternoon's rutting in Ymirsfjord. No more than that. But after two weeks in the Danish town, she had broken that private vow, hoping to... hoping to what? Hoping, perhaps, to feel something more profound than the simple rush of animal sex; hoping perhaps to recapture the sweet feeling of their togetherness on campaign in Saxony all those years ago. She did not fully understand her own actions, if she was honest, and that irked her. But whatever she was seeking from Widukind, now, almost every day, she found herself drifting into Ribe, alone and on foot, and sidling up to the door of the grand house near the king's hall and knocking.

Sometimes he was not there, and she went away disappointed and feeling hurt, as if she had been slighted by him – taking out her frustrations in long rides into the hills to the east of Ribe, driving her horse hard, heedless of the falling rain or sleet.

Sometimes he was there and, somehow, that was worse. She came into his house like a beggar, cajoling him for love, offering herself. And Widukind never refused her and they would spend an hour or two in his bed chamber, coupling like wild beasts, urgently, repeatedly, then, both spent, drowsing exhausted in each other's arms. She felt almost contented then, for a while, after the act itself, only for it all to come to ashes when she had to leave his bed and return to the cheerless compound outside Ribe and the mundanity of ordinary life with her own Ymirsfjord folk. It was surely a sickness – and Widukind was the cause of the disease and somehow its only cure.

She hated him sometimes, for casting this love-spell over her. For making her his mistress, for her enthralment to his body, his bed, his touch and his smell. She hated him for his kindness and his skill as a lover – for his methods of lovemaking had changed a great deal since she had been with him in Saxony. Had his wife Geva schooled him? He was more tender, and more languorous. Yet vigorous, too, at just the right time, and lavish with praise for her. She felt mired in his being. Drowning.

The worst aspect of her situation was that she could not tell anyone about it. He was Widukind, that ridiculous Saxon popinjay, that sad hanger-on at the Danish court. Many folk viewed him almost as a walking jest. The penniless speech-maker, the self-regarding pretender and glib persuader who claimed to be rightful ruler of his southern homeland, but a man who, in truth, had no more than a few dozen warriors at his command – mostly Danish shield-men gifted to him by his patron Siegfried.

How could she look up into Bjarki's big, red, foolish face and say that she had spent all afternoon between Widukind's sweaty sheets? She could not do it. Her big brother had enough on his mind without that image, too. She watched Bjarki covertly sometimes, just sitting there and staring into space – thinking his thoughts. He sometimes looked a little blank, as if he was just awaking from some dream. But it was not his preoccupation with his strange inner life that bothered her. It was his character. If she told him about Widukind, Bjarki would be kind; he would be understanding; he would be supportive. He would try very hard to genuinely like Widukind, for her sake. Which would be intolerable.

Then there was Edith – lovely Edith, with her two perfect children, the two little ones who made Tor's heart skip a beat every time she laid eyes on them.

How could she tell Edith that she was now fucking her brother? And that her feelings were perhaps becoming something a little more than just ordinary lust? Edith would immediately begin planning, scheming. A wedding, a big celebration – and who should be invited? Which of the many *gothi* of her acquaintance should be asked to officiate? Not Abbio – that man gave Tor the shivers just to look at. While she had seen him around the court and in Ribe, Abbio seemed to be avoiding all contact with them. Furthermore, it would be a slap in the face after Bjarki had stolen Edith from him, to ask Abbio to officiate. And she did not want to *wed* Widukind, just bed him.

In truth, most of all, she simply wanted to be free of this terrible sickness. To go back to being her old tough self, independent, proud, beholden to no man.

She could not continue in this honey-sweet but horri-fying connection. He was so wrong for her, she could barely speak to him. They rutted, and slept, and rutted again – they rarely conversed. Each time he opened his mouth to talk of his wild hopes and dreams, she was forced to kiss him just to shut him up.

He desperately wanted to retake all of Saxony – he truly believed the folk of his homeland would rise up and embrace him as their leader, even now, with Frankish Red Cloaks in three hundred fortified *castra* across the land, and with their own Saxon jarls baptised and confirmed in their position with the Frankish title of count. How could Widukind speak of pushing back the Christian tide? Saxony was gone. How could he cling so stubbornly to the lie that he might one day defeat Karolus?

And now Widukind was gone. Gone south to pursue his absurd fantasy of the reconquest of Saxony. And that was the worst blow of all. She actually ached for him. She longed for him. She even missed his silly talk, his stupid boasting, his rash promises. He wanted to rule, he said, he had been born and raised to rule wide lands. It was in his blood, his bones, he could not be happy unless he was lord of a realm. He was dying in Ribe, he told her. He *must* regain his lands… and so on. All she could think of was the feeling of his strong arms round her, his hands on her body…

'What?' she said. 'What was that you were saying just now, Bjarki?'

Her brother frowned. 'I was asking if it would be right to wear my bearskin to the audience with Siegfried this afternoon. But if you are too busy to…'

Bjarki was holding up the item he had mentioned. It was a shrunken flap of moth-eaten fur, originally a dark chestnut, almost black, but now it was streaked yellowish in places, orange in others, badly torn by dozens of enemy blades in battle, about half the size of the original magnificent garment, which had been a lush, ankle-length cloak. It looked more like a filthy rag used for washing the hall floors than the revered badge and effective armour of a *berserkr* warrior.

'Don't think so, oaf,' said Tor. 'You should wear your green cloak with mink trim. We'll be taking part in a royal ceremony, not an ale-house brawl.'

–

Bjorn Hildarsson, known by all as Bjarki Bloodhand, the Rekkr of Ymirsfjord, entered the king's hall at Ribe, flanked by his sister Torfinna Hildarsdottir and his old friend Valtyr Far-Traveller. He had indeed chosen to wear his fine green woollen cloak, trimmed with black mink fur, and he had a well-made Frankish sword belted at his waist and a seax hanging from two straps across his loins.

His head was aching, the pain unusually intense. He felt as if he had drunk a whole barrel of ale the night before, and then been beaten about the skull for several hours with an iron bar. Yet he had had no more than two cups of watered ale and been in bed only a little after sunset. He was just very tired, he supposed. His nightmares had been especially bad of late, so much so that, at night, he almost feared to fall asleep. After a few days of rest he would doubtless be completely well again.

The king was seated at the dais at the end of the hall with his steward Mundi standing beside him and there were a dozen other warriors scattered around the hall, including two big scarred brutes standing before the dais, Danish bodyguards who stepped smartly aside when Bjarki approached. He looked up at the king, at his familiar face, and noted that he now looked almost impossibly old: his almost translucent skin was wrinkled, sagging and mottled with brown spots around the eyes;

his sparse, wispy white hair had been combed and stuck to his pink scalp with water. There seemed almost to be ancient cobwebs all over his features, which made them seem oddly indistinct.

The Rekkr had been well coached by Valtyr as to what to say in this ceremony of reconciliation, and while Bjarki had initially balked at the words, indeed, he flat-out refused to say them, both Edith and Tor had persuaded him that he must, and with sincerity, or he might as well pack up and sail home to Rogaland that same day.

Bjarki knelt before the throne on the dais, his head bowed in humility, and said: 'Mighty King, Sovereign Lord, Father of the Nation... I beg your pardon for all the grievous wrongs I have perpetrated, for the crimes I have committed against your person, your people and your peace; and for the insults I have offered, which stem from my evil ways, my ungoverned greed and malice. I seek your forgiveness, lord, admitting my own unworthiness, but desiring you, in your wisdom, to grant mercy.'

Bjarki looked uncertainly up at King Siegfried, who was looking down on him haughtily from his throne. This next part he particularly dreaded, yet it must be done.

'I prostrate myself before you, O King, humbling my body in your presence, submitting to your lawful justice and entrusting my life to your royal benevolence.'

Bjarki got down on his knees, then lay down flat on the hall floor, pressing his face into the layers of filthy floor rushes. For a long while there was silence in the hall. Bjarki lay there, arms outstretched on either side of his prone body. His greatest fear was that someone in the audience would laugh.

He was aware, too, that he lay helpless before the two bodyguards, and that if Siegfried refused his humble request for reconciliation, he was a dead man.

He heard a creaking sound, the sound of a wooden chair being pushed back across a wooden surface, and then to his intense relief he heard the king saying, 'Arise, my good and faithful servant, and be assured of my forgiveness. Let us be reconciled, one with another, and go forwards together in friendship and brotherhood.'

Bjarki did not move.

One of the spearmen stepped closer. 'On your feet, Fire Born,' he said.

Bjarki lay still, his face down in the rushes. Valtyr swiftly stepped forwards.

'The king has forgiven you, Bjarki. You are reconciled – in his highness's good graces again. Get to your feet and embrace him like a son, as discussed.'

Bjarki's whole body gave a little ripple, and then a bigger spasm, and then his massive arms and legs began to shudder and shiver. His back arched upwards, revealing a grey-hued face and froth-spattered lips. His mouth opened and his lips peeled back to show tight-gritted yellow teeth. His whole body was now jerking, rhythmically, along with his swift heartbeat, eyes closed, arms flailing, his long legs kicking. He flipped on one side, then the other side, like a just-landed fish.

He lurched up to his knees, unclenched his grinding teeth and vomited copiously all over the floor before the king's dais, and again, a thick, brown stream, then his whole body went limp and he collapsed to the floor into his own stinking mess.

The hall was frozen by this astonishing turn of events. Suddenly everyone was moving forwards, everyone was talking very loudly, all at the same time.

Tor was hard by Bjarki's side, on her knees, wiping the vomit from his mouth with her sleeve to clear his windpipe, and whispering softly in his ear.

Valtyr went towards the king, avoiding the pools of sick. One spearman tried to stop him, and stepped in his path, but Valtyr irritatedly pushed the man's spear shaft aside and stepped past. 'It is clear, highness,' he said loudly to the dais, 'that Bjarki Bloodhand is unwell. I will take him to his bed, as soon as it can be arranged, to see what can be done. I am known for my skills as a healer.'

'It could not be clearer,' said Siegfried, staring at the huge warrior in his fine clothes, now streaked and stained, being helped quivering to his feet by his sister. 'Take him away, Valtyr – and tend to him. Perhaps it was something he ate?'

'Perhaps,' said Valtyr. 'May we assume reconciliation has been effected?'

'What?' said Siegfried. 'Yes, by the gods. I don't want to do all that again.'

–

Tor took her station beside her brother. She sat on a low, three-legged stool by his bed under the eaves in the rear of the hall in the compound at Ribe.

Bjarki had been put to bed after the reconciliation ceremony, still mumbling about a terrible headache, his skull splitting, and been given a strong medicinal draught by Valtyr to ease his pains. Tor sat beside him and kept her long watch over his sleeping body. She took turns with

Edith, each woman watching Bjarki for half a day or half the night, as he snored, muttered, and tossed about in his sweaty blankets.

For two days Bjarki slept, and when he woke on the morning of the third day, he sat up, opened his eyes and looked at Tor with total incomprehension.

'Who are you?' he said. And then: 'Where am I?'

Tor, when she allowed herself to admit this, was shocked and hurt by the fact that he did not know her. She said: 'I am your sister Torfinna – you know me, Bjarki. We are in Ribe, or just outside it, as guests of King Siegfried.'

'Yes,' said Bjarki. 'I remember. I was ill in the king's hall, and very sick.'

'How do you feel?'

Bjarki slumped back down on the bed. 'Weak,' he said. 'I feel very weak.'

He slept for another half day and then, when Edith came to take over Tor's watch, he awoke again, sat up and swung his bare feet off the bed, to the floor.

Tor looked into his face. He seemed to have lost weight, and all the healthy colour from his ruddy skin. His eyes, once bright blue, now seemed darker, the colour of the sea before a big storm. They seemed opaque, too, as if Bjarki was half-blind or like a very old man. His body was leaner, as well, the scars and burns, the marks left by the stitches from his many, many wounds, now all seemed to be thrown into a sharper relief by the angular slabs of springy muscle.

'Do you know who I am?' she said. Bjarki nodded, then winced, as if his sore head was still paining him. 'Of course I do, Tor. How long have I been asleep?'

Edith let out a sob and rushed to him and enfolded her husband in her arms.

They gave him broth and watered ale, and sent a servant off to find Valtyr. When the one-eyed old man arrived, he gently took Bjarki's right hand in his and felt the beat of his heart through the thick, blue veins in his wrist.

'When you were asleep, Bjarki, did you dream?' he asked.

The Rekkr slightly inclined his head.

'Of your *gandir*?'

'They were talking,' said Bjarki, 'but in their own language. About the many battles they had fought with me, I think. About the times when they had possessed me and given me strength. About the people they had killed. Then there was something else. A bitter argument. They were talking about a threat. To them. Something evil coming from the World of Men into the Spirit-Realm. They were bickering about the arrival of this evil thing but I could not really understand all that they were saying.'

Valtyr made Bjarki drink a quantity of water and gave him another draught of his powerful medicine, then they left him to rest. The old man and the two women withdrew to the body of the hall and sat at a table, where Valtyr called for ale.

'What is wrong with him?' asked Edith. 'He was in fine health last week.'

Valtyr looked at Tor. 'You remember Brokk from the Groves of Eresburg?'

'The Rekkr?' said Tor. 'He was Bear Lodge – Bjarki knew him a little. He has spoken of him anyway. He died heroically at the battle in the Thursby *castrum*.'

'That's him. He lived a good long time for one who had been a Fire Born. He must have seen thirty summers or more before he was killed in battle,' said Valtyr.

'Bjarki said Brokk was very nearly Galálar,' said Tor.

'He was,' said Valtyr. 'If Brokk had not died at Thursby then…'

'No! No! Are you saying that Bjarki is…' said Tor.

'I cannot be sure,' said Valtyr. 'But maybe.'

'What are you talking about?' asked Edith loudly. 'What ails Bjarki?'

Tor and Valtyr looked at each other, but neither spoke. Valtyr shrugged.

'Speak to me,' Edith's voice was harsh. 'Speak to me. What ails Bjarki?'

Tor said: 'There is a disease. A condition, which afflicts *berserkir* – some of them anyway. My father – Bjarki's father and mine – he developed this same evil condition. It is sometimes known as going Galálar. A Fire Born who has seen too much of battle, and survived it, can be stricken, can become withdrawn, silent. That would be fine, but they also, as the disease takes a firmer hold in their hearts, lose their humanity and become uncontrollably violent. A warrior who goes Galálar kills indiscriminately – anyone who comes within reach of his blade. It doesn't matter if the victim is a loved one, a wife, son or best friend. When a Rekkr goes Galálar the only thing to do is to kill them. Immediately. Before they kill the innocent. They must be put down like a mad dog.'

'Bjarki is not like that. Bjarki would *never* behave like that,' said Edith.

'He has had brushes with this same condition in the past,' said Valtyr.

'He nearly killed me once,' said Tor. 'Long ago, in a prison in Aachen.'

'But he did *not* kill you, Tor,' said Edith. 'And he would never hurt you.'

Tor and Valtyr said nothing.

'No,' said Edith. 'You are wrong. Bjarki has not gone Gal-whatever. He is tired and needs a rest, that's all. He will be fine after a few days in bed. He just needs rest.'

# Chapter Eight

## Thor and the three trolls

For Bjarki it was a slow awakening, a gradual dawning, one that took place over several weeks. He knew he was awake, indeed he even sometimes spoke with real, living people, although he rarely retained what they said to him. He even participated in events such as the grand feasts they held over the period of Yule with the king. But he showed no great pleasure, nor did he hold any memory of it afterwards. Tor chided him several times for saying nothing during the many elaborate meals and during the various festivities. He simply sat and stared at the entertainment, at the jugglers and the tumblers, or listened impassively to the skalds, and had to be nudged by Edith when it was time to show appreciation by clapping his hands or pounding the table.

He spoke rarely, if at all, during this time, and always after a considerable pause. And the dreams he had at night, almost every night, were still terrifying. He recalled every man he had killed, and the women too. He recalled their screams, the bright splash of their blood, the expressions on their terrified faces. He particularly remembered the lovely features of Yoni, his lover in the Auxilla, who had had the misfortune to face him in battle in Saxony. He recalled what he did to her in his rage.

Yet he *was* recovering, slowly, and one morning in the frozen month of Thorri, a few weeks after Yule, he sat up in bed just after dawn and saw a large child sitting on the stool beside it.

He stared at the boy for a while, and the child solemnly stared back at him. He was an ugly, lumpy creature, Bjarki thought, with a head too big for his thin body and slanting brown eyes under a thatch of straw hair. He did not seem malformed, no, not quite ugly, just oddly proportioned. His hands were too big. His shoulders were too wide. Upon a second glance, Bjarki reckoned he was in truth a fairly well-made lad, and tall, probably, when he stood up, if a little pudgy from lack of exercise. Bjarki judged the child to be about eleven winters old.

'How did you get all those scars?' the boy asked.

Bjarki looked down at his naked torso, at the rips and tears, the welts and stitch-marks, and the smooth pale patches where he had been burned by fire long ago.

'Fighting,' he said.

'You can't be very good at it, if you let your enemies cut you up like that.'

Bjarki could think of nothing to say to that.

'Do they hurt?' asked the boy.

'No,' said Bjarki. 'They did hurt when I took the wounds – they hurt a lot – and for a long time afterwards. But not now.'

The boy pushed back his left sleeve and showed a white line across his forearm. 'My father gave me that,' he said. 'He punished me with a red-hot poker.'

'Did your father beat you often?'

'Often. More after my mother died. I don't think he cared for me much.'

Bjarki grunted sympathetically. His mouth felt sour, gummy and unpleasant. He looked around the bed for something to drink. The hall was surprisingly quiet this day, he noticed this only now. The usual chatter and hum of people, the ordinary clink of metal and the clunk of wooden objects was entirely absent.

'Where is everybody?'

'At the king's hunt. A great she-boar has been spotted in the woods to the north – a real monster – and everyone has gone with the king to see his huntsmen kill it.'

'You're not interested in hunting?' asked Bjarki.

The boy shrugged. 'Old One-eye told me to stay here and look after you. Fetch anything you asked me for. Bread, ale, cheese, porridge, whatever.'

'Old One-eye – you mean Valtyr?'

'Yes, my master Valtyr Far-Traveller told me to stay here all day with you. To learn something if I could. He said I should study you and learn things.'

'What things?'

The boy shrugged. 'He didn't say. Maybe how not to get cut up so badly.'

Bjarki grunted. 'What is your name?'

'Erik.'

'Well, fetch me some ale and a piece of bread, Erik, and when I have eaten my breakfast we will go outside and I will show you a few ways to stop your enemies hurting you. Got a shield? Got a sword? Must have a knife at least?'

The boy shook his head at all three.

'I'll dig out some gear for you. Now go, fetch bread and ale, and be quick.'

-

The snow had been cleared from the courtyard, swept into big dirty piles, in the corners of that large space, and Bjarki and the boy Erik squared off against each other. Erik held a short, blunt, rusty iron sword and a light, round ash-wood shield. Bjarki had a long stick of elm, stolen from the kindling pile under the eaves and a full-sized but battered, unfaced lime-wood shield. And before too long they had both worked up a good sweat in the freezing air of the courtyard.

The boy was fast, Bjarki recognised that immediately. Fast and strong, despite his ungainly body and layers of puppy fat. He was clever, too. He could tell when Bjarki was making a feint, and anticipated the true strike, and in his turn he tried his best to strike his teacher with his rusty old sword, unlike some Bjarki had trained who instinctively pulled back from delivering a full-strength blow. But he had no sword-skill, none at all. He flailed the blade like a ploughman wielding an ox-goad. And after Bjarki had absorbed a dozen wild whacks on his shield he stopped the bout.

'Did your father never teach you how to use a blade?'

Erik shook his head.

'Then we had better start from the very beginning,' said Bjarki.

They set aside their shields and standing shoulder to shoulder, Bjarki slowly, almost ritually, demonstrated the twelve basic strokes of the sword in the chilly air – the high and low blocks, the parries, the strikes and the lunges – and had the boy Erik repeat them again and again until they became smooth and natural. Then Bjarki picked up his shield again and invited the boy to try the moves he had learned against a real live opponent. The boy learned quickly and after an hour or so they set aside their swords and progressed to the basic foundations of spear-work.

'This is a more important weapon than the sword,' said Bjarki. 'Firstly, it is more deadly: you can kill a man with a spear before he gets close enough to you to use his sword. Secondly, you can keep horsemen at bay with enough friends around you. Master the spear, and you are halfway to becoming a warrior.'

The shaft of the ash-wood spear Bjarki produced was too long for Erik, which made the weapon unwieldy, so the Rekkr found a second weapon with a broken shaft and showed the boy how to use it in combination with the shield, overhand and underhand. How to deliver a killing jab, without yielding control. Before he knew it, dusk was falling at the close of that short winter's day.

'We made a good start, youngster,' said Bjarki, cuffing the boy on the shoulder. 'But don't rush to join any shield walls yet. A long, hard road lies ahead.'

'You will show me some more spear sequences tomorrow?' asked Erik.

'If I have time, but my sister Tor would be a far better person to...'

At that moment the gates of the compound burst open and a wall of people surged in. Kynwulf was in the lead, with a massive haunch of hairy boar slung over his shoulder, and behind him an excited Valtyr, waving an ale flask in one hand, and then came Tor, glowering as if she had just been mortally insulted. Even Father Alwin, his cheeks red as apples from the cold fresh air, came bursting in with them. And something about the sight of these cheerful faces – and the folk behind them, too, people whose company he enjoyed – made Bjarki smile for the first time in weeks.

It was not till that night, with a greasy wooden platter that had once held roast boar before him, a crumb-strewn table, and a horn of ale in his right fist, as he sat and listened to Valtyr begin one of his old stories, that he realised he was himself again.

'Once, when the world was fresh,' said Valtyr and, at the back of the hall, someone struck a dramatic chord on a harp, 'the mighty god Thor was making a difficult journey through the tangled depths of the First Forest in the height of summer. He had heard tell of a beautiful Saxon maiden, the most beautiful in all the Middle-Realm, who lived on the eastern bank of the river Elbe. She was said to have hair like a bolt of pure yellow silk, huge eyes like glowing sapphires, and a sweet body, as lush and fertile as a meadow in high summer. And so Thor wished to see this paragon of Saxon beauty for himself and, if she was indeed as perfect and as lovely as he had so often been told, to carry her off to his bed.

'Thor travelled, as he always did in those days, in a two-wheeled cart pulled by two huge, magical goats, pure white animals that never tired and required no food nor water, save for a drop of Thor's own sweat given to each every nine days. They were ferocious beasts, and devoted to Thor, and they were called Tanngrisnir and Tanngnjostr, Teeth-Snarler and Teeth-Grinder. And wherever these animals travelled, their iron-shod hooves and the iron-rimmed wheels of the little cart made the terrible sounds of rolling thunder.'

'Like you in the latrine of a morning, Valtyr,' yelled a drunken spearman, before being shushed by friends. Bjarki sat back. He closed his eyes to hear the story better.

'Thor and his goats passed through the low-lying Saxon lands, the valleys of the Lippe and the Ems and, after crossing the wide, serpentine river Weser, he longed for the higher ground where the wind might cool his sweating brow and blow away the biting insects that plagued him and his goats. So he drove his cart up on to the wooded heights known as the Süntel Hills above the insect-ridden riverlands. Even as he did so, Thor knew he was taking a risk, for this high, hilly place was the preserve of the ancient giants, the *jotun*, some men call them, while others call them trolls.

'But Thor was not afraid. No, no, he feared no creature, not even trolls, for he always carried with him his mighty hammer Mjolnir, a fearsome weapon which he could use to strike any enemy dead with a single blow – dead even before they hit the ground. And it was up in these hills, amid the elm, the pine and dwarf beech of the First Forest, that Thor found himself with his cart and his goats as the sun grew red and slowly sank over the western horizon. So the god halted his goats and began to make his camp for the night.'

Valtyr gestured in the air with his empty ale cup, and a servant came hurrying forwards and refilled it. Bjarki took a sip from his own cup and looked over at Tor, who was fiddling with a thong attached to her belt. She seemed oblivious to the tale.

'Thor made his camp, and tethered his goats, and built a fire to warm his bones throughout the chill of night, and he ate up his porridge and drank his ale, and presently he fell fast asleep. However, during the night, while Thor lay peacefully snoring, his camp was visited by three huge mountain trolls, who saw the thunder god lying there in his blankets and crept towards him. They were hungry creatures, as trolls always are, but none of them are too clever either. Thor was unaware of them because this was their land, and they knew ever branch and rock, every leaf and fold in the ground, and so they moved towards the god as silently as bird-stalking cats.

'Thor slept, and while he was deep in his slumbers, the trolls advanced upon him. Then, at the very last moment, one of the goats, Tanngrisnir, opened one of his yellow eyes, saw the three trolls and let out a very loud bleat of alarm. Thor stirred and slowly began to awaken. But the trolls, now abandoning all stealth, ran forwards as quickly as they could and the first one seized Tanngrisnir in his huge hairy hands and swallowed the goat whole, leather harness, horns, the lot. The second troll snatched up Tanngnjostr, and swallowed down Teeth-Grinder as if he was no more than a morsel of honey-cake. And the third troll, who was the youngest and stupidest of them all, grabbed the little wooden goat cart, wheels, leather traces, wooden yoke, everything, and following the example of his two older brothers, crammed it in his huge mouth and swallowed it down without chewing once.'

There was a good deal of laughter in the hall at this part of the story – even though many of the folk gathered had heard the tale many times before. Bjarki even saw Tor look up from gazing at her lap and crack a small grin.

'But Thor was wide awake now, and on his feet and preparing to fight the trolls. They were a fearsome trio, so even mighty Thor hesitated before charging straight at them. He said: "You have eaten at my campfire, and filled your bellies, which means you must be my guests. So I have an obligation to entertain you gentlemen after the feast. And what I propose is a game of riddles. I will tell you three riddles and if you guess them all, you will win. And if you do win, you can cook and eat me, and I shall not resist at all. But if I win, then you must go from this high place and leave me here in peace. Do you agree?"

'The trolls looked at each other. One gave a little goaty burp. They rumbled on for a bit in their own tongue, then, "Agreed," said the oldest troll. And so Thor began the riddle game:

"'When I am alive I do not speak.

Anyone who wants to, takes me captive and cuts off my head.

They bite my bare body

I do no harm to anyone unless they cut me first.

Then I soon make them cry."

'One of the trolls laughed, then, the sound of jagged rocks grinding against each other. He said: "Everyone knows that ancient riddle, even the little troll children know that one! The answer is – an onion!" And Thor admitted that this was indeed the true answer. So then he told the trolls his second riddle:

"'My home is not quiet but I am not loud.

My lord has meant us to journey together.

I am faster than he and sometimes stronger,

But he keeps on going for longer.

Sometimes I rest but he runs on.

For as long as I am alive, I live in him.

If we part from one another

It is I who will die."

'The three trolls discussed this for a while, and then the oldest one barked out happily: "The lord is a river, and the answer is… a fish."

'All three of them rolled on the grass and laughed like drunken men. "We have answered two riddles," said the young troll, "if we answer another, we can eat you!"

'"That was the bargain I made," said Thor. "See if you can guess the last:

I emerged angry from the red womb.
Beaten as a child by others of my kind.
Drowned by my father to make me harder.
Impaled on a branch to make me stronger.
In battle, I strike at the heads of my enemies,
And drive them deep into the wood."

'The trolls gathered together in a huddle and there was much scratching of heads, and angry trollish arguing. And while they talked and disputed with each other for an age, it seemed that not one of them knew the true answer to the riddle and, while they were distracted by their quarrelling, Thor attacked them. He threw himself at the nearest one and with a mighty swing of Mjolnir, he struck the first troll a terrible blow in the small of his back, and the surprised creature immediately coughed up the goat Tanngrisnir, whole and hale, if astonished to be alive. Thor struck again, another mighty blow to the second troll, and that one then vomited up Tanngnjostr straight away, and with a third hammer-blow deep into the soft belly of the youngest troll, up came the little wooden cart, traces, yoke and all.

'"The answer to the riddle is – hammer!" cried Thor and, as he swung Mjolnir around his head, lightning cracked and lit up the darkness in the Süntel Hills. Thor was ready for battle, but the three trolls were already crippled and dying from the powerful magic-hammer blows they had just suffered. And soon they were all dead.

'Thor stacked the corpses of the trolls into one great, stinking heap, one creature on top of another, and then he pounded them with his hammer Mjolnir and squashed them all flat. Then, having soothed and comforted his faithful goats, and given them a little of his sweat to drink, he went back to sleep beside his fire.

'In the morning, he found that the first rays of the sun had turned the pile of dead trolls into one gigantic stack of stone, very high, and flat on top. And to this day that great stack of stone-turned trolls stands at the western end of a mountain spur in the Süntel Hills, looking out over all the valley lands below.

'The locals used to call that place the Troll Rock, after the legend of Thor and his three stupid foes; but now it is called the High Stone. The Hohenstein. And it is said by wise men that if you shove your head into one of its many cracks and fissures on a stormy night, you can sometimes, if you listen hard, hear the terrible wails of the three dead trolls lamenting their stupidity in their trollish afterlife.'

–

'You are sure you are recovered from your sickness?' asked King Siegfried. 'There have been no more episodes, like the one that happened here last...'

'I am much better, thank you, highness,' said Bjarki.

He was sitting on a stool in the king's private quarters, with the lord of the Dane-Mark in a chair opposite him. Widukind, Duke of Saxony, was leaning against the wall and, on the other side of the small room, Valtyr was sitting on top of an apple barrel, humming to himself and trimming his nails with a fruit knife.

'You understand why I have to ask, Bjarki. I am proposing to name you as my heir at the full-moon feast, to proclaim you as the man who will be the next King of the Danes, and I cannot name someone who is sickly, or even believed to be sick or suffer from any weakness, or worse… um, not be entirely, that is fully in command of all his senses. I'm sure you can understand my concerns.'

'He's fine,' said Valtyr. 'It was one episode – it hasn't been repeated. I think it may have been caused by a bad oyster, rotten pork, or some other kind of spoiled food. Nothing to worry about. I've dosed him regularly and he is healthy as an ox.'

'That is most reassuring,' said the king. 'And you are minded to accept my nomination, Bjarki? You will make the oaths, fulfil all your royal duties and so on?'

'I am,' said Bjarki. 'I would like to say, too, highness, I am grateful…'

'Tell him about the thing we discussed last night,' said Widukind, rudely interrupting Bjarki. 'Tell him all that first, and make sure he fully agrees before you promise him the whole Middle-Realm on a polished silver platter.'

'Tell me about what?' said Bjarki, looking hard at Widukind. There was something in the Saxon Wolf's bitter tone that almost sounded like jealousy.

There was an awkward pause. Valtyr raised his head and smiled at Bjarki. Not a nice smile. He looked like a schemer whose plan is about to bear fruit.

'The King of the Danes must be a Guardian of the North,' said Valtyr.

'Yes, I am afraid Valtyr is right,' said Siegfried. 'After I die, you will have to take my place among the Guardians. Will you agree to that? Will you join them?'

Bjarki thought about this for a moment. The Guardians of the North was a group of nine very powerful men who swore to ward and protect all the various peoples of the North. Valtyr, Siegfried and Widukind were all Guardians, as well as six other men that Bjarki did not know. Yet Bjarki had no quarrel with the role they played in preserving the laws and customs of the North. If he was to be a king again, he would have to behave in a similar manner towards all the people of the Dane-Mark. That was not the problem. The thing that slightly soured the moment for him was that the Guardians were initiated into their secret society with a ceremony involving the sacrifice of human beings, usually disobedient thralls or unfortunate prisoners of war, alongside a variety of animals, nine cockerels, nine sheep, nine horses, and so on. Nine men would die when he became initiated as a Guardian. But then, if he did his duty, and kept the peace, how many lives might he and the Guardians preserve?

'I agree,' he said. 'I will be a Guardian, but I must choose the victims for the sacrifice. They will only be the very worst criminals. Men who truly deserve death.'

'Agreed,' said Valtyr and the king as the same time. Widukind noisily cleared his throat. 'Tell him about the other thing, highness,' he said. 'About Lippspringe.'

'Ah, yes,' said Siegfried. 'The duke has recently returned from a visit to his southern homeland. A successful visit, he tells me. He has travelled all over Saxony to, em, I forget the name… to Forder, or was it Verdo? Then to Or-something.'

'Shall I tell him, highness?' drawled Widukind. 'It might be quicker.'

Bjarki felt a shaft of pure dislike run through him. Widukind's impatience with the venerable king was more than just rude, it was bordering on the insolent.

'I went south by sea to Frisia,' said Widukind, looking at Bjarki. 'Small boat down the coast of Jutland, very discreet. Then up the river Elbe to the town of Treva, meaning to stay at Jarl Ulf's hall. You remember him, Bjarki?'

Bjarki shrugged, wondering what all this travelling talk had to do with him.

'Only it's not Jarl Ulf's hall any longer. Old Ulf is dead. His son Guthrum is the new Jarl of Nordalbia. A very different man to his father. Ulf wanted peace with the Franks at any price, as long as it kept them on the far bank of the Elbe. Guthrum is a vigorous young man, looking to make a name for himself. Much more warlike. You would like him, Bjarki. I stayed two nights with Guthrum in Treva, then I headed on south, disguising myself as a fisherman, to Verden, to the place where the rivers Aller and Weser join. You must remember Verden, at least?'

'The hall of Jarl Brun, lord of the horse-raising Angrians,' said Bjarki. 'Who if I recall is a Frankish count, a baptised Christian and a staunch ally of Karolus.'

'Not staunch,' said Widukind. 'Not staunch at all. Jarl Brun is unhappy. The Franks take all his best horses as tax and send them away to mount the troopers of Karolus's *exercitus* – his standing army. Jarl Brun is not a happy ally.'

'Why are you telling me? Why do I care whether a jarl is happy or not?'

'Let me finish. Next I disguised myself again as an itinerant peddler and went upriver to Orhum, to the hall of Jarl Hessi – the leader of the Eastphalians is also no longer quite so enchanted with life under the Frankish yoke. In short, I have been all over Saxony this winter, visiting all the leaders of my people great and small, even to my former family lands in Westphalia, and gathering solid information. This is what I have learnt: all Saxony is ripe for rebellion.'

Bjarki made a scoffing noise.

'You doubt me, Rekkr, I can see that. So I invite you to see for yourself.'

'What? I'm not going to Saxony!' Bjarki felt his face flushing with anger.

'It will be quite safe,' said Widukind. 'I personally guarantee your safety.'

'Don't start all that again.'

'Karolus has called a Grand Assembly,' said Valtyr.

'A grand *what*?' asked Bjarki.

'It's like a Thing but a hundred times bigger,' said Valtyr. 'A thousand times, perhaps – it is a great meeting of Karolus's subject peoples at a specific time and place. The King of the Franks will dispense justice, issue laws and reward his faithful followers. It is also a way for him to demonstrate his power, since armed contingents from all his realms will be there. It will happen in a month or so at a place called Lippspringe, about a day's march due north of the Groves of Eresburg, site of the Fyr Skola. That place I *know* you remember.'

Bjarki was about to say something but memories of the place where he had trained to be a Rekkr, where he had in a way become a man, overwhelmed him.

'Karolus has invited a representative of the Dane-Mark to attend his Grand Assembly,' continued Valtyr, 'under a flag of a truce, guaranteed by Karolus.'

'You want *me* to go?' said Bjarki, incredulous.

'If you would be my heir, Bjarki,' said Siegfried, 'then I would ask you to represent the Dane-Mark on my behalf. I am not strong enough to travel so far.'

'And while you are there,' said Widukind, grinning slyly, 'you might speak to the Saxon leaders – they have all been invited, too. And you can form your own opinion of their mood – and whether or not they wish to be free of the Franks.'

Bjarki looked at the faces of the three men. He knew then he had indeed walked into a trap when he came to Ribe. Still, he struggled to escape their net.

'Unfortunately, I cannot go to Lippspringe,' he said, lifting his chin in defiance. 'The last time I put myself in King Karolus's power – and *you* may remember this, Widukind, since I went as your emissary – I was thrown into a stinking prison cell. If you don't believe me, ask Father Alwin, or ask my sister. If I went to Lippspringe, I would no doubt be immediately thrown into gaol again.'

'Karolus had offered us a hostage, an important man, to guarantee the safety of our Danish envoy,' said Siegfried. 'And speaking of your Father Alwin, I thought we might dispatch him to fetch the hostage here to Ribe before you set off for Saxony.'

'But I don't want to go,' said Bjarki. And as he said it, he realised how childish his protest sounded – and how useless it would be. 'I don't want to go to Saxony.'

'You remember when we spoke of your debt to me in Ymirsfjord. The bride price owed for Edith?' asked Widukind. 'You acknowledged it, if I recall. Well, I do not want your money, Bjarki. I want this. This is my bride price. Go to Saxony – you will be quite safe – go and meet the Saxon leaders and measure their mood, and if anyone has a message for me, you are to relay it. Do this and your debt is repaid.'

# Chapter Nine

## Enough is enough

Tor had charged into bristling shield walls on many occasions and faced the blades of her foes without showing a shred of fear. Yet today she was frightened.

She stood in the street, twenty yards away from the door of the big house beside the king's hall, and she could feel all the cowardly symptoms: sweating palms, racing heart, that awful sick feeling in the pit of her belly. It was fear and she knew it.

And why?

Because she was going to go inside that house where her lover, Widukind, freshly returned from his travels in Saxony, resided with his few servants and bodyguards, and she was going to look him in the eye and tell him she wanted to end their relationship. She would tell him that she no longer wanted his hard, muscular body pressed against hers beneath the linen sheets. That there would be no more afternoons of animal rutting, then cuddling together half-asleep. Enough was enough. She was done with love. She had feasted on him like a greedy woman at a lavish banquet – and now she was uncomfortably full.

She straightened her spine, squared her shoulders and began to walk towards the dread portal. As she was about to reach out and knock, the door swung open and a man, his face partially covered by his hood, stepped out and bumped into her.

She glared into his deep hood and recognised, to her astonishment, that he was Father Alwin, the thrall priest she had captured in Dorestad and whom she had given to Edith as a gift – and whom Bjarki had freed. And yet here he was, still teaching Bjarki's children their letters and, apparently, also paying friendly visits to her lover – her soon-to-be-former lover – Widukind, the penniless Saxon Wolf.

'Greetings, Tor,' said Father Alwin. 'May you be healthy and happy this day.'

Tor just gaped at him. Father Alwin smiled, nodded and gently pushed past her, beginning to walk down the street towards the gate in the walls of Ribe. Tor pulled herself together, and called after him: 'Yes, Father. Healthy and happy. And you too!'

*What is the Christian priest doing with Widukind?* she asked herself. Then she shrugged it off, recovered her poise, pushed open the door and went inside.

She had hoped to find the duke alone, indeed her strategy that day depended on it: she would say her carefully prepared words, the stuff about the lavish banquet and now being full, kiss him once on his cheek, and walk away with her head held high.

What she was not prepared for was to find Widukind and his weird crow-like creature Abbio standing together over a large table which was covered with sticks and stones and coloured ribbons and little wooden discs with runes carved on the flat surface. At first, she thought they were engaged in some dark magical practice – Abbio had a sinister reputation for exactly that kind of thing. But no, apparently not.

'Tor, come over and look at this and give me your opinion,' said Widukind.

Intrigued, despite her firm intention, Tor went to the table and stared down at the collection of objects that were laid out. She picked up the nearest wooden disc and looked at it.

Abbio hissed: 'Don't move the piecessss.' He grabbed her hand in his dry little claw and retrieved the disc and, after a moment's thought, he replaced the token at the bottom of the table on top of a length of curling blue ribbon.

'What is all this?' asked Tor.

'Saxony!' said Widukind triumphantly. 'That piece you just picked up was the fortress of Buraburg, the place where that snake Livinus made his claim to be Archbishop of Saxony, and that blue ribbon was the river Eder. We fought a battle there years ago. Remember? Not one of my greatest triumphs, if I recall.'

Tor remembered. It had been a bloody catastrophe, with the Saxon infantry mauled by Frankish heavy cavalry – the *cabellarii* – the Black Cloaks wielding lance and sword who had erupted from their hilltop fortress to slaughter Widukind's men.

But the Saxon Wolf was still talking excitedly. 'See, here is the Groves of Eresburg – now a mighty fortified Frankish garrison. And there is another of their fortresses, Sigiburg, which *you* captured for me, Tor. They have taken that back too, unfortunately.' Widukind suddenly seemed to lose the keen edge of his enthusiasm.

'What is that stick there?' asked Tor, pointing to a short length of thin ash branch lying horizontally across the table.

'That is the Hellweg, the great road that leads due east from the river Rhenus – which is that thick piece of rope over there – as you will recall it is the main route along which the Frankish troops will advance into Saxony. See, it leads here, north of the Groves of Eresburg, directly to Lippspringe, where Karolus is holding his Grand Assembly next month.'

'What are all these pebbles?' asked Tor, pointing to a concentration of round stones to the right and above the stick that did duty for the straight Hellweg road.

'That is the Süntel Hills, where we will muster our...'

Abbio stepped close to the duke and put a claw-hand on his arm. He whispered something sibilant in Widukind's ear.

'Oh, nonsense. She is trustworthy,' said the duke. And then he looked at Tor and frowned. 'But I have bored you long enough, my dear, with my Saxon affairs. Let us go through into my chamber and have a cup of warmed wine.'

He took Tor by the hand and drew her away from the table. She found she had lost her voice, and meekly followed him into the chamber where he slept.

She would tell him tomorrow. First thing, she would tell him it was over.

–

Valtyr was behaving very oddly, Tor thought. He was drunk, but that was not the unusual thing: he was excited, he was even, perhaps, triumphant. Something had occurred between him and Bjarki when they went to see the king which had made him very happy. He had two spots of colour on his normally sallow old cheeks, and the black eyepatch he wore seemed to be set at a jauntier angle.

Bjarki was to be named heir in a ceremony at the full moon, in ten days' time, her brother had told her that much, and Father Alwin had been sent south into Saxony to escort a very important but mysterious guest of King Siegfried's back to Ribe.

Yet there was something else that was making Valtyr so happy these days – and Bjarki so very unhappy. Her brother sat on a stool in the corner of the hall staring into space day after day, nether drinking nor eating, apparently lost in his own deep, dark contemplations. When she had tried to engage him in conversation, he had looked at her as if he had never seen her before in his life. She had suggested that Bjarki come with her when she took the *hird*, the fifty spearmen they had brought with them to Ribe from Ymirsfjord, out into the fields for some much-needed exercise and battle-practice. But he had refused and then, when she persisted, had told her quite roughly to leave him in peace. His voice troubled her. It was deeper and darker than before, almost gravelly. Even Edith could not seem to reach him, although she tried to be cheerful around him and make him eat from time to time, and drink an occasional cup of ale. She confessed to Tor late one evening that she was equally worried about him.

Bjarki seemed to be recovered from his attack in the royal hall, and there had been no repeat of the episode, but he seemed a changed man. One terrible word kept occurring to her, bobbing up in her thoughts, a word she could not bear to say aloud – Galálar. Was her brother in danger of succumbing to that blood-soaked horror?

Mercifully, Bjarki seemed to come back to himself for the full-moon feast, when it finally arrived, and he carefully washed and dressed himself in his finest clothes. He donned a tunic of green silk, and matching baggy green-and-black striped trews, and a fine white woollen cloak trimmed with midnight sable. His polished, knee-high leather boots were as soft as butter; his belt had a large gold buckle, and he even wore a small circlet of gold round his brow, to keep his long blond hair away from his face.

He looked every inch the Golden Viking.

There were sometimes advantages to being rich, Tor thought, although she herself wore her old leather jerkin and trews that day and her boots were shod with iron and more suited to the breaking of a shield wall than the naming of a king's heir.

The hall was filled with revellers when she and Valtyr and Bjarki squeezed through the wide-open door and began to make their way between the crush of elbows and backs of the chattering people of Ribe who had flocked to be feasted so royally by their sovereign. They were halfway up the length of the hall and nearing the high dais when Valtyr swept out his staff, striking the broad back of some red-faced ploughman, and called in a loud voice: 'Make way, Danes, for the Erfingi! Make way for the man who will one day be your lord and king!'

Tor could see Bjarki frowning at that unlucky presumption but a rough path did clear before them, with people moving away on either side as swiftly as if a pair of curtains were being dramatically pulled apart. And now Tor could clearly see the raised dais, and old King Siegfried sitting up there in the centre with Duke Widukind on his right hand, dressed almost as regally as the king himself, and with an older Danish jarl beyond the Saxon duke, a senior fellow she knew as the Master of Hellingar and

Warden of the Dane-Work, and to the left of the king, to his left…

Tor stopped dead, and clutched at Bjarki's fine cloak, halting him too. Her brother spun round to look at her with an expression of intense irritation.

'You see him, Bjarki?' she asked. 'Beside the king. That's… that's…'

It was Valtyr Far-Traveller who answered her: 'That is Bishop Livinus, the so-called Archbishop of Saxony. That is the Frankish hostage we will hold here in Ribe to guarantee Bjarki's life when he goes to the Grand Assembly.'

For Tor, this was new and largely unwelcome information. Too much for her to digest immediately. The feast became just a blur. She was seated at the very end of the table on the high dais, beside a grim and silent Bjarki, far to the right of the king, yet she could not help but keep sneaking glances down the long, heavily laden board to Bishop Livinus, who was eating and drinking and conversing with Siegfried as if they were already old acquaintances. Which, Tor realised belatedly, they were.

This was not Bishop Livinus's first visit in the Dane-Mark: he had come north as part of an embassy nine years ago, when Widukind had been recruiting Danes to fight for him in his first doomed attempt to evict the Frankish legions from his homeland. That had been at Hedeby, a wealthy trading port on the south-east coast of the Jutland peninsula. But the bishop had stayed in Siegfried's realm for several weeks, with the king as his host, while they discussed various bits of diplomatic business and, it seemed, their relationship even now was at the very least cordial.

Should Tor be worried about the fact that Bishop Livinus was among them? She pondered this while she ate, and the conclusion that she came to surprised her.

No, he was not a threat. He might be a manipulative shit-weasel but he had no power in the North. Indeed, *he* was now in Siegfried's power. If anything were to happen to Bjarki in Saxony, then Bishop Livinus was a dead man.

She recalled something that Father Alwin had said to her before he departed from Ribe on his southern mission. 'I am happy to be of use in this delicate matter. It's a time-honoured practice, the swapping of hostages. Without it there could be no peace discussions, no parlays, no arrangements at all made between realms.'

Bishop Livinus's presence was reassuring, Tor concluded. He was an important man in Francia, Karolus's chaplain and chancellor, the king's right-hand man. And while Livinus was being held in Ribe, no one in Saxony would dare harm her brother.

If her conclusions about Livinus surprised Tor, it was as nothing to the surprise that came when the platters of meat and broken bread had all been cleared away by the servants, and with the help of his bald steward Mundi, Siegfried slowly, stiffly got to his feet to address the great mass of revellers seated at the long benches beneath the dais – the common Danish people of Ribe in their raucous hundreds.

'My friends and subjects, good Sword-Danes and stout husbandmen, I have today an announcement to make to you all. One this day of the full moon, in the month of Góa, I have gathered you here to commend my friend, my long-time ally, my strong right arm, Bjarki Bloodhand to you, and to announce it is my will to adopt him as my son, having no other, and to endow him with all the rights and duties, titles and lands which are mine, and to ask that you all acclaim him as my heir this day and confirm him as your lawful sovereign after me.'

There was a cheer from the crowd. And several folk began shouting out Bjarki's name. Tor had not realised until now that her brother was so well liked. She knew there were many stories about him circulating in the ale-houses and told by a hundred hearths but, since she herself paid scant attention to popularity, she had overlooked the high regard in which Bjarki was held by ordinary folk.

'Therefore, according to the ancient laws and customs of this realm,' the King continued, 'I ask you to come forwards and speak now if any among you knows good reason why Bjarki should not be adopted as my son and named as the heir to the kingdom. Speak now, if you have cause, or for ever after hold your tongue!'

There was a silence in the great hall, with several of the seated common folk looking around and at each other. And then, to Tor's astonishment, a man near the back stood up, and took a few stumbling steps towards the dais.

He was an ordinary-looking fellow, of about five and twenty years of age, medium height with nondescript brown hair. He looked intensely embarrassed, but also determined. And Tor suddenly realised that she recognised him. He was one of the king's servants. One of the people kindly provided by Siegfried, who served food and ale inside their own hall outside the walls of Ribe.

'Highness,' said the man, 'if you will forgive me, I have cause to speak.'

Siegfried peered into the gloom at the middle of the hall. 'Speak now, and speak up, young man,' he said. 'Tell me your name and what you wish to say.'

'You do not know me?' said the man, and it seemed he now had anger in his quavering voice. 'You – who of all men should – do not recognise my face?'

'Who are you?' asked the king.

'I am called Halfdan – Halfdan Siegfriedsson. And I came here to serve you, to know you, and have you know me. I came here months ago from our steading on the coast in Frisia, and your steward there offered me bed and board for my labour as a servant. You have claimed today, O King, that you have no living son, and would adopt that big, scarred lump sitting with you up there. A man who is sick in his mind, as all his own people know. His illness is the talk of all Ribe. Yet you choose him over me, claiming that you have no son. I am here to tell you that is a lie. I am your son, Siegfried. I am your flesh and blood, born of my poor mother, Heilka. I am your only living son, King Siegfried. And I come here today to demand my rightful inheritance.'

# Chapter Ten

## The silence of the bears

They were quarrelling again. Mochta and Garm, his two *gandir*, grunting and growling, and giving the odd bark, talking in their own tongue that Bjarki could almost, so very nearly, understand – the meaning just slipping out of his grasp each time he thought it securely held. He listened to their talk all through the day and through parts of the night as well, on and on, barely aware of the World of Men, as he thought of it, oblivious to the splash of the waves, the harsh sting of the salt spray on his ruddy cheek, the regular creak and groan of the rigging.

When the boat changed tack, and the heavy boom came swinging across at head height, Kynwulf put a warning hand on Bjarki's shoulder, and muttered, 'Highness, beware,' and Bjarki ducked his head obediently to allow the bar of wood to slide over it without cracking his skull, before the wind filled the loose, flapping sail and smacked it taut once more. Rask, the most sea-skilled of his *Felaki* bodyguards, had the tiller, at the stern of the skiff, and Halfdan sat in the prow looking balefully back at Bjarki and Kynwulf amidships. All their baggage, including the gifts for Karolus, was piled in the middle of the boat.

It had taken them three days sailing more or less due south to reach the wide, marshy mouth of the Elbe, and another two days to sail – and when the wind was against them to pole and row the little boat – south-east down that great river to the hall of Jarl Guthrum at Treva. And during that time the number of words that Bjarki uttered could have been counted on his ten battle-scarred fingers.

Treva was a fortress built on an island in the centre of the wide river, with a wooden bridge leading to the north bank where there was a larger, more spread-out settlement of perhaps two thousand people. When they tied the skiff up at the harbour front on the north side of the island, Bjarki, stiff from sitting still for so many hours, stumbled out on the dry land like an old man, and Kynwulf was forced to steady him with a quick hand to stop him falling back into the water. Bjarki just caught the look of contempt on Halfdan's face and found to his surprise that his own was flushed with shame. He made an effort to pay attention to the World of Men, to shut out the constantly bickering bears for a little while.

'It is not Jarl Ulf who rules here,' said Bjarki to Kynwulf, as if they had been in the midst of a long conversation. 'Jarl Guthrum has this old place now.'

'Any fool knows that,' Halfdan sneered.

Bjarki looked at him from under his brows. A blank, inhuman expression, his blue eyes seeming opaque, a look that caused Halfdan to quickly turn away.

Bjarki knew who this rude fellow was. This was the man who had popped up at the feast in Ribe and claimed to be Siegfried's son, got on a Frisian girl more than a score of years before. He even recalled what had happened next.

The hall had fallen silent after this man's words, and Bjarki, who had been listening to his two *gandir* bicker in the Spirit-Realm, jerked himself back into the hall in time to follow what had occurred after that. The hall had erupted in noise, with many people shouting Bjarki's name, and others calling for the man – this Halfdan – to fully explain himself. Siegfried had quelled the uproar merely by remaining standing and waiting patiently for silence. Gradually, quiet had returned to his hall and the king then asked the young man: 'Is your mother Heilka? A free woman of Frisia?'

'She is, and she was your lover for a few weeks twenty-six years ago, when you visited Lord Raedbad, the grandson of the last king of Frisia. You hunted eider duck in the marshes with Raedbad by day, and by night you made love to my mother. She remembers you fondly, and sends you her kiss; but I do not understand why. You treated her shamefully, as a worthless whore. That is no matter: I am your son and, if you would choose an heir, he should be one of your own and not some half-mad *vikingr*.'

He pointed at Bjarki.

The king said: 'I would speak with you, young man. I would hear a little more of your tale. Just you and Mundi will join me in my private chamber.'

That had been the abrupt end of the feast. For two days, Bjarki had not known what was to happen until another summons came from the king, and he, Mundi and Valtyr convened in the large room at the back of the hall where King Siegfried held his private court and which also housed his large, wooden-framed bed.

'I believe he has a claim on me,' said Siegfried, when his two guests had been seated on stools and wine had been fetched. 'His mother was pretty, and I did bed her, this is true. The boy has her looks – I see that. But he's been raised to grow cabbages. In truth, I cannot see him leading Sword-Danes to victory against their enemies.'

'With all respect, highness,' said Mundi, 'you did not yourself lead the army at Norrkoping. He might appoint a good *Armathr* to command his spears in his place.'

'Siegfried was a sword-champion in his youth, a fearless warrior-king of the highest renown,' said Valtyr. 'At twenty-five years old, he was respected right across the North. He met the Sjaelland hero Valmar Iron-skull in single combat and slew him. This cabbage-seller, this Halfdan, is now in his prime fighting years, at the peak of his youth and strength, and he has no renown as a warrior *at all*.'

'Thank you, Valtyr,' said Siegfried with a smile, 'for remembering that.'

The one-eyed man sipped his wine and inclined his grey head in response.

'I could fight him, if you like,' said Bjarki. 'A duel. A *holmgang*. The winner to be named heir. That would resolve the issue, one way or another. If he won the bout, if he bested me, he would immediately have renown, if not...'

'It would end with Halfdan dead,' said Siegfried. 'My last son dead.'

There was a pause, then Siegfried said: 'Bring Halfdan in here, Mundi.'

A few moments later the young Frisian stood awkwardly by the door beside Mundi looking at the three older men, all seated together beside the fire.

'I cannot make you my heir, Halfdan,' said Siegfried. 'I have promised that honour to Bjarki. And it would not be right to deny it to him on a whim.'

'My lord king,' said Halfdan, 'I am of your own flesh and blood…'

'Be silent,' snapped Siegfried. 'I shall tell you now what is my judgement.'

The king collected his thoughts for a few moments. 'I cannot make you my heir, Halfdan – not yet,' he said at last. 'I do not know you well enough. I know not what is in your heart, what courage, strength or wisdom you possess. So I must put you to the test. This is my decision – this is my royal decree: you will go along with Bjarki to Saxony to the Grand Assembly that the King of the Franks has called. Neither of you shall be declared my heir. But you will both be my envoys, each of equal rank to the other. And I must insist that you both comport yourselves as befits ambassadors, with all courtesy and honour. When you return here to Ribe, we shall see how matters stand.'

So Halfdan had come with Bjarki. And Valtyr's last words to Bjarki before they embarked still rang in his ears. 'Just shove him over the side on the way, Bjarki, or cut his throat one night at camp. Shouldn't be a problem for you.'

–

Jarl Guthrum was a vigorous young man with a mop of black hair, muscular arms that gleamed with gold rings and a loud, confident voice that belied his lack of any meaningful experience both in the fields of governance and warfare.

He greeted Bjarki and Halfdan in his huge candlelit hall on the fortified island in the middle of the Elbe with an unconcealed, indeed, almost puppyish enthusiasm.

'A *berserkr*,' he said, 'a true Rekkr, reborn from the flames of the Fyr Skola – I am honoured. And a son of King Siegfried to boot. My hall is yours!'

Guthrum introduced them to his family, his mother, Jarl Ulf's widow, a sour-faced, white-haired, grim-looking woman, and his pretty younger sister Minka. He had no wife yet and few interests and, so far as Bjarki could tell, his chief pleasures were hunting deer, drinking large quantities of ale and telling long, extremely dull stories about ancient, heroic battles. He talked a great deal – which was fortunate because his mother said not a word beyond a mumbled greeting, and his sister Minka had eyes only for young Halfdan – and while a succession of lavish dishes came out from the kitchens to the large round table at which they all sat, Halfdan and Minka murmured shyly to each other, and Bjarki sat and nodded as Guthrum bored endlessly on about the Battle of Hellingar, in which Bjarki had fought nearly ten years ago.

This battle had been a great Saxon and Danish victory over the Franks at the Dane-Work, a great long earth wall and ship-channel, which divided Saxony from the Dane-Mark. Jarl Guthrum had a host of opinions about that famous battle, which he reeled out endlessly and which from time to time he asked Bjarki to validate.

'Of course, it was the reckless but ultimately successful attack by Duke Theodoric that sealed the great victory for us,' he said, looking sideways at Bjarki, who was nodding along. 'He was Fire Born, did you know, Bjarki? Boar Lodge, I think. And what a truly noble death! A fine ending. How I wish I had known him.'

The Rekkr jerked his chin up and down. He was with the two bears in the Spirit-Realm, they were talking about something more agreeable this time, he thought, but part of his mind knew exactly when he was expected to agree with his young host.

'So it shows that they can be beaten: that's what my father never grasped.'

Bjarki sat up, hauling his mind into the World of Men with some difficulty.

'You think we could beat the Frankish army in a full-scale war?' he said.

'Yes, indeed. Karolus sent the cream of his army – ten thousand legionaries of his famed *exercitus* – up to Nordalbia ten years ago, and we threw them back at the Dane-Work. If we were united, Dane and Saxon, Nordalbian, Angrian, Westphalian and Eastphalian, we would be a match for any force the Franks could muster.'

'Has Widukind been talking to you?'

'He was here last month. A prince of great vision and courage. I believe he is the man who could finally break us free from the hated yoke of the Franks.'

Bjarki discovered then that with his growing anger came a wonderful clarity.

'He's a spoilt, smooth-talking dreamer – no, he is worse than that, he is a clever word-wielder who uses other folk, manipulates them shamelessly, and spends their lives to further his personal ambitions; a dangerous man, Jarl Guthrum, who will get you and your people killed. Do *not* listen to Widukind.'

'I'm surprised at you, Bjarki. I would have thought that you – a Rekkr of the highest renown, one of the very few Fire Born alive in the Middle-Realm – would be in favour of a good, bloody fight against our ancestral enemies!'

'I've seen Francia. I've travelled over a good part of it. And I tell you Karolus commands multitudes. He could field a hundred thousand spearmen, if he chose to.'

Jarl Guthrum scoffed. 'There are not that many spears all in the Middle-Realm!'

'You don't know what you're talking about, sonny. For a start, there were never ten thousand Franks at the Dane-Work, but perhaps only half that number. Also, we *were* united then, and we still only just managed to defeat them from behind the greatest fortification in the Middle-Realm. We won that fight – just barely – but who won the war in Saxony? I will tell you this now, and you should remember it: if you go to war with Karolus, you will lose. You may enjoy a victory or two. But, in the end, you will lose and you will be destroyed.'

The air in the hall seemed to become a great deal more chilly after that and Bjarki soon made his excuses and went off to bed. But as he lay in the dark with the bears quiet for once, he thought about his conversation with the warlike young idiot.

Only a few years had passed since the long string of disasters in Saxony that Widukind proudly called his campaign of liberation. It had largely been a catastrophe. Widukind's combined Saxon army had been forced to flee – time and again – from Karolus's much larger pursuing force, and their apparently 'loyal' Saxon allies – including Guthrum's father, the deceased Jarl Ulf – had all slipped away, one by one, from the main force and then, even more quietly, surrendered to the Franks. But all of the hard lessons of those dark days, it seemed, had already been forgotten: certainly by mad young firebrands such as Guthrum. Now nobody seemed to remember that, despite a small victory at Lubbecke, Widukind had been hounded from his homeland.

Did they plan now to do that all again?

There was no way the Saxons could win against the Franks. The idea was madness. The foe were too strong, too organised – and there were simply too many of them.

This was Bjarki's honest view, an opinion gained over many years and many encounters with this enemy. Yet he found he still thrilled to the thought of a Saxony free of its oppressors. Of the happy homeland of Widukind's fathers.

*Was there a way in which this could be achieved?*

—

Bjarki, Halfdan and their small company bade a curt farewell to Jarl Guthrum the next day and set out on the road on foot, travelling south and a little west, making for Verden, a royal hall and settlement at the junction of the Weser and Aller rivers. They travelled for three days in fine weather through open country with horses galloping free in the pastures on either side of the road and sheep dotted about on the hillsides. It was a cosy, and familiar landscape, one Bjarki had journeyed over before, yet also subtly changed since last he was here.

The villages seemed a little poorer, the Saxon people they met a little more ragged and gaunt, more wary. There were fewer smiles, and from time to time, quite often, in truth, he saw red-cloaked soldiers lolling at their ease in the sunshine outside ale-houses, and once a squad of grim-faced Black Cloaks on horseback stopped them and asked them their business in Saxony, allowing them to pass only when they admitted that the Grand Assembly called by King Karolus himself in Lippspringe was their final destination.

The greatest differences in Saxony were the signs of Christianity, which had sprouted up everywhere like mushrooms after rain. At several junctions in the roads, where once there might have been a small shrine to a local deity or spirit, with a meagre offering made of berries, bread or meat and a cup of ale, they found that large, freshly cut stone crosses had been erected, and that some of them had been garlanded with flowers. There were new churches too, small wooden buildings in the most part, but usually with a shaven-headed brown-robed priest and his female Saxon acolytes in attendance. The sound of church bells regularly rang out across the green pastures, and they heard singing, more than once, coming from inside these Houses of God.

As they walked further south, Bjarki felt clear-headed for the first time in a long while, and his thoughts became unusually lucid. His display of anger in the hall of Jarl Guthrum seemed to have cleared his fogged mind. Yet perhaps it was that he merely slept much better in the open air after a long, hard day of walking than he had in his soft bed in Ribe. Certainly, his nightly rest on the road had been entirely without the horrific dreams of bloodshed and ruin that had plagued him so often in the Dane-Mark. Perhaps it was simply hard travel, motion with a purpose, the fact of walking, that was the medicine he required.

During the long days on the march, he recalled what Edith had said to him before they left Ymirsfjord about his duty to his children. If King Siegfried *did* make him his heir, then one day Hildar would be the King of the Dane-Mark. That was a thought. Imagine: that pudgy infant, now struggling to walk, with the bright eyes and enchanting smile, one day ruling thousands of Danes!

And, of course, Lili would be a royal princess, too – well, that he could easily imagine. She was already an imperious, wilful little creature. But all this would only come to pass if this fellow Halfdan was not made heir in his place. He looked at the young man, stumping along a few paces in front of him. He would not be hard to kill, just as Valtyr had said. He had no battle skill. But, no, no, Bjarki could never do that. It would be a dishonourable thing to do. He could never do that. Could he?

Their party arrived at Verden on the evening of the third day and Bjarki was immediately swept back ten years by the sight of the dying sun casting its rich light on the whitewashed walls of the great hall and the adjoining buildings, painting them an exquisite golden colour. This was the very comfortable home of Jarl Brun – now styled *Comes*, or Count Brun, since he had submitted to Karolus, been baptised and become a Christian, just days before Bjarki's victory at the battle of Lubbecke.

His meeting with Brun was an awkward affair. Bjarki tried hard to forget that this man, after professing loyalty to the cause of free Saxony, had quit Widukind and made his own arrangements with Karolus. He made no mention of it, and Brun, too, seemed disinclined to revisit the deeds of his pagan past.

He greeted them with grave courtesy and, after a brief tour of his domain – which included, Bjarki could not help but notice, a new-built Christian church – Brun led them into his hall where he fed them a modest feast of roast river pike, brown trout and wild duck. When the best wine was being served out, after the meal – much better stuff than the common quaff, so Brun claimed – and their greasy plates and scraps of food had been cleared away by the servants, their host leaned forwards in his chair and enquired politely about Halfdan's family.

The question seemed to surprise his young guest. 'Oh, Siegfried is a good old stick,' said Halfdan. 'A little set in his ways now but with a kindly heart. Of course he is getting on a bit, but he is still very spry. And his mind is sharp as a well-honed seax. However, these days he seems to be worried primarily about his legacy; he spends a lot of time thinking about how the Middle-Realm will remember him when he is gone. He need not fret, I will make sure Siegfried is honoured after death...'

'I meant your mother,' said Brun. 'I've known Siegfried fifty years. I was at Ribe six months past with a dozen brood mares for him. He was well then.'

'Ah, yes, my mother. My mother Heilka is, um, in excellent health, thank you.'

'She has a small steading, I understand. Grows turnips, is that correct?'

Bjarki watched as a faint pink stain crept up Halfdan's neck. He felt genuine pity for this peasant-born man then, despite their conflicting interests.

'Cabbages. The best white cabbages in Frisia,' said Halfdan, recovering fast.

'You must be *very* proud of her,' said Brun, straight-faced, with absolutely nothing in his voice to indicate mockery nor the slightest degree of contempt.

Halfdan's cheeks were bright red and Bjarki felt compelled to intervene.

'How are your famous horse herds faring, jarl? Do you mind if I call you Jarl – or do you prefer *Comes*, since you are, well, now a servant of Karolus?'

Brun looked at him, his eyes hard as stones. After a little while he said: 'Jarl is fine. And I note *you* are no longer one. As for my horses, they are well enough; they breed and multiply, and there is ample pasturing for them on my lands. But the hand of my overlord, the king, lies heavy on my shoulder.'

'How so?'

'The king's marshals come every spring to take away the best colts for the *exercitus*. They took away five hundred last year, and they will be here again to take another crop of yearlings in a week or two. I am left with the lesser animals, the slow ones, the lame, the ones with narrow backs and poor wind.'

'I am sorry to hear that,' said Bjarki, keeping his tone even. 'Have you complained to your king? Begged for mercy? Christians are keen on mercy.'

'All complaints must go through the office of the chancellor. A high prelate, and Karolus's right-hand man. He has his dirty little fingers in everything. He calls himself the Archbishop of Saxony — Livinus is his name. He ignores my complaints then he sends his men to pick over the few horses that remain. Tithes, they call it.'

Bjarki grunted, then, and this time in genuine sympathy.

'It is one of the matters I will petition the king about at the Grand Assembly,' said Jarl Brun. 'But I do not know if I shall be heard by him. The bloodlines of my stallions and brood mares are much depleted, with the best foals taken year after year. Maybe soon there will be no horses grazing on the Angrian plain. Only sheep.'

A week later, Jarl Brun, Bjarki Bloodhand, Halfdan Siegfriedsson and the rest of their fifty-strong travelling party rode up to the wooded crest of the hill and looked down at the valley of the river Lippe below, where an array of humanity had been assembled from all four corners of Karolus's domain. They had been supplied with their mounts by Jarl Brun — his famous herds were not yet extinct — and in the three days of hard riding it had taken them to travel south from Verden to the north ridge of the Lippe Valley, Halfdan had fallen off only four times. Which Bjarki reckoned not bad for a man who had never sat a horse before, travelling at speed over rough country, including a day spent struggling through the dense undergrowth of the First Forest. Not once had Halfdan complained, which Bjarki marked in his favour.

Halfdan was, however, almost comically slack-jawed at the sight of the Grand Assembly laid out in the valley below them now. The tents of the multitude that had gathered at Karolus's command stretched for three miles both east and west along the valley floor on both sides of the shallow river.

They came in all shapes and sizes, from the white waxed linen shelters, set out in neat lines, of the Frankish cavalry *scarae*, to the black conical yurts of the Avar tribesmen from the great plain beyond the Danube, far to the east of Francia. There were brushwood shelters made by the green-cloaked mountain troops from the snowy Alps, and the great round red-and-gold striped pavilions of the proud noblemen of wealthy Aquitaine. And the badges that proclaimed the identity of each martial contingent also came in every possible hue and shade, from pennants on fluttering spear shafts, to big vertical banners attached to cross-pieces, to painted shields slung between two trees, to flapping, bedsheet-sized standards on tall, ship-like masts.

Halfdan, his eyes popping from his skull, said: 'I have never seen such a crush of folk in one place. The whole Middle-Realm must be assembled here.'

# Chapter Eleven

*Lesson from a wise old crone*

'Is it true, Tor,' said Erik, 'as I have been told, that your brother Bjarki can transform himself into a bear in the heat of battle? That cannot be true, can it?'

Tor fractionally lowered her shield. 'It's a bit complicated, young—' But before she could finish her answer Erik launched a savage attack on her, his wooden sword lancing out towards her eyes. Tor just blocked the blow in time, rolled away from the strike to her right, and whacked Erik hard across the buttocks with the slender ash wand she was carrying.

'Nice try,' she said. 'You almost fooled me. First position again. Ready?'

They were in the courtyard of their compound in Ribe, on a bright spring morning, with a chill in the air and a beautiful blue sky. Erik had approached her just after Bjarki's departure and asked to be schooled in the arts of warfare and, for want of anything better to do, she had agreed. It was better than mooning around outside Widukind's house hoping to 'accidentally' bump into the Saxon duke – for she had vowed that she would no longer go begging for his love by knocking at his door.

She liked the boy, and since his master Valtyr seemed to spend all of his time either in the ale-houses of Ribe or sleeping off his ale in the *Felaki* house, and had ignored Erik almost entirely since their arrival in the Dane-Mark three months ago, she felt the lad had been neglected. If he was ever to make a decent spearman one day, she ought to at least show him the correct way to hold a blade. Occasional lessons had become a routine, an hour each day before the midday meal, and Tor began to look forward to each session. The boy was keen and coming along well.

'No, I mean it, Tor. Tell me about it. How did Bjarki come to be a Rekkr? He seems so quiet, so gentle...'

'It's noon. Let's set aside our weapons, and sit on the bench by the kitchen with a bite of something and I'll tell you all about the Rekkr of Ymirsfjord.'

Tor lowered her shield and tucked the ash wand in her belt. Erik passed her his half-sized shield, and just as she took it, he jabbed her hard in the belly with his sword. She grunted in pain and swiped a roundhouse fist at his head, but missed by a good six inches as the boy laughed and danced nimbly out the way.

'You should never put up your blade while facing a dangerous opponent,' he said, chuckling. 'A wise old crone once taught me that bit of knowledge.'

'I taught you that, you ungrateful little shit,' said Tor, and charged him. Her shoulder hit him mid-chest and knocked him down in the dirt, and a few moments of frantic wrestling later, she was kneeling on his back, both his arms locked painfully behind him, with his face pressed into the courtyard mud. Yet he was still laughing.

'I'll teach you to call me an old crone,' said Tor, but she was grinning, too.

'Peace, Tor, peace,' mumbled Erik with a mouthful of mud. 'I surrender.'

They sat together, mud-smeared and content, and shared a loaf of bread and a hunk of cheese and a handful of spring onions. Tor told him at some length about the Fyr Skola, the holy place where both she and Bjarki had trained to become Fire Born, although her attempt had been unsuccessful.

She told him that someone who wished to become a Rekkr had to learn how to summon a *gandr* – the spirit of a wild animal – into their heart, as well as undergoing various harsh tests of endurance and passing through a sacred fire in a ritual that symbolised death and rebirth – which was why they were called Fire Born. Both she and Bjarki had undergone this but only Bjarki had managed to summon a *gandr*, which gave him his powerful bear-like ferocity in battle.

'The Golden Viking has a bear spirit inside him? Even now?' Erik asked.

'In truth, he has two,' said Tor, 'a bear mother and her full-grown cub.'

'Two *gandir*. That seems a bit... greedy,' said Erik.

Tor laughed again. 'I do not begrudge him his two *gandir* – not at all.'

'I think I'd like to become a Rekkr,' said Erik, 'and have all men fear me.'

'Be careful what you wish for,' said Tor.

She was about to elaborate on the perils of *gandr* possession when Valtyr came wandering over to them, with an empty jug dangling from his right hand.

'Go and fetch me some more ale, boy,' said the one-eyed old man. And when Erik glanced at Tor, to seek her permission, he said. 'Don't look at her – you serve me. Go get some ale. But take your time, I need to talk to her.'

The boy trotted off with the empty jug and Valtyr sat by Tor on the bench.

'Bishop Livinus,' he said.

'What about him?'

'That man is poison – a draft of lethal *eitr*. You know he's been given a house on the far side of Ribe? A big place to accommodate his whole retinue?'

'I did not know that.'

'Well, he has, and he has consecrated it himself with magic water or holy oil or something, and now he is holding Masses there. He is offering to baptise any Dane who wishes it, and welcomes anyone who seeks to learn about Jesus Christ. All new Christians receive gifts of food, ale, even silver coins. The house is full of our folk.'

'What does Siegfried say about this?'

'He doesn't want to intervene. He says a Dane should be free to follow any god he chooses. But the truth is that he does not want to antagonise Bishop Livinus while he is here. Not just because Bjarki is in the Frankish lands now, but because if any insult were offered to this bishop, it would give his master Karolus a fine excuse to come north and attack the Dane-Mark.'

'We need to consult Father Alwin,' said Tor, and she turned her head and bellowed her former thrall's name in the direction of the hall. A moment later and Alwin's tonsured head poked out of the doorway.

'We need your advice,' shouted Tor.

Erik returned with the ale as she was explaining the situation to Alwin.

'I think this may have been the very reason he volunteered to be a hostage,' said Alwin. 'He would count it a worthy martyrdom if he was killed by pagans in the Dane-Mark and was the cause of a successful war of conquest –

one which resulted in the conversion of all the Danes to the True Faith. The Church would greatly honour him – and he would be assured a place in Heaven. And Pope Adrian might even declare him a saint in due course.'

'How can we stop him then? We obviously can't just kill him.'

'Stop him?' said Father Alwin. 'My lady, I do not wish to stop him. I am a priest of the Catholic Church and I pray that through God's grace all people will come to love Christ. I don't wish to *stop* Livinus saving souls from damnation.'

'I thought you were on our side,' said Tor.

'I am on God's side. I like you and your brother, and his wife and children; I respect you and wish you all well. But do not ask me to choose the pagan side over the Christian. It would violate my sacred vows. I could *never* do that.'

'Livinus clearly seeks to provoke a war between the Dane-Mark and the Christians,' said Valtyr. 'If that war breaks out, thousands of men, women and children will die. Is that what you want? Do you want Bishop Livinus to spark a conflagration that will destroy the lives of so many innocents on both sides?'

Father Alwin frowned and thought for a while.

'I will go and see him,' he said, 'and ask him to be more discreet, and moderate his activities. He should not be enticing converts with gifts anyway.'

'I will go with you,' said Tor.

–

The doors of the longhouse were wide open when Tor and Alwin arrived there about an hour later, and the noise of the revellers could be heard from two streets away. There were drunken Danes everywhere, and bare-breasted bawds accosting them. Two men were brawling in the mud of the street a dozen yards from the entrance. The fine guest accommodation that Bishop Livinus had been given resembled nothing more than the lowest kind of ale-house. No effort was made to stop them entering, although Father Alwin's tonsure, wooden pectoral cross and plain brown hooded robe received a sharp glance from one of the two Black Cloaks who stood on either side of the open door, leaning on their spears. But nothing was said as they entered the hall.

Inside, the longhouse seemed to be filled to the rafters with Danes, some seated at the long benches by the tables, and some standing around the walls. Every man – and quite a few women – seemed to have a foaming horn in their hands, and was chatting or arguing with a neighbour. A group of men in the corner were singing, and the tables were covered with crumbs and dirty plates, piles of bones and scraps of fat and gristle, and small lakes of spilled ale.

At the far end of the longhouse, Tor noticed a long queue of folk in front of an enormous wooden barrel, in which a man was standing, soaking wet, as another man, a lean, handsome prelate of middle years in a tall, stiff white hat and gorgeous robe of gold and scarlet, poured a cup of water over the bathing man's head and mumbled some unintelligible words. Tor recognised the prelate as Bishop Livinus – and this ceremony as the Christian baptism. A few yards away, another Dane, wrapped in a blanket but still dripping from his cold plunge, was standing to one side of the barrel, where a tonsured clerk in a black robe presided over a table covered with a black-and-white chequered cloth on which stood several stacks of silver pennies. The dripping man held out a hand, the clerk asked him a question, dipped his quill in a pot and made a note on a piece of vellum. Then he handed the wet Dane a few pennies.

Behind the bishop, all along the back wall, was a line of armed Black Cloak troopers, and half a dozen also stood beside the clerk at the money table.

Father Alwin was already moving forwards, pushing his way through the crowds until he reached the barrel, where Livinus was helping another Dane enter the water.

Tor followed in the priest's slipstream.

'My lord bishop,' said Father Alwin. 'What is the meaning of this?'

'Father Alwin,' said Livinus. 'You grace us with your presence. I would have thought you might have come before now to pay your respects to your spiritual lord in this benighted land, if for no other reason than to pray with me.'

Tor could tell that the two men disliked each other. She wondered why.

'My lord, I have other duties in the house of my patron. But I see I should have come to you sooner. I might have been able to prevent this travesty.'

'A travesty, you say? How so?'

'You are buying these souls with silver. They are *paid* to be Christians.'

'They are saved none the less. Do you dispute Church doctrine with me?'

'No, lord. But what would Christ himself say? He who chased the money-lenders from the Temple. Our Lord would be angry. You use a love of Mammon...'

'Be silent, man! You would chide *me* – your superior – citing the actions of Our Lord? I told you when we last spoke to get out of Francia. But I see you did not run very far. And now you seek to correct me, to chastise me when I do the Lord's work in this pagan wilderness. At the very least, shame at your own failure in a similar task should curb your tongue. Be silent – speak no more!'

'My lord, that is grossly unfair…'

'Say one more word, Father Alwin, and I shall have you excommunicated. Do not test me, priest! I will have you defrocked, disgraced and damned for all eternity. You have the temerity, the sheer effrontery to come here – and in the company of a known witch, the sister of a demon-worshipper, whose grubby pagan children you instruct, you have the gall to lecture *me*. The Archbishop of Saxony, the king's chaplain…'

'I'm no witch,' said Tor. 'Nor does Bjarki worship demons. And if you call me that again, or impugn my reputation at all, I shall prove you a liar at the point of my seax. You are not in Francia, bishop. Karolus does not rule here.'

There was a stiffening among the Black Cloaks, those who had been leaning against the wall took a step forwards. Tor eyed them all contemptuously.

'I remember you well, Torfinna Hildarsdottir,' said Livinus. 'I recall you once accepted baptism in Aachen, in my presence, and then you broke your sacred oath to the king and fled his realm. You are therefore apostate, which is a serious crime in Francia. A crime punishable with death. And while I am perfectly aware that Karolus does not rule here – perhaps one day he might.'

'Do you threaten me, Christian?' said Tor.

'No more than you threatened me, woman, with the point of your seax!'

'Could you hurry it up a bit, please,' said a voice. 'I'm getting cold here.'

Tor stared at the Dane who had spoken; he was naked and dripping, having emerged from the barrel. She made a loud, scoffing sound and turned to Alwin.

'Let's go,' she said, 'and leave these *nithings* to sell their souls for silver.'

# Chapter Twelve

## The king's justice

They found a patch of ground on the north bank of the river Lippe, a little way up the slope of the hillside, left Jarl Brun's grooms to see to their horses, the servants to set up the tents, and then set out on foot to explore the camp of the Grand Assembly. Bjarki and Jarl Brun led the way, with Halfdan, Kynwulf and Rask close behind them, with half a dozen wide-eyed young Angrian spearmen trailing along, too.

The camp was a confusing maze of tents and other shelters, with a few paths between them and a babble of a score of different tongues in Bjarki's ears. But gradually he came to see that the layout was all structured in loose rings of increasing size around one huge central tent – a vast blue edifice of waxed linen and wool, with tall golden tent poles holding the flaps open on all four sides.

They all stopped at one of the entrances of the tent and stared inside, and there, only twenty paces away, sitting on a gilded wooden throne, was Karolus himself with a dozen Black Cloak guards around him and various officials and priests hovering nearby. Any competent bowman, Bjarki thought, standing right where he was, could render the most powerful man in the world stone dead in the blink of an eye, just as long as he cared nothing for his own life.

Bjarki, Brun and Halfdan pushed their way in and left the rest waiting outside the royal tent. There seemed to be something of a disturbance on the far side of the royal tent, where a pair of black-cloaked soldiers were dragging in two bound prisoners, with another man, a more richly dressed Frank coming into the tent behind these four. They all stopped in front of Karolus's throne, with the bound men forced to kneel, and a buzz of excitement rippled through the two hundred or so people inside the shelter and just outside of it.

'What is going on?' Bjarki whispered to Jarl Brun.

'From the look of it, I would say the king is about to dispense royal justice to his subjects. Under Frankish law, any free man who has been found guilty of a crime can appeal personally to the king to look again at their deeds and the punishment to which they have been sentenced. Karolus will make the final decision. Take a look at those two Saxons on the ground, look at their faces.'

Bjarki craned his head and looked at the two men, kneeling dejectedly on the floor before the king's throne, arms bound behind their backs. Their hair was matted with dried blood, and their faces were marked with cuts and bruises, several days old. They had been beaten severely, perhaps during questioning.

The king was calling for silence, and the Black Cloaks were echoing his call.

'My friends,' said Karolus, and Bjarki was dragged back into his own past by the man's familiar silky tones, 'I am required to adjudicate today on a case brought to me by my servant Gallo, Count of the Stables, who has brought two malefactors before me, men from the Osnabrucke region, who were charged with theft and later sentenced to lose a hand each as their punishment. The sentence was passed by Gallo himself, who is their lord, and who governs the county of Westphalia on my behalf.'

'I know Gallo,' said Jarl Brun, 'his men are all mounted on my horses.'

The king continued: 'However, they have appealed for mercy from me, as is their right, claiming the sentence is too harsh, and accordingly we shall hear their case and pass judgement upon them. Count Gallo, are you ready to speak?'

'I always stand ready, highness,' said the count, a barrel-chested fellow with cropped hair, wearing a hauberk, with a beautiful purple-and-gold cloak flowing from his shoulders. He had a fine sword on his hip with a gold pommel.

'Then you may begin,' said the king.

'I have known these two Saxons for some months, highness, they are father and son and both are born trouble-makers. They come from a farm near Osnabrucke, and they have given me nothing but insolence from the very first...'

'That is not true,' shouted the older man, 'we gave you your due...'

One of the Black Cloaks punched the man hard in the side of his head.

The king said, 'You shall have your chance to speak. Until then be silent.'

Gallo continued: 'They were not accustomed to pay their land taxes, nor their tithes to the Church, and my men and I were forced more than once to remind them of their duty. As their contribution to the efforts to build the new cathedral dedicated to St Peter in Osnabrucke, contributions that all peasants in the region are obliged to pay – according to your laws, highness – they gave two dozen chickens and a milch cow. But, in the dark of night, on several occasions, they came to the Church farm and stole eggs from the chicken coop, and milked the cow, before making away with their booty. They were apprehended by my men in the commission of their crimes and brought before me as their count for a fair trial according to the laws of the land. That is all I have to say, highness. There men were caught stealing, found guilty, and sentenced to the usual punishment set down in the statutes for the crime of theft.'

Gallo stepped back and bowed to the king, looking pleased with himself.

'I thank you for your succinct account, Gallo,' said the king. 'Now let us hear from the accused – do you dispute the facts as presented by your lord?'

'Yes – no – well, not all of them,' said the older man before faltering.

The younger man spoke up. 'They told us one day we had to pay the tithe for the cathedral, but we had already paid the usual amount in butter and cheese. Armed men came to our steading and, when we told them we could not pay the new amount, they took possession of our milch cow Ursula and all our chickens and left us with nothing. A tithe is supposed to be one tenth of the crop – but they simply took it all.

'So, yes, highness, we stole a few eggs, and yes, when we came across Ursula in the byre we milked her and took a little of her sweet cream. We were starving, and my little sister is sick and needed a posset, and Ursula did not mind being milked – and certainly the bishop did not notice that he lacked an egg or two. And for that the count says we must lose a hand. How can we feed ourselves with one hand apiece?'

Karolus put his chin in his palm and regarded the two men before him.

'You freely admit you are guilty of theft,' he said. 'There is no dispute about that. But the circumstances of this crime must also be taken into account.' Karolus paused for a while, thinking, and the whole tent seemed to fall silent in anticipation.

'Hmm, very well, you have appealed to me as your king, and therefore I must give you my considered judgement. You are guilty of the crime of theft. But you are also guilty of the crime of stealing from Holy Mother Church, which is a far more serious matter. Therefore, an example must be made of you. You will both be taken to a place of execution and have your heads severed from your bodies – and may God have mercy on your souls. Take them away!'

To Bjarki's astonishment, half a dozen Black Cloaks immediately fell on the two bound Saxon men, lifted and dragged them struggling out of the tent.

A large proportion of the crowd followed after the knot of Black Cloaks around the prisoners, and they did not go far, merely a couple of dozen yards to the river's edge, where the two men were forced to kneel on the grass. Bjarki and Jarl Brun were swept along with the mass of people, hemmed in in the crush so they could barely move. So Bjarki watched as one of the Black Cloaks – an officer, he knew, because of the black plume on his helm – drew his long sword and without a word hacked off the first man's head with two hard, grunting blows. The head tumbled, the torso began jetting gore and the second man shouted, 'No, wait – I beg you, wait a moment.'

Two Black Cloaks seized him, then, one man on each shoulder, and while the first man's body was still pumping his life's blood on to the turf, the officer raised his gory sword in the air. 'Karolus is a filthy tyrant,' shouted the second prisoner. 'He is a murderous bully, gorged on Saxon blood. We only stole eggs, a couple of eggs...'

The officer's sword swept down and, with just one powerful blow, the man was dead, his blond head rolling away like a ball to splash into the Lippe River.

The watching crowd let out a collective sigh of relief, or sadness, or shock.

Bjarki turned to face Jarl Brun and simply stared at his companion in disbelief.

'We must make ourselves known to the king,' said Brun, 'and be entered by his clerks among the names of those men who have attended the Grand Assembly.'

'Not now,' said Bjarki. 'I cannot look at that man. I need to get away.'

For the rest of that day, and the first part of the next, Bjarki moved through the assembled throng looking for the encampments of people that he knew and greeting them, and occasionally asking help to seek out those people he could not immediately find.

He tracked down the tent of Hessi, lord of Eastphalia, with no great difficulty, the next day a little after sunrise.

'What are we doing?' asked Halfdan, as they stood outside a low, deer-hide tent. Two big, heavily bearded spearmen stood by the entrance, eyeing them warily, with their hands on their hilts. Jarl Brun and the rest were still in their encampment, and Bjarki had agreed to return by noon, when they would go to the royal tent and present themselves to Karolus and give him the expensive gifts they had brought from the Dane-Mark. Kynwulf loomed behind Bjarki's right shoulder, giving the two spearmen the same hard eye the three visitors were receiving.

'Jarl Hessi is an old comrade from the Saxon wars. We campaigned together in the old days. He is lord of wide lands in the east, beyond the Oker.'

'I meant – why are we meeting him?'

'Widukind asked me to find him. He said Hessi might have a message for him.'

The sound of a barked order came from within, and one of the hairy Eastphalian spearmen bent and lifted the flap, beckoning the visitors to enter.

It was dark inside the small space, and oppressively malodorous, the air heavy with the stench of stale ale, urine and old farts; the only light coming from a lamp on a small folding table which was burning some kind of rancid fish oil. Several round shields were stacked against the central tentpole and there were piles of war gear in one corner of the space. At the folding table sat two men, grey-bearded Hessi, who was bare to the waist, whom Bjarki greeted cordially with a wide flap of his hand, and another younger fellow with long moustaches dressed in grey half-cured leathers.

'Back in Saxony, eh, Rekkr?' rumbled Hessi. 'Not had your fill of the Franks yet?'

'I'm not here by choice. Widukind sent me. I'd rather be home in Rogaland.'

'Widukind – how is that silver-tongued old glory-monger? Still spouting nonsense about a united North, is he? Still talking his bollocks about *victory*?'

Hessi gave the last word an unpleasant sardonic twist.

'He hasn't changed at all,' said Bjarki. 'Unlike some. Are you enjoying being a meek little Christian? That was the grubby deal you made with Karolus, was it not?

149

Undergoing baptism? Swearing to serve him? Are you enjoying gathering tithes and taxes for your overlord, building churches for Eastphalians to pray in?'

Hessi laughed bitterly. 'The only person I truly serve is me. The only cause I support is that of my own tribe. You mock me, Bjarki Bloodhand – and that is fair. I chose to live, to survive. Soon after we left Widukind at Braunsberg my five hundred Eastphalian spears found ourselves with an army of five *thousand* Frankish *cabellarii* up our arses and a couple of thousand savage Obodrites to our front. So yes, I made a deal with Karolus, yes, I allowed them to wash me in his holy water and swore to be a meek little Christian. It was that or total annihilation. We are not all death-or-glory seekers like you Fire Born. I wanted to live; I wanted my people to live too.'

Bjarki looked at him. 'How do you feel about Karolus now?' he asked.

'When he stands over me with a drawn sword, I am his loyal, whimpering lap-dog. But am I a Christian? Fuck no, I piss on the cross, I shit on all the tax-collecting silver-stealing Franks – recently I ordered all the new churches in Eastphalia to be burnt to the ground. Sometimes with their congregation inside.'

Bjarki heard Halfdan give a sharp intake of breath at Hessi's words.

'I heard about that,' said Bjarki. 'So – you have a message for Widukind?'

'Tell him, yes. Tell him I am in. Tell him exactly what I told you just now.'

'I will do.'

The other man at the table, the one with the long moustaches, spoke for the first time. 'I also have a message for you to deliver to the Lord Widukind.'

The man spoke the Saxon tongue but with a strong Slavic accent.

'Who are you?' asked Bjarki.

'I am called Witkojc. I was born beyond the river Elbe. I am the headman of the Zyrmunti clan.'

'He is a Sorb,' said Jarl Hessi. 'He is a neighbour of mine to the south.'

'Why do you wish to send a message to Widukind?' asked Bjarki.

'The Franks press upon us, too,' the Sorb said. 'They have built a fortress, what they call a *castrum*, at the meeting place of the Elbe and the Saarle rivers. There is a filthy Frankish church there, as well. Lord Widukind came to see us only a few months ago. He came with many gifts. He spoke most beautifully to me and to my people. And before he left, he asked me one question. I will give you my answer: "Midsummer's Eve". That is my message to the Saxon Wolf.'

Bjarki and Halfdan went to the royal tent at noon, to pay their respects to Karolus and his court and be entered in the clerks' lists. Jarl Brun had already made his obeisance and given his gifts and they spotted him in the crowd at the back of the tent. They gave their names to one of the Black Cloaks clustered around the throne and were told to wait. They sat on a bench at the side of the airy space while a stream of people were received by the king, a surprising variety of nations and tribes. There were Avars from the great plain, who strutted forwards bowlegged from a life perpetually on horseback, not subjects of Karolus, not quite allies either, just a neighbouring folk who were eager not to anger the powerful Frankish king but to do him all courtesy.

There were many different kinds of Frankish noble too – Austrasians and Neustrians, Burgundians and Swabians – many of them close kin to Karolus, but still men required to bow and hand over rich tribute to their lord. There were close allies of the vast Frankish realm present here as well – Lombards, Bavarians and even a lonely duke from little Carinthia – allies who were never to be fully trusted but were a necessary presence nonetheless if only for the look of it. It was nearly dusk before the little contingent from the Dane-Mark was beckoned forwards by the steward and allowed to make their bows before the throne. They were announced by a mumbling courtier and Karolus stifled a yawn as Bjarki laid out his treasures for the king, thick furs of fox and sable, jewelled brooches and silver hair pins for ladies, and a pair of swords with the hilts inlaid with precious stones, with a pair of matching daggers.

As he laid out Siegfried's gifts, Bjarki discreetly observed the king from under his brows. Karolus's curly red-gold hair was cut short and encircled by a tall, golden crown that flashed in the candlelight. He wore a pair of long moustaches that draped either side of his mouth but no proper beard, which reminded him of the Sorb he had met that morning. The king's eyes were larger than most, bright and expressive, but his defining feature was, as it had always been, his great, long, curved beak of a nose.

Suddenly, Karolus jerked straight upright in his seat. 'I know you!' he said, pointing a long and much be-ringed finger at Bjarki. 'I thought this was an embassy from the Danish king – and who do I see but my old friend Bjarki Bloodhand. The one all the common people used to call the Beast-Man. Bjarki, bless my soul! So you are the envoy

Bishop Livinus is standing hostage for in Ribe. They did not provide us with a name. Are you well, Bjarki? One of Siegfried's *hird*-men these days, are you?'

'Greetings, highness,' said Bjarki. 'I am well, I thank you.'

'Bjarki – happy to see you. Why it must be a seven, eight years since…'

'Since you locked me and my sister in a rolling wooden cage?'

Karolus frowned at him.

'Since I released you from that most-necessary cage and sent you to give a message to the rebel Widukind. You had broken your oath to me – and I do not usually allow oath-breakers to have a second chance. Every man deserves one chance at redemption but no man should be granted two. You were lucky I did not have you beheaded. Perhaps I should have done so. I heard that you later took up arms with that vagabond Saxon prince and fought against my *scarae* at Lubbecke. But let us not dwell too much on our past mistakes. Both yours and mine. The war is over. All Saxony is at peace, at last. How is your fiery sister?'

'Tor is well, I thank you, highness. She is in the Dane-Mark at present.'

'Good, good. And you Bjarki – did you marry? Have you made children?'

'I have a lovely wife, a fine baby son and a beautiful daughter. All in good health when I left them. And your highness, how is your lady wife Hildegard?'

'She is with child – again,' said Karolus. 'It will be our ninth, God willing.'

'I heartily congratulate you, highness.'

'A man should have children, Bjarki. That is what makes him a man.'

'Indeed, highness, but I'm not here to talk about family. I am here to present these gifts to you along with the compliments of Siegfried and to express his heartfelt wish that the Dane-Mark and Francia shall live in amity together for ever.'

'Hmm. We would have better amity if predatory dragon ships from the Dane-Mark did not raid our shores, burn our ports, slaughter our monks and carry away our goods and silver.'

'I will mention it to Siegfried. I'm sure he has no desire to anger you. Yet there are many *vikingir* who sail those seas. Siegfried has no way to curb them.'

'He had better start trying to curb them, or I shall become angry indeed.'

Bjarki held his tongue and bowed. Halfdan said: 'And I shall personally make sure that King Siegfried is aware of your great displeasure, highness.'

'Who are you?' said the king.

'I am Halfdan Siegfriedsson. I am the only son of King Siegfried.'

'Oh yes, the cabbage-grower. I've heard of you,' said Karolus witheringly.

Bjarki was impressed. It would seem the Franks had spies in the Dane-Mark and they were earning their pay by keeping their royal master informed.

'I am honoured that you have heard my name,' said Halfdan. 'Perhaps one day we shall meet as fellow monarchs, when I come into my inheritance.'

Karolus ignored him. 'Tell Siegfried this from me, Bjarki,' he said. 'It is important: my missionaries will be visiting the Dane-Mark in the months to come, honest Christians, pious men, driven by their love of God, and desire to bring the light of Christ to the North. I require that he offer them his protection. They are to be treated as my envoys.'

Bjarki said: 'The Dane-Mark is not Saxony, highness. I do not think Christian monks – or missionaries, as you call them – would be welcomed by common folk. We cleave to Odin, Frey and Thor and do not take kindly to being told which gods we may or may not worship. I think your missionaries might encounter resentment. They might arouse hatred, perhaps even violence.'

'That is why I require King Siegfried to grant them his protection.'

'I understand, highness. But I do not think we are able to guarantee the safety of missionaries. It might be better, if they did not come north at all.'

'They *will* come north. And if they are injured or molested or, God forbid, killed, I will hold Siegfried, and perhaps you, Bjarki Bloodhand, to account.'

Bjarki stared at the king. He knew he was no good at all this courtly back-and-forth and he found he was struggling to control an urgent desire to take a couple of steps forwards and punch Karolus very hard on his beaky nose.

'I will give your message to Siegfried, highness,' said Bjarki, bowing.

'I, too, will ensure that the king is fully alive to the situation,' said Halfdan.

'Do so,' said Karolus. 'And one more thing. I suggest you both remain close for the next day or so. I shall be proclaiming the new Capitularies for Saxony, that is to say, the new laws governing this land. You would be well advised to listen closely, take note, and follow these new laws to the letter while you sojourn in my domain.'

# Chapter Thirteen

### 'Old One-eye will be angry'

Tor was furious. She had done it, she had finally found the strength to say what she needed to say to Widukind, and he had acted as if he were indifferent to her.

She had gone to his house in the early morning, knowing she had many things to do that day so she would not be tempted to linger and lose her self-control. She had arranged that morning to go out and train the men of Bjarki's *hird* who had remained in Ribe. They had been idle for months and needed to shake off their sluggish winter torpor and be taken through their paces, now *Harpa*, season of war, was upon them.

Widukind had welcomed her as usual in a jovial fashion. 'You are here very early, Tor,' he said. 'Do you want some breakfast first? Or a cup of wine?'

'No. I just want to say this to you: we are done.' She did not care for his use of the word 'first'. She went blundering on: 'I cannot continue with our relationship, such as it is. You and I are not well suited. We are finished. That is all I have to say.'

'Very well,' said Widukind. 'You sure you wouldn't like a cup of wine?'

'No wine. I just want to make sure you understand. We are done.'

'Yes, you said that. We are done. It is just as well, in truth, Tor. Because war is coming, and I suspect I may soon not have the leisure to entertain you.'

Then Tor had left. White with anger. The idea that Widukind had been merely 'entertaining' her these past few months made her feel sick. Had their loving times together meant so little to him? Had she been no more than a troublesome guest, a stranger whom he was forced to entertain with his body? Well, she cared not. She had been simply using him for her own pleasure, too, had she not? And now it was over.

She stomped furiously through the gates of their home and across the courtyard to the hall, where she pushed through the main door of the long, narrow building in the middle of the east wall. She did want a drink now, a big cup of ale, maybe two, to calm her troubled spirits before she took Bjarki's *hird* out into the hills for training.

She looked left and right to see if there was a servant at hand and saw Erik, leaning on a broom, next to a pile of swept-up dirty rushes from the hall floor, and staring at the group of people a few yards away in the far corner of that long space.

It was Father Alwin, Edith with the toddler Hildar in her arms and Lili.

The priest was writing something in chalk on the piece of smooth black slate that he had set up on a wooden stand. The symbols meant nothing to Tor but as she watched, Father Alwin finished writing and said something to Lili. The girl, to Tor's surprise, in a high, clear voice said: '*Canis... custos... est... domus.*'

'Good, Lili,' said Father Alwin. 'Now who can tell me what this means?'

And to Tor's even greater surprise, Erik lifted his hand in the air.

'Ah, yes, my young friend. Can you interpret what was Lili saying then?'

'The dog is guardian of the house,' said Erik.

Tor found herself drifting close to the group in the corner.

'Very good. Let us try another…' said Father Alwin. He began writing again.

Tor said quietly to Erik: 'You can read Latin, then, the Christian tongue?'

Erik flushed. 'I have been eavesdropping on Father Alwin's lessons for many weeks now. I am sorry. I will get on with my work. Do not tell Valtyr.'

Tor said: 'Father Alwin, do you object to adding one more pupil to your little school?' And she jerked a thumb sideways at Erik.

'No, no, not at all. Erik is a fine lad. Come, set aside your broom. Join us!'

'Old One-eye will be angry with me,' said Erik.

'I will speak to Valtyr,' Tor said.

–

Tor found Valtyr in the *Felaki* house, snoring on a straw-stuffed mattress. She awoke him with a gentle kick to the ribs. While he was waking up, she pulled over a stool and sat next to his bed. She noticed a jug of ale beside it, picked it up and took a sip. The ale was stale and sour-tasting.

'What do you want?' said Valtyr.

Tor indicated the open doorway, where a bar of sunshine was spilling into the house. 'It's mid-morning. It is past time for you to rise and greet the day.'

'Why?' said Valtyr. 'Why should I rise when you say so? Am I a child?'

Tor made a see-sawing motion with her left hand to suggest that Valtyr's childishness was a matter for debate. 'You don't behave much like an adult.'

'What do you want?' Valtyr repeated.

'I would like you to stop drinking like a thirsty fish every day from the moment you wake until the hour you fall unconscious – wherever that happens to be.'

'I'm not going to change my ways for you.'

'You are killing yourself.'

Valtyr gave a glimmer of a grin. She looked at him closely for the first time in a while. His skin was yellow, tight against his skull, his eye bloodshot, his breath foul.

'You have it the wrong way around, Tor,' he said.

'What do you mean?'

'I *am* dying, but not from drinking good ale. I went to see a wise woman, some years ago; before we all went off to seek the Loki Sword. She told me that I had the Crab in my belly; that he was eating me from the inside. I feel him now. The pain.'

'That is why you drink so much?'

'It numbs my belly. And well, because... why not? I'll be leaving this Middle-Realm soon, I see no need to suffer overmuch in the time I have left.'

'I am sorry to hear this, Valtyr. Are you sure this is true?'

'I can feel it myself. In my belly, my bowels. I know the end is near.'

They sat in silence for a while. Tor found her eyes prickling with tears.

'Pass that ale jug,' said Valtyr.

'The ale is stale.'

Valtyr laughed and made a beckoning gesture. So Tor passed the jug over.

'I want to talk to you about Erik,' she said, eventually.

'I thought you might,' said Valtyr. 'You have realised who he is, I expect.'

'What? No. Why? Who is he?'

'He is Bjarki's son. Your nephew. Fathered on Freya, Bjarki's girl in Bago. Before she went off with the *nithing* Freki. I thought you'd have noticed his looks.'

'I did not know. Does Bjarki?'

'If you did not, I very much doubt Bjarki has worked it out.'

'Why did you not tell my brother?'

'It amused me. And I wanted to put Erik in Bjarki's company first, to see what Bjarki made of him. I found him on Bago – Freya was dead and that *nithing* Freki was beating him cruelly. So I bought him from Freki, and carried him away from there. I thought he might have the potential to be a Rekkr one day. Alas, it seems he has not inherited Bjarki's *berserkr* blood.'

'He is still a fine lad. Got the makings of a spearman. He is clever, too.'

'Will you tell, Bjarki?' said Valtyr.

Tor fell silent. 'I think not. Not yet. Let us see what Erik is made of. If he proves a weakling or coward, it would be best never to tell Bjarki that Erik is his son.'

'So will *you* look after the boy, when I am… when I am not around?'

Tor shrugged. 'I'll get him to bring you some fresh ale,' she said.

They worked on the ambush. In the sun-filled woodlands among the hills of central Jutland, Tor and Bjarki's *hird* practised position, concealment, and all the silent hand signals required to spring the jaws of a trap on a column of enemy.

'Stop moving your big shiny bald head about, Sambor,' shouted Tor, who was standing in the centre of a dappled glade playing the part of a cautious enemy scout. 'When you move it about trying to get a better view of me, you idiot, the movement always draws my eye. If you must move, do it when I'm looking the other way.'

The *hird* had been split in two, with twenty-six warriors on each side of the clearing now attempting to conceal themselves in the underbrush. A track ran up the middle of the glade, the road that led back to Ribe, five miles to the west. Apart from being a little too obvious, it was a perfect spot for an ambush.

She turned to Erik, who, his lesson with Father Alwin completed, was employed as her runner, the fleet-footed messenger every commander required.

'Go find Joralf and his people on that side and tell them they are too far back. They need to be out of sight but within two yards of the treeline. Go on!'

She could see it now. Watching the boy speed over the grass, she could clearly see Bjarki in him, in the set of his shoulders and the way his long legs drove him forwards as he pelted away. It seemed strange she had never seen it before.

She was also surprised at the amount of affection she had for him. Was that not odd? She had liked Erik before, admired his boyish tricks, but now that she knew he was her own blood, a whole new world of raw feeling opened up inside her heart.

She heard the soft thudding of horse hooves behind her and turned to see two riders approaching, a man and a woman: Widukind and his sister Edith.

They reined in in front of her, with Edith giving her a warm sisterly smile. Bjarki's wife was in fine fettle: her cheeks were pink from riding and looking magnificent in a dark blue gown with a silky sheen, a gold brooch pinned at her shoulder, and a leather-lined sky blue cloak trimmed with brilliant Arctic fox fur.

She looked like a genuine princess, Tor realised, and then she wondered how difficult it must have been for this woman, raised as a duke's daughter, to have spent so many years in a rough *vikingr*'s lair on the uncivilised western edge of the North. Obviously, Edith relished the chance to revert to her previous ducal splendour. And Bjarki was certainly rich enough to indulge her in a few fine dresses. Tor too, now that she remembered it, also possessed a modest fortune. Perhaps she ought to visit some of the clever tailors in Ribe and buy something pretty to wear, something to make Widukind stare. No, there was no point. It would only get torn and muddy.

'All alone, Tor?' said Widukind, looking down at her from the saddle. 'They said you were with Bjarki's *hird*. Have they all abandoned you for something better?'

'Not quite all of them,' said Tor, and jerked her head at Erik, who was trotting towards her over the empty glade. Inside her heart, she said: *Sambor, if you move your fat head even an inch, I swear I'll remove it from your shoulders.*

'You're lucky to have Erik with you,' said Edith, looking at the approaching boy. 'He's a quick one. He puts all the rest of Father Alwin's pupils in the shade.'

Erik smiled at Edith.

'When you catch up with the rest of Bjarki's *hird*,' said Widukind, 'I want you to ask them this: if you and Bjarki were to give them leave, a free choice, would they then choose to seek glory in Saxony with me as their commander? I would welcome them. Tell them from me all past crimes will be forgiven to any warrior who elects to fight with me, and he will be given lands in Saxony when the Franks are defeated.'

'Why don't you ask them yourself?' said Tor. She reached her right hand high in the air, all her fingers extended as if waving. Then she clenched her fist.

The treelines on either side of the glade erupted. Dozens of screaming warriors poured out from conceal-ment. They charged from both sides straight at Tor, Erik and the two Saxon riders, yelling war cries and bran-dishing weapons. The glade was transformed from a place of peace and beauty to a fair approximation of a battlefield.

Edith's mare became skittish under this unexpected assault, shying and rearing, and she had to work hard to calm it. The animal began to run, but she kept it tightly reined and turned it, and turned it, speaking soothing words until it understood that there was no danger. However, Widukind's horse was utterly terrified by the surprise attack and began bucking, crabbing sideways and trying to gallop away. Widukind very nearly lost his seat. The animal got halfway down the track back towards Ribe before the Saxon Wolf managed to right himself in the saddle and curb its flight, hauling on the reins hard and turning it back towards Tor. It was only when, a few moments later, they were back in the centre of the glade surrounded by a mob of laughing, jubilant *hird* folk, that Widukind brought the animal fully under his control.

'Reckless hussy,' he snarled. 'You could have killed me with your game.'

'Yet neither of you is harmed,' said Tor. 'You wanted to address the *hird*?'

Widukind stroked the sweat-gleaming neck of his horse. He was badly out of sorts. Then he looked around at the more than fifty flushed, excited faces.

'I am glad to see you men in such high spirits,' he said. 'War is coming. War in Saxony. And I am certain it will test your enthusiasm to the limits. I trust you will be as high-hearted when you come face to face with the Frankish foe. Indeed, I know you will be. The Christians have oppressed our folk for years – now it is time to fight back. I expect all you brave warriors will be eager to join in this struggle for the North.'

There was a puzzled silence at his words.

'We are not Saxons,' said a *Felaki* called Oddvin, a young man. 'And we do not fight for you, duke. We follow Bjarki Bloodhand and Tor. No others.'

'But if Bjarki were to go south to fight in Saxony, you would follow him?'

'We would,' said Oddvin. There was a chorus of assent from the others.

'Then I shall have to convince Bjarki Bloodhand himself to fight with me,' said Widukind. 'And I believe I have just the argument to persuade him.'

# Chapter Fourteen

*Crimes punishable by death*

Since the day was bright, for the reading of the Capitularies the King of the Franks abandoned his huge tent in the centre of the encampment and took to a hillside to the south of the river Lippe. A wooden platform had been built halfway up the grassy slope to give the king and his ministers somewhere to stand above the assembled masses, so that all the *hersirs*, jarls, bishops, lords, *comes*, dukes and officials of the Frankish realm might be able to clearly see Karolus and hear his wise words.

They numbered in their thousands and Bjarki – standing with Jarl Brun and Halfdan, on the left bank of the river in roughly the centre of this vast, chattering mass – was amazed at how many folk the king could address in this casual, open-air manner. It was, as Valtyr had said, like a Thing, only a hundred times bigger.

'Who is that standing on the right of the platform?' Bjarki asked Brun. He was pointing at a tall, lean man with a receding hairline and very large ears, dressed in a gorgeous blue cloak, fringed with golden tassels that he had swathed about his body but leaving his right shoulder and arm bare to the elements. The big-eared man held his chin high, and peered down his long, bony nose at the mass of folk beneath him.

'That is Adalgis. He is Karolus's chamberlain – and a bit of a pompous arse. He believes himself a brilliant cavalry commander, a man of great talent and vision; he reads a lot of history and encourages his men to describe him as the new Alexander.'

'The new who?' said Bjarki.

'It's not important. He's an arrogant fellow. Dangerous, too, if he thinks you are a threat to any of his interests. You remember that fellow, Gallo, who had those two poor Saxons beheaded for stealing a few eggs? He's Adalgis's lieutenant, and chief supporter. Between them they command a large part of the Frankish cavalry.'

'So Adalgis is the chamberlain – is that a higher rank than Bishop Livinus, who is Karolus's chancellor? I thought our Livinus was the next big dog after the king.'

'There is no clear hierarchy. The king likes it that way. Karolus is in charge, and only him. But his minsters each have areas of influence. But Bishop Livinus is Archbishop of Saxony. He has responsibility for all lands to the east of the Rhine. He advises Karolus on all foreign matters, and on all religious affairs. Which gives him a lot of ground to claim his own. He is probably the biggest dog, as you put it, but there are three others – Adalgis, Gallo and Worad – who are not far behind. I'd say Adalgis is Bishop Livinus's biggest rival. I have been reliably informed that they absolutely loathe each other.'

'And who is the other fellow, the short, dark one?'

'That ugly little bastard is Worad – he is the Count of the Palace, and he is also the King's Shield. He is in charge of the Black Cloaks and responsible for the king's protection from harm. He is influential but, mostly, he is just the king's strong right fist. Don't ever cross him. He *will* have you killed. Poisoned, or a knife in the dark.

Or a dozen Black Cloaks dragging you from your bed to behead you in your own yard.'

'How do you know all this, Brun?'

'When I yielded to Karolus after Widukind's Saxon army fell apart, not only did I have to be baptised a Christian, but I had to live for three years in the king's court. I mingled with these people. I still have nightmares about them.'

'Who else has power, apart from Adalgis and Worad? Whom should I fear?'

'Don't dismiss Gallo. He may be subordinate to Adalgis but he's a vicious brute, too. Then there is Count Thierry – he is with the *exercitus* in the camp just outside Aachen. He is not very bright but he commands all the infantry, the Red Cloaks. But he is the king's first cousin, and is trusted by Karolus. That makes him dangerous.'

Now the king himself was climbing up on to the platform, helped by a couple of Black Cloaks and Worad, the King's Shield. Bjarki had forgotten how tall Karolus was, perhaps even taller than Bjarki himself. He towered over the other tall man on the platform – Adalgis – and he made Worad look like a particularly stunted dwarf.

Adalgis stepped forwards: 'Silence for his highness the king!' he bellowed, then bowed and backed away, and Karolus came forwards to the edge of the platform.

'My subjects, my citizens, my dear friends, I would like to thank you all for gathering here in such harmony at Lippspringe at this most joyous and fecund time of the year,' he began. 'It is at moments like this that we are all made aware, by witnessing the physical presence of our fellow noblemen, that no matter how exalted our rank, or how illustrious our birth, we are, in truth, only constituent parts of one great whole. That we are, in truth, one nation of good and decent men, one people, united in our common purpose and desire for a strong peace and security for all of us. And that while we might have been born in Septimania, or Swabia, or even right here in Saxony, we are all Franks, part of a brotherhood, a family, joined by faith and love of God. For we all share a shining dream: the inevitable triumph of Christ on Earth.'

Here the king paused, and Bjarki watched as Adalgis and Worad on either side of the king began to clap and cheer his words. He looked around him and saw that about half of the audience below the king was also applauding, and that those who were not were looking around uneasily; and then, as realisation slowly dawned on them, hastily beginning to applaud the king's sentiment enthusiastically themselves.

Bjarki tucked his thumbs in his belt and turned to look at Halfdan. The cabbage-farmer's eyes were glinting with rage, apparently shining with tears of his emotion.

'It falls to me,' said Karolus, his powerful voice ringing out, 'to reward those of my faithful servants who have been most diligent on my behalf, but also, with a very heavy heart, to chasten those who have fallen short in the performance of their duty.'

A silence fell over the masses. 'It pains me to tell you that Count Vigilus of Fulda has displeased me over the past year. He has failed to provide justice for his people and several grave accusations of corruption have been levelled at him by a number of honest men. I therefore decree that Count Vigilus be removed from his offices as of this day, and his lands be forfeit. I may also tell you today that a truly remorseful Vigilus has thrown himself on my mercy and I have allowed him to be sequestered in the monastery at Fritzlar, so that he may repent and do penance for his sins.

All his lands and titles will go to my loyal friend Count Worad here, whom I have no doubt will prove a far better servant to me and better master to his people.'

'And what is all that about?' Bjarki asked Brun.

'Worad wanted to marry Vigilus's pretty daughter but the old Count of Fulda foolishly refused him. So Worad accused him of stealing the king's taxes and paid three witnesses to speak at his trial. Vigilis is lucky to have escaped with his life.'

'Does Karolus know that the witnesses were paid?'

'Probably. He's no fool. But Worad is much more important to him.'

Bjarki listened with a mingled astonishment and mild outrage as officials he had never heard of were mentioned by the king as failing in their duties, or proving to be dishonest. Their lands, their titles and sometimes their lives were forfeit, and on a number of occasions their fiefs were allocated to Adalgis, Gallo or Worad, who were much praised. Gallo, Adalgis's lieutenant, received a new title: Count of Westphalia, which made Bjarki smile to think how furious Widukind would be when he heard.

Bjarki grew bored after a little while – he did not know these people and was not much interested in their jostling for power and lands – and began to look around him, and estimate the numbers of folk gathered here. He thought it must be two or even three thousand people. And he began to do the sums in his head. The lowliest *hersir* might command fifty men, a *lith*, as this unit was called; while a *comes*, or count, might command five hundred men, but a bishop or a duke might have a few thousand... Which meant that gathered here in this valley were some two thousand lords, great and small, who might command as many as, what? – a hundred men each. More? More than two hundred thousand spears in total?

No, that could not be right. If each lord had, on average, eighty men…

At that point, Jarl Brun elbowed him sharply in the ribs. 'You will need to pay attention to this part, Bjarki,' he said. 'Karolus is about to read the new Capitularies, a fresh batch of laws for Saxony. King Siegfried will be interested to know about these, as will your friend Widukind.'

Up on the platform, a priest of some sort, probably a high bishop from his gold, scarlet and purple robes, was intoning a prayer, and Karolus and his two ministers, Adalgis and Worad, had their eyes closed and their heads bowed.

When it was done, the priest stepped down from the platform and a cleric in a plain black gown passed a scroll to Worad, who passed it over to the king.

'Know this all of you and harken to my word,' said the king, reading from the vellum scroll in his hands, 'these are my laws and Capitularies pertaining to my territories east of the river Rhenus and south of the river Elbe, to the land known to men as Saxony, and applying to all my subjects and all denizens of any rank or condition in this land, as set down by my scribes in Aachen on the fifteenth day of the month of May in the Year of the Incarnation Seven Hundred and Eighty-Two.'

Karolus paused for a breath.

'Firstly, it is my decree that all churches of Christ now being built in Saxony and consecrated to Almighty God shall have not less, but indeed greater and more illustrious honour than the pagan shrines where the worship of idols has hitherto taken place.

'Secondly, that if any one who shall have entered a church by violence and shall have carried off anything in it by force or theft, or shall have burned the church itself, let him be punished by death.

'Thirdly, if any one, out of contempt for Christianity, shall have despised the holy Lenten fast and shall have partaken of flesh, let him be punished by death.'

'What is the Lenten fast?' Bjarki whispered to Halfdan.

'It is forty days before Easter when you must not eat any meat.'

'Why?' asked Bjarki.

'Shhh,' said Jarl Brun. 'I missed that last one.'

'Fifthly,' the king was saying, 'if any one shall have killed a bishop or priest or deacon, let him likewise be punished by death.

'Sixthly, if any one in accordance with pagan rites, shall have caused the body of a dead man to be burned and shall have reduced his bones to ashes, let him be punished by death.

'Seventhly, if any one of the race of the Saxons hereafter has concealed among them any who wish to remain unbaptised, and who have scorned baptism, and still wished to remain a pagan, let him be punished by death.

'Eighthly, if any one shall have sacrificed a man to the Devil, after the manner of the pagans, he shall be punished by death…'

Bjarki stopped listening, his mind reeling with rage and hatred. He could hear the king droning on, reading out more and more of his laws and decrees, but the true meaning of these Capitularies was already crystal clear in his mind.

To steal from a church, to kill a priest, to cremate a dead family member, or to sacrifice to the gods in the old manner, to resist baptism, or hide anyone who did not wish to be baptised, to eat meat during Lent – whatever *that* was – all these were now deemed the worst kind of crimes, and therefore capital crimes. Karolus had with a few brisk sentences made it illegal – and punishable by death – to be a pagan in Saxony.

Bjarki turned and began to force his way through the crowd. Jarl Brun quickly caught up with him, and stopped him with a hard hand on his shoulder.

'Where are you going?' he said. 'The king has not yet finished speaking.'

'I have finished listening. And I'm finished with Saxony. I'm going home.'

'To Ribe?'

'To anywhere but here. I need to get away from this madness – away from a land where they would kill you for eating meat at the wrong time of year. Or for setting a dead king on his funeral pyre. Or for refusing to be baptised. And when I am gone, I'll never return. I swear I will never set foot in Saxony again.'

# Chapter Fifteen

*A formal request from a hostage*

Tor had been a little surprised by the royal summons from Siegfried, since she had no standing in court, nor in the Dane-Mark. She was a foreigner, a Svear, and only here because she was Bjarki's half-sister. But she obeyed nonetheless, when a breathless messenger came to the compound and informed her the king wished to speak to her.

Valtyr was with the king, as well as his steward Mundi, when Tor presented herself in his hall, and after she had made her bow, she was invited to sit with the three old men in a corner of that great space, and a cup of wine was brought to her.

'I would like your advice, Tor,' said the king. 'About our illustrious guest Bishop Livinus.'

Tor tried not to sneer. 'What has the hostage done now? Has he been buying up more Danish souls for his feeble Christian god?'

'No, well, yes, but that does not concern me. If Livinus is stupid enough to give away his silver, I'm sure my folk are clever enough to take it from his hand. I do not think that, in itself, is the problem. My steward Mundi here has been speaking to Olaf Blackfinger, his cousin, an oat farmer from up Rødding way, who has been baptised three times, so far. He's coming back this afternoon for his fourth wash in that holy barrel. He gives the Frankish clerks a different name each time: last time I believe he claimed his name was Siegfried Siegfriedsson, the impudent dog.'

'You don't think the converts are genuine in their love for Christ, then?'

'I think,' said Valtyr, 'if I were a Danish ploughman and someone said to me, I'll give you three silver Frankish deniers to have a quick wash in this barrel, I'd be out of my clothes before you could sneeze. I have always liked being given free silver. Particularly by my enemies. And I'm certain I'm not alone in that predilection.'

'My cousin Olaf says they make jokes about the ceremony when the bishop and his guards are out of earshot,' said Mundi. 'But he does admit that some of the newly baptised folk, a few, are true believers. Some even feel that it is a matter of honour, they made a vow to worship Jesus Christ and so will honour that promise till death.'

'What are you going to do about it?' asked Tor. 'Can you not simply forbid Livinus to convert more Danes? Or outlaw the religion, say, on pain of death?'

'I cannot tell a free man what to believe,' said the king. 'That is quite absurd. How could I hope to control what is in his mind? The idea ridiculous. My task as their king is to guide and protect my folk, not tell them to whom they can or cannot pray.'

'Then Livinus will continue to baptise folk in his unruly ale-house,' said Tor.

'Until he runs out of coin,' said Valtyr.

'Not quite,' said Mundi. 'He will ask permission to build a church in Ribe.'

'No,' said Tor, 'no, it cannot be allowed. Surely, highness, you will deny him.'

'Bishop Livinus is coming here, to my court, today, in an hour or so, to make his formal request to build a Christian church and, as an envoy of Karolus, King of the Franks, as well as a hostage, I must graciously receive him – just as Karolus must graciously receive Bjarki and Halfdan at Lippspringe. The Black Cloak he sent to me used those words, I suppose to remind me of our people's vulnerability in Saxony.'

–

Bishop Livinus entered the great hall of Ribe as if *he* were the king, rather than the white-haired old stick who was slumped on his throne up on the high dais.

The king had been ill again, another chill in his chest, and was only recently recovered and strong enough to sit on his throne. Bishop Livinus was evidently blooming with good health and dressed that day in his full episcopal finery: a tall, peaked hat made of stiff linen, a magnificent robe of purple and scarlet, and a kind of scarf of thick green silk, embroidered with the symbols of his faith. In his hand he held a bejewelled shepherd's crook, which appeared to be fashioned from solid gold.

Mundi stood beside his master, one hand on the back of the throne, as if to steady himself, with his mouth clamped angrily shut as he took in this vision of Christian splendour. Valtyr, who had earlier collected his own jug of ale, and Tor sat on a bench to one side, observing this entrance with a more cynical eye. The great hall had been relatively empty that afternoon, a few servants moving about at their usual chores, and a guard or two, snoozing on benches beside the lime-washed walls, but when Livinus entered the space it suddenly seemed full, full almost to bursting.

Because the man claimed to be the Archbishop of Saxony, Christ's anointed representative in the North, Livinus did not enter the hall alone. He came in with a pair of clerks, tonsured and wearing simple brown robes and sandals, one of them bearing a small pile of scrolls, and half a dozen well-armed Black Cloaks, and about a dozen ordinary Danish folk who entered the hall behind the great bishop singing a hymn.

It was a painful dirge, something about sacrificing a lamb to God, and Tor found that the tune jarred on her ears. The processions stopped in front of the high dais, and Livinus stepped forwards and made a small inclination of his head towards the throne, which might perhaps just pass for the respectful obeisance required by any monarch.

'Greetings, Bishop Livinus,' said the king, his voice sounding weak and reedy, 'you are welcome in my hall. But, kindly tell me, what is the purpose of your visit?'

'Lord king,' said Livinus. 'I give you my greetings in return. I wish also to thank you for the kindnesses you have shown me since I have been your guest in the town of Ribe. You have made my sojourn here pleasant and comfortable.'

'I am pleased to hear that,' said Siegfried, 'since your time with us is drawing to an end. I am sure that you will report back to Karolus that we are civilised folk up here in the North, who have treated you with all due grace, respect and courtesy.'

'My time with you is drawing to *an end*?' said Livinus. He took a step back as if stunned by this revelation. 'But surely you do not seek to expel me from your realm, lord king? What can I have done to offend you, highness?'

'You have done nothing to offend me, bishop. And you are welcome to remain here as long as you desire, of course... But the Grand Assembly in Lippspringe must be drawing to a close soon, and my envoys Bjarki Bloodhand and Halfdan Siegfriedsson will be returning to the Dane-Mark. Therefore, I expect you will be eager to return to your home, and to your own king's side.'

'You are very good, lord king, to allow me to remain in the Dane-Mark for as long as I desire. I shall, indeed, avail myself of that most generous offer. As I am sure you are aware, my presence here has awakened the souls of many of your subjects – a substantial number of whom have come to love Jesus Christ and have been baptised by me and my priests. Which brings me to the purpose of my visit today.'

Bishop Livinus paused and looked around the hall then. His eye fell on Tor and he gave her a small, smug smile.

'I am here to ask you, lord king, for your gracious permission to build the first church of Jesus Christ in these northern lands. The numbers of our Danish Christian brethren now far exceeds those that we can comfortably accommodate in the longhouse in Ribe you so kindly provided for our comfort. Put simply, we need a bigger space in which to worship the Lord of Hosts. I have in these scrolls here the names of five hundred Christians who have willingly undergone baptism and who now require a place to peacefully serve God and worship His only son Jesus Christ. However, I can promise you, lord king, that our new, and much larger church will cost you almost nothing. All we require from you, highness, is a little land to be set aside, near the town – ten acres of farmland would be perfect. I shall pay for the construction of the church myself, and its upkeep, and the living of the priests shall be provided by the tithes we will gather from the congregations in the surrounding—'

'Enough!' Tor was on her feet and striding forwards. 'No. You cannot build your filthy church in this kingdom. I shall not allow it. I shall never allow it.'

'I believe I was addressing the lord king, not some ill-mannered hoyden.'

'Tor, this is for me to decide,' said Siegfried.

'Well,' said Tor, turning on the king, 'decide then. Decide. Tell this gaudy pimp to take his foul religion and fuck off back to Francia. Tell him, Siegfried.'

'It's not that simple, Tor,' said the king. 'The bishop is the envoy of…'

'It is that simple. Who rules in the Dane-Mark, you or this shiny prick?'

'You should show respect to your king, woman! This is most unseemly.'

Tor turned on Livinus. 'Let me make this clear. You and your religion are not welcome here. You will not have a church in this land. And, if you do build one, I shall raze it to the ground and kill any cowering priests inside. Me, not the king, not his spearmen. Not my brother. Me, Torfinna Hildarsdottir. I shall personally burn your church and slay your priests. Have you understood that?'

'Men of God fear not death,' said Livinus, and he knelt before Tor and stretched out his chin, exposing his white, wattled neck. 'Here, Tor, here is my neck, ready for your devilish knife. Kill me, if you wish, grant me the blessed martyrdom I so desire. Kill me and allow me to go to my heavenly reward.'

Tor already had her right hand on her seax handle.

'Stop that, Tor,' shouted the old king. 'Step away from the bishop. Now!'

The Black Cloaks were moving in now, they too had their hands on their hilts, and a trio of Siegfried's spearmen were also hurrying closer. Tor could hear wild laughter, and turned to see Valtyr convulsed with mirth on his bench, clutching at his ale jug.

'Go on, Tor, slit his throat. Ha-ha-ha! Do it for me! Do it as a favour for me.'

Tor took her hand off the seax and took two long strides backwards.

'If my brother Bjarki were not in peril in Saxony, bishop...' she said.

–

Three days later Bjarki, Halfdan and their party returned to Ribe. And Siegfried dispatched his steward Mundi to the longhouse to tell Bishop Livinus and his servants that their welcome in his realm had worn thin. It was time to depart.

'I'll gladly tell him,' Tor offered. 'It would be a pleasure, highness.'

'No, no, Tor, you have done enough. I think Mundi would do this more... how can I put it... gracefully. If Livinus refuses to go, then you can take a *lith* of my spearmen and escort him and his men to the border with Saxony, down to the Dane-Work. But do not kill him. I do not wish to spark a war with Francia.'

'I'll go with you, Tor,' said Bjarki, 'if it comes to that. I would very much like to see Bishop Livinus and his priests removed from Danish soil for good.'

However, perhaps surprisingly, Livinus packed up his possessions, held one last Mass in the longhouse – sparsely attended, Tor was told – and meekly left Ribe, without the necessity of being removed. If he had not gone, Tor was quite sure she would have given him his blessed martyrdom, sooner or later.

Tor, Bjarki, Halfdan, Widukind and Valtyr met the king in his quarters behind the great hall on the evening of the day that Livinus departed, and the king invited Bjarki to relate what he had learned at the Grand Assembly in Saxony.

To Tor's eyes, despite the rigours of the journey from Saxony, Bjarki seemed his old self. He seemed less withdrawn, more cheerful, even happy. The dark bags under his eyes had gone, and he seemed full of his old vigour.

'Three important things I gathered from Lippspringe,' Bjarki said. 'Firstly, the Franks are even more powerful than I had thought…' He went through his mental tallying of the number of the lords and the men they might command.

'Two *hundred thousand* Frankish spears?' said Siegfried. 'That is absurd!'

'But those spears would be spread all over Francia and allied territories,' said Widukind. 'If they all stayed in one place they would soon starve. Each region would only have at most two thousand men to call on in time of war.'

'Perhaps,' said Bjarki. 'But if there was a war they might well concentrate their forces. Judging by the turn-out at Lippspringe, they could do that with ease.'

'What else did you learn, Bjarki?' said the king.

'Well, Karolus gave me a message to give to you, Siegfried: he said his Christian missionaries would be coming north and you should treat them as envoys of Karolus himself. So, while you might have got rid of Bishop Livinus, more of his ilk are certainly coming here.

Karolus says he'll hold us – you and me – personally responsible if any of his missionaries are killed or harmed. Do you hear that, Tor?'

There was a gloomy silence after that.

'What was the third thing you learnt?' asked Widukind.

Bjarki told them about the Capitularies, and recited all the ones he could remember. Then he said: 'It is clear Karolus will kill anyone in Saxony who is not a Christian. Anyone who still follows the old gods will be caught, tried and executed.'

'Good,' said Widukind.

The others all looked at him with astonishment.

'Why is that good?' asked Bjarki, his eyes narrowing dangerously.

'Because Karolus has shown us his true heart. I have spoken to many Saxons who claim that life under the Franks is not so bad. They pay a little tax, sometimes they have to go to church. But, broadly, they say, they can carry on as normal, doing things in the way they have always done them. After these disgusting Capitularies, they can no longer claim that. The King of the Franks has just declared war on all the Saxons. My people will never accept his stupid Christian laws. Karolus has just lit a spark that will ignite the raging fire of rebellion all across my land.'

Tor noticed that Bjarki was now smiling to himself.

'What are you so happy about?' she asked.

Bjarki looked at her, then at everyone in that small, cramped room.

'I am happy,' he said, 'because I've made up my mind. I have at last come to a decision. After everything I saw in Saxony, and from what I have heard from you about events up here, I have decided what I will now do. I am going to go back to Ymirsfjord, and I am going to live there quietly on the treasure I have accumulated, watch my children grow, and perhaps, from time to time, play the *vikingr*. And I mean to die there many, many years from now, after one last, great, glorious seafaring raid against a worthy and wealthy foe.'

'But what about Saxony?' said Widukind.

'What about the Dane-Mark?' said Siegfried.

'What about them? Saxony is doomed to be a Christian nation, ruled over by the Franks. And they will soon rule up here in the Dane-Mark, too. Karolus as good as told me that – he means to come north with his vast armies, when his missionaries are duly insulted, or on some other feeble pretext, and conquer the lot of us. He used the phrase "the inevitable triumph of Christ on Earth". That is what he believes in. That is what he is always working towards. To make the whole Middle-Realm Christian.'

The silence in the room was a solid thing.

'So Karolus will come up here to the Dane-Mark,' Bjarki continued. 'But I won't be here. I shall be in Rogaland; I shall be far, far away in Ymirsfjord, where I can live my life exactly as I choose. Therefore, I hereby renounce any claim I may have advanced to be your heir, King Siegfried. I thank you for it, but I no longer desire that high honour. I suspect you were going to make Halfdan here your heir anyway, in due course. Do not try to deny it. He is your own blood, after all. And not such a bad fellow, as I came to realise in Saxony. He has a good heart. I am content for Halfdan be next King of the Dane-Mark. And I fully expect he will one day be king here... That is, if Karolus allows him to keep his throne.'

# Chapter Sixteen

### The fires of rage in his eyes

Bjarki slept badly that night. Whether it was because he was back in his hall outside Ribe and no longer travelling, or because of his outburst at the king, or because he knew, in his heart, that he was running from a fight – whatever the cause he slept little and when he did he dreamt of the bears. They were fighting this time, growling and tearing at each other, with bloody tooth and claw. But when he looked closer, he saw it was a figure of a man they were attacking, crudely made, a doll-like object, stiff-limbed, with the face of Bjarki. Both the bears were tearing at it, trying to destroy it. Growling, biting and tearing at the man-sized doll that looked exactly like him.

These terrible images kept on coming, all night long. He tried to speak to the bears to plead for them to stop. But he found his words made no sense as they came from his mouth and neither could he understand the *gandir* when they spoke to him. They seemed to be trying to communicate something urgent to him. Something vital. Then, when they saw he could not understand, they would attack the doll-object once more. When he woke, sweating in the middle watch, these images stayed with him.

He tried to drink himself to slumber, sinking two full jugs of strong mead, and merely made himself sick, but then he drowsed a little and when he awoke in the grey light of pre-dawn, he felt feverish and weak. Which was unfortunate because that day he was given no time to recover his wits, nor to sleep off his horrible mead hangover.

All that day, people kept coming at him, relentlessly, mercilessly.

One type of assault after another.

First it was Widukind, who visited him as he was washing himself in the courtyard a little after dawn, the boy Erik sluicing him with buckets of water drawn from the well. Bjarki was freezing and naked when the duke began his harangue.

'I am astonished, quite astonished, Bjarki, that you can turn your back on the Saxon nation, knowing the hardship they suffer under the cruel tyranny of the Franks, and knowing this, still abandon them to their fate. I'll not say you're a coward...'

'You'd better *not* say it,' growled Bjarki, with his wet hair over his face.

'All I will say is this is not the behaviour I expected from a Fire Born warrior. A true hero of the North. What would Angantyr, that legendary King of the Goths, and your own revered ancestor, whose ancient sword I now so proudly bear – what would King Angantyr have to say about your shameful conduct in this Saxon matter?'

Erik handed Bjarki a rough linen towel, and while he scrubbed his body dry, the Rekkr of Ymirsfjord glanced over at the old sword with the big blue jewel set in the pommel that hung at Widukind's left side. He knew that antique blade very well.

'Honestly, I do not think Angantyr would be very pleased with his descendant,' said Widukind. 'I think your long-dead hero ancestor would be restless in his grave.'

Bjarki ignored him. He turned and went into the hall to find some clean clothes, but Widukind, never one to take a hint, followed after him, still talking.

'You've felt the weight of the Frankish yoke first hand; you have seen what life is like now in Saxony,' he went on, as Bjarki pulled on his leggings, the cloth sticking to his still-wet legs. 'You heard Karolus himself read out those Capitularies. You know that an innocent man can be executed for eating meat – eating a little slice of life-giving meat – in what Karolus decrees to be the wrong season!'

'You are wasting your breath, duke,' said Bjarki, finally deigning to reply. 'I owe the Saxon people nothing. I have fought, bled and suffered for them. In the last rebellion, I nearly died, so did Tor – and many of my good friends and comrades did indeed breathe their last in the cause of Saxon freedom. That old sword you carry cost me the lives of many loyal companions, too, when I retrieved it from the Avar Khaganate, and much of my own blood, as well. And I gave the Loki Sword to you; so you could use it to free Saxony. Why don't you wield it, duke? Rally the Saxons, draw the sword and use it, if you seek a great victory over the Franks. If the legend is true, you'll be victorious. That's the power of the Loki Sword.'

Bjarki did not mention the second part of the legend connected to the sword – the sword that was forged by the Dwarf-Masters for the trickster god Loki. The second part of the myth claimed that the warrior who wielded the Loki Sword would gain victory – but victory would come at the cost of his own life.

Widukind did not reply. He just looked very disappointed in Bjarki.

'There is something else,' said Bjarki, shrugging his body into a long woollen tunic, and reaching for his belt, 'something I forgot to tell you.' He looked at Widukind. 'I met a Sorb in Lippspringe – a neighbour of Jarl Hessi.'

'Was his name Witkojc?'

'Something like that. He asked me to pass on a message to you.'

'What message?'

Bjarki looked closely at Widukind, and saw that now he was keyed very tight, waiting, intensely interested in whatever Bjarki would say next.

'It was very short. Midsummer's Eve. That was all the message he gave me.'

'Oh, that is good, very good. Midsummer's Eve, he used those words?'

'He did. What does it mean?'

'Oh, nothing. It's not important. I simply wondered when the Sorbs had their most important annual festival.'

It was obvious, even to Bjarki, that Widukind was lying through his teeth.

Then the duke said: 'Tell me, Bjarki, of all the Saxons you spoke to, did any of them seem to be content under Frankish rule? Did you find even one?'

Bjarki thought for a moment. 'No,' he said, 'I did not meet even one.'

'They are ripe for rebellion,' said Widukind. 'Saxony is ready to boil over like a cook-pot left too long on the fire. You know it, Bjarki, deep in your heart. And I know it, too. When I raise my battle standard – and I will raise it soon – they will flock to me. My own Westphalians will rally to me as their rightful Saxon lord. Jarl Hessi and the

Eastphalians will also come to me; Jarl Brun of Angria will send his horse people galloping to join my banner. And young Jarl Guthrum of Nordalbia – well, he has already promised me a thousand of his prime spearmen. But I need you as well, Bjarki Bloodhand, I need you staunch by my side, I need your ferocity, your war experience. I need your fame and battle-renown. You can inspire Saxons to fight and die to finally free their lands from their oppressors. They say you have four hundred *vikingir* in Ymirsfjord – and I need them too, whatever they have done in the past. Bring them all and come and fight with me. We can win this time, brother. I know it. We can have our victory. Join me, Bjarki, and win such renown that it will echo down the ages. Your name will be spoken of with awe – until the breaking of the world!'

'It might well be true that the Saxons will all rise up and join you but I've made up my mind, brother,' said Bjarki. 'I wish you all the good fortune there is. And I pray that Odin grants you a glorious victory; that Thor destroys the enemy host with a dozen of his thunderbolts. I hope that you win the freedom for all Saxon peoples... But I am going home to Ymirsfjord, and if you will be kind enough to give me some peace, I need to start packing my possessions.'

Edith came at him next. A much softer and more subtle appeal.

'Bjarki, I love you – you are my husband,' she said, 'and I will go where you go, and live where you live, and if you say that we must spend the rest of our days together in Ymirsfjord, I'll go with you and raise our children there.'

'You don't like Ymirsfjord?' Bjarki was genuinely surprised.

'I don't dislike it. But it is a place of exile. A place of hiding. We fled there to escape the wrath of Siegfried and my brother. But there is so much more of the world for our children to see, so much beyond that one small village in a fjord filled with uncouth, drunken *vikingir*. I, too, would like to see more of the Middle-Realm, experience more of its joys, understand a little more of its many mysteries. But whatever you decide, my husband, I will assent to.'

Edith drew breath, then. 'Only, I beg you, Bjarki, think of the children – of Lili and little Hildar – think of them, and be sure of your choice. I will say only one thing more: if the Franks can be driven from Saxony, as my brother claims, it will benefit all of us in the North. If we can keep the Christians from our lands, we can raise Lili and Hildar as honest northern folk – as proud Danes or even as Ymirsfjord people. Not as the creatures of Karolus and his Christ God.'

The conversation with Tor was short, and to the point. 'There is a big fight brewing in Saxony, a fight against our enemies. It is going to happen and we have a chance to play a part, a large part, in its success or failure. Are you really going to turn your back on that and run off to Ymirsfjord and do… what? Drink and tell stories and sleep all day? Or will you give Karolus the massive kick in the balls he so badly deserves? I will fight beside you, of course, and so will all our people, here and back in Ymirsfjord, you know that. So you only have to consider one thing, brother: do you want to live for ever? One day you *will* die, and when you do, you will want to go to the Hall of the Slain. So ask yourself this: was there ever a warrior invited to feast eternally with Odin who shirked a good, bloody fight?'

An hour later, Valtyr came shuffling into the hall. The old man looked around and noticed Father Alwin in one corner with Edith, Lili and Erik, all gathered round his teaching slate, and he gave a sniff of disapproval, then he looked at the far end of the hall where Bjarki was standing quite still, staring at a small round object that he was holding in his hands.

Valtyr limped towards Bjarki, leaning heavily on his tall staff, his grossly swollen belly shooting white-hot streaks of pain up into his chest and all the way down his right leg, but he was intrigued, and diverted from his agonies, to see that Bjarki had no awareness of anything around him. He was immersed in his own world. He stood there like a marble statue and stared down at the thing cupped in his hands.

As Valtyr drew closer, he looked at the object, a ball-like leather thing, like a purse, but with tufts of what looked like hair, protruding from the open top.

'What do you have there, son?' asked Valtyr.

Bjarki slowly turned and looked at him. For a moment he seemed not to recognise his old friend. His bright blue eyes were a dull, greyish colour and seemed to be covered with a milky film, like a blind man. But he was surely able to see. Bjarki stared at Valtyr for a long, long while. Then he said: 'It fell. It fell from the thatch. Up there.' And he jerked his head up at the sloping roof above his large wooden bedframe, now stripped of its mattress, to expose the bare rope lattice-work.

Valtyr moved with astonishing swiftness. He swung the staff in his hand, and with commendable accuracy struck the leather pouch from Bjarki's hands.

It thudded dully to the floor.

'Aah!' said Bjarki, shaking his hands and stung fingers. He glared at Valtyr, and for one instant, the old man felt a shiver of pure terror. Bjarki stared at him, his eyes, now clear of their dull sheen, and seeming to glow with some black inner fire. His lips curled back in an animalistic snarl to expose his yellow teeth. And Valtyr was, for that brief moment, convinced that Bjarki was about to launch himself at his old mentor and rip his pain-ridden body apart with his bare hands.

'It is a *seithr* curse-charm,' said Valtyr, trying to sound calm but taking a firmer grip on his staff. 'Do not touch it. They are very powerful, and can even be deadly.'

To Valtyr's intense relief, Bjarki relaxed his rictus mouth, tried to smile in a mechanical sort of way, and the fires of rage slowly faded from his blue eyes.

Edith was with them now. 'What is going on here?' she asked.

'This thing fell out of the thatch above our bed, my love,' said Bjarki. 'Some magical doo-dah. Someone was playing a silly joke on me. Maybe a prank.'

'I have heard of these things,' said Edith. 'They are said to be dangerous.'

'This is no prank,' said Valtyr. He was crouched down beside the object, staring at it. He poked at it with the end of his staff, as if it were a dead rat and he wanted to see if it still lived. 'We must be rid of it, and as soon as possible.'

'I can do that,' said Father Alwin, and he reached down and picked up the leather ball. 'I'll toss it in the midden at the back of the hall, shall I?' he said.

'No,' shouted Valtyr. 'Do not touch it. The magic is very strong.'

'I am not afraid of sorcery,' said Father Alwin, and he turned and began to walk towards the door. 'Almighty God wards me from all the Devil's work.'

'Not the midden, then,' said Valtyr quickly. He was torn between admiration at the Angelcynn priest's courage and his fear of the lethal power of the *seithr* curse-charm. 'It needs to burn. That fell thing needs to be consumed by cleansing flames.'

'Easily done,' said Alwin, changing direction and walking over to the long, central hearth. He threw the little leather ball into the heart of the hall fire, and then took a step back in astonishment, as the object flared green and blue as it burned away.

'Who would bring such an evil thing into our house?' asked Edith.

'It was probably just someone playing a trick on us,' said Bjarki, and he looked over at Valtyr with bright eyes that pleaded for him to follow his lie.

Valtyr said nothing, and Edith said: 'I will do a cere-mony of purification this evening. I have a powerful ritual I learnt from a cunning man in Uppsala. It should cleanse the curse from the house, chase any evil clear out of here.'

'Whatever you think best, my dear,' said Bjarki. But, when she had gone back to the chalk and slate with Father Alwin and the children, he gripped Valtyr's skinny elbow. 'Someone wishes me ill,' he said. 'Or wishes harm to come to me and Edith.'

'Yes. They hoped to kill you with this *seithr*. I've seen this happen before. Unexplained deaths – men and women who never wake up from their sleep.'

Bjarki looked at the old man, then looked down the length of the hall towards his family. Lili was holding year-old infant Hildar on her lap and feeding him with a horn filled with goats' milk, saying, 'Good boy, hungry boy,' while Edith looked at them lovingly. Even Father Alwin stopped his scratching on the slate for a moment to smile at the children and enjoy the sweetness of the scene.

'I don't want to die like that,' said Bjarki. 'Not now. They need me. My family needs me. Who could it be, Valtyr? Who hates me and wishes me dead?'

Valtyr shrugged. 'You do not lack for enemies. A relative of someone you killed in battle? Someone who resented your *vikingr* raids? It could be anyone.'

'But it has to be someone in Ribe,' said Bjarki, 'to have put it there, above the bed. Someone who is in and out of this hall.'

'That does not make it any more obvious. There must have been two hundred people in here since you came to Ribe. Could be any one of them.'

'Edith and I will be much safer when we're back in Ymirsfjord,' said Bjarki.

'I want to talk to you about that,' said Valtyr.

'Not you, too,' said Bjarki. 'Why does *everyone* want me to fight in Saxony?'

Valtyr said nothing for a while. Then: 'When I met you in Bago, all those years ago, I thought I saw something in you, Bjarki.'

'You thought I had the potential to be a Rekkr. To become a Fire Born.'

'Aye, but do you know *why* I wanted you to become Fire Born?'

'To defend the North. To fight and die as one of your warriors. Are you saying I owe you? That somehow, you made me, and I am beholden to you?'

'There was no need for me to stop in Bago. True, I had promised your father I would look in on you, and help you if I could. But I could have come back the next year, or the one after. What would have happened to you, if that had been the case?'

'I'd be dead. They would have hanged me. You *are* saying I owe you.'

'No, *you* are saying that. You were to be sacrificed at that old oak tree dedicated to Odin. You would have been hung up on that tree to die like the All-Father himself. But something guided my footsteps to Bago, on that exact day, on the day you were destined to die. Something told me to purchase your life from the angry *hersir* who wanted you dead. I say some*thing*. I mean some*one*. The One whose oak tree it was.'

'I have fought and killed and bled for you, old man,' said Bjarki. 'Many times. Almost all my life, I have been bound in service to you and to your ideas about the North and my duty to save it from its enemies. Now I am saying no. At last, I am saying no. I do not want to slaughter red-cloaked Franks because you and Widukind require my *berserkr* strength to achieve *your* purposes. I am not a tool, to be used like a hammer or a chisel to make something. No, I say no. I will go back to Ymirsfjord. And nothing you say, old man, no debt you claim, no cunning persuasions you employ will make me change my mind.'

'You are not a tool, Bjarki. You are a free man who can make his own choices based on the thoughts in his own head, and the opinions he forms as to what is the best course of action, what is the best thing to do with his brief span of life here in the Middle-Realm. You have been given a gift by Odin – your *gandir*, your strength, comes from the god. But all strength is borrowed, Bjarki. And one day it must be repaid. Only you can choose how to use your strength, while you have it. Saxony will rebel.

That vain fool Widukind will lead those good, trusting men and women into battle against the Franks – against the Christians. Maybe he will win, maybe he'll lose. But you could help him win. And if you do *not* help, and Widukind loses, and all those good Saxons lie broken on the battlefield. Will that be an end to it? I do not think so.

'The Christians will not be content with Saxony. They want the whole world to bow down to their ridiculous nailed god, they want every man and woman, boy and girl to worship at their altars, to pay their tithes, revere their priests and humbly admit to their own sinfulness. When Saxony is subdued, the Dane-Mark is next. Bishop Livinus has already sunk his claws in this Danish kingdom. The priests of Jesus Christ will rule here, in Ribe, in Viby and Hedeby, eventually. Karolus may even be King of the Danes in a few years' time – you said as much yourself to Siegfried. The Dane-Work will not keep him out for ever. And after the Danes, the Svear will fall to his Red Cloaks. And after that, the North-Way. Rogaland. Ymirsfjord.

'How long before Ymirsfjord has its own priest, and your little temple to Odin is a chapel? And your children, who learn their Latin from a Christian priest here in Ribe, become priests themselves? Even you must see it. What was the phrase you said Karolus used? His foretelling… the inevitable triumph of Christ on Earth.'

'I cannot see into the future,' said Bjarki. 'Neither can you, Far-Traveller.'

'No, but you *can* see the threat to our way of life. And your response to the threat is to run away and hide in Ymirsfjord and hope it does not come to pass.'

Bjarki simply stared at Valtyr. He could find nothing to say to the old man.

'Five years ago, in Vastergotland, by the river outside Lodose, when you were the king, and still believed in honour, you asked something from me. Do you remember? You asked for a favour. You asked me to go to Uppsala and extract your sister Tor from the grip of Sigurd Hring. You begged me to do it.'

Bjarki could feel a coldness rising within him, lapping in his empty belly.

'And I said that I would do it, old and sick as I was. But only if you would make me a promise. You swore to do my bidding – only one time but without question – when I called upon you to do a task for me. And you duly swore that solemn oath to me, did you not?'

Bjarki's throat felt choked and somehow swollen. 'I did,' he said thickly.

'Therefore, I now remind you of your oath and ask you to do my bidding,' said Valtyr. 'And you will do this for me, if you have any sense of honour left in you at all. I ask you now, Bjarki Bloodhand, to go to Saxony with the spears of Duke Widukind and join in his rebellion with all your heart and mind, all your will and strength. Slaughter the Franks. Save the Saxon homeland. Stop the Christians there before they despoil all that you hold dear! Will you do this for me, Bjarki? Will you?'

# Chapter Seventeen

### 'Only he will suffer its malice'

'What in the name of Thor's veiny hammer is an *amanuensis*?' asked Tor. She was standing in the parlour of the grand house that stood next to the royal hall in Ribe and addressing three men – Widukind of Westphalia, Abbio the Crow, his counsellor, and Father Alwin, who had just been described as an *amanuensis* by the Duke of Saxony.

'It means I will be writing many letters in Latin from the duke to his correspondents,' said Father Alwin, 'and helping him generally in some other administrative matters.'

'This should not have to be pointed out,' said Tor, 'but he is a *Christian priest*. He is a spiritual leader in the religion of our foes. I ask you, Widukind, are you mad?'

'Be calm, Tor,' said Widukind. 'Father Alwin is not our enemy. He is not a Frank – he is an Anglecynn, of good Saxon blood. We are not seeking to make war on the worship of Christ or any deity. That is what separates us from the Franks – after the Capitularies, they have declared war on the worship of all gods but their own.'

'I like you, Father Alwin,' said Tor, nodding at the priest, 'I do, and I trust you to teach Latin letters to Bjarki's children. But why do *you* need him, Widukind? Why are you taking him along when we go to...' Tor stopped.

'There isss no need to be coy,' said Abbio. 'The priesssst knowss that we plan to go to Sssaxony. And he hasss agreed to help usss, for a ssshort time.'

'I believe that Karolus is quite wrong to compel people to come to Jesus Christ at the point of a sword,' said Father Alwin, 'or, like Livinus, with the promise of a gift of money. Folk seduced in that way will never become true Christians. And I don't believe that Our Saviour would ever approve of these crude, brutish methods.'

'But why do you need him, Widukind?' said Tor.

'If you must know, I am writing in secret to many counts, dukes and princes, and not all of them are speakers of the Saxon tongue. I am communicating with Sorbs and Swabians, Bavarians and Lombards, Avars and Moravians, and inviting them to join me in rebellion. To rise against their cruel overlords at the same time that we do.

'I have spoken to many of these lords already, very discreetly. Over many months and years of travelling. We will send out our messengers and, when the time is ripe, they will give these letters to our potential allies, stating the date for the revolt. Imagine this, Tor – an insurrection in Lombardy to reject their Frankish king and, at the same time, we raise the rebel battle standard in Saxony. Think of riots in Thuringia, a *scara* of Red Cloaks ambushed in Frisia, a bishop's fortress attacked in Bavaria...'

'So Karolus will not know in which direction to march,' said Tor slowly, 'nor where to dispatch his swift-riding *cabellarii* – with confusion, war and riot breaking out in so many parts of his empire, he won't know which way to turn.'

She was impressed with the plan, in spite of herself. She knew Widukind had been plotting his moves for years, but this was *clever*. And it might – and she could barely allow herself to think this – it might even prove successful.

'Do not fear, Tor, for the education of Bjarki's wife and children,' said Father Alwin, 'I shall leave some writings for them to study – not Christian teachings but a work by the Roman poet Virgil on agriculture. Edith knows enough to be able to read it. I can continue to instruct young Erik while we are on the journey south to Verden. After Verden, I cannot say, for I feel it may be a suitable time for me to complete my pilgrimage to the village of Brema, which is only a few miles from Verden. I dearly wish to see the lands of my Saxon forefathers before returning at last to my home in Angleland.'

'All will be well, Tor,' said Widukind. 'Trust me. Father Alwin is a son of Saxony by blood, even if he mistakenly worships the wrong god! Ha-ha-ha!'

Tor watched as Father Alwin's face make a strange, twisted grimace of disagreement. But the Angelcynn priest said nothing to contradict his new lord.

'Isss all ready for departure?' said Abbio. 'I heard there wasss sssome difficulty with sssorccery in Bjarki's hall some days ago. He isss well, I trust?'

'We found something in the thatch, an evil talisman of some kind. Maybe nothing. We destroyed it. All is well. Bjarki is well again. Since that foul object was burned to ash, he has shown a remarkable transformation. And our own ships from Ymirsfjord will arrive in Ribe in just a day or so, with the rest of our spearmen and all our war gear – and then Bjarki and I, and all our people, will be ready to depart.'

*All our people*, thought Tor, and her mind went back to the short meeting with Siegfried the day after Bjarki agreed to keep his oath to Valtyr and fight in Saxony.

'You have changed your mind?' said Siegfried. 'You will join Widukind?'

'It was changed for me,' said Bjarki, glancing sideways at Tor and Valtyr. 'But yes, I will fight – with your blessing, O King – with Widukind against the Franks.'

'You have my blessing. But I desire one more thing from you, Rekkr, before you leave. I ask it as a boon, although you may believe I no longer have the right to ask, now that I have decided that Halfdan shall be my heir...'

The old king stopped. He seemed very uncertain, perhaps fearing a refusal.

'What is it that you want to ask me? What is this boon?'

'Halfdan is my blood – and he must be my heir. But I have not yet told him this. Nor have I told anyone of my decision, save for you this day. Halfdan is no kind of warrior – if it were known that he is to be my heir, then there would be those who would object and would try to deny him his birthright. My full-grown son has never seen the spear-tips dyed red with the blood of men. He has never heard the screams of the wounded echo through the cold night. He has never stood in the *skjald-borg* and felt the thunder of the hooves of the enemy cavalry rising up through his boots to shiver his bones. So I ask you this boon, Bjarki Bloodhand, not on my behalf, but in the name of the Dane-Mark, in the name of this land of your birth. Help me to make Halfdan into a fitting ruler for this Kingdom of Sword-Danes.'

'What are you asking me, O King?'

'Take my son to war. I know he has seen twenty-five winters but I want you to teach him, to guide him, to allow him to carry your shield on the march, permit him to stand beside you in the storm of battle, and learn to face the foe without fear.'

Bjarki said nothing for a while, he stood there staring at the king. For a moment Tor feared that he had gone again into that dark place where he listened only to the talking of the *gandir* and heard nothing else. At last Bjarki spoke.

'I will do this for you, my king, and for the Dane-Mark, too,' he said. 'And I swear that I will not harm Halfdan myself, nor will I allow any others to harm him. I will also do my utmost to shield him from injury in the maelstrom of war. But, if your son *were* to fall, if he were to succumb to the swords and spears of the Franks – for the danger will surely be great – if Halfdan were to fall, and I were to live, then I require your oath that I shall be named heir in his place.'

'I give you my oath,' said Siegfried. 'You will be my heir if Halfdan falls.'

—

The ale-house was of the meanest sort, a draughty shack on the edge of Ribe, mouldy smelling, with a spongy floor, and a loose plank in the east wall that clapped with the wind – a place that dispensed a sour brew, stale bread and very little good cheer.

Abbio the Crow sat at a table at the back of the room, nursing a cup of ale. The other patrons in that miserable place took one look at his shaggy cloak, his tattoos and rat-tail hair, his grey teeth sharpened into points, and stayed well clear of him.

A fat merchant sat at the other end of the room, his round face bent over a bowl of greasy bean soup. He made loud, sucking noises as he ate, and rarely looked up. A raggedy drunk snored by the far wall, his head tilted far back, mouth wide. Two lean murderers, men from the wild heathlands to the north of Ribe, whispered darkly in the far corner, one of them surreptitiously fingering the hilt of his long knife.

The door slapped open, and a dark, shapeless figure came inside the room, clothed in a baggy woollen robe, his whole face shielded by a deep, dark hood, giving only the impression of gleaming eyes inside its dim recesses. One of the murderers turned around and sneered at the newcomer by the door, before turning back to his accomplice. The soup-eater looked up quickly, and went back to his beans.

The hooded man walked quickly over to the table where Abbio was sitting. There was no sign of the tavern owner, but the hooded man was neither hungry nor thirsty. Merely resentful at being summoned to the sorcerer's presence.

'I did exactly as you asked me,' he said. 'I put the object in the thatch above his bed. And he slept under it many a night. Your *seithr* does not work.'

'Do you criticissssse me? You wissssh me to prove my powersss… on you?'

'No,' said the hooded man. 'No, I believe in your arts. But Bjarki lives!'

'Do not ever sssay hisss name. Even in thisss place.'

The owner of the tavern came stumbling out from behind his counter, rubbing the sleep-sand from his eyes. He tore a dusty jug from its peg and bent to fill it from the ale barrel. The two men said nothing as he came over and put the slopping jug and an extra cup on the rickety pine table. Without a word, he staggered back to his counter, and into the dusty room beyond without pausing.

The hooded man poured himself a cup of ale, took a sip and grimaced. He spat the ale back into the cup and set it on the table, sliding the vessel away.

'We mussst continue,' said Abbio. 'The task is only half-completed. He wasss made very sssick by the *ssseithr*; it weakened his bonds with his *gandir*. He began to ssshow the firssst signsss of madness. Now the curse-charm isss gone: he recoversss.'

'How then can we continue?' said the hooded man.

Abbio smiled, exposing his dingy sharpened teeth. 'Thisss isss for you.'

The sorcerer passed a small wooden object across the wet table, pushing it towards the hooded man's hand. It was a tiny, crude figurine of a man, but the body had been painted with stripes of brown and yellow. Two small iron nails had been hammered into the figure's chest and the top of the head, where a scrap of yellow silk cloth fell from the crown like the drape of long blond hair.

The hooded man quickly retracted his hand from touching the tiny doll.

'What is it?' he asked warily.

'The sssame but more powerful,' said Abbio. 'Take it. It cannot hurt you. I've whissspered hisss name into the flamesss. Only he will sssuffer its malice.'

'And what must I do?'

'Hide it. Near him, touching him, if you can. Hide it in hisss clothing or hisss gear. Put it close to him for just a few dayss and watch him sssicken and die.'

The hooded man opened a leather pouch in his belt, leaned towards the table, and using only the edge of his hand he swept the talisman into the pouch and buckled it shut. 'If it does not work, Abbio...' the hooded man began.

'If it doesss not work, you will not receive your heart'sss desire. Place it well.'

–

One week later, they rowed out of Ribehaven in five ships – four of them containing the men and women of Ymirsfjord. Tor was in the leading ship, *Fafnir*, but for once, she was not at the prow-beast end but at the helm in the stern, with the long tiller clamped under her left armpit. She looked back at the other vessels following in her wake. Widukind was in the one just behind her lead dragon ship, and she thought she could make out his fair head and the wink of the golden coronet that he seemed to wear most days now, as he bent low to speak to one of the straining men at the oars.

She had always known Widukind possessed no true power of his own. His gift was simply his ability to persuade others – convince other men to supply the spears, cajole them into fighting and dying for his causes. He had just done so with Bjarki, persuading Edith and then Valtyr to work on Bjarki – Tor too, now that she thought about it, had been influenced by him. Had she done the right thing? Surely she had. The Franks were the enemy and their relentless advance north must be resisted. For a brief moment, she considered that she might be wrong and Bjarki right. That this war in Saxony was not their business. That it would be better to stay out of this fight to save a foreign land.

No. She and Bjarki had strength in their bones and courage in their hearts, and so it followed they must fight on behalf of those who had neither. This was the warrior code that she – they – had always lived by. The strong defend the weak.

As she looked back at the following ships, the clear disparity of military strength between Widukind and Bjarki had never been starker than on that brisk summer morning, with the gulls shrieking overhead, and bracing packets of spray drenching her face, when the choppy swell slapped against the larboard side. Bjarki had four hundred fighting men packed into those four ships, including *Fafnir*. Widukind, on the other hand, had a bare sixty manning the oars of his only vessel, the *Lady Edith*.

Widukind was not a coward: he would stand firm and fight bravely when required to do so. And it was not that he would rather talk about the fight than roll in the bloody dust with his foes. But there was still something unmanly about him. Words were all very well, and it was true that they had their own power. But if an army of *cabellarii* were thundering down upon her, Tor knew that she would far rather have Bjarki standing at her side than Widukind.

She had lost her concentration, and realised the ship was now angling too close to the muddy shore of Jutland. She cursed herself for daydreaming like a child and made a small adjustment to the angle of the tiller. It would be time to raise the sail, soon – the wind was freshening in the west – and then Kynwulf could take over in the stern and she would return to her customary position by the dragon's head.

In a day or two they would be in Treva, on the Elbe, at the riparian hall of Jarl Guthrum, and they would begin their journey south into Saxony on foot.

Widukind had decreed that the force under his command – which was so overwhelmingly made up of Bjarki's warriors – must proceed into Saxony on foot in small groups of no more than fifty, in other words, bands no bigger than a single *lith*. This made sense. They would go into Saxony in small companies, which were less likely to be spotted by the Frankish patrols, who might raise the alarm. These groups would then make their way independently and discreetly to a rallying point, somewhere deep in south Saxony, in the endless First Forest.

At this location, Widukind would raise his battle standard and declare his intention to overthrow the rule of the Franks in Saxony. What Tor found to be strange was that this small seaborne army still had no idea where they were heading for. Widukind had refused, absolutely refused, to tell anyone their destination. Even when he practised his speeches, and Tor had heard him do this several times, he used vague phrases such as 'the meeting place' when talking about the rendezvous in Saxony.

Tor knew that Abbio was behind this. He seemed to be obsessed with secrecy, with spies and treachery, these days. Tor reckoned that only three men in their whole fleet knew the location of the rallying point, and those three men were Widukind himself, Abbio, of course, and Father Alwin – whom she assumed had written all those letters to potential allies inviting them to join in.

Even Bjarki had no idea where they were going. She certainly did not.

'Kynwulf,' she yelled forwards. 'Make ready, War Chief, to hoist the sail!'

As she watched the old warrior begin making his way down the crowded centre of the war ship, squeezing between rows of burly rowing shoulders, she spared one last thought for Widukind. She realised that she had been pondering the Saxon Wolf, his few strengths and many weaknesses, for more than an hour now, and not once had she thought about bedding him.

Perhaps, at last, she was indeed cured of her sickness.

# Chapter Eighteen

*Boots, boss-hollows and the joy of battle*

It seemed strange to Bjarki that a wealthy man, the lord of four hundred warriors, with not one but *two* shield-bearers, should have to cut his own leather boot-strappings from a sheet of cured cow hide and attach them to his footwear by the flickering light of only one cheap, smelly, tallow candle.

However, he supposed it was not the shield-bearers fault. Erik rarely wore any shoes at all, and when he did, they were shapeless, clumpy, leather foot-bags, crude items that weighed almost as much – when covered with claggy Nordalbian mud – as Bjarki's saddle. The boy knew nothing of the upkeep required for a pair of riding boots. But neither had Bjarki at his age. No one had them on Bago; for no one rode.

Halfdan, on the other hand, a king's son, should at least know how to wear riding boots. But it seemed there had been no use for them on his cabbage farm.

'Halfdan, go and ask Guthrum's steward for a big jug of ale, and another candle. Two more candles, if you can get them. I need light for this fine work.'

The heir to the throne of the Dane-Mark – although, of course, he did not yet know about that momentous decision – strode willingly away into the darkness of the crowded hall in search of the senior servant who was in charge of the running of it.

'Erik, come here and watch me do this. You should know how to replace boot-strappings by now. Watch!'

Using his own seax, which was razor sharp – putting a keen edge on a blade was something that Erik *had* clearly mastered – Bjarki cut several strips half an inch wide and a yard long off the hide, trying for an even width all the way down the strip. By the time he had two he was satisfied with, Halfdan was back with the candles and ale.

Bjarki patiently showed the two young men how to thread the strap in the loop at the back of the wide top of each riding boot so they fell an equal length to the floor, then how to bring them round and back several times and gradually down towards the ankle so they formed a nice, even, criss-cross pattern of straps over his shins and calves. When the straps' ends were pulled tight and tied at the back they gripped each leg like a garter and prevented the boot from sliding down to puddle around his feet.

'Now bring my shield, and I'll show you both how to pad a boss-hollow.'

This next lesson – watched closely by Erik and Halfdan, all three siting on the hall floor and enjoyably sipping ale – involved padding the iron bowl that formed the centre of Bjarki's wooden shield with scraps of woollen cloth. The shield itself was made of lime-wood boards, covered in a sheet of leather which was painted with Bjarki's device – a brown bear on a yellow background. The round iron boss was fitted in the centre of the wooden boards and had a slim, vertical iron bar across the open side, which the shield-wielder gripped in battle, as well as a stout leather strap for his forearm, nailed to the boards on the inside of the wood. The wielder's bare knuckles inside the boss were in danger of being knocked or rubbed against the iron of the boss-bowl – hence the cloth padding to protect the fingers. It was a matter of taste for each warrior, but Bjarki preferred a large amount of padding, solidly wedged in the curved space inside the boss, because his hands were usually covered with cuts and bruises after even a short training session with an unpadded boss.

'Pack it in good and tight, Halfdan,' he urged his shield-bearer, 'and remember, sometimes it is useful to carry extra padding into battle in case…'

A shadow fell over his face and he looked up to see Tor standing over him.

'Having fun?' she asked.

'Educating these lads in the important things of life,' said Bjarki. 'Sound boot-strappings and padded shield bosses – not messing about with Latin poets.'

'Speaking of which – Erik, time for your lesson with Father Alwin. Go.'

The boy reluctantly left them. Halfdan said: 'You want me to go, too?'

'No, you need to hear this. Widukind is making a speech tonight, after supper. I think he means to tell us at last where the rallying point in Saxony is.'

'I hope so. We are marching off in our little groups tomorrow. It would be useful to know where we are going – and what we are expected to do when we get there.'

–

Bjarki rested his scarred forearms comfortably on the table in front of him, and smiled at the world. He had found something in his pack just as he was washing himself before the meal and this object sat on the oak boards in front of him.

It was a plain earthenware pot, about the size and shape of an apple, of the kind used to store preserved fruit or, as in this case, honey. The top was sealed with wax, melted and poured over the string that kept the wooden plug in place.

Bjarki did not plan to open the pot, at least not just yet. His belly was still full of the roast pork, apple sauce and mashed turnips and a full jug of excellent ale he had had for his supper. But he enjoyed looking at the little honey container and musing on what it represented. It was a parting gift from his wife Edith, slipped into his pack while he was preparing to leave Ribe and travel south to war. It was, in truth, a small, tangible piece of Edith's love. A symbol of the sweetness of their loving union.

The pot reminded him of Ymirsfjord, of his wife and children, and the reason why he was here, embarking on a war and plunging into danger. The honey pot was a little piece of home in this strange land, in this stranger's hall.

The parting from Edith and the children in Ribe had been sad but sweet, Lili had cried and asked why he had to leave them, and why he could not stay and play with her, and so he had taken her into his arms and held her, hugged her and smelled her hair. He promised her he would bring her back a present from Saxony. Something pretty. Hildar had no notion of what was happening, and when Bjarki knelt, tousled his hair and said goodbye and urged him to be a good boy for his mother, he had smiled happily at his father. And Edith – Edith was a shaking bundle of nervousness, tear-stained, trying to be brave, and she hugged him to her fiercely.

'What if you never come back to us?' she said, only just holding back her tears. 'What if my stupid urging you to go results in… It would be my fault.'

'I will count the days until I can come back to you, my love,' he said. 'And, if I were to fall in battle, you would surely have a good home here in Ribe for as long as you need it. Siegfried will protect you, I know that; and there is Ymirsfjord, too, if you want to get away from here – and more money than you could possibly spend.'

'I care nothing for all that. I want you. I want you alive, beside me, in my bed, at my table, I want you there till we are both fat, grey and grandparents.'

Bjarki could think of no way to reassure her. 'I'll be back, my love, back by autumn,' he said. 'When we have taught the Franks a lesson they will not forget.'

He picked up the honey pot and stowed it in his pouch and, as he tucked it safely away, he made an effort to examine the other emotions that were in his heart that evening. Was he frightened of what was to come? No. When he was younger, he might have felt anxious about going into battle, even fearful; he might have felt a growing sense of discomfort about this long, unstoppable slide into the bloody chaos of war, but this night, perhaps because of the gift of the honey pot, he felt at peace.

He had faced death so many times that his fear of it was like an old friend, something sitting in the corner of his heart, waiting and murmuring quietly, 'I am your Fear. Here I am, no need to pay any attention, just know I'm with you.'

He had fought this enemy, these brutal, warlike Christian Franks – with their arrogant, inflexible ways, their domineering desire to control all men and punish any who dared to oppose them – almost all of his adult life. And he had almost always been ultimately bested by them. Yet here he was again, facing the same formidable foe but with an instinct that this time, *this time*, they might just win the fight against these invaders who believed they had the right to rule all the northern lands. The brutal Capitularies were the spark that would this time rouse the whole Saxon nation. What decent Saxon man could accept them? The people must now surely all rise up and join Widukind in his rebellion.

He was surprised to discover that, in his heart, he actually believed the Saxons could triumph, and Widukind had not even started spouting out his shimmering, intoxicating words.

Bjarki smiled at his own silent joke.

The Saxon Wolf was at the high table with Jarl Guthrum and his mother and sister. Valtyr sat up there, too, his old face strained with pain and flushed with drink. Guthrum had pointedly not invited Bjarki to join them, he was evidently still smarting from the Rekkr's rudeness on the last visit, but Bjarki did not care: he was content to sit at the common benches with his comrades, with Kynwulf and Tor, with Oddvin, Rask, Joralf and Sambor. Captain Mogils and some of the other *Felaki* were at other tables nearby and, despite the fact that Guthrum had packed the hall with his own grim Nordalbian warriors, everywhere Bjarki looked he saw a friendly face. He was content to sit with a full belly and watch the high and mighty from the lowly benches; to sit there quietly, absorbed by his thoughts.

Now there was movement. Widukind at the high table was getting to his feet, and Bjarki prepared for a long oration, filled with stirring, glittering exhortations to victory and appeals to his warrior's sense of duty and pride.

The Duke of Saxony held up both his empty hands, palm out. There was a murmur of excitement rippling through the hall but, gradually, silence fell.

'My friends,' Widukind said, 'we stand here this night perched on the lip of Saxony, ready to plunge ourselves into the cauldron of battle, into the chaos of red war. Behind us lies the free North, before us is a freedom-loving land in Frankish chains. We must not shrink from this fight; indeed, we shall not shy away from it. Saxony will be freed. By you, and by me. Tomorrow you will all go south in your groups, you know already who your *lith* captains are; you already know what your task is to be – to bring down ruin and destruction upon the enemy. But you do not yet know your destination. Travel light, travel fast and make your ways to the Süntel Hills. The rallying point is the Hohenstein, the High Stone on the plateau. We meet there on Midsummer's Eve. Ten days' time. This is where we shall congregate, this is where we will be met by our friends and allies. My own people, the warriors of Westphalia, three thousand spears, will meet us at the Hohenstein. And once our full strength is mustered, we will launch our assaults on the enemy strongholds and conquer them, one by one. So tonight, as we stand on the cusp of war, I bid farewell to you, and ask the true gods to speed your feet. Till we meet happily again in the Süntel Hills!'

And then, to Bjarki's astonishment, he sat down.

A storm of applause erupted. Jarl Guthrum's men cheered and shouted the duke's name. Some were slapping the table or drumming their booted feet on the floor.

Others beat their hilts against their wooden platters. It was deafening.

–

Bjarki peered out from behind the trunk of the ancient oak and surveyed the huts and longhouses of the Saxon village a hundred yards away. Between him and the open gates set in the wooden palisade were a half dozen grubby tents, simple triangular-ended white-ish shelters made of waxed linen. Around and among the tents were a dozen or so soldiers, red-cloaked and at their ease, sitting by fires, sleeping on the grass, polishing their arms. They were Franks.

Bjarki turned to the man beside him, a small, leather-tough warrior called Rask, one of his *Felaki* bodyguards. 'How many?' he said quietly.

'They sleep six to a tent,' said Rask, 'so… thirty Red Cloaks. Forty? Two officers. I don't know if the villagers will take up arms with the Franks or not.'

'If they willingly fight for the foe, we are lost. The rebellion is doomed.'

'We could retreat,' said Rask, 'pull back into the forest and circle round. They would never know we passed by. Never know we were here at all.'

Bjarki and his small group – his fifty Ymirsfjord warriors, with Rask as his scout and Oddvin as his second – had set off three days ago, following the left bank of the river Elbe south-east until it came to the First Forest, a vast largely untouched expanse of virgin woodland in the heart of Saxony. Tor commanded another group of fifty warriors, as did Kynwulf, and Captain Mogils, and four other Ymirsfjord leaders. They had all chosen different routes from Treva to the Süntel Hills and left hours between their departures from Jarl Guthrum's hall.

Once Bjarki's *lith* had reached the forest, they followed its margins, roughly south-west, always staying close to the trees. Early on, Bjarki had sent Rask ranging out in front to scout for danger and his plan had been that, should they come across a force of Franks, say, a patrol, they would either flee into the depths of forest or fight. It depended on how strong the enemy force was. There was no point in them being slaughtered in some soon-forgotten skirmish before they got to the Süntel Hills.

Before Bjarki could reply to his scout, he noticed a commotion in the open gates of the village, a knot of Red Cloaks seemed to be manhandling three scruffy-looking Saxon villagers, dressed in filthy rags. Their faces were battered and bruised and it seemed their arms were tied behind their back. They were coming, through the lines of tents, towards the edge of the forest – right towards Bjarki's hiding place.

'Tell Oddvin to make sure everyone is well back from the treeline and out of sight,' Bjarki whispered to Rask, 'but tell him to be ready. And send my two shield-bearers to me. Quietly!' The little scout nodded and silently backed away from his lord, and disappeared into the gloom of the trees.

Bjarki stayed exactly where he was behind the oak, occasionally peeping out to watch what was happening with the Red Cloaks.

The three Saxon prisoners were kicked and shoved past the last linen tent to the open grassy space before the treeline, and there they were forced to kneel, their heads bowed. A priest pushed through the ranks of the Frankish warriors and stared down haughtily at the three bound, kneeling men. He began to recite a long list of their crimes, which Bjarki could clearly hear. Insolence to the Red Cloak captain, refusal to work on the construction of the new church, failure to pay their tithes in a timely manner, and the worst crime of all – they were accused of tending a small shrine to Nicor, a water spirit that inhabited a local stream. This was blatant Devil worship, said the priest, and there could only be one punishment for such wickedness.

Bjarki heard a rustling sound behind him and turned to see two nervous-looking faces: Halfdan and Erik. 'Are you ready?' he said.

Both shield-bearers nodded.

'Keep shields up. Keep your distance and use your spears,' Bjarki said.

The Red Cloak officer stepped forwards and drew his sword from its scabbard, a long, straight-bladed weapon. He raised it high and gripped the hilt in both hands. A pair of Red Cloaks came forwards to hold the first condemned Saxon securely.

'Have you anything to say before you meet your maker?' said the officer.

'Now,' said Bjarki, and stood up. He stepped from behind the oak and charged, a Dane axe in his right hand, his left fist in the well-padded boss-hollow of his shield.

He had no helmet, and only a knee-length mail shirt to protect his body. He felt no stirring from the two *gandir* at all; the creatures who had once dominated so much of his life were silent this day. Yet he was full of the ancient battle joy, nonetheless. He was doing what every self-respecting warrior must do. He was wielding his strength and courage in defence of those weaker than him.

He screamed as he charged, a meaningless howl of rage, and threw himself straight at the officer with the drawn sword. He did not know nor, in truth, did he care, if the rest of his *lith* were charging out of the trees behind him. His mind was fixed on the officer with the drawn sword. He hurdled a kneeling man, a prisoner, and crashed straight into the Red Cloak officer, barging into him with his shield, the iron boss crunching into the Frank's mailed chest, with Bjarki's full weight behind it.

His opponent, his sword already poised, struck down at him, a chopping blow, but Bjarki swept the sword away with an upwards surge of his shield, and shoved him over backwards. The officer fell, landing awkwardly on the turf, and Bjarki hacked down with the long-handled axe and buried it in his belly.

As he pulled the gory blade free, he looked around and saw that the *lith* were all around him. Halfdan was poking at a Red Cloak with his spear, timid, tiny jabs. The Red Cloak smashed the spear shaft out of its line and ran forwards, his sword slashing at Halfdan's head, but mercifully, the heir to the Dane-Mark had remembered Bjarki's words and upheld his shield. He blocked the wild sword blow and Bjarki ran a few yards towards him and swung the Dane axe, long-armed, at the Frank's back leg, the blade slicing across his calf and crippling him. The man screamed and fell to his knees on the ground, his left foot barely connected to his leg, and Halfdan came running in and delivered his first decent strike: he rammed the spear into the man's open mouth, the blade blooming like a flower out of the back of the fellow's neck.

Erik, too, was in the thick of the combat, despite his lack of years. A Red Cloak was hammering on his shield, and the boy was only just managing to absorb the blows, when Rask danced in from nowhere and shoved his blade in the attacker's groin. There were Franks coming from all sides, now, emerging from tents, running out for the open gates of the village, brandishing weapons, but the *lith* were swarming too, thundering out of the trees, eager to show their lord their prowess.

The two sides met among the tents, hacking and slashing at each other, cracking their steel against wooden shields, shouting in rage or pain. Oddvin stood in a space between the shelters directing his warriors to their enemies with a pointed sword and snapped order. A pair of Red Cloaks rushed at Bjarki. He took the blow from the nearer one plumb on his shield boss, and swept the legs out from under the second man with his axe a moment later. The second man was down, and shouting in pain. Bjarki absorbed a second sword cut from the first Frank on the iron rim of his shield, hacked at him with the axe, and was blocked by his opponent's shield.

The Rekkr hammered at the Frank again, and again, two hacking downward blows, but each time the Red Cloak blocked him. The man jabbed at him with his sword and he felt the steel slice across the iron links of his mail. Bjarki gave a roar of frustration and a mighty blow, and his axe chopped through the top rim of the Frank's shield, and carried on to smash into his collar bone. His arm went loose, the shield dropped, and Bjarki sliced laterally into his neck, dropping him to the turf. He looked down at his side and saw that his mail – the most expensive a rich man could buy – had kept out the Frankish steel. He examined the inside of his heart. There was nothing from the bears, no speech, no indication of their presence. They were fast asleep.

However, it soon became perfectly clear which side had the upper hand in the skirmish. The Ymirsfjord warriors, having greater numbers as well as the element of surprise, overwhelmed the Red Cloaks in less than the time it takes to hard-boil a hen's egg, and Bjarki soon found himself standing flat-footed, deflated, casting around for more foes to fight. Just then, a terrified young Frank popped out from behind a row of tents and ran straight at him, yelling something about God and forgiveness, and at the same time driving at him with his spear. Bjarki dodged, only just in time, and the instinctive counter blow from his axe caught the man across the small of his back as he ran past the Rekkr, severing his spine, felling him like a tree.

Then it was all over. All the Red Cloaks he could see were down, dead or wounded; someone had decapitated the priest – his tonsured head lay two yards from the rest of his body – and the villagers were now flooding out from their gates, men, women and children, flitting like ghosts between tents and stooping quickly to slit the throats of any fallen Frank who yet lived and rob his corpse.

An elderly man, hobbling slightly, dressed in a raggedy rabbit-skin vest, came up to Bjarki, and peered up at him, smiling, full of joyful curiosity.

'Are you Duke Widukind?' he said. 'Are you that mighty warrior, lord? We heard tell that the great Saxon Wolf was coming home to us at last.'

# Chapter Nineteen

*'My business is murdering Karolus'*

Tor stumped up the long, steep slope, on a track through the thick woodland, the midsummer sunlight dappling the path in a way that might have seemed quite beautiful to her in other circumstances. She might have appreciated her forest surroundings a little better if she had not recently lost three good men due to her own stupidity, combined with a misplaced sense of direction and certainty in her own skills in rough country.

Three Ymirsfjord men were dead – and it was all her fault. If she ever made it back to the little settlement at the end of the long fjord in Rogaland, she would have to face the pretty wife of one of them, and the formidable mother of another, and tell them how idiotic she had been and why the blood of their men was on her hands.

She had thought she knew the First Forest – not all of it, of course, but this part, south-east of the town of Minden on the right bank of the Weser. She had once lived wild near here for some weeks, as part of a dangerous spiritual test during which she had hoped to become a Rekkr. She had marched through this part, too, retreating from Karolus's armies seven years ago, before fighting a battle at Lubbecke, a dozen miles to the north-east. But she had been wrong. It turned out that she did not know it at all. The forest seemed to have changed, shifted itself, configured its many valleys and rivers, its cliffs, glades and meadows into different, indeed, entirely alien patterns.

Tor had led her *lith* down a steep defile, against the advice of Joralf, her second, a tall, lean, dark warrior, a very handsome fellow, who had a reputation in Ymirsfjord as a swordsman – in both senses of the word. Joralf had said he had heard the distant sound of horses' hooves, the distinctive strike of iron shoes on stone, but when Tor had stopped and listened, she had heard nothing at all. They were running late – the long journey on foot down from Treva had taken longer than she had anticipated. And Midsummer's Eve was the next day. The nearest road or track that a horseman could use was a good five miles away towards Vlotho; this part of the First Forest was uninhabited, she believed, a densely wooded hilly wasteland only traversable on foot, and even then with great difficulty. She had ordered the *lith* to move forwards down the narrow valley, against Joralf's advice, and at the bottom of the slope she had found not only a new road, levelled by Frankish engineers and finished with a surface of crushed rock, but a patrol of thirty Black Cloak *cabellarii* trotting along it.

There had been a brief fight, and three of her men, those nearest the enemy heavy horsemen, had been cut down before Tor had got the rest of the *lith* up the slope again and into the trees where the horsemen could not approach them. They had fled north. And wasted two days losing their pursuers, but thankfully with no further loss of life.

It was inexcusable. She had broken her own iron rules for advancing in enemy territory, lost three good men, and alerted the Franks to the presence of rebels in this region. Now she went forwards more slowly, with a great deal more caution: three scouts out front and two on each flank, and even one man trailing behind the column.

At least now they were nearly there, if a day late. She was almost certain that the day before had been Midsummer's Eve – it had taken long enough for the sun to sink behind the hills to the west, anyway. And now, as she slogged up the path through the trees to the Hohenstein, the heavy shield which was slung across her back tapping painfully against her spine, she wondered what Widukind would say about her tardiness, and thinking of his disapproval made her even more angry.

'Halt or I shoot,' said a young man. A figure in hunting leathers with a bow and an arrow nocked to the string stood before her on the track, just thirty paces ahead.

'State your name and business,' said the man, his tone commanding.

'Fuck off, sonny, I am not in the mood,' said Tor.

'State your name and business,' the young man repeated, now less certainly.

On either side of the rack there were rustling sounds and a dozen hidden archers emerged from the trees. Tor's own people, also armed with bows.

'Or what?' said Tor. 'What will you do if I refuse to tell you my name?'

'I'm sorry, Tor,' said the young man, 'they make us say that to everyone.'

Tor squinted up at the man through the slanting sunbeams. The face was familiar; for a moment, she couldn't quite place his name. Then she remembered: he was one of Widukind's Danes.

'You know my name, Nils – now you want to know my business, too? It is killing Franks; it is stirring up rebellion. It is murdering Karolus and his priests.'

'Pass, friend,' said Nils. He saluted and stepped off the path into the trees.

–

Tor was relieved to see that she was not the last of the Ymirsfjord *lith* to arrive at the Hohenstein. Captain Mogils's company was unaccounted for, although Bjarki said he had seen them on the banks of the Aller, and they had shared a camp for one night before continuing their separate ways in line with Widukind's orders.

'He's probably got lost in the First Forest,' said Tor. 'It is easy to get turned around in the trees. I don't think Mogils has ever been to Saxony before.'

'I hope he's careful,' said Bjarki. 'The Franks are patrolling the roads.'

'We met Black Cloak *cabellarii* on the way,' said Tor. 'Lost three men.'

Somehow she could not bring herself to admit to her big brother that it had all been her fault. She'd tell him some other time. She'd tell him if he asked her.

Bjarki made sympathetic noises. He passed her the ale sack. They were in their own camp, the Ymirsfjord folk, a few hundred yards east from Widukind's smaller group. The duke had made his camp inside a newly built fortress – his handful of household troops, many of them Danes who had been gifted to him by Siegfried, had been the first to arrive on this long, thin spur of high land in the Süntel Hills, and they had not been idle. The rest of his Westphalians – three thousand spears from the rich, flat

222

county on the left bank of the river Weser – had been delayed, the Saxon Wolf told her. They would be joining them soon and then the fun would start.

In the three days they had been here, Widukind's men had felled a good deal of local timber and constructed a simple, square, defensive redoubt, with four chest-high timber walls a hundred paces on each side and only one small entrance, a little way back from the Hohenstein rock formation. Above the narrow entrance to the fortress was a tall pole atop which fluttered a blood-red standard, depicting a large grey wolf standing on its back legs: the Saxon Wolf – Widukind's personal battle standard.

The fortress had no roof, but luckily the weather was fair, the skies beautifully clear and blue by day and speckled with a dizzying, dazzling array of stars at night. And while Widukind's fortress was little more than a huge wooden box, it could easily be defended from attacks by both Frankish cavalry and infantry. If she was honest with herself, Tor was impressed by Widukind's industry and his foresight.

The plateau on which the Hohenstein stood ran roughly east–west with a slight curve to the north in the middle. The Troll Stones were at the extreme western end. A lookout standing atop the stacked rocks of the Hohenstein could see for miles in all directions and particularly over the whole wide Weser Valley, which lay to the south-west, the nearest part of the green, winding river itself being some three miles away.

The approach of any enemy could be seen long before they could come to blows, and any attacker would also have to scale the steep sides of the plateau before they could assault the Saxons – that is, if they attacked from the north, east or south. The only feasible approach to come at the rebels on the Hohenstein spur was from the east – along a muddy track that ran through the dense trees of the First Forest.

It was, Tor conceded, almost the perfect spot for a forward attack base, from which Widukind's warriors could raid the surrounding Frankish lands with impunity.

That silver-tongued Saxon had chosen his rallying point extremely well.

And the Saxon people *were* rallying to it. Small companies of warriors trickled in every day, coming from all over Saxony – some, like the dozen recruits that Bjarki had picked up after his skirmish at the village at the edge of the First Forest, were untrained farmers who had heard rumours of the rebellion and sought to revenge themselves for the hurts they had suffered at the hands of the Christians. Others were true believers, folk who were committed to Widukind's vision of a return to the old ways, to a Saxony free of tyranny. Others were bad men, outlaws or men shunned by their own communities, who had sniffed an opportunity for plunder on the wind.

They came to the Hohenstein and Widukind welcomed them all. Soon he had more than two thousand warriors on that narrow little spur of land. Jarl Brun came in on the fifth day after Midsummer's Eve, with five hundred Angrian spearmen who had marched from Verden. The jarl claimed that he now had too few horses to mount his famous Angrian cavalry. But, even if he were lying, and Tor thought it most likely, five hundred more shields was a welcome addition to their growing army.

On the sixth day, Jarl Hessi arrived. And he came in with three hundred Eastphalian spears and, far more importantly, with fresh tidings from the east.

Widukind had begun sending out raiding parties in groups of a hundred or two hundred warriors, whose task it was to collect food and fodder for the army of the Hohenstein. There were now three thousand hungry mouths to feed on the plateau. They collected generous contributions of bread and meat from the local farmers – and Widukind thought it best not to enquire too much about their methods of extraction – and one bold group, captained by a young Saxon from Eastphalia called Detlef, even attacked the fortified villa of a Frankish nobleman outside Minden with great success.

Detlef removed three wagonloads of grain and other food supplies from the wealthy villa, murdered its owner and his whole Frankish family and burned the place to the ground – with the large church newly built beside the compound the very first building to be torched. Other Saxon raiders soon discovered that Christian churches were a fine source of loot and booty and, enticingly, that they were often completely undefended. And so Houses of God were soon burning from Minden to Orhum.

On the seventh day after Midsummer's Eve, Widukind summoned a council of war to his campaign tent inside the square wooden fortress he had built. He invited the leaders to join him so they might plan a campaign and allocate responsibilities.

When Tor and Bjarki came into the tent, it was already filled with the hum of excited people – for some twenty warriors from across Saxony and the North were gathered there. Widukind and Abbio had set up a table in the middle of the tent on which was the same collection of stones and twigs and ribbons, which depicted the features and landscape of Saxony and the locations of the major enemy garrisons. Tor noticed that, at the back of the table, the Loki Sword in its leather sheath was displayed on a purple velvet cushion, where anyone might pick it up and wield it.

But she was more worried that day about Bjarki than how the Saxon Wolf chose to furnish his command tent, for since their arrival at the Hohenstein, her brother had gradually become more and more silent and withdrawn by day, and he complained that his terrible blood-filled nightmares had returned to plague him when he slept. She had hoped his illness had abated, and perhaps been cured by Valtyr's medicine, or that the threat had ended when they burned the curse-charm in the hearth-fire. Valtyr had insisted that the hidden object was the cause of his malaise – although Tor still wondered if her brother was suffering another illness. One she did not like to name.

'My friends,' said Widukind, calling the council to order. 'Before I reveal what I plan to do over the next few weeks and months, I would like to call upon my good friend Jarl Hessi to give us his tidings. He has come to us from his hall in Orhum, beyond the Oker. He has news of recent events in that region.

'My friends, I give you, the courageous Jarl Hessi,' said Widukind and he began to applaud. The warriors in the room were nonplussed for a few moments but scattered claps soon filled the air, enough to rouse Bjarki from his torpor.

'Eh?' he said. 'What's happening now?' He looked at Tor in puzzlement.

'Hush, brother, Jarl Hessi is going to speak to us,' said Tor.

'I have tidings of the Sorbs,' said Jarl Hessi, 'particularly of my friend and ally from the banks of the Saale, Witkojc, chief of the Zyrmunti tribe. Seven days ago, on Midsummer's Eve, he and his fellow warriors sacked the Frankish *castrum* at the junction of the Saale and Elbe rivers. They slaughtered all the Red Cloaks inside and utterly destroyed it with fire. Witkojc is a fine, jolly fellow, but he also likes to take heads – he has sent a message to say he has collected two hundred Frankish skulls.'

Now the applause, the cheering even, in the tent was more enthusiastic.

'Wait, my friends, wait – that is not the only good news,' said Widukind.

Jarl Hessi resumed speaking: 'We, that is me and my Eastphalian brothers, were recently asked by the Frankish king's chamberlain – an arrogant prick called Adalgis – to guide a powerful force of *cabellarii* eastwards to the Saale River to punish the rebellious Sorbs. What Adalgis did not know is that I have long had an agreement with Witkojc, and we are both also allied with our good friend Duke Widukind here.'

There was silence in the tent. Many warriors were not sure how to respond.

'So you are saying that you, Hessi, guided Adalgis and his cavalry *scarae* east to attack your allies the Sorbs?' said Tor. 'Who are also on our side?'

'No, well, yes, I'll explain,' said Hessi, but he seemed to run out of words.

Widukind spoke for him. 'I asked the Sorbs to attack the *castrum* on Midsummer's Eve, to suit our plans. Bjarki relayed their answer, didn't you Bjarki?'

Tor saw her brother was staring into space like a simpleton. He made no acknowledgement of Widukind's question. But the Saxon duke did not notice.

'When the Sorbs attacked the *castrum*,' continued Widukind, 'I knew it must provoke a strong response from Karolus – it was an act of war – although I did not anticipate he would ask Hessi to be his guide to take the *cabellarii* east.'

'What happened then?' asked Jarl Brun. 'They attacked the Sorbs?'

'I tricked the Franks. I abandoned the Frankish horsemen in the Saale Valley east of Hoheseeburg,' said Hessi. 'I rode out of their camp at midnight and circled back to collect my men and came to join you in the Süntel Hills.'

'I don't understand,' said a young Saxon captain. 'You are boasting that you played some childish trick on the Franks, is that it?'

'Come on, everyone, this is not so difficult,' said Widukind. 'Adalgis – the king's chamberlain – and *two thousand* of his best Black Cloak *cabellarii* – along with his lieutenant Gallo, and Lord Worad, the Count of the Palace – are nearly two hundred miles away in Thuringia now, chasing their tails on the Sorb border, trying to find an enemy that has already withdrawn beyond the Elbe into their own heartlands. Two thousand Frankish heavy cavalry, by far the biggest threat to us, are now out of the game. I am told Bishop Livinus, smelling a great victory against the Sorbs, and never one to allow any passing glory to slip through his sticky fingers, is joining them on the border with another three *scarae* of his light horsemen.'

There was a murmur of general approval in the tent.

'And if that were not enough to raise your spirts, my Saxon brothers, then know this: Karolus himself is at present down south in Bavaria with all his unoccupied household troops, preparing to attack the Avars. I had word from Duke Tassio of Bavaria last night. A response to one of Father Alwin's letters,' said Widukind, making a grand sweeping gesture towards the priest, who was standing in the corner, smiling shyly.

'Abbio's friends in Francia have reported that the *exercitus*, a thousand Red Cloak spearmen under the command of Count Thierry, are still in their camp in Austrasia, outside Aachen. When the Westphalian shields arrive here, we will have an army six thousand strong. We have a free hand, my friends. *A free hand!* We face no serious opposition from the Franks in this entire part of Saxony. Our enemies are confused and scattered from the Rhine to the Elbe. It is time to strike a blow for freedom.'

And the whole tent was set a-roar with the cheering of Saxon warriors.

—

'Bjarki, pay attention, you great oaf, I am trying to talk to you,' said Tor.

The council of war had ended after several jubilant, drunken, talk-filled hours during which Widukind and his commanders had considered various bizarre strategies which ranged from the slightly absurd to the utterly insane.

'We march to Aachen, destroy Karolus's capital, capture all his royal women!' one Angrian captain had suggested. Another proposed marching down to Bavaria to attack King Karolus himself, just as he was about to invade the Avar Khaganate, to take him completely by surprise. But it was finally agreed that the nearest target – and the one with the most symbolic value – was the great Frankish fortress of Eresburg, once known as the Groves of Eresburg. This was the erstwhile home of the Fyr Skola, and the place where once the mighty Irminsul, the World Tree of Saxon beliefs, had soared into a pagan sky. After much loud, heated discussion, it had been agreed that winning back the Groves of Eresburg from the Franks should be their first major objective.

'Bjarki, you must rouse yourself. Bjarki, wake up, Valtyr is asking for you,' said Tor. 'You should speak to him before… before…'

Bjarki was sitting on the cold ground beside their little campfire. He had been sitting there and staring into the flickering flames for hours as it gradually grew dark, unmoving, unspeaking, unblinking. Yet Tor was more worried about their old friend. Valtyr had not risen from his blankets for the past two days. And now he was calling for Bjarki, saying he had something important to say.

Perhaps there was something in the urgent tone of Tor's voice that reached through the fog in the Rekkr's brain, a hint of panic, maybe, but she was relieved to see her brother slowly turn his head and look into her face – partially himself again.

'What does Valtyr want with me?' said Bjarki.

'Ask him yourself,' said Tor. She reached out to haul Bjarki to his feet.

Valtyr lay in sweat-drenched blankets in a small make-shift tent, a cloak on a few sticks, erected to keep the sun out of his eyes. He seemed to have lost even more weight, and was now no more than bones and skin – yellowish waxy skin, at that. His one working eye appeared huge and he had lost the black patch over the other, so he now presented a scarred, pinkish cavity below his frosty eyebrow to the world.

He had taken no nourishment, it seemed, not even his beloved ale, for many days now, and Tor knew that he was near the end. Nevertheless, he roused himself when

Bjarki and Tor came into his tiny tent, crowding in under the cloak-covering, and both plumping down beside him.

Valtyr reached for Bjarki's paw and cradled it in his own stick-like claws. He seemed to have trouble breathing, for even that tiny movement exhausted him.

'Do you want a drink?' asked Tor. 'Shall I get Erik to fetch some ale?'

'No,' quavered Valtyr, 'no more ale. I must say this… have to talk to…' He broke off in a series of wet wheezes. 'Bjarki,' he said, 'is that you here?'

'I'm here,' said Bjarki. 'Tor and I are with you. We will stay with you.'

'You are… a good… boy,' said Valtyr. 'I'm… sorry you are… so ill.'

'I think you are a little sicker than I am, old man,' said Bjarki. 'But you will feel better soon. Get some rest – eat something, eat some nice hot soup…'

'No,' said Valtyr, with more strength than Tor had believed he possessed. 'No food, no lies. This is my end. Listen, Bjarki… listen to old Valtyr one last time.'

Bjarki cocked his big head on one side. 'Speak then, old friend,' he said.

Valtyr took some more wheezing breaths. 'I'm dying,' he said, and he tensed his jaw and seemed to summon up all his strength. 'All strength is borrowed and now I must make the final repayment on that debt. The Crab has eaten me, all of my insides, my belly, my lungs. I can feel him. Scuttling. I'm sick in body, but you, Bjarki, you are sick in your spirit. And your sickness has been created by another, by *seithr*.'

'But we found that horrible leather thing,' said Bjarki, 'in the thatch above my bed. Father Alwin threw it into the fire. It is gone. Burnt to nothing.'

231

'And yet... your illness is back, Bjarki. It eats you, eats at your spirit.'

Tor's brother said nothing. His big paw stirred slightly in Valtyr's brittle grip and the old man tightened his skinny fingers around Bjarki's meaty digits.

'I can feel it in you, my son,' Valtyr said. 'The curse-charm was destroyed but the one who placed it is still with us. They have made another, much more powerful charm... and set it somewhere near you, in your bed... perhaps in your clothes... The evil magic... the curse-charm is designed to drive you mad, make you... Galálar. But you must... fight it... the *seithr* will also kill your *gandir*, it will silence the bears for ever, and send you utterly mad... fight it... find the one who would destroy you.'

'How do you know this?' said Bjarki.

Tor could feel the hot prick of tears behind her eyelids. She sniffed.

'I know it because... I am close to the Spirit-Realm... nearly gone from this world. The dead speak to me; they tell me their secrets... For I will soon join them. I fear not death... No fear... I will find my place in the Hall of the Slain beside the All-Father. Oh, yes... I have played my part in defending the North... and much, much more. Odin will hail me as a worthy comrade... and welcome me to his Hall.'

Tor though she saw a faintest smile of satisfaction on Valtyr's grey lips.

'My greatest gift to Odin...' the old man said, and broke off, panting. 'My greatest gift to the All-Father... was you, Bjarki Bloodhand. I gave the world a Rekkr, a true Fire Born. And I will not allow some *seithr*-wielding maggot... to remove my gift from this Middle-Realm.

Find… find the traitor, Bjarki, find the… one who seeks to harm you. Seek them out… find them… destroy them.'

Valtyr gave a small jerky start, a kind of twitch, and he stopped speaking.

Bjarki and Tor thought the old man was dead. But Valtyr gripped Bjarki's hand fiercely, opened his one eye and said: 'May the Bear guard you, my son.'

And Bjarki replied gruffly: 'May the Bear guard you, too, Far-Traveller, wherever your journeying takes you next.'

Valtyr's hold on Bjarki's fingers slackened. His body seemed to relax, to slump and sink in on itself, to subside like the settling earth on a fresh grave. And all the living air still in his lungs came rushing out in one defiant, rattling breath.

And thus Valtyr, Guardian of the North, departed from the Middle-Realm.

# Chapter Twenty

### Return to the Groves of Eresburg

Sometimes he thought he could almost understand them, grasp a little of their talk, anyway. But much of it was growling, grunting ursine sounds, incomprehensible to his human ear. Yet some of the bear words seemed to resonate with him, if Bjarki paid very close attention – not exactly as language, but as some kind of deep feeling, combined with complex emotions, muddled and confused, but no less powerful for it.

Mochta was very tired and sleepy, and did not want to go anywhere, but the younger one, Garm – a friendly creature that Bjarki had raised from a cub – wanted to go off somewhere else, somewhere much more exciting, to another country, to some foreign land, it sounded like. Bjarki did not understand where Garm wanted to go, and why his mother should want to stop him leaving, but that was the basic meaning of their quarrelling this day. Stay or go. And there was some satisfaction for Bjarki in being able to understand even a part of their discourse.

'What do *you* think?' asked Tor. 'Bjarki, I would just like your opinion.'

'I think Garm should be allowed to go,' he said. 'Why not? He is young.'

'What are you babbling about? I want to know what you think of Father Alwin.'

Bjarki could feel himself slowly coming back from the Spirit-Realm, leaving the conversations of the bears behind him, and emerging into the World of Men, the world of his sharp-tongued sister Tor and all the other noisy people who demanded difficult things from him day and night. He was sitting on a stool beside the campfire. It was daylight. About noon. The hot sun above him.

'What about Father Alwin?' he said vaguely.

'Do you think that Father Alwin could be the one who is using *seithr* to make you go...' Tor did not say the word Galálar but Bjarki was just about present enough in the World of Men to understand exactly what she meant.

'Why do you think it might be him?' Bjarki was trying to form a mental image of Father Alwin. He was a nice man, he thought. Skinny, with a shaven bald patch. Foreign, but not a Frank. He was teaching Bjarki's children – the girl and the infant, and Edith – to make Latin letters so they would all be clever.

'He's a Christian, oaf. He's a *gothi* of the religion of our enemies. And he has been in and out of the compound in Ribe since we got there. He could easily have put that horrible thing in the thatch above your bed. And perhaps done something on the march south with us from the Dane-Mark, too. He has always been around us, unobtrusive, trusted; around Edith and the children every day. Part of the family.'

'He is helping Widukind. He is helping us. Why would he want to harm me? What does he know of *seithr*? I don't think Christians use magic, do they?'

'I don't know. Maybe he hates us. Hates you. If so, he is good at hiding it.'

235

They sat in silence for a while.

'Are you hungry?' said Tor. 'I could get Erik to bring us some soup from the kitchens, maybe some bread and cheese, too. Wait – Erik! It could be Erik.'

Bjarki just stared blankly at her.

'It could be Erik who is using *seithr* to hurt you,' said Tor slowly, and watched puzzlement spread over Bjarki's big, red face. He did not reply to her.

'You have to fight this, Bjarki,' she said. 'You have to try harder to stay with us. I'm suggesting your shield-bearer is the traitor Valtyr talked about.'

'Why would he do that? He is a stray boy and we have been kind to him.'

Tor bit her lip. 'There is something you do not know about Erik,' she said.

Bjarki cocked an eyebrow at her. 'What is that, Tor?'

'Valtyr picked Erik up on Bago,' Tor said. 'He is your son, by Freya. She died and that *nithing* Freki used to torment him. So Valtyr brought him to you to care for. It could be that Erik is resentful that you left him in Bago with his mother for so long. Maybe he wants to take his revenge on you for that. With *seithr*. The weakling's weapon. For he could not hope to fight you by ordinary means.'

Bjarki said nothing. He stared into the dancing flames of the fire.

'Bjarki? I've just told you that Erik is your son. Have you nothing to say?'

'I knew this already,' said Bjarki. 'I knew he came from Bago – we had a long talk in Ribe, and he told me all about himself. And when I asked, he said that his mother's name was Freya. He was born a few months after I left Bago with Valtyr. He looks just like her – and a little bit like me, too,

I think. So I knew he was my son. Or guessed it. But I don't think he knows. I don't want to tell him, not yet, I don't want to disappoint him. He will be disappointed and upset when he finds out that his famous Rekkr father is… that he is Galálar.'

Tor looked at him in surprise. Bjarki felt his world become completely steady. Fully real at last. He fixed his steady blue gaze directly on his sister.

'Erik is not the one who seeks to hurt me,' he said. 'He likes me. I can tell that. I can see it in his eyes. He wants me to like him, too. He's not trying to drive me insane with magic. I'm surprised that you think he might be the one.'

'You see! If you fight it, you can beat it,' said Tor. 'You're still Bjarki. Don't listen to the bears, brother, don't stay in their world. It means death for you. Be here, be present here as much as you can. We will find the source of this poison and we will destroy it. But you have to do your part – you must stay with us in this world.'

–

They set off in the afternoon, a thousand spears on foot and a few mounted scouts, heading south down the wide Weser Valley, with Bjarki in command as *Armathr* – as Widukind's proxy general – and Tor, his second, buzzing annoyingly around him. He kept Tor's advice in the front of his mind and when he did find himself lapsing into a silence, he hoped that the other commanders, and Tor, believed that he was simply considering the wisest course to take next.

Widukind had given him his battle orders – and they were very clear.

'The Groves of Eresburg, Bjarki,' the Saxon Wolf had said to him. 'You know as well as I do what they meant to the Saxon people. It was once the beating heart of our homeland. Our holiest place. And it could be once again... If you can retake the Groves for me, my friend, I would be for ever in your debt. But, on the other hand, do not do anything too rash. Don't embrace your death-or-glory Fire Born creed. Don't take stupid risks. If you spend my spearmen's lives against that rock – and fail to take it – we will be in a worse position than if you had never attempted to take it at all.'

What Widukind was saying, Bjarki realised, was: 'If you manage to take Eresburg I will claim the credit – but if you fail, you alone will bear the blame.'

On the march, Bjarki noticed that Kynwulf and Rask flanked him at all times, on Tor's instructions, he suspected, and all the other *Felaki* were also always within calling distance. And so Bjarki did his best to appear normal, in perfect control of all his fraying faculties, giving crisp, almost brusque instructions to his subordinates, sending out scouts, and listening carefully to their reports. He greeted veteran warriors he knew in the throng with a wave and a jest, only occasionally prompted by a nudge in the ribs from Tor. He had listened to her advice and was indeed fighting hard to stay in this world as much as he could.

They saw no sign of the Franks, not even their scouts, on the first day of the march – although in the dense trees of the First Forest on either side of the road they might easily have been watching from cover undetected – and Bjarki began to hope that Widukind's crowing prediction at the war council, that they had a free hand to do whatever they pleased in this part of Saxony, was true.

The Franks in Saxony, it seemed to him, were all bottled up inside their fortresses. The others were all far away in Austrasia, Thuringia and Bavaria.

Bjarki gave orders to camp for the first night at the shallow ford over the Weser at Braunsberg, where they had once nearly fought a pitched battle, and, although there were still several hours of good daylight left, Tor, to his surprise, agreed with his decision. They were not trying to catch the garrison of Eresburg by surprise – even if the Frankish armies *were* bottled up or far away, they must know already that the Saxon tribes were in rebellion. All those razed villages and burnt churches would have trumpeted that story far and wide. The fortress of Eresburg would be full of refugees. The *scarae* inside Eresburg – and no one knew how many Red Cloaks were there – would know that they were a target.

On the second night, they camped again at the junction of the Diemel and Weser rivers and Bjarki found that he was actually enjoying himself. He felt perfectly fine. Happy. He had decided to travel very light, wearing only a knee-length jerkin, cloak and trews, with a sword on his hip and a seax slung across his loins – he abandoned helm, shield, axe and mail, giving them to Erik and Halfdan to carry for him – which was their duty – and he felt light-bodied, light-hearted and, most importantly, clear-headed. The bears were silent, and they might almost be absent from his heart. Perhaps it was movement that was beneficial, as he had discovered in Treva earlier in the year when he was on his way to Lippspringe. Moving, walking, made him feel good. He tried not to think about the bears and his sleep that night was untroubled.

A long day's march the next day took them to within sight of the Groves of Eresburg and, as the sun dipped low in the west, Bjarki borrowed a scout's horse and with Kynwulf and Rask running along behind him he went forwards to look upon the place that had changed his life as a young man and which, he discovered, still meant so much to him now. As the rest of his small army was still advancing up the valley behind him, Bjarki, giddy with his light-bodied freedom, gazed up at the place that had once housed the Fyr Skola, the institution that had made him what he was today.

The lowlands below the scrub-covered limestone cliffs of the Groves of Eresburg – that jutting, oval rock formation that sprang unexpectedly out of the Diemel Valley – were deserted, but there were plenty of signs of recent activity. A ramshackle village of longhouses and sheds had sprung up to the north of the fortress, and kitchen gardens had been dug in the earth beside the river.

There were even a few fields sown with oats and barley on the margins of the First Forest. Bjarki frowned. He had helped to bury a large number of his comrades right there, good men and women slaughtered by the Franks in a horribly one-sided battle ten years ago. A dozen Fire Born from the Fyr Skola had perished in that fight; they had died heroically, according to the one man who had survived it, a friend of Bjarki's called Gunnar, but there were no signs of their graves now. The new villagers, the incomers, probably Frankish colonisers, had dug them up, or ploughed them further into the rich earth, which caused him to feel a flare of anger in his belly.

There were no people or animals visible, and when he got off the horse and kicked open the door of one of the larger huts, he saw that it had been emptied of all its valuables, pots, pans, knives, all the food was gone too. The hut had been so recently vacated that a linen rag he found beside a basin full of cold water was still damp. Perhaps his Saxon army had been observed on the march down here by hidden Frankish scouts, after all. And all the villagers were now up in the Grove above him.

Coming out of that dark space, into the gloaming of the river valley, he looked upwards at the palisade which ran all the way around the summit of the Eresburg outcrop. And saw the tiny lights glowing now along the top, lanterns or candles, or maybe flaring pine torches, which had been lit by the defenders.

He had built that wooden wall himself – although he could see it had been more strongly reinforced since his day. There were several new tall towers, crenelated, set into the walls, and far more solid looking than anything he had built. That was where the local people were. Up there, snug and safe, so they believed.

They were up on there with an unknown number of Red Cloaks, or Green or Black. He would find out in the morning. Maybe he would send up some envoys and talk to them, invite them to surrender. Maybe he would simply storm the high walls.

He slept well once again, and the nightmares were mercifully absent, and after breakfast he took counsel with Tor, and Kynwulf and a square-faced Saxon leader called Hrothgar, a fellow from Nordalbia, one of Jarl Guthrum's senior *hird*-men.

'Our enemies are up there,' Bjarki began, 'and we all know how hard it will be to climb up and overwhelm them. Ladders and ropes and straight up the cliff sides, or up the main road and an assault at the gate. Any way we do it, it will be a hard fight.'

'How many foes are we facing up there?' asked Hrothgar. 'Do we know?' He scratched at a white scar that neatly bisected his raven-black bearded chin.

'Maybe five hundred – maybe six,' said Kynwulf. 'I counted heads on the palisade at dawn, when they would have made all the troops on duty stand to.' The grizzled *Felaki* was looking more than a little pleased with himself. 'I reckon maybe about one third of them would have stood-to, and I counted two hundred heads.'

'If *we* were up there with six hundred spearmen,' said Bjarki, 'could we defend the Groves against a thousand Red Cloaks down here, men who had to come up ropes and ladders into a storm of arrows, lances and boulders?'

'We could certainly defend the Groves with six hundred spears,' said Tor. 'But we are better, braver warriors than they are.'

'Are we?' said Bjarki. 'I saw Black Cloaks up there this morning, as well as their Green Cloak mountain troops. They are better than the Reds, usually.'

'We could do it… but it would cost us a sea of blood,' said Hrothgar.

'It may be costly in lives, but I say we must attack,' said Tor. 'These are the Groves of Eresburg – when Karolus took this place, he captured the heart of Saxony. If we take it back, we will have won much more than just a fortress.'

'I need to think on this,' said Bjarki. He got up from his stool and walked away. Kynwulf and Rask followed him at a distance as Bjarki began to plod a circuit of the plateau, keeping a prudent arrow-shot from the walls at all times.

It took him the best part of two hours, with frequent pauses to stare up at the fortified plateau above him, looking at the angles, tracing possible paths of ascent up the cliff sides. There were gulleys and crevices; caves, too, he remembered. Might they serve to access the summit without too much loss of life?

There were so many other memories that came rolling back when he stared up at that high plateau, walked on a few more steps and looked some more from a fresh angle. He had learned to fight up there, with Tor patiently instructing him in sword and spear. He had also fought a boy with his bare hands and been badly bitten on the face. He had charged through the flames of the Fyr Pit – and been acclaimed as brave by none other than Angantyr, Father of Bear Lodge.

He remembered, too, months before that, when Valtyr had first brought him here, as a callow, nervous boy, agog at all the world – ah Valtyr, poor Valtyr, his grief rose in him like a tide – Valtyr had brought him here from Bago, directing the course of his life. Valtyr had also half-drowned him, once, in a cave pool – *was it that one just up there beneath the alder bush growing from the rock face?* It was. Valtyr had tried to drown him in there, hoping to rid Bjarki of his *gandr*. It had not worked.

Valtyr had been his true father, Bjarki realised, not Hildar – Valtyr had been the one who had always been there, advising him, criticising and helping him – meddling in his life, as Tor would no doubt say. And now he was gone.

Valtyr would have told him to capture this place, no matter the cost. Valtyr would have said – just as Tor did – that the Groves of Eresburg were worth more than the lives of any number of Saxon spearmen. Valtyr would have had no doubts. But what did Bjarki think? Could it be done without decimating his people in the assault?

'Highness,' said Kynwulf, tapping his arm. 'A rider. A flank scout, I think.'

The rider was galloping towards him, his horse sweat-lathered and blown. Something urgent, then. The man reined in in front of Kynwulf, and slid from the saddle. '*Armathr*,' he said, panting, 'I come from the hills to the south.'

Bjarki struggled to remember the scout's name. An Angrian, he thought.

'Make your report,' he snapped.

'Horsemen. Black Cloaks. Frankish *cabellarii*. Many hundreds of them. Possibly even thousands. They looked like an army to me. But no infantry with them. And they are coming north at speed on the road from Fritzlar Abbey.'

'Are you sure? That there are indeed thousands of them?'

The scout shrugged. 'Too many to count. I think it is Adalgis and Gallo.'

'How soon before they get here?'

'Two, maybe three hours. Their swifter outriders will be here sooner.'

'That's it then,' said Bjarki.

—

The retreat was orderly, which was pretty much all that could be said for it. Bjarki wasted no time. He simply began giving orders, and Tor, who was silently fuming beside him, had to wait until he had issued them before he gave her his explanation.

The orders given, the various contingents began hurriedly packing up their belongings and setting off back down the Diemel Valley on the route they had advanced up only the previous day, the withdrawal protected by a screen of skilled First Forest archers, and a rearguard of a hundred experienced axemen.

'We would not have had enough *time* to make a successful assault on the heights and capture the Groves,' said Bjarki later, when they were on the march. 'The Black Cloak cavalry were at our throats. Very nearly upon us. You must understand, Tor.'

'If we had attacked at first light, or last night,' she said, 'we'd be up there, looking down on the Frankish horsemen and thumbing our noses at them.'

'But we did not. So, there was not enough time. If we had not pulled back, we would have been caught between two fires. And if the first assault up the cliffs did not break through their defences, our strength would have been seriously weakened when we faced the *cabellarii*. Remember what happened last time foot soldiers faced Frankish cavalry in this valley? Skymir, Angantyr, and the rest of the Fire Born – all the others too – they were slaughtered here. The only thing we could do was to retreat.'

'Widukind is not going to be happy with you,' she said.

# Chapter Twenty-one

*'I chose this position with care'*

Widukind was not happy. Three days later, back on the Hohenstein spur, Bjarki related all the events that had occurred in the Diemel Valley. The Saxon force had withdrawn quickly, and in good order, the rearguard of axemen and archers managing to keep the Frankish heavy cavalry at bay for a dozen miles, before the horse-borne enemy chose to disengage and return to the Eresburg fortress.

The Saxon Wolf made a small show of criticism, saying, as Tor had done, that if Bjarki had been speedier in his assault on the Groves, or quicker in his advance, then the story would have been very different. But Tor had backed up her brother, pointing out that the sizeable force of Black Cloak cavalry would have, at the very least, badly mauled the Saxon infantry, and then they would have had to pull back anyway.

And, Tor pointed out, if the Red Cloaks in Eresburg had sallied forth from their stronghold, Bjarki's force might have been destroyed. There was no way they could have fought and won. Bjarki, she said, had done the right thing in the circumstances.

So while Widukind was unhappy, he was in truth less angry with Bjarki's cautious actions in the Diemel Valley than worried about two other things. The Westphalian contingent – the promised three thousand spears – had not yet come to the Hohenstein. And there was bad news, too, from another quarter.

'Father Alwin is gone,' Widukind told Tor, pouring her a big cup of wine. Bjarki had finished his report, accepted his official scolding and gone back to the camp to rest, but the duke had asked Tor to stay behind and speak with him alone. Her mind was filled with troubling thoughts at the invitation, but she had accepted it.

'What do you mean – gone?' said Tor.

'I mean he's not here,' said the Saxon Wolf. 'I spoke to him three days ago in this very tent, and then today, when I sent a servant to summon him, I found out that he is no longer present anywhere in the camp. No one knows where he is but one of the sentries said he passed through the lines two days ago, with a walking staff and pack on his back. No one thought to stop and question him.'

'Which way was he going – north or south?' asked Tor.

'South,' said Widukind.

'Towards the enemy,' said Tor. Widukind had lost a little weight on the march, perhaps because of the strains of command. It suited him, she thought. He looked striking this morning, his fair hair held back by a gold circlet, his cheekbones prominent, skin tanned a golden colour from the road, blue eyes bright with worry.

'We shall not see Father Alwin again,' said Tor. 'And you must assume that our secrets are known to Karolus and his generals. The Franks must have a full understanding of exactly where we are in these hills and in what strength.'

'You think we should run, Tor?' said Widukind. 'Run from the Franks as quickly as possible, just like your brother Bjarki in the Diemel Valley?'

Tor winced at the way he expressed this thought.

'I do not,' she said stiffly.

'I don't think so, either,' said Widukind, smiling at her to show he was joking. His smile made something flip over in her belly. 'I think we should stay here and fight them. I chose our position here on the Hohenstein with the very greatest care.'

'You're hoping to fight them *here*?' said Tor.

Widukind nodded. He beckoned her over to the table in the corner of the tent, to the bizarre arrangement of stones and twigs and ribbons. 'See here, Tor. If they come at us from the south, west or north – from here, here or here – they have to climb up the steep slopes to get to us, while we roll giant rocks down among them and shower them with javelins and arrows. It would cost them more in blood than... well, than Bjarki trying to storm the Groves of Eresburg. If they try to come at us while we are up here on the Hohenstein from any of those three directions, north, south, or west, we will slaughter them – we will completely eviscerate them.'

'So they *must* attack us from the east?'

'That is so. There is only one road through the First Forest in the east, Tor. So, they must come that way. And since we *know* they will attack us from that direction, we have the advantage over them. But I shall need your help to secure us a complete victory. This is why I wanted you to stay behind. This is what I wanted to ask you, Tor. A favour. I want you to pick out five hundred of our best and bravest warriors and give the attacking Franks a fitting welcome.'

'And the rest of the army?'

'We wait for them here,' the Saxon Wolf said, and grinned smugly at Tor.

'Father Alwin has gone,' said Tor.

Bjarki was lying on his bedding in their little camp, his eyes open and staring up at the endless blue sky, and Tor feared that her brother had gone back into the place where she could not reach him. But he quickly turned on his side when he heard her voice, and he looked directly at her with a clear blue gaze.

'You think the priest has gone over to the enemy?' he said.

'I think Father Alwin was always on the side of the enemy,' said Tor. 'From the start. Moreover, I also think he was the person who tried to poison you with *seithr*.'

'We have talked about this, Tor. Why would he wish to do that?'

'Let us imagine that Father Alwin – like any normal man – resented being captured, carried away and made a thrall. Let us imagine that Father Alwin, trapped in the North, held as a slave, felt anger and hatred, as anyone would, but that he did not chose to show it to the world. He is a very clever man, after all. His hatred would be concentrated on those who enslaved him, and the enemies of his own people, the Christians. He hated us. I think he always hated us. Nobody could truly be that cheerful all the time. We have harboured a venomous snake in our house all along.'

'But I gave Father Alwin his freedom. I told him he could do whatever he wished. He chose to stay with us, to help us, to teach Edith, Lili and Hildar.'

'He must have known war was coming – a war against the Christians. Perhaps he felt his revenge could be better served if he stayed with us, earned our trust, learned our weaknesses, all the better ultimately to betray us.'

'Hmm,' said Bjarki. 'I don't know. Where did he get that horrible *seithr* object? How did he know how to use it to hurt me?'

'There are a dozen wise women and cunning men in Ribe, any one could have sold him a curse-charm. Or perhaps the Christians have their own magic.'

'He was not afraid to handle the charm when it fell from the thatch. He picked it up and would have thrown it in the midden. Even Valtyr was too afraid to touch it.'

'There, you see,' said Tor. 'He was not afraid to touch it because he had *already* touched it. He put it in the thatch above your bed. And he offered to throw it in the midden... because it could easily be retrieved and used again.'

'Perhaps you are right,' said Bjarki.

'Do you feel better or worse, since Father Alwin has gone?' asked Tor.

'Better, a good deal better.'

'There you are! Have you searched your belongings for another curse-charm? Valtyr said it might be something that you wear, some item close to your body.'

'I have – Erik and Halfdan helped me do it. We went through everything – from my spare hose to my sun hat. We shook out all my bedding too, and my dirty clothes, everything, we even examined the seams of my cloaks. We even looked at my riding boots. We found nothing out of the ordinary in any of it.'

'Let's hope Father Alwin took whatever it was with him when he fled.'

'I do feel better. More... alive,' said Bjarki.

'I think your much-battered spirit is finally mending, oaf,' said Tor.

Tor took Hrothgar, Rask and half of the Ymirsfjord *vikingir*, as well as four *lith* of Guthrum's Nordalbians and a hundred bowmen, mostly First Forest hunters.

She led these warriors eastwards along the spur of hillside on which their camp was situated. They marched for about a mile east along the rough track that passed for a road, with thick woodland on either side, until Tor found exactly what she was looking for, a section to the north of the track with a steep cliff to the south, dropping sharply to a stream. The river below her position was called the Long Pine Brook, one of the hunters told her, an older man who knew this area of the First Forest well.

She gathered the leaders of the various contingents, all of them sitting on the earth or crouched beneath the low-slung branches of the trees – a strange, squat local variety called the dwarf beech. Then slowly, even painstakingly, she told them what she wanted to do. There were questions, many of them, but finally Tor managed to get across her plan of attack, and all the tactics and manoeuvres she had previously agreed with Widukind, and eventually she was sure that everyone fully understood it.

Then she sent out scouts in pairs to the high places to watch the valley below, and the mountains to the east, and told the rest of the force to make themselves comfortable.

'We will be camping here until the Franks attack,' she said. 'It could be a day or two. Make all your usual preparations, ready your weapons, paint your shields, pray to Odin or whomever and wait. Hrothgar is in command, and Rask is his second. I will be back here in the morning. Or before then, if the enemy comes up sooner.'

Tor returned to the camp at the Hohenstein just in time for the evening council of war. Widukind was standing in the centre of his tent, beside the twig, stone and ribbon table, with Abbio standing beside him in his hairy cloak, glowering from under his mop of matted hair at all the assembled warriors.

Tor entered the tent, and went to stand beside Bjarki. Widukind gave her a warm, welcoming smile, his eyes twinkling. But Tor only nodded coolly at him and glanced up at her brother, who was also intently watching Widukind. Bjarki had girded himself for war already, presumably with Halfdan and Erik's help. He was wearing a full mail byrnie that covered him from his elbows to his knees, stout war boots reinforced with iron strips, a long sword at his waist, seax across his loins, and his big, round bear-device shield slung over his back. He had a good steel helm, tucked under one arm, and he looked as if he expected to fight a full pitched battle within the hour. *Perhaps*, thought Tor, *he is right to be so thoroughly prepared already*.

'My friends,' said Widukind, 'the day of battle is nearly upon us. I'm told that the Franks are within a few hours' march of our position. My adviser Abbio has used all his cunning in the gathering of information to give us a picture of the Frankish forces in this region of Saxony, and their intentions with regard to making war on us. The enemy, he says, are below us, in the valley of the Weser and, with Abbio's permission, I shall outline what he has told me of their dispositions.'

Tor looked properly at Abbio then, a disagreeable and bedraggled creature, a man who filed his teeth into beast-like points – and for no good reason that Tor could think of. Despite dressing like something half-human that had recently crawled out from a swamp, Tor knew that Abbio the Crow was extremely gifted in the clever deployment of spies and informers, and that the information he gave Widukind was most likely to be correct. It had been proved so, time and again, in previous campaigns. Spying and torture, she knew, and bribery, too – these were Abbio's usual methods of information gathering and some whispered that he employed the dark arts, as well, to good effect.

'The situation as of this afternoon is thus,' began Widukind. 'There are *two* large Frankish armies at present below us in the Weser Valley...'

There was a general stirring of unease in the tent at this news.

'...the first Frankish army is a heavy cavalry force commanded by General Adalgis, the king's chamberlain, and by Adalgis's loyal lieutenant Gallo, the Count of the Stables. Just cavalry in that one. No infantry. They are joined by another noble called Lord Worad, the Count of the Palace, a rising man in Karolus's court, and also by a man that many of us already know – Bishop Livinus, Karolus's chancellor, who calls himself the Archbishop of Saxony.'

There were several boos in the tent at the mention of Livinus's name, and one man shouted out: 'He's a bastard, that bishop. The worst of the lot of 'em.'

Widukind held up his hand for silence. 'These men have a force of perhaps two thousand highly trained Black Cloak heavy *cabellarii*, and three hundred light horsemen too, provided by Bishop Livinus. And this very powerful force is, in my view – and my view aligns with that of Abbio – the main threat to us. Adalgis, in particular, is impressed with his own skills as a cavalry commander. He invites his men to call him Count Alexander, after some ancient Greek general.'

Widukind paused for a moment. One of the Saxon *hersirs* put up his hand.

'Yes, Herzog, what is it?'

'Forgive me, highness, but what exactly is a count?' the man asked.

'It is more or less the same as a jarl,' said Widukind. 'But don't ask me what different task each of these counts performs. Just know that these four men – Adalgis, Gallo, Worad and Livinus – are the commanders of the cavalry, and all four of them are very dangerous foes.'

The Saxon Wolf continued: 'The second Frankish army is an infantry force of fifteen hundred Red Cloaks under Count Thierry, who I'm told is a greedy man, eager to win glory in battle. He is no friend to Adalgis – they had a dispute over a territory that both men claimed and nearly took up arms against each other last year...' Widukind looked over at Abbio. 'That's right, isn't it?'

'Karolusss made them reconcile but they sssstill hate each other.'

'Count Thierry has also fallen out with Bishop Livinus over some matter of church doctrine, which I don't understand. He hates Livinus more than Adalgis.'

'He can't be all that bad, this Thierry, if he hates Livinus!' shouted Jarl Brun.

There was laughter in the tent at this quip, a release of the tension.

'You are right to mock and be merry, my friends,' Widukind said, 'because our enemies are indeed risible. They are not only arrogant and over-confident but also divided among themselves. The Frankish commanders are filled with mutual animosity and suspicion for each other – and Karolus is not here to keep the peace between them!' He said this last part with relish, then looked round the tent to see who there followed his train of thought.

Tor said: 'So you mean to play the commanders off against each other?'

'Exactly,' the Saxon Wolf replied. 'Exactly. Well done, Tor. Abbio tells me that Adalgis is fearful that Count Thierry will try to steal all his glory when they have vanquished us. And the king's chamberlain will not willingly share it with anyone. You will note that there is no suggestion in Adalgis's little mind that they will *not* be victorious against us. He is confident of his success. And I plan to use this grave error against him.'

'You want the Frankish heavy cavalry to attack us,' said Tor. 'But only the cavalry. That's your strategy, isn't it?'

'You are as wise as you are beautiful, Torfinna,' said Widukind. 'As you have just heard, my friends, that is my plan, my strategy. I will spell it out in the plainest terms for those of you at the back who may not have heard Tor clearly.'

*Or who may be too stupid to have understood*, thought Tor. She felt a glow at Widukind's words of praise, and scowled ferociously to disguise her feelings.

'Our scouts report that the heavy cavalry force under Adalgis has already crossed the Weser, and are heading up into the hills, to the east of us. We think they are making for Hohe Egge, the highest point in the Süntel Hills, which is about three miles away from here, eastwards, as the eagle flies. I estimate that they might even be ready to strike at us by tomorrow morning. However, the slower Frankish infantry are still down in the valley, to the south of us, about five miles away. They have also crossed the river but seem cautiously to be building a fortification in case of attack. The enemy seeks to come at us up here in a crab-claw movement – Adalgis from the east, Thierry from the south. They think they're being clever by coming from two directions. But I say they have divided their force in the face of the enemy. A mistake. One we shall punish.'

Widukind gestured to a servant who brought him over a cup of wine, which he drained in two large, quick swallows. 'Our task,' the Saxon Wolf continued, 'as Tor has so cleverly pointed out, is to encourage Adalgis and his heavy cavalry to attack us – *without the support of the Frankish infantry*. If we can persuade them to do that, to attack on their own, for the cavalry to charge in without the help of the infantry… we can crush them here at the Hohenstein.'

'Forgive me, highness,' said Jarl Hessi. 'But Franks are not idiots. Adalgis is an arrogant arsehole, yes indeed – I know this because I have spent days in his company. But he is not *completely* stupid. The speed with which he turned around in Thuringia and came back here after that wild goose chase I led him on is surely proof that he is no man's fool. Why would he attack us unsupported?'

'I do not claim Adalgis is stupid,' replied Widukind. 'I only say we must persuade him to attack us, convince him that he can win a quick victory without help from the infantry. He already wants to win without Thierry's help, so all glory will be reserved for him. He wants to cut Thierry and his Red Cloaks out of the game, and out of the fame that will surely follow from *his* victory!'

'How do you mean to persuade him to do that?' asked Jarl Brun.

'We come out of the Hohenstein fortification, we come out of these protective walls and offer ourselves up for destruction. We act, in short, as bait.'

There was a flicker of movement beside Tor, caught out of the corner of her eye, and then a heavy thump and she turned round to see her brother lying flat on the floor of the tent, his eyes staring into nothingness. And then he began to twitch and writhe, and a creamy foam began to form at his chewing mouth.

'Give him some room,' shouted Tor. 'Get back, all of you.' She shoved hard at a warrior who was looming over Bjarki – peering at him as her brother jerked and wriggled on the ground. A circle of curious men was formed around Bjarki, at least a yard from his madly twitching body. Tor got on her knees, as close as she dared, and called out his name.

'Bjarki! Get a hold of yourself. Bjarki, come back to us now!'

The Rekkr stopped, and Tor truly feared he was dead. He lay there unmoving, eyes open, the creamy froth sliding from his lips and slipping down his neck.

'No!' shouted Tor. 'First Valtyr, now you. No – I will not have it.' She slapped Bjarki around the face, a solid blow that rocked his big head over.

Bjarki blinked and turned his head to her. 'You stupid, fucking bastard,' Tor yelled. 'You frightened me, oaf.' She slapped him again, a gentler blow.

There was no shortage of warriors who offered to help get Bjarki back to his bed in the campsite. As always, Tor was amazed at how popular her brother was with... well, with everybody. Some offered words of comfort to Tor, as she accompanied the six men who carried Bjarki's dead weight out of the tent.

At the entrance of the tent she looked back inside and saw Widukind frowning at her across the space, and Abbio beside him, grinning, as if he had seen something funny. Or something that gave him a great deal of pleasure.

It was dark by the time she got Bjarki settled, with Erik attending him, a pitcher of water by his head and a bowl for his vomit, should he need it. Bjarki had not spoken since the fit; he had looked at her, tried to smile, then fallen into a deep sleep.

Tor paced up and down outside their tent, in short jerky steps – racking her brains for something to do. She missed Valtyr Far-Traveller terribly during that long, long night. The old man would have known exactly what to do. Tor did not. In the end, knowing she would not sleep, she walked back to the tent where Widukind had held his council, pushed open the flap, and went inside.

Widukind was there with Abbio the Crow and a couple of servants, and Tor said loudly: 'All of you, just fuck off, right now. Go on, go, get out!'

The servants stared at Tor, and Abbio gave her a sharp-toothed sneer.

'Leave us,' said Widukind, and a few moments later Tor and Widukind were alone. They stared at each other, eyes locked, but neither spoke for a time.

'You want some wine first?' asked Widukind, indicating a jug on a table.

'Yes,' said Tor, 'give me a very large measure of wine… first.'

# Chapter Twenty-two

*'We will shield you from evil'*

Bjarki was lying on his back, looking up at a wide blue sky. His whole body was constrained, somehow, and he felt hard stone uncomfortably under his spine. He looked around, rocking his head from side to side as much as he was able. And saw he was in a beautiful meadow with a babbling stream running down the middle and thick woodland in either rising flank. Somewhere in the First Forest, he thought. But not somewhere he recognised. He was chained to a large stone with many links of iron, in the middle of that forest valley, and naked as a baby.

He could see an object in the sky now, a dark thing flying. It came closer to him and now Bjarki could see that it was an enormous eagle, golden brown in colour shading to copper at the tips of its wings. The bird landed heavily on his bare belly, the talons as sharp as knives, digging painfully into his skin and muscles. The bird looked at him, down its long razor-beak, furious avian eyes seeming to measure him.

Bjarki felt the fear then, the drowning terror of a helpless victim under the executioner's blade. The massive bird tightened its talons in his belly flesh and the Rekkr grunted; he could feel the trickle of his own hot blood running down his sides.

Then the eagle struck, the beak hammering down at his chest, the sharp, curved point hacking in, and punching through his solid chest bone, cracking it like a walnut under an axe. The bird reared back, its beak bloody, and pecked down again, and Bjarki screamed with the pain and horror of it all. He could see that the bird now had a gobbet of bloody flesh in its beak, a piece of his heart, which the creature greedily gobbled down. The eagle struck again, and Bjarki could feel it now tearing at his living heart, ripping away chunks of his flesh, rearing back, opening its throat and swallowing it down. Three times the bird struck him, three times it ate a portion of his heart. He screamed, he howled like an animal – a long, wordless bubbling cry of raw anguish.

Then he heard them. A huffing, rumbling growl. A pounding of feet. A deep roar of rage and a lighter bark of outrage. And the bears were around him.

He saw Mochta claw at the eagle, swinging one massive black paw at the bird. Which easily dodged the strike. But Garm was there, too, and a chomp from his teeth closed on the end of the eagle's long copper wing. The bird leapt into the sky, scattering feathers. And Bjarki saw that the eagle was not, in truth, an eagle at all, but a huge, shaggy crow, black as midnight, with vicious eyes as red as blood. The massive bird hovered above his open, bleeding chest, cawing, cawing, seeming almost to cackle in glee at his misfortune, and the she-bear rose to her full height and roared at the creature, a mighty blast of sound, swiping up once again with her lethal claws.

And the malevolent crow fled. Flapping away into the empty blue sky.

The she-bear sank back on to its haunches, panting, and when she had recovered she looked into his face, from inches away, the once-jet hairs showing white at her blunt muzzle, the eyes rheumy and old. Bjarki could not hold her terrible gaze; he looked away to his left and saw that Garm was now licking at the blood that tricked down his naked ribs – not eating him, not savouring to taste of his essence; healing the deep wound in his body with his ministrations, with the careful licking of his hot tongue.

Mochta moved. She shoved her grizzled snout forwards and down his body and breathed out on the still open wound, a huff of hot, meaty breath, and the hole in his chest seemed to move, to quiver and close, to knit itself, and Bjarki could feel his arms and legs become free at the same instant, the chains melting away. He sat up on the rock, and looked at his chest, at the pink patch of fresh scar tissue over his heart.

'You saved me,' he said, wonderingly. 'You saved me from that thing.'

'For now,' said Mochta. 'You are safe, for now, man-child. But that evil creature is not yet defeated. Nor is it destroyed.'

'Only fire can do that,' said Garm. 'Only fire can expunge the *seithr*. Or your own death. But the malignant one is gone for now, Bear-brother. You are safe here with us, your *gandir*. Fear not this *seithr*, for while we are with you, we will shield you from its evil; while we walk beside you in friendship, you are protected.'

'I can understand you,' said Bjarki. He was still bewildered. 'I thought I would never comprehend your tongue again. Today I understand every word.'

'The *seithr* came between us, man-child, just as it was designed to do by the evil one,' said Mochta. 'The one who wove his dark spells to ensnare you knows you well.

He knew the source of your power and sought to deprive you of our strength.'

'He failed in that task,' said Garm. 'For this is not the first battle we have fought with that evil. Yet I say again, Bear-brother, the *seithr* is not defeated.'

'But you will protect me from it, my *gandir*? You will stay beside me?'

'I will be with you, man-child,' said Mochta, 'with you for ever. You sought me out at the Fyr Skola, beneath the spreading boughs of the Irminsul, and, in the First Forest, you killed my sickly, dying body in the deep snows. You cut off my head and stripped my magnificent skin from my body for a warrior's cloak. You have called on my strength in battle, many, many times, and used my ferocity to slay your enemies. I am in you, Fire Born, as you are in me when you wear my skin. We are joined inseparably. We will be together, you and I, for ever – for we are both one and the same. Our twin spirits are fused into one far greater entity. Man and bear, bear and man: *berserkr*.'

Bjarki said, 'But tell me, Mochta, and tell me truly, I beg you. Am I going mad? Am I going, as we sometimes call it in the World of Men… Galálar?'

'No, man-child. You are not mad; you are not Galálar. The *seithr* was designed to make you appear so, but it has been repulsed. Fear not, Rekkr, that is not your fate.'

Bjarki felt a vast sense of relief, of joy even. His deepest fear had been allayed.

'And you, Garm, will you, also, be beside me for ever, come what may?'

'I will always be your Bear-brother,' said Garm, 'but I cannot make you the for-ever promise.' The young bear sounded sad. 'I have other lives to live. Other worlds to explore. But I shall always remember you as my first man-child – as the cheese-giver, as my merry playmate and my beloved childhood friend.'

–

Bjarki opened his eyes. He was lying in his own bed and by the freshness in the air and milky greyness of the sky, he knew it was just after dawn. Tor stood over him, dressed, with a cup of something. She knelt down and looked intently into his face.

'How do you feel, brother?'

'Tired,' he said. 'Weak. I dreamt of the bears again. A terrible dream, at first. The *seithr* was eating me. Then the bears came to rescue me. They spoke to me.'

'Drink,' said Tor, and put the cup into his hand: warm wine with honey and spices. Bjarki immediately knew where she had come from with this morning gift.

'We must fight today,' he said. 'The Franks are upon us, Widukind says.'

'You won't be fighting anyone, brother. Not in your condition. You collapsed last night, don't you remember? You fell. You are to stay here in the camp, and rest today. There are plenty here who can do the fighting in your place. You must rest.'

'Don't be silly, Tor,' said Bjarki, and he began to climb out of his bedding. Then he stopped. Someone, presumably Tor, had stripped him in the night of all his armour and war gear, and he found he was naked. He looked at his chest but while there were plenty of old scars, there was no fresh pink one over his heart. Tor put her hand on his broad chest, and pushed him down into the blankets.

'You are in no right state to fight anyone,' she said. 'And you could be a danger to our own folk in the battle, if you go...'

263

She could not bring herself to name the illness from which Bjarki suffered.

'We can win this fight with one less warrior,' she said, smiling at Bjarki. 'Even without *this* famous warrior, a Rekkr as impressive as you, my brother.'

'I'm not going Galálar, sis,' he said. 'The bears told me that was not my fate.'

'Nevertheless, you are not in your full strength,' said Tor. 'Do not do anything. Rest. We can manage without you, Widukind is confident of success. I will be back when the battle is done. And I think I know who is behind the *seithr* attack.'

'Who?' said Bjarki.

'I do not have the time to go into it – I need to get back to my people in the woods – and I don't want to argue with you. We will talk after the battle, yes?'

Bjarki nodded and lay back down in his blankets. Then Tor did something that surprised him. She leaned in, embraced him, and kissed his bearded cheek.

He watched his sister collect her bow and a quiver of arrows, her shield and a spear, from the stack of their weapons. She waved as she walked away.

Bjarki sat up. The sip of hot honeyed wine had given him a taste for something sweeter. He crawled over to his pack and delved in it for a few moments, and found the pot of honey that Edith had given him. He held it cupped in his hands for a few moments, feeling the texture of the rough earthenware with his fingers, and then he peeled away the wax covering, levered out the wooden plug and dipped a finger in the golden depths.

The taste of the honey was an explosion of sensation, and not only of sweetness. He was instantly transported back to Ymirsfjord, to those idyllic late summer days with his wife and young family. He could hear Lili singing an idiotic little song as she munched on a dripping piece of comb, and recall his wife's loving scolding for allowing Little Hare to become so sticky and dirty.

He put the pot of honey to his lips and drank down the viscous liquid in a few slow, delightful gulps, wallowing in this simple pleasure, and feeling the honey's golden power in his empty belly, and its strength filling his limbs.

He finished the whole pot, wiped up the last sticky traces with a finger, licked that digit and the rest of his hand completely clean, then he rose from his mess of blankets, stood upright, naked, and called loudly for his shield-bearers.

'Erik! Halfdan! To me. Fetch my armour. We have a battle to fight today!'

An hour later, he stood before Widukind, fully dressed once more, in byrnie and helm, his bear-device shield slung by a leather strap over his back. He had added vambraces of leather and iron to guard his forearms. And his old bearskin, sadly reduced to a cape-like yellow-brown rag, was draped over his shoulders. He held a long Dane axe in his right hand, and the long seax he habitually wore hung across his loins. He looked like a man ready, even eager for the fray. In truth, he felt exhausted.

'No, Bjarki, no, I want you here inside the fortress, behind the barricades,' said Widukind. 'That will be your battle position on this day.'

'But you are forming up your battle lines *outside* the walls – I've seen your Saxons getting into their positions. We had to pack up our camp stuff and move it into the woods to keep out of their way. You are making a battle line out there, a *skjald-borg*. My people and I should be joining your wall. You need us.'

'I am not going to argue with you. Do as you are told. You will *not* join the shield wall. You will stay inside the fortress with a small reserve – your two hundred Ymirsfjord men ought to be enough. And maybe some archers. I will give you Ulrich the Bow-Master's men, too. All right? They can shoot over the walls and over our battle lines, too. Stay here inside the barricades until I call for you, understand?'

'Did my sister tell you to do this?'

Widukind did not reply. But his blue eyes shifted guiltily to one side. 'I command here, Rekkr. This is my Saxon army, not yours, nor hers, and I have given you orders. You will stay inside the barricades as a reserve. If I need you, I will call you. Now, get out of my tent. If you cannot tell, I am very busy.'

Bjarki did not move. 'Will you use that today?' he asked.

'Will I use what?' asked Widukind.

'That.' Bjarki pointed to the table with the ribbons and stones and twigs. At the back of the table, the sheathed Loki Sword was lying on a large, purple cushion. 'Will you use the sword of my ancestor Angantyr this day to guarantee that you win a great victory over the Franks?'

'That old thing? No. I have a much better, sharper sword of my own. It's a Harva blade. Superb. That old one would probably shatter at the first clash of arms. I won't need the Loki Sword's magic today. If indeed it even has any. We are going to win a great victory. I just like people to see I have that old blade with me.'

'So it is only for show, then?'

Widukind looked at Bjarki, sensing his disdain. 'How about this, Bjarki? You carry the Loki Sword today. You

266

keep it safe for me here in the fortress. Keep it safe behind the barricades. Don't try to wield it – and don't lose it.'

Widukind went over to the cushion and picked up the sword in its sheath. He handed it casually to the Rekkr. 'Now, will you please go away, Bjarki? And do just as I told you. I cannot afford to waste any more time on your nonsense.'

–

Bjarki leaned his vambraced forearms on the top of the barricade, and looked east over the torn turf that had once been a campsite. The Saxons were forming up in three main battle blocks about fifty yards away, outside the fortress, facing east, the only direction, he had been told, from which the Franks could attack the Hohenstein.

He could remember almost nothing of the night before in the command tent, save for Widukind's early comments about there being two powerful Frankish armies pitted against them. But Widukind seemed confident of victory. And Tor was equally confident that the Saxon Wolf knew what he was doing; and he trusted Tor's opinion.

He also knew, in his heart, he was in no condition to direct a battle that day. His head was pounding; he felt dizzy, sick and weak, and he could hear a low droning, a persistent buzzing sound, which might have been the bears talking in their own language in his head or it could have been a swarm of wild bees inhabiting his ears.

Thinking of bees made him think of Lili once again and their delightful honey-collecting trips in the hillside above Ymirsfjord: would he ever return there, he wondered? Would they ever collect honey again, just the two of them? Would he ever see his Little Hare again? He brought an image of her sweet face into his mind. Not clean and shining, not beautiful, but smeared with honey, dirt and wax, her bright blue eyes gleaming with mischief. He fought for her today, he knew that now. He would fight the Franks here in this unfamiliar place in the middle of the First Forest for Lili, for his Little Hare, so that she might grow up a free woman of the North. He made a silent promise to himself then, that if he lived, if he survived this coming battle, he would sail back home as soon as possible and never leave Ymirsfjord again.

He and Edith would stay put in Rogaland and watch their children grow tall – he would watch Hildar rise into manhood, and Erik too, his other son, if the boy chose to live there with them all. And when Edith felt the seductive pull of the bigger towns and their crowds and markets, when she grew bored with ordinary life in their remote home, he would give her a good ship and a crew to sail away to the Dane-Mark, or Svealand, or even to her homeland Saxony, if the Franks were expelled and it was safe once more for travellers. He might even go with her. Or not. No. Most likely not – maybe he would ask Tor to go along with Edith, to keep her safe from any dangers.

Tor worried too much, Bjarki thought. He knew he would fight today and be a part of the great victory. He also knew he would not go Galálar. He understood this deep down. As for the *seithr*, well, the bears were with him, they would guard him from its evil. He just wished he did not feel quite so sick this morning. It was not a good day to be weak.

Kynwulf was at his shoulder now, asking him something. Asking him to say something encouraging to his troops inside the Hohenstein fortress.

Bjarki turned around to look at him, and at the other *Felaki* who were gathered about the War Chief. There was Haugen Half-hand, and Black Ivar and Oddvin. There were his two young shield-bearers, Halfdan and Erik. And beyond that the stout warriors of Ymirsfjord – Sambor the Polans, Captain Mogils and Joralf the Swordman – and dozens of other folk he knew well, and beyond them in their own gathering were the archers that Widukind had put into his hand.

Yes, he should say something encouraging to them before the fight. They might have been worried by his sudden illness and collapse in Widukind's tent.

He clambered slowly up on to the wall of the fortress, using toe-holds in the layers of wood, and stood up on the top surface, looking westwards, down at his folk inside the barricade. He opened his arms wide, and smiled at them.

'We are going to fight today,' he bellowed. 'Our enemies are coming here. And we are going to fight them and we are going to slaughter them – we will slay every one of them because they are evil, and the enemies of the North.

'We will be victorious – I know this in my heart. The gods have told me so. We will win a great victory today for Saxony and for the North. But before we hazard our lives and bloody our blades there will be a little fear. Even for the bravest of you. You will feel fear. This is normal. Some of you will sense the cold hand of death on your shoulder and tremble. And to those of you who feel this, I will tell you something that my good friend Kynwulf once told me, years ago, in a place very far away from here… "Fear not death, for the hour of your doom is set, and no one can escape it!" So this is my message to you on this day, this red day. Fear not death. Your doom is already set. If it is your time to die, fight well, fight hard, and I shall meet you in the Hall of the Slain at Odin's feast. And if it is *not* your time, why – what then is there to fear?'

Then he jumped down from the wall, and called to Halfdan. 'Bring us some ale, man, let us drink heartily before we fight.' He turned to Kynwulf, and said loudly: 'You will drink with me before we slaughter the Franks, won't you, O War Chief?'

Kynwulf held up one finger. 'Listen,' he said, 'do you hear it, highness?'

Bjarki listened, straining his ears, ignoring the buzzing, and heard, on the westerly wind, the sounds of thousands of hooves pounding the earth, the chinking of metal bits and buckles, faint shouts and cries. The sound of cavalry.

# Chapter Twenty-three

*'I will never doubt you again, my lover'*

Tor and Rask lay side by side in the undergrowth about ten paces back from, and to the north of, the only track that led eastwards towards the Hohenstein. They had covered themselves with branches and leaves, and their faces were smeared with mud to hide their pallor.

If Tor twisted her head, she could see the Saxon battle line less than a mile away to her right, the rows of warriors, loosely formed for now, some even sitting on their shields, and fifty yards beyond the lines of men – and a tiny sprinkling of women – she could see the upper part of the front wall of the fortress, and the battle flag of Widukind – a grey wolf standing on hind legs on a field of blood.

It was mid-morning, and Tor had been lying here for two hours, trying not to move at all. Behind her, ten yards back, was a line of archers, hidden in the trees, and beyond them the *liths* of Ymirsfjord warriors and Nordalbians under the command of Hrothgar. She hoped he would keep them all quiet. There had been some tension between the different groups, with some of the Ymirsfjord men calling the Nordalbians traitors because they had abandoned the Saxons in the last war. Tor had shut it down quickly but it was clear the two groups did not like each other. The most important thing was that they were quiet. No arguments, no fights. She hoped Hrothgar had them under control. If the enemy became aware of them, the plan would fail.

'Mistress, what if they don't come this way – at all?' Rask whispered in a voice that was just audible, even though his mouth was inches from her ear.

Her second had voiced her own deepest fear. When she and Widukind had discussed this plan, after making love in his bed the night before, the Saxon duke had made it all sound so very simple. The enemy could only attack from the east, he repeated, they could not easily come up the steep slopes to the north, south and west. Her mind lingered on the glib word 'easily'. It would not be impossible for the infantry under Count Thierry to fight their way up the slopes, it could be done, at a high cost in Frankish blood, and if that were combined with a cavalry attack from the east, their crab-claw attack would crush the Saxons like a ripe blackberry between two rocks.

'General Adalgis is eager for glory – he is arrogant, over-confident – and he does not want to share his victory with Thierry,' Widukind had said to her. 'If we offer him a nice, juicy Saxon target outside our own fortification, unprotected, apparently weak and helpless – he will take the bait, I'm sure of it.'

Widukind was sure of it, thought Tor. But maybe, just maybe, the Saxon Wolf was the over-confident one today.

'If they are not here by noon,' Tor whispered back to Rask, 'I will send you out to find them. Just you, for a discreet look. Head to Hohe Egge and…'

Tor stopped. There was a rumbling sound, and the noise of clinking metal, tinny in the distance. *I will never doubt you again, my lover*, thought Tor.

The noise became louder and resolved into the thudding of hooves and the chink of iron bits and stirrups and other metallic cavalry gear. Right in front of Tor's eyes, a thick line of Black Cloak cavalry appeared, Karolus's famous *Scholares*, his finest horse-borne troops. And they stretched right across the track to the cliffs beyond.

They halted at a signal from one of the men in the centre of the front rank, and sat on their snorting black horses, as the rest of the *cabellarii* came to a halt behind them. *Of all places to stop*, Tor thought. *Right in front of my hidey hole.*

There were now hundreds of Black Cloak cavalry a stone's throw from Tor's nose, and when she turned her head very slightly, very slowly to the left, she could see hundreds of troops coming up on the halted leaders' position. She could clearly make out the accoutrement of the rigs of the stationary horsemen, just a dozen yards away – the two Frankish swords, one long, one short, the pair of javelins they carried in a tall bucket holster on the right side, beside the horse's withers. They wore shiny scale-mail, and calf-high leather boots, and steel helmets polished to a gleam, with a thick steel ridge running down the centre, fore and aft, to give their head-protectors extra strength, and on a few of them to provide mounting for an officer's plume.

Some of the *cabellarii* carried shields, iron-rimmed with a sharp pointed iron boss. And of course, the famous black cloak that was their badge, a heavy garment flowed down from their shoulders and spread over their horses' rumps.

Rask touched her arm gently, and she slowly turned and looked at him. He raised his eyebrows in an obvious question – should we spring the ambush?

And she, again very, very slowly, shook her head. No. Not yet.

There were too many here to attack. She had five hundred warriors with her, and there must have been two thousand cavalry in front of her. Besides, she had specific instructions from Widukind – and she intended to follow them.

'Do not hinder their attack,' he had said. 'We *want* them to attack us. Your task is to chew up the rear of the column, Tor, then come in to join us in defeating the main force at the Hohenstein. Most importantly, do not disrupt their attack!'

The man in the centre of the front rank was drinking from a flask. He was a tall man, bare-headed, with a receding hairline and rather large ears. His fine armoured coat had some of the steel scales replaced with golden ones which caught the light and made him stand out from the rest. Beside him, on his left, was a lieutenant, a stunted, barrel-chested dark fellow, carrying a tall flag with the golden man's personal sigil, three yellow birds on a blue background, and on his other side – on the big-eared man's right – Tor was more than a little surprised to see Bishop Livinus, in scale-mail, purple, scarlet and gold cloak and wearing a shining steel helm. He was riding a magnificent bay stallion. And the brown horse marked him out as different. All the Black Cloaks rode black horses. Widukind had mentioned that Karolus's chancellor and chaplain had joined up with the Black Cloak commander – what was his name? Adalgis – but it had slipped her mind. She had not been thinking about individuals, just thinking of the enemy as a mass of hated Franks, fodder for her bow and blades.

But here was Bishop Livinus, right in front of her, a man she loathed more than any other in the Middle-Realm: the man who was trying to infect the North with his filthy religion, buying and bullying folk to get his way, the so-called man of God, who had imprisoned her twice, tricked and humiliated her and Bjarki – and with whom she had never had a proper reckoning. Today he was on the field of battle. Today there *would* be a reckoning, if Tor had anything to do with it. For a brief, reckless moment, she even considered springing the trap early. It would catch Bishop Livinus in its jaws. She could go out there and kill him now, if only she were willing to give the order. But that would surely spoil everything. She bit her lip, and did not move. Blood trickled over her chin.

The big-eared man offered his wine flask to Livinus, who shook his head. All three men were looking intently at the Saxon lines a mile away, which Tor noted were now hurriedly coming into formation, joining their shields together to make one huge wall – a *skjald-borg* – in front of the fortress, a wall that was a good three hundred paces long and five men deep, and which stretched from one steep slope in the north to another in the south, right across the end of the narrow spur of land in front of the Hohenstein fortress. There must be three thousand shields in the Saxon formations, Tor guessed, the bulk of Widukind's troops. And if the Frankish cavalry could break that shield wall, then the day was surely lost – indeed, Widukind's whole campaign was finished. The Saxon cause would be dead, along with thousands of butchered Saxon warriors.

Widukind *must* know what he was doing.

'I urge you to proceed with caution, my lord,' said Bishop Livinus. He was speaking to the man with the golden scales – Adalgis – who was drinking again from his flask. 'This smells wrong to me. Why would they be *outside* the fort?'

'Because they are Saxons, they are pagans and, therefore, they are stupid,' said Adalgis. 'They were foolish enough to rebel against King Karolus. And now they are gathered before me, ready to be crushed like ants under my boot.'

'I have spent much time in pagan halls, trying to bring the love of Christ to their benighted lands,' said Livinus, 'and while they are stubborn in their idolatrous beliefs, and clearly wrong, I would not say they were particularly stupid.'

'There are the Saxon *rebels*, my lord bishop,' said Adalgis, 'peasant scum. We fight with Almighty God on our side. We will ride them into the dust.'

'Perhaps it might be better to wait for Thierry to come up,' said Livinus. 'If he were to attack up that hill and engage the enemy from the south at…'

'That would take another day, maybe two. There are the enemy, my lord bishop. *There!* If you do not wish to fight the enemy, why did you join my force? If you wish to wait for Count Thierry, go back down into the valley and join him. But my men will attack the enemy, scatter them, and the victory will be mine – and mine alone.'

'I did not say I would not fight today, only that…' Livinus began.

But Adalgis had already stopped listening to him. He turned to the stunted, barrel-chested standard bearer and said, 'Sound the trumpet, Gallo – the order for a general advance. On my signal, we charge! I shall ride these rebels into the earth and teach them a lesson they will not soon forget. Let us go forwards!'

Trumpets squealed, the brash sound rippling back over the dark mounted ranks. Orders, too, were barked all the way down the lines of horsemen. And the whole jingling, leather-creaking mass of Black Cloak cavalry began to move off. And Bishop Livinus was swept forwards with them, and out of Tor's sight.

Tor felt a touch on her arm again, and looked round again at Rask.

'Now?' he mouthed.

'Wait, man!' she whispered back crossly.

It took a painful amount of time for most of the *Scholares* under Adalgis's command to trot past their hiding place but, finally, when she reckoned the rearmost ranks of the Black Cloak column were at hand, Tor jumped to her feet.

'Archers!' she shouted. She had her own strung bow already in her hand, and she plucked a shaft from her quiver, nocked it to the cord, drew and loosed.

Tor's arrow thwacked into the ribs of a passing *cabellarius* at a distance of only twelve paces, punching him right out of the saddle simply with the force of the strike and tumbling the mortally wounded trooper to the ground.

Around her the undergrowth was alive with rustling, as Saxons popped up from their concealment with cries of wild excitement and began shooting their deadly arrows at the last ranks of the passing Franks. Tor had timed it perfectly – the last few hundred *Scholares* had been level with her position when she sprung the ambush, and a hundred of her most experienced bowmen were now standing on either side of her on the fringes of the thick forest, showering the enemy with a lethal hail of shafts.

The arrows flitted out of the trees, with a continuous zip and twang of strings, and sliced horizontally into the enemy tail like a huge, invisible scythe. The black-clad warriors on gleaming, jet-coloured horses were skewered and punctured, their flesh torn, their skin ripped and lacerated by the flying iron arrowheads, even their bones snapped. It was sheer bloody carnage, the black horses mad with pain and fear, bucking, leaping, neighing in terror, trying to buck off their riders, amid a lethal hail of shafts.

The air seemed filled with hissing arrows, shouts of anger and raw screams of fresh pain. Tor saw one Frank take a shaft to the side of his head that went straight through his right cheek and out of the other through the left one. Some men were already stuck with dozens of arrows like enormous hedgehogs, although some shafts, if striking obliquely, bounced off their excellent scale armour and skittered away into the road. Other Black Cloaks were clearly dead and being dragged along the road, one foot stuck in a stirrup, by a pain-maddened galloping mount. One fellow with a bleeding face, his shield struck with five arrows, took a shaft through his thigh that pinned his leg to the saddle. He went down yelling something about God's mercy.

A final Saxon arrow pierced his throat and silenced him for ever.

The Black Cloaks had been surprised by Tor's ambush, with three dozen killed in a few heartbeats. But they rallied soon and quickly realised what was happening. Once they knew the situation, they were swift to organise a counterattack. An officer with a black plume on his helm was shouting for his horsemen to form a line, and charge straight into the trees. To kill these treacherous

Saxon bastards regardless of the cost. Tor took her time and calmly put an arrow right through the centre of his forehead, crunching the iron point deep into his skull under the helmet rim. But the Frankish counterattack line was still swiftly forming up in the road, the *cabellarii* facing their foes – a dozen men, now twenty, now twenty-five, thirty of them ready, eager to fight.

The Franks were getting ready to charge the enemy and trample the line of archers in the trees into bloody ruin. Tor plucked another arrow from her quiver, drew and loosed, striking a big man at the end of the line, a fellow who was shouting and waving one arm in the air. The shaft caught him in his belly and he doubled over, grunting. But the cavalry line was moving, all their bright swords drawn, cantering across the road at the line of archers half-hidden in the trees.

Tor was a step ahead. 'Ymirsfjord!' she yelled, momentarily forgetting the existence of the Nordalbians. 'Ymirsfjord! Charge them! Take them now!'

The forest wall erupted with men on foot. Four hundred warriors came roaring out of the trees behind the line of archers, led by a boldly yelling Hrothgar, and they swarmed out towards the remaining enemy horsemen. The two lines crashed into each other on the verges of the road into a scrum of shouting men, chopping blades and neighing horses. Tor saw Hrothgar almost immediately felled by a Frankish swooping blade, but then saw him rise again, bloody but still shouting out orders, and another Frankish rider chop his sword into the back of the Nordalbian's head.

He dropped like a stone. Tor plucked a last arrow, nocked and loosed it at the rider who had killed Hrothgar – the shaft smacking into his back, high up and to the right of his spine. The rider spurred away, the shaft still stuck in his shoulder blade.

Beside her, Rask threw aside his bow, and drew his short sword. He yelled, 'Odiiiinnnn!' and charged out of the trees along with the rest of them.

Tor felt giddy with battle rage, the blood singing in her veins. She shouted, 'Y… mirs… fjord!' and, following Rask's example, discarded her bow, grabbed a spear and hurled herself into the middle of the boil of chaos on the road.

She ran straight at the nearest Black Cloak rider, a spear in her right hand, a sword in her left, her shield completely forgotten, discarded in the thick weeds by her hiding place. She hurled the spear as hard as she could at the Frank, the iron point catching him under the right armpit, and plunging deeply into his torso. But a furious horseman rode at her and she had to block his strike with her own blade. Another rider slashed wildly at her head and she ducked. There were Ymirsfjord warriors all around her, and Nordalbians too, three or four to each Frankish horseman, and in a matter of only a few moments, the enemy were all dragged from their mounts and swiftly put to the sword, the savage Saxons hacking into their torn corpses long after they were dead.

Yet some of the foes still fought on savagely: she saw one Black Cloak hack down and split the leather-covered skull of a Nordalbian with a single blow, then ride on and slice open another Saxon's shoulder. But the rest of the Franks were soon overwhelmed. Some now were galloping madly back down the road the way they came. A few Black Cloaks tried to escape down the steep slope to the Long Pine Brook, their horses sliding on their rumps in clouds of dust on the loose scree.

A line of a dozen archers formed up on the lip of the slope and showered them with jeers and lethal arrows as they fled in panic from the battlefield.

There were dead and dying littering the road, and Tor almost tripped over a badly wounded horse, kicking its hooves in agony. She stepped back from the poor beast and looked west, towards the massive Saxon *skjald-borg*, and saw that the Black Cloaks had not halted their full-on assault. They were still thundering heedlessly towards the wall of shields at the full gallop. A huge black mass of men and horses. She could feel the ground shaking under her boots even at this distance. The first black block of cavalry, a *scara* of some three hundred riders, was a mere seventy yards from the Saxon battle lines. Then the Franks unleashed their favoured tactic, their most lethal manoeuvre, in a display of prowess that astonished even Tor's war-wearied eyes.

At the full gallop, as hundreds of Black Cloak horsemen were bearing down on the thick Saxon wall, each Frank in the first squadron managed to pluck a javelin from the holster on his horse's withers, draw his right arm back and launch the spear high in the air – with no visible slackening of speed at all – hurtling the lethal missile towards the waiting line of enemy shields.

Hundreds of javelins rose in the blue sky, like a vast flock of slender black birds, or a rain of thunderbolts, and their needle-tipped shafts soared, then descended on the packed ranks of Saxon warriors. The effect was immediate and devastating. Scores of Saxons in the front three rows of the shield wall fell to their knees, skewered by the rain of spears. Dozens of men fell out of the line, some staggering sideways with spears sticking from their chests or shoulders. One man had a slim lance right through his eye socket and out the back of his head, and fell to his knees clawing at the long, embedded weapon. Two Saxon men were transfixed by the same javelin, falling together out of the lines like yoked oxen.

Even more astonishingly, the foremost Franks managed to repeat the manoeuvre, just moments before they crashed into the Saxon wall. A second wave of death floated up high and swooped down the shield line, and many dozens more good Saxon men were instantly felled by the falling Frankish bolts.

There were gaps in the *skjald-borg* now, spaces where one or two warriors had stood before being struck down, which their comrades shuffled in to fill.

But the heavy cavalry were upon them, the Franks driving their black muscular war-horses into the ragged holes in the Saxon wall, their bright swords, drawn from the scabbards, rising and falling, hacking down at Saxon heads, and coming back bloody. Slowly widening the gaps and shoving their mounts further into the mass.

The second *scara* of Frankish cavalry was hard on their heels. Another three hundred men. They, too, plucked out their javelins, and hurled them over the heads of the struggling melee at the face of the Saxon wall. Tor could see the whole *skjald-borg* moving, swaying back and forth as the second mass of Black Cloaks hit them. Then, as the third *scara* came galloping in, javelins flying, she saw that the wall was wavering; holes, then channels were forming, the whole structure was coming apart, dissolving under the massive Frankish assault. Yet more black-clad riders were galloping in to join the slaughter. The heavy horses' bodies crashing into the thin, wavering line of infantry. And another *scara*, another cloud of flying javelins. Another score of Saxons dead. Still more Franks coming after them, crowding in to crush the Saxon foe.

Tor yelled out: 'To me, Ymirsfjord. Nordalbians, to me. Archers, too!'

When Rask popped up by her side, a spatter of blood across his eager little face, Tor said to him: 'We must gather everyone and support our folk. There!'

She pointed at the eastern end of the spur. 'We have to try to aid them.'

# Chapter Twenty-four

*Nothing in his heart but silence*

Bjarki slipped his forearm through the leather strap, and put his hand into the padded boss of his shield. He gripped the iron bar that formed the handle, and immediately felt a strange sensation, a kind of tingling feeling that started in his fingers and began to spread slowly up his left arm. The touch of the iron also seemed to make the buzzing in his ears worse. He ignored his petty problems, hefted the heavy shield, gripped his Dane axe with his right hand and went forwards to the barricade, with Kynwulf beside him and Erik and Halfdan, both garbed for war in leather armour and helms, shields in their left hands, spears in their right, dutifully following their lord.

Bjarki looked out over the field from behind the chest-high barricade and saw in the distance a wall of black, with glints of silver, and the occasional flapping flag, moving towards them. Cavalry. *Cabellarii.*

The Franks were riding in to do battle with their foes.

He spotted Widukind in the centre of the Saxon line, shouting orders and forming his warriors into their battle ranks, shields overlapping, each wall-soldier touching shoulders with the next. On the left Jarl Brun, with his core of Angrians, was doing the same, with young Jarl Guthrum beside him. On the right Jarl Hessi was standing out in front of his wing, haranguing them about duty and honour and proving themselves to be the heroes he knew they truly were. His fierce easterners were already formed, tight-packed and ready, and as Bjarki watched, Hessi gave one final exhortation – 'Remember, men, the gods are watching us. Make them respect you this day!' – and shoved his way into the front ranks in the centre of his people.

The three blocks of formed warriors, each one nearly a thousand strong, now shuffled towards each other and linked up their shields to form one massive unbroken wall that stretched, north to south, from one side of the Hohenstein spur to the other. A *skjald-borg* five men deep, three hundred paces long with impassable slopes on either flank. Bjarki had never seen a wall like it.

'Highness,' said Kynwulf, and when Bjarki looked at him he jerked his head behind them, and when the Rekkr turned he saw that a small, balding man dressed in a plain tunic and wearing no armour was standing staring at him.

'Yes?' said Bjarki.

'Uh, you are the Rekkr?' said the man. 'The one they call the Bloodhand?'

'That's me,' said Bjarki. His left arm felt very hot, as if it was burning.

'I'm Ulrich the Bow-Master,' the bald fellow said. 'Widukind said I should look to you for my battle orders, when the time came.'

'How many archers do you have?' asked Bjarki, a little unnecessarily, since he could clearly see a group of men standing in the centre of the fortress, most of them clutching long bows and with full quivers hanging at their waists.

'Seventy-four,' said Ulrich. 'Seventy-five including me.'

'What is the greatest distance you can shoot?'

'About two hundred paces.'

Bjarki looked out over the barricade at the long battle-field. He measured the distance by eye and reckoned that two hundred paces was just about where a large, lopsided pine stood, on the north side of the road at the edge of the forest.

'Form a single line behind me, along here, and you shoot – at your longest range, mind – when I give the signal. Stop loosing only if we make a sally, or if you think you are in danger of hitting our own people, you understand me?'

'Yes, lord,' said Ulrich.

Bjarki turned back to the field. The cavalry had leapt closer, the enemy were six hundred paces away, and had increased the horses' gait to a canter.

He looked back at the archers now forming their line, drawing arrows from quivers and examining them for straightness. His left arm was buzzing, and felt sore and swollen; but apart from that, he felt alert, bright-eyed, ready to fight.

The weakness he had felt that morning seemed to have gone: the dizziness, the buzzing sounds in his ears, the tiredness too, and had been replaced by a sense of excitement, a flow of joy like strong mead running through his veins. He looked inside his heart and said: 'Are you there, Mochta? You there, Garm?'

There was no reply.

The Franks were nearly at the lopsided pine. He heard Widukind's voice bellowing from the centre of the shield wall, but it echoed all over the field: 'Stand firm for

Saxony, my friends, stand fast here for your wives and lovers, for your children, stand strong and we shall have our victory!'

A cheer broke out along the whole Saxon battle line. 'Wi... du... kind,' they all shouted, 'Wi... du... kind, Wi... du... kind!'

Bjarki turned his head. 'Ulrich,' he said. The man looked at him attentively. Bjarki glanced back at the field, counted to three, and said: 'You may begin...'

The thunder of the hooves was growing louder; Bjarki could make out the faces of the oncoming riders, the snarls of rage, or gritted teeth of terror. By Thor, was that Bishop Livinus, on the left, in the front rank? Could it be him?

A flight of arrows rose gracefully into the air and fell like dark rain upon the charging Franks, and a dozen saddles were suddenly empty. One horse, arrow-struck, went mad and, turning sharply left, charged over the edge of the slope, disappearing with his Black Cloak rider frantically hauling back on his reins. And, almost as if in response to this opening barrage of arrows, the front ranks of Frankish cavalry reached for javelins, drew back their arms and hurled their missiles.

The bad time began.

The arrows of Ulrich's men and the Frankish javelins crossed in the air but it was the missiles' effect on the Saxon *skjald-borg* that occupied all of Bjarki's vision: the hail of javelins tore into the mass of Saxons, striking scores of them, and moments later another hail of bolts smashed into their ranks. Bjarki could see a dozen wounded men, leaning on their friends, and another score fallen to the lethal rain of spears and, much, much worse, spaces were immediately beginning to appear in the ranks. The first rank of *cabellarii* struck, the horsemen piling into the weakened line of shields. More gaps were created. Now there were Black Cloaks in and among the Saxon shields, hacking down on both sides, widening the gaps into which more of their comrades forced their snorting, frightened black horses.

Widukind was shouting – yelling in truth – telling his men to push, push hard, push the enemy out of the Saxon ranks, to force the horsemen back, but then a second *scara* of Franks crashed into the face of the shields. Some Franks were launching javelins from just yards away; some thrusting these spears into Saxon faces.

A third squadron of Franks, another three hundred men, charged the Saxon line on the right. Javelins were hurled, swords drawn, and the always-unequal fight began between mounted man and the foot soldier beneath his blade.

The whole centre of the Saxon line was now a jumbled melee, all the careful linked structure was gone. Saxons edged backwards, frightened men taking one pace to the rear and losing shield-contact with their comrades. The wall was disintegrating. It had been astonishingly quick, the collapse.

Karolus's horsemen chopped into the Saxon ranks with a brutal efficiency and scant thought for their own safety, hacking down foot men left and right, then spurring over their corpses to slice into the next file. The heavy stink of hot blood and fresh ordure filled the air, so thick it was almost visible. Bjarki caught a glimpse through the struggling, shifting, shouting crowds of Bishop Livinus, pounding at a cowering Saxon's helmet with a war mace, a cruel spiked club. Widukind, on the right, was duelling with a man on a huge black horse. The Saxon Wolf blocked a savage blow and stabbed the Frank through the left thigh and he screamed and pulled his horse away. Yet more and more Franks were piling in, showering javelins, jumping their horses over fallen Saxons.

The jarls on either wing of the Saxon line were shouting for their men to close up, close up. But the centre was gone now, destroyed. Only one thin, wavering line of shields remained where there had been five ranks of linked warriors. Where they had stood was a crowd of milling Black Cloaks, crawling wounded, both Frank and Saxon, and splayed everywhere, the reeking corpses of men and beasts.

Bjarki heard a dark voice inside his heart: 'You called me, man-child?'

'You called me too, Bear-brother,' said a lighter one. 'You desire our aid?'

A fresh Frankish cavalry squadron crashed into the left wing of the Saxon line, hammering Jarl Brun's men with their javelin barrage, once, twice, then barging their big horses into the ranks. The entire left wing began to tremble and fray; Bjarki saw one man on the very end running back towards the fortress. The remains of the *skjald-borg* seemed to creak and cringe before the relent-less *cabellarii* onslaught. As the horsemen charged in once more, blocks of Saxons were splintering off, splitting apart the once-tight, solid formation. Bjarki could hear several men screaming in agony, all their voices mingling. One man was singing a traditional Saxon war song. Someone else howled.

'Yes, my *gandir*,' said Bjarki, 'I do desire your help.'

He started to hum, the ancient tune of summoning, and over the vibration of his own vocal cords he seemed to hear Garm repeating something he had said to Bjarki in his dream: 'Fear not *seithr*, Bear-brother, for while we are with you, we will shield you from its evil; when we walk beside you in friendship, you are protected.'

He shook the big shield loose from the loop on his left arm, still humming his tune, and taking the heavy, round wooden disc on both hands, he hurled it spinning high over the barricades and out towards the bloody melee beyond.

'Yes, my *gandir*,' repeated Bjarki. 'Come to me. I now require your aid.'

Then everything changed.

–

As quickly as she could, Tor gathered her people together into a Boar's Snout: she retrieved her shield and took the point with Rask, and the Ymirsfjord men, wholly familiar with this battle formation, lined up on her flanks in a V-shape. The Nordalbians soon grasped what she wanted, and filed into place. In the centre of the V she placed the lightly armoured archers, who needed the most protection, and could shoot over the heads of the outer warriors. Then they slowly began to advance, east, towards the Hohenstein.

They tramped forwards, trying to keep together as best they could, some four hundred warriors of the North – for Tor had simply left the wounded strewn on the road behind them to care for themselves as best they could, and the dead did not care any longer what she did. They made good progress and soon the rearmost ranks of the Frankish force were a few hundred paces away. There she stopped, and reformed the Boar's Snout. 'Keep it tight, lads – and always keep it going forwards,' she yelled.

The rearmost squadron of Black Cloak *cabellarii*, waiting for their turn to attack the crumbling Saxon lines, were almost caught unawares. Almost.

Two hundred paces out, one of them turning to look behind, gave a shout of alarm and, instantly, the rearmost squadron was wheeling, and reforming, and a heartbeat later, three hundred *Scholares* were spurring hard towards them.

'Shields and spears!' shouted Tor, and she demonstrated by bringing her shield up to meet the rim of her helm. On her right, Rask, whose shield was behind her right shoulder, cocked his spear and clamped it under his elbow, and the man behind him did the same. On the right flank the Boar's Snout was an impenetrable line of spears, on the left, an invincible wall of linked shields. And on they marched, tramping forwards, straight forwards into the seething battle in a tight formation shaped just like a killing arrowhead, aimed straight towards the mass of swift galloping Franks.

A shower of javelins rattled against the shields, most bouncing right off, or embedding themselves in the wood, but the cries of pain from the centre of the Boar's Snout indicated that some of the lightly armoured archers had been struck. Then the horsemen were on them. Thudding down the flanks of the swift-moving formation slashing, with their swords at their raised shields and spears, clanging helms, but doing little damage.

'Keep it tight, keep going forwards!' yelled Tor. 'Just keep going!' She could see the next rank of horsemen ahead of her. They, too, were now looking over their shoulders, back towards the rear attack. Beyond them were the Saxon shattered lines, and the shapeless mess of hundreds of struggling men, a vast heaving scrum of blades and blood, and terrified horses and screaming enemies battering each other to death.

'Keep going forwards!' Tor could see the black-cloaked horsemen parting in front of her. A rider swooped in and thwacked the face of her shield before passing on down the line. The Boar's Snout forged on straight in the midst of a boiling sea of horseflesh. One rider kicked at Tor's helmet with his boot and she felt something else clang dizzyingly against her helm. But on they all went.

Nearly there. Tor could see that the centre of the Saxon line was gone and the once monolithic shield wall had been cloven in two. Widukind was on the left, with Jarl Hessi and a ring of several hundred shields; she recognised it as a traditional hedgehog configuration, all the spears outwards. A pack of Black Cloaks were gathering, ready for another charge at them, hoping to overwhelm this last redoubt.

Jarl Brun on Tor's right was in a confused mess of Black Cloaks, his men all scattered, each individual fighting for his life. Jarl Guthrum, with a bloody face, was still yelling defiance at the Franks. A javelin took him in the dead centre of his chest and he fell to his knees. The Nordalbians around their brave young jarl gave a huge shout and surged forwards. But the Franks clearly had the upper hand now; the cavalry using their height advantage to rain killing blows down on the Saxons. And beyond them, Tor could see the gates of the Hohenstein fortress, slowly opening – why where they opening? Why?

The gates were being dragged apart and there – there was Bjarki, tall and blond and red-faced and draped in his raggedy yellowing bearskin. He charged. He surged out of the fortress at the head of a large screaming mob of Ymirsfjord warriors, his long-handled Dane axe grasped in both hands, his features horribly contorted, the pure rage coming off him almost visibly, like steam off a boiling kettle. He was filled to the brim with the vast, majestic power of his two *gandir*.

—

The stinging soreness in Bjarki's left arm faded to nothing and he experienced a sudden feeling of complete emptiness, as if he were a dry jug waiting to be filled with ale. He felt icy cold, freezing all over his body, down to his bones; he heard the sound of rushing water in his ears, loud like the noise of a tumbling waterfall. He found he was still humming, deep in his throat, that simple four-note tune he knew so well. His vision became blurred, then tinged with red, then suddenly very, very sharp.

Then it came, his *gandir* power, a tumbling, pouring rush, roaring through his veins and belly and filling all his limbs with a delicious icy fire. He could hear the sounds of the two bears growling somewhere deep in his chest. He felt buoyant, weightless, but stronger than a mountain troll, faster than a hunting hawk, fiercer than a she-weasel, so powerful he could leap up and touch the sun.

With the last drop of his humanity, he looked over at Erik and Halfdan through his blood-tinged eyes and growled. 'Follow me. But... stay... back.'

Erik said: 'Yes, lord.' Halfdan nodded, looking terrified, then the heir to the Dane-Mark made a very curious gesture with his right hand. He quickly touched his forehead, then his heart, then his right shoulder, and then his left.

Bjarki turned to Kynwulf. 'Open... the... gates.'

And that was all the speech he had in him.

He roared out of the gates at the head of the Ymirsfjord men, Kynwulf beside him, Halfdan and Erik just behind the War Chief. And they piled into the mass of struggling men on the left wing of the shattered shield wall around the fallen body of Jarl Guthrum and his furiously battling Nordalbian followers.

Bjarki seemed to move at the speed of lightning, hacking effortlessly through the Frankish mounted ranks with his long Dane axe. He sliced the living heads from their war-horses with a single blow of his blade, he reached up with the long-handled weapon to slash and hack and slice and eviscerate the terrified enemy horsemen. He smashed away everything in his path and the response from the battered Angrians and Nordalbians of that part of their shattered *skjald-borg* was a howl of approval.

With the Ymirfsjord men in a pack behind him he wiped the Frankish cavalry from the field, with all the Saxons surging forwards along with him.

A javelin took Bjarki in the side, punching through his mail and snapping two ribs, but he merely growled and snatched it out from his own flesh and hurled it at a passing rider, burying the bloody point deep in his back.

He charged into a knot of Frankish horsemen, his axe swinging, the gore flying like a summer rainstorm. A *cabellarius* hacked at Bjarki from the left, a mighty blow that thudded against his excellent mail. Bjarki just snarled, turned, and cut the horseman in half at the waist in his saddle.

A pair of Black Cloak riders targeted him, both coming in at the same time, their long swords swinging. Bjarki chopped the forelegs from the nearest horse and, as it fell, his backswing took the head off its rider. The second horseman hacked at Bjarki's blond head, met the wooden shaft of the Dane axe and severed it. The blade tumbled to the earth and, before he could withdraw, Bjarki dropped the shaft and leapt up at him like some kind of giant ape, and was tearing at his face with his bare hands, ripping at his eyes with his nails, and then he began biting his neck, tearing out the sinews and veins in his throat with his snapping teeth. The man's screams bubbled through his blood-filled windpipe. The Rekkr lifted the fellow out from the saddle and threw him into the middle of the baying Saxon crowd, where he was hacked apart in moments.

Now, the jubilant men of the *skjald-borg* were all chanting his famous by-name, 'Blood… hand, Blood… hand, Blood… hand!'

Bjarki stood tall on the saddle of the terrified, galloping horse, his balance on the moving animal a thing of wonder all by itself. He was covered in gore and filth and dripping from half a dozen wounds. But he was grinning madly. He pulled the Loki Sword from the scabbard on his belt and acknowledged the cheers of the Saxon warriors below him, lifting his sword hand and his empty left both high up in the air.

The frightened horse raced away from the ruins of the shield wall, from the scattered blocks of Saxons, from the mess of bloody and broken bodies, and back towards the mass of Franks, now regrouping fifty yards back from the carnage. Some of the *cabellarii* were fresh, those who had still not yet been committed to the fight.

The maddened horse instinctively ran back to its own kind, bearing Bjarki, wobbling but upright on the saddle, into the very centre of his foes. The ancient blade seemed to glow in the sunlight, the jewel in the pommel flashing sparks of violet fire, and the Fire Born warrior was engulfed by the dark tide of his foes.

The Saxons, all who could, with one wild animal roar, surged in after him.

# Chapter Twenty-five

*The* coup de grâce

Tor ripped her eyes off her brother as he slashed and snarled through the mass of Franks like a blood-spraying whirlwind; she had enough troubles of her own without worrying about him. The Black Cloaks were all around her, and she was taking pounding blows on shield and helm from a dozen Frankish swords. She felt a crushing blow on her shoulder and saw blood start oozing from the torn links of mail. Beside her Rask gave a strangled cry and dropped away, and when she looked round, she saw him on the ground looking up at her with a gory slash across his face. She reached down with her right hand and seized a bunch of his mail coat at the chest and hauled him upright with a surge of strength, but the cohesion of the Boar's Snout had been lost. The V-shape had flattened into a line as the men of Ymirsfjord battled on.

'Forwards,' she shouted, drawing her sword. 'Keep going. To Widukind! To the hedgehog. We must link up with the Saxon Wolf!'

She batted a riderless horse out of her way with a smack from the flat of her blade on its rump and saw that, only fifty yards ahead of her, a small part of the battlefield was clear of enemies, and the grim ring of spears and shields, three men deep, that was Widukind's mighty hedgehog stood staunch against the foe.

Her lover was looking right at her, his face pale but determined, and there was Jarl Hessi beside him, looking furious. She guessed that some eight hundred Saxon warriors were still under their firm control in a tight, steel-point-bristling formation.

'Follow me,' she yelled, and with all the men of her Boar's Snout who could still run she sprinted towards Widukind. The ranks of the hedgehog opened like a massive door, dozens of men moving aside with the grace of trained dancers, and she and hundreds of her running people flooded gratefully inside.

A few heartbeats later and she was in Widukind's arms, wincing as he squeezed her wounded shoulder. He kissed her hard and she kissed him back, careless of what any disapproving eye might see. She had thought she was free of her feelings for him. But, at the sight of Widukind, hale and whole, they all came flooding back. And now she was weeping just because he was alive.

'No time for that, Tor,' said the Saxon Wolf, holding her out at arm's length, but smiling at her. 'The battle hangs in the balance. Can you still fight?'

Tor nodded and cuffed at her snotty nose with her hard, mailed sleeve.

Widukind strode to the front of the hedgehog and looked out at the enemy ranks. Tor came forwards and joined him, standing at his side and looking out over the heads of a triple line of spearmen with locked shields, front rank kneeling, second and third ranks standing. The field of battle was thickly strewn with dead and wounded, men and horses, all about them. She could clearly hear the piteous cries of the wounded, and smell the stink of shit, piss and curdled fear. Over on the left, the battle still raged, a moiling scrum of warriors waving blades, as Saxon and Franks still battled each other, the mass moving back and forth like a stormy sea. Somewhere in that bloody stew of humanity was Bjarki – if indeed he still lived. And she felt another huge wave of emotion roll through her at that thought. She took hold of herself, cursing. Directly ahead of her, the ranks of Frankish horsemen were formed for another charge, seventy yards away, but their ranks were far thinner than she expected, only a couple of hundred of them left, she thought, and a short, ugly man, some kind of Frankish leader was haranguing the ranks of riders from his saddle.

'Who is that officer?' she asked. 'The dark-haired fellow out in front?'

'He is called Worad. A commander – he is Count of the Palace, I'm told.'

'The what?'

'Not important. I think they are ready to break, what say you, Tor?'

Tor looked at the ragged lines of horsemen. They looked frightened, pale, some were blood-spattered, some were wounded, they were very far from the neat ranks of men who had ridden past her hiding place less than an hour ago. They looked with despairing eyes at Worad, the count of something, who was still shouting at them.

Yes, she thought. Oh yes, they were ready to break.

They unfurled the hedgehog into a phalanx, a horizontal bar of shields and spears, opening the wings of warriors on either side of Widukind, with the Ymirsfjord folk behind the hard men from Eastphalia, Angria and Nordalbia.

They made three straight ranks across seventy paces of ground, shields tightly linked, spears extended – and Tor had never been so proud of her own people. Then, at a shout of command from Widukind, they began to advance against the Franks in a slow, measured tramp. Shields high, spears out front, a walking wall of wood and steel. Arrows started to fall on the enemy horsemen and Tor, snatching a glance behind her, saw a body of archers, who had emerged from the fortress, begin showering the enemy with their lethal shafts.

They sang 'The Death Song of Tiw' as they walked, a miserable, ancient dirge, but well suited for the slow march of attacking warriors, hitting each beat with the thump of their boots, and once they got within thirty paces of the shifting, uneasy line of horsemen, Widukind yelled out, 'Saxons, now, for the honour of our homeland – charge!'

And they rushed at the enemy as fast as their tired legs would carry them.

To Tor's relief, she saw several horsemen on the extreme right of the Frankish line turn their horses and ride away, galloping eastwards back down the spur. Count Worad was shouting something, trying to halt their flight, but more and more of the exhausted, arrow-stricken Franks had decided that they had had enough, pulled their horses' heads around and ran. Soon the entire force of *cabellarii* was cantering away, some recklessly guiding their horses to the right, southwards down the steep wooded slopes towards the Weser Valley. And Worad went along with them, his black mare slipping and sliding on the loose earth, still shouting commands to his beaten cavalry.

Yet Widukind had not finished his advance. 'Halt!' he shouted. 'Left turn.' Then, 'We will sweep them away, too!' He was pointing left, towards the boiling mass of battling Saxons and Franks, many of whom were now unhorsed.

'Left turn!' the Saxon Wolf yelled, and those who heard him, those men who had tasted victory, obeyed, turned and charged afresh into the wild melee.

Tor ran beside Widukind, on his left side – she had lost Rask somewhere but there were a dozen Ymirsfjord warriors nearby. She was looking for Bjarki.

Then she saw him. He was badly wounded, on his knees, his bare head bowed, bloody, exhausted, in the centre of a ring of Franks on foot, with Bishop Livinus standing over him, a mace held in both hands, spikes filthy with blood and flesh. Livinus lifted his mace, preparing to give Bjarki the *coup de grâce*.

–

Bjarki felt as if he was truly flying. He rode the frightened horse effortlessly, upright on top of the saddle, into a sea of black-clad enemies. And he embraced them all. He leapt from the saddle, a two-footed bound, and crashed into a horseman with large ears and a haughty expression, knocking him right out of his seat and sending them both sprawling to the turf. Bjarki bounced up, picked up the Loki Sword, which he had dropped, and looked over at the funny-looking fellow. He was shouting, 'Kill him – kill the demon!' to his comrades.

Big-ears looked familiar, Bjarki thought, he had seen this one before. A young Black Cloak with a spear came running at him and the Rekkr slipped sideways to avoid the lunging point and hacked the Loki Sword into his extended arm, severing it and leaving the youngster clutching at his spurting stump with his remaining hand;

another cheeky fellow was trying to stab him in the back with a sword, and the Fire Born turned fast and smashed in his nose with a left-handed punch, then jammed the Loki Sword deep into his side.

Big-ears was still shouting at him, so he jumped forwards and swung the ancient blade, double-handed, and hacked off his shouting head with one blow.

Despite its antiquity the Loki Sword sliced effortlessly through Adalgis's neck and set his big-eared head rolling away across the bloody ground. Another Frank came thundering in towards him on horseback and hurled a javelin at Bjarki's unprotected back from three yards away. Bjarki felt its impact as it punched right through his tatty bearskin and his fine mail and into his left lung.

He plucked out the offending missile, tossed it away and rounded on his Frankish attacker, snarling like a wolf. He stabbed the man's horse through its broad chest with the Loki Sword and, as the dying beast fell, he swarmed all over the Frank, hacking at him with the ancient blade, again and again. The man's arm came free and blood jetted into Bjarki's eyes, momentarily blinding him. He could hear the two bears growling with excitement; Mochta saying: 'Open the meat-bags, open them all up for me, man-child!'

So he tried to oblige the Mother of Bears, his protector and friend, bounding back into the crowd of frightened Franks, where he immediately slashed open a man's belly and thrust the Loki Sword through another man's throat, skipping and dancing through the throng, splashing blood wherever he went. There were friends around him now, he sensed it. There was good old Kynwulf, battling a horseman. So Bjarki cut the horse's off-hind hoof away, and the whole lot, horse and rider, came tumbling down.

Kynwulf hacked at the man's shoulder, then stabbed him through the face.

There was another man he knew near him – a priest, this time. No, no, he was a bishop. And this Christian fellow was an evil man, an enemy. The Rekkr knew him, he could even smell his evil, a stench of marsh gas and rotting meat. The gaudy bishop was yelling at his fellow Franks, ordering them to kill Bjarki and Kynwulf, beckoning them, urging them all to come forwards and fight. A Frankish spearman plunged his blade into Kynwulf's back and the older man roared in anger; the spearman pulled out the bloody steel and plunged it in again. The Rekkr knew this Frank must be punished for that. So he jumped in and cut off the man's leg. But the bishop – Livinus, that was his name – swung hard and caught him a crunching blow on the shoulder with his mace.

Someone punched a sword deep into Bjarki's side and made quite a hole, and while the Rekkr was killing *that* man, chopping away several parts of his head, slicing them off, another fellow came running in and dealt a great blow of some kind to his head from behind. Bjarki found himself suddenly on his knees, looking up at the evil man, this bishop fellow Livinus who was standing in front of him with his spiked mace in his blood-smeared hands. He was now saying something gloatingly, something bad, and insulting, but the Rekkr could only hear the loud buzzing of bees in his ears – and yes, he could taste wild honey.

The bishop was saying something – oh, he liked to talk, this one! Bjarki remembered that. Now he was lifting his spiked mace, and he looked as if he wanted to hit Bjarki with it. Bjarki couldn't have that. No. That wouldn't do.

Faster than a striking snake, Bjarki lunged forwards with his right hand. The Loki Sword flashed out, still seeming to shine brilliantly despite its coating of gore and filth, and the blade plunged deep into Livinus's open belly. Bjarki stood up, the blade still in the bishop's body. With a sideways flick of his wrist, Bjarki ripped the blade out of Livinus's side, spilling out a stinking mess of blood and entrails with the movement, the gory pile splattering across the grass.

Bishop Livinus never spoke again. He fell to his knees, and collapsed on the torn ground, his mouth flapping but no sounds coming out. Bjarki giggled, and turned to find more enemies. But they were running way. That was no fun.

They were running north, off the spur and down the hill towards a little stream, still some scores of them, all a-foot. Bjarki staggered after them, blood streaming from his many, many wounds. He found a spear lying on the ground and picked it up, he would use it as a staff. He was feeling very sleepy now, his legs felt heavy and sluggish. He looked at his body and saw that he was covered with gore, drenched in his fluids and others'. He would need a bandage, maybe more than one, and a nice long sleep. Tor would help him mend. In time. She always helped him do that.

*Did you watch me, Odin?* he thought. *Did you witness all my great deeds?*

He saw his shield-bearers were with him, his boy Erik and the other one.

He suddenly felt very tired. He would just sit down for a moment, just a moment, and rest his legs. He dropped the spear and sat down on the ground, his head hanging loose between his shoulders. Blood began to puddle around him, staining the grass.

Halfdan and Erik were standing over him and looking at him, gawping at him, but his eyes were growing dim, he found he could not see them properly.

He felt the *gandir*'s strength go out of him, leaving him flat, deflated, empty. The buzzing in his ears stopped. The pain began to swell and shimmer. A scarlet bubble of screaming agony growing, expanding around his whole exhausted body. He longed to sleep, to sleep for a very long time.

Erik came forwards: 'Bjarki, did you know? We won – we have won the battle. Widukind is victorious. Can you hear them cheering? Because of you. We won because of you. Look – that is the last of the enemy down there.'

Bjarki just managed to lift his heavy head. He looked down the slope at the valley below where a group of Franks were standing in a loose circle, no more than a handful of them, under the branches of a dwarf beech beside a stream. They looked frightened but still defiant. Widukind was speaking to them, making a speech – how like Widukind! – but whatever the Saxon Wolf was saying, the encircled Franks did not like. Their leader refused, shaking his head.

Widukind shrugged. He turned to his men and gave an order. Bowmen drew back their bows, and loosed. The arrows flew, flicking out, skewering the men under the squat tree, then a dozen Saxon warriors rushed in and cut down those Franks who were still standing. A few moments later, Widukind stood over their fallen bodies. He spat on one corpse. Bjarki could see the dead men's blood seeping, flowing, coming together and trickling down into the stream below. He could not keep his tired eyes open.

'I'm going to sleep,' he said, not sure who he was addressing.

'Don't sleep, Bjarki, you must try to stay awake,' said Erik. The boy was kneeling before the Rekkr and Bjarki could see there were tears in his eyes.

'Erik,' he said. He was now fighting the growing darkness with all his remaining strength. 'Erik, my boy, there is something I must tell you…'

'Don't speak, save your strength,' said Erik.

Halfdan said: 'Go and get help, I'll stay with him. Fetch a healer or a *gothi* or someone.'

'I want to stay with him,' said Erik.

'Go, boy,' said Halfdan. 'You will help him more by bringing a healer.'

Erik looked uncertain.

'Go, you stupid child – and be quick!' said Halfdan. 'Or Bjarki will die.'

Erik got up and raced away up the hillside.

Halfdan crouched beside Bjarki and looked into his face.

'Still there, big man?' he said, grinning. 'Not for much longer, I think.'

Bjarki was able to hold his eyes open just a fraction. He stared at Halfdan.

'I don't think there is any doubt *now*,' said Halfdan, 'about who is heir to the Dane-Mark.' He let out a little laugh. 'I have waited long for this moment. I do not know if the *seithr* worked or not but… it matters not. You will not be in the Middle Realm another hour. And once I return to Ribe, King Siegfried will not live another week.'

'You,' said Bjarki, his voice dry and whispery. 'You are the evil one. You are the one who put the curse-charm in the thatch… to drive me to madness.'

'They all said you were stupid. A big, dumb ox. And they were right. But even I was a little surprised that you never, ever suspected me – not even once.'

Bjarki found the last spark of strength left in him. His right hand reached for his seax, slipping and fumbling for the bone handle at his waist. But Halfdan was far quicker. His hand covered Bjarki's and his youthful strength easily overpowered the spent Rekkr's feeble movements. He effortlessly removed the seax from Bjarki's grasp and held it up, tantalisingly out of reach. 'You want this knife, don't you, big man? You would like to kill me with this blade.'

Halfdan looked up and around. There was no one at all within thirty yards.

'The Bible says thou shalt not kill,' Halfdan said, leaning in close. 'But I think the Lord of Hosts would make an exception for you, demon-worshipper.'

He took the seax blade and pushed it into Bjarki's belly, shoving through the iron links of his mail, then he ripped it out. A trickle of blood followed. Bjarki gave a groan, but made no other sound. He panted a few times, slowly, then he began a faster rhythm, making a horrible wheezing noise in his throat.

'That's it, big man, time to die,' said Halfdan. 'And know this, Rekkr: you are heading off to burn in Hell for the rest of time.'

But Bjarki's panting wheeze continued. 'He... he... he-he-he-he!'

'Are you laughing?' said Halfdan. 'Are you actually laughing... at me? You great blundering idiot – how dare you think you can laugh at *me*?'

'The king... had already... decided... to make you his heir,' panted Bjarki. 'He-he-he!' He was still making the horrible laughing sound. 'There was no... no... no need... to kill me... and now... they, Tor... or someone else... will... kill *you*. Now... you will... never... be... king. He-he-he... huh.'

Halfdan shouted: 'You have no right to laugh at me! Not you, you demon-worshipping imbecile!' Once more he plunged the seax into Bjarki's belly. Then, once more, he slammed it home, punching the blade into bloody mush.

'What are you doing? Stop!' said Erik. 'Halfdan, why did you do that?'

The Rekkr toppled over on to his side, his body relaxed, limbs sprawling on the grass. He let out a long, last breath, and Bjarki Bloodhand was no more.

# Chapter Twenty-six

*'He was the best of us'*

Tor stumbled across the torn and bloody field, exhausted, stepping over the bodies and the wounded alike. She had charged the enemy with Widukind but had barely lifted her own sword even once. The Franks had been overwhelmed, and many had fled even before the Saxon avalanche hit them, some escaping into the First Forest, others trying to make a stand beneath the dwarf beech by the stream at the bottom of the hill.

The ones who had not fled had all been cut down without mercy.

She was looking for Bjarki now. He must be alive, although badly wounded, because she had seen what remained of Bishop Livinus's ruined body, the torso almost severed in half, the purple, red and gold robes soaked in his blood. Her big brother had come through several impossible fights before, particularly after summoning his *gandir*'s power. He was unkillable, she reckoned. Bjarki had been hurt but he had always managed to survive. He must be alive, somewhere, must be.

There were hundreds of dead and wounded scattered all over the battlefield and scores of folk like her wandering about, searching for their friends and comrades. Tor sidestepped a moaning, belly-wounded Frank, who was reaching for her boots, scrabbling at them, begging for water, and kicked something curved and wooden.

She looked down. It was a shield.

The shield was broken. It looked as if it had been trampled by hundreds of horses, she could see the over-lapping prints of their iron shoes, and the snapped pieces of lime-wood board were only held together by scraps of painted leather. She stared at the battered shield; the device painted on the leather was scratched and scuffed by the pounding of many hooves, but it was still just recognisable. The image was of a brown bear on a yellow background. It was Bjarki's shield.

Tor picked it up. The iron boss fell out from the centre of the broken wood and thudded to the hard ground. Tor bent again to pick it up. The cloth padding inside the curved iron bowl of the boss had come loose and, as Tor picked it up, something fell from the material: it was a tiny, crudely carved figurine of a man. The little wooden body had been painted with stripes of brown and yellow. Two small iron nails had been carefully hammered into the centre of the figure's chest and into the top of the head – where a scrap of yellow silk cloth fell from the crown like the drape of long blond hair. As Tor held it in her fingers, it seemed to burn her skin by its touch. She quickly wrapped it up again in the boss-padding cloth and shoved it in the pouch on her belt.

A Saxon archer approached her, walking towards the fortress. His arm was bandaged and hanging in a sling, and Tor called out to him as he came nearer.

'Have you seen my Rekkr brother? Have you seen Bjarki Bloodhand?'

'Someone said he went down the north slope after the last of the Franks. Wounded but still full of blood-lust. He's a fearsome killer, that Fire Born, isn't he? A true *berserkr*,' said the man approvingly. He walked on past Tor, making for the fortress, where she could see and smell the smoke of cooking fires.

Tor went north then, towards the slope, and as she began to descend it she spotted Erik and Halfdan, and a large shape lying sprawled on the bloody grass between them. She began to run.

Then the world took a very strange turn.

As she ran, Tor saw the still, blood-soaked shape – the body of her brother, and surely dead, she had no doubt now in her mind – was beginning to shimmer, like a vision of a cool lake on a hot day. There seemed to be a kind of steam or mist – no, it was thicker than that, a grey smoke coming from his slumped corpse, boiling off him and collecting in the air above Bjarki's body. The tendrils of smoke seemed to twist around themselves, and thicken, become denser, somehow harder, and formed a shape, a humped shape with snout and paws and short legs.

The shape of a bear.

Tor was sprinting now, and her eyes were blurred by her tears, but she was sure that she saw the smoke-bear rise up into the air, hover for an instant over Bjarki's body, and then dive into the middle of the chest of the boy Erik, the smoke or mist or whatever it was funnelling into his body and completely disappearing. She stopped a dozen paces off, cuffed her eyes to wipe away the streaming wetness and, when she looked again, there was no sign of smoke or bear-shapes, but Erik was on his feet.

The boy seemed to be filled with a vast and glowing fury. His face was contorted with rage, twitching, his skin a bright, unnatural red, mouth chewing, and a creamy froth was now appearing at the corners of his lips. Erik reached down at his feet and plucked up a spear, which had been lying right beside her brother's corpse, and before Tor could react, the boy stepped forwards and slammed the point of the spear into the belly of the other shield-bearer Halfdan.

The heir to the throne of the Dane-Mark screamed and curled round the spear tip, and Erik, consumed by his battle-rage, pulled out the spear and struck again. The blade plunged into Halfdan's chest, knocking him down to the turf.

Tor stopped running. She stared in disbelief as Erik, standing tall over the fallen form of Halfdan and holding the shaft in both hands, repeatedly stabbed the point down into his body, six, seven, eight times, the blade hacking and tearing at the fallen man's flesh. Erik punched the spear into his enemy one last time: with a shout of pure fury, he drove the spear right through the lifeless bag of meat that poor Halfdan had become, and deep into the soft ground beneath.

Tor kept her distance, and one hand warily on her seax handle. And after a while Erik released the shaft of the spear, which was still standing bolt upright in Halfdan's body, tottered away a few steps and slumped down on the grass.

He began to weep. Heart-wrenching sobs. And Tor slowly edged closer.

She sat down on the grass a yard or two away from the crying boy, waiting for him to notice her. Eventually, he looked over at Tor from red-rimmed eyes and said: 'Bjarki is dead, Tor. That one, Halfdan, murdered him. I saw it. My father is gone.'

'Not all of him,' said Tor, and she went forwards to embrace her nephew.

–

Erik could only just feel the wiry arms of Tor tighten around him. He was consumed by his grief at Bjarki's death and the tears would not stop falling. But there was also another feeling brewing inside him. Horror at his own brutal actions, yes, disgust at the way he had mutilated Halfdan's body long after the man was dead, certainly. But also something else. Something extraordinary, something that he had never felt before in his whole life. He could feel a being growing inside his own body, inside his beating heart, perhaps, or on his head. He could not exactly tell. But something was there.

'Who are you?' he said silently.

There was no reply.

'What are you?' he said. The being stirred in a dark corner of his heart.

'Tell me what you want with me?'

A voice replied. A mellow voice, pleasant and sweet-toned. 'I would be your *gandr* and your friend,' said the voice. 'As I was *gandr* and friend to your father, my Bear-brother. I would give you all that I gave to him, and more.'

–

They built a pyre on the flat top of the Hohenstein and laid Valtyr Far-Traveller on the left side of Bjarki's body, and Kynwulf the *Felaki* War Chief on his right. And though the night was bright with similar fires and mournful gatherings, hundreds of warriors drew near to stand beside the Troll Stones for a while to watch the flames consume the last of the Fire Born. Before she kissed his cold cheek one last time, Tor had placed the Loki Sword in her brother's grasp and whispered, 'May the Bear guard you, oaf. And may the Bear guide you to the Hall.'

Then Erik passed her the flaming torch.

They stood together, Tor and Erik, united by their grief, with Oddvin and Rask, his face heavily bandaged, and Sambor the Polans, and Captain Mogils, and Joralf the Swordsman and scores of others who had followed Bjarki in life. And when the flames were licking high, dancing up into the night sky, Widukind came over to stand beside her, with Abbio the Crow lurking beyond in his master's shadow.

The Saxon Wolf gripped her shoulder and said, 'He was the best of us, Tor. He gave us victory and it cost his life. He feasts with Odin now, for ever.'

But Tor found that she had no words to say, and only tears to shed.

–

In the morning, they marched north.

Tor, walking beside Erik at the head of the column of surviving Ymirsfjord warriors, said: 'If in doubt, go north. Your father used to say that sometimes.'

'I don't understand,' said Erik.

'It means it is better to have a plan – any plan – than to be snared by indecision. And the North is where we come from and where we must return.'

'No, obviously, Tor, I understand *that*. I meant why are we now retreating north when we have won a great battle and destroyed all the Frankish cavalry?'

*He is not his father*, Tor reminded herself. *And Bjarki did say he was clever.* She pondered her response, selecting which of several truths to tell him.

'Because cavalry, although it can be a very powerful arm, is not everything in warfare. I think we have just proved that point in the Süntel Hills. Although it cost us dearly. We lost more than half our battle strength in that fight. And the second army – the Red Cloak infantry of Count Thierry – is still down there waiting in the Weser Valley. If they come at us, when we are exhausted and weak from the last battle, I do not think we will survive. So we must pull back now, make a tactical retreat north.

'Also, Abbio's spies tell us that Karolus is coming up from Bavaria with all his finest household troops, at speed and full of wrath. The Avar Khan should be thanking us, Erik – the invasion of his land has been called off, so Widukind says.'

She did not mention the other piece of information that Widukind had imparted to her: that his own troops from Westphalia were no longer coming to the Hohenstein. That the commander of that force – of the promised three thousand spearmen from the territory that had once been Widukind's fief – had sent a message saying they were still in the north of Saxony. Still north of Osnabrucke.

'So where are we going?' said Erik.

'Verden – we're going to Verden, to the hall of Jarl Brun, lord of Angria.'

'What happens at Verden?' asked Erik.

'We rest, we recuperate, we rearm. We will be joined by many more Saxon fighters. Our victory should encourage others to join Widukind's rebellion.'

–

It took the column three days to reach Verden, for they did not push themselves hard. Despite the melancholy due to so many deaths, and with so many warriors nursing their wounds as they limped on, the days on the road were joyful and short – easy marches filled with laughter, jests and much drinking around the night-time campfires. The Saxon warriors who had survived the battle, more than a thousand of them, were in a jubilant, almost hectic mood of celebration.

They had taken on the might of the Frankish empire, the cream of their heavy cavalry *scarae*, and had resoundingly triumphed. General Adalgis had been slain by Bjarki, as had Bishop Livinus. So two of their most powerful officials – the King of the Franks' chamberlain *and* his chancellor – had been destroyed in just one battle. Gallo, the Count of the Stables, had also fallen – Jarl Brun, lord of the horse-lands, was particularly pleased about that. And some twenty other high and mighty Frankish noblemen had also lost their lives along with more than a thousand well-trained Black-Cloak horsemen.

The only significant Frankish noble to escape was Worad, the Count of the Palace, and he lived only because he ran from the fight like a cowardly *nithing*.

No wonder the Saxons sang as they tramped northwards to Verden; no wonder Widukind's name was toasted each night around the fires with foaming horns of ale; no wonder Karolus had rushed back from Bavaria, filled with fury.

Tor made camp with the Ymirsfjord folk on the fields outside Jarl Brun's compound at Verden. Widukind invited her to stay with him in the comfortable guest hall next to the longhouse, where Jarl Brun planned to hold a feast, but Tor declined.

She did not wish to celebrate. She held her grief tight to her, like a flame cupped in her hand while the winds of joy blew all around her. And, anyway, she did not plan to spend very much longer in Saxony. She wanted to return to Ribe and speak to Edith, and see the children again, as soon as she could. She wanted to be the one who told Bjarki's widow how her brave husband had died. By her reckoning, she had made her sacrifice for the cause; she had paid her dues in full. She had struck a hard blow for the North, as had Bjarki. Now, she reckoned, it was time for Saxons to stir themselves and fight their own battles. If they wished to be free of the Frankish yoke, it was now within their power.

The people of Saxony agreed with her. Every day a trickle of folk came into Verden to volunteer for Widukind's cause, young men looking to prove their valour; canny older warriors who could see that the Saxon Wolf had the upper hand in this war, and who hoped to befriend him, so they would not be ignored when the spoils were divided up after the ultimate Saxon victory.

However, the army of Westphalia, the promised three thousand spears, still did not arrive. And when Widukind came to seek Tor, at her camp in the field of the Thing-Mound – the place where the Angrians held assemblies – and brought her wine, bread and a brace of smoked river fish to eat, she greeted him coolly.

'I want you to train up a new regiment of Saxon light troops for me from the recruits,' he said, through a mouthful of fish. 'They are to be archers and scouts, mainly, but I want them able to stand in the battle line if called upon.' He beckoned to her to pass him the wine. 'I thought we might call it Tor's Scouts. Unless you think we should honour Bjarki. The Bloodhands, perhaps?'

'I'm not staying,' she said. 'I'm going to the Dane-Mark to see Edith.'

'I am going north myself,' said Widukind. 'If you worry that my sister does not yet know about poor Bjarki's fate, you can rest easy. I have already sent messengers to tell her. And I am going to see Siegfried, anyway – after our success, I want to try to persuade him to give me some more of his spearmen.'

'I will tell Edith myself about Bjarki's death. I need to be with her, so we can feel it together.'

'I can give her the details as easily as you,' said the Saxon Wolf. 'I'll make it sound suitably heroic, if you like. A ring of dead Franks piled at his feet, his bloody, broken sword in his strong right hand... You should stay here and start licking Tor's Scouts into shape. We are going to need them, I assure you. It seems my reinforcements from Westphalia are not able to join us quite yet.'

Tor looked at him across the campfire. She had forgotten how insensitive and even rude he could be when people did not do what he wanted them to do.

'I'm leaving in a few days, when my shoulder feels a little better,' she said. The wound she had taken in the Boar's Snout was paining her badly that night.

'Stay, rest if you need to, I'm sure Joralf or Rask could begin the training.'

'No,' said Tor.

'Then wait a week and come north with me. I'm getting a ship from Treva after the full-moon feast. Come with me; the travelling will pass pleasantly.'

Tor was, in truth, too tired to argue with him, so she agreed that they would travel together to Ribe, after the moon-feast. But when Widukind suggested they spend the night together, she refused, pleading her wound.

'I should not mention this, Tor,' said Widukind, as he was preparing to return to Jarl Brun's hall, 'but I have come to an agreement with the King of the Dane-Mark. I may have good news to share with you soon.' He winked at her.

Tor sat up a little straighter. 'He is going to make you his heir,' she said.

It was not a question.

'I cannot say,' said Widukind – but he grinned at her and winked again.

–

Would-be Saxon warriors were not the only visitors to Verden that summer. Three days after the conversation in the Thing-Mound field with Widukind, Father Alwin came to Jarl Brun's hall. He came into the compound bearing a white flag on a pole, carried by a terrified monk, and announced himself as the official emissary of the King of the Franks.

By chance, Tor just happened to be in the hall when the Angelcynn priest made his entrance. She was playing *tafl* with Joralf, killing time while they waited for a chance to speak to Jarl Brun about borrowing some horses for the journey to Treva.

Father Alwin strolled into the hall as if he had never been away, greeting those he knew and giving Tor a cheery wave when he saw her on the benches.

'I should have you taken outside and hanged by the neck for a traitor,' said Jarl Brun, looking down from his throne at the priest in his dusty brown robe.

The monk who had accompanied Father Alwin made a whimpering sound.

'But then, jarl, you would not hear what I am about to say,' said Father Alwin. Tor found herself admiring the priest – he showed no fear at all. 'And shall we wait till Widukind has been summoned, lord?' he continued. 'Save me repeating myself?'

At that moment, a red-faced Widukind came bursting into the hall and made his way hurriedly to the front. He found himself a stool on the dais next to Jarl Brun.

'I come to you from Karolus,' said Father Alwin, 'who dispatched me knowing of my familiarity with you, thinking it would help me make his case.'

'Why would we trust you – or believe anything you say?' said Widukind. 'You befriended us then betrayed us to our enemies. You are foresworn.'

'I take issue with that,' said Father Alwin mildly. 'I am not foresworn. I made no oaths to you, Duke Widukind, nor to any of you. Furthermore, I never hid my true allegiance at any time. Which was, and remains, solely to the Church of Our Lord Jesus Christ and to His Holiness Pope Adrian in Rome.

'I left you at the Hohenstein when it became clear to me that your war was not with the Franks, as you had claimed – who are not, in any case, my folk – but with Christianity itself. You burned churches, and not just one or two. Many. It was your practice and your policy. I lost count of the number of gleeful Saxons who reported that they had razed some unfortunate House of God, and slaughtered their priests and congregations. I could not stay with you. However, I bear none of you any ill-will, and I hope that the same is true on your part. I made, I hope, some good and true friends during my interesting time in the North. I come to you today as a friend.'

'Just tell us what you have to say,' said Widukind. He sounded very tired.

'But, if we don't like it, we may well hang you afterwards,' said Jarl Brun.

'As I have said, I am the emissary of Karolus, protected by all the usual laws of parley and customs of war,' said Father Alwin. 'And the great king who sent me will punish severely any man who harms me. But that is all by the by, because I fear not death at your hands, for God is with me. He guides my feet.'

'You will not be hanged, nor will you be harmed,' said Widukind. 'Say what you have to say, Father. What message does Karolus intend for our ears?'

'The King of the Franks' message is the same eternal Christian message of forgiveness and mercy. He wishes to parlay with you, to speak with you about your grievances. To understand them and to address them. He wishes to discuss with you a harmonious settlement between the Franks and the Saxons, one that does not explode into calamitous warfare every few years. For too long the blood of both peoples has been needlessly shed. And Karolus says enough is enough. It is time to make a peace, a lasting peace, fair and equitable for both sides. And, to that end, he offers you his forgiveness for the events in the Süntel Hills, and for the churches that you have burnt, and the Christians you have slaughtered, and he promises you mercy, providing that you show contrition for your warlike actions, and swear never to take up arms against him again.'

Father Alwin's words sent the whole hall into an uproar, with every man who heard his words of peace speaking at the same time.

'Silence,' roared Jarl Brun, 'I will have silence in my hall. Be quiet all of you.'

Order restored, Jarl Brun said: 'Tell us exactly what Karolus proposes.'

Father Alwin said: 'If you will submit to the king, come before him without arms, in a spirit of genuine contrition, kneeling before him humbly and admitting to his authority over you, he will offer you forgiveness of your sins and grant you mercy.'

'Where exactly is Karolus at this present time?' asked Widukind.

'He is ten miles south of here, with all his household troops, and with the Red Cloaks of Count Thierry,' said Father Alwin. 'And he is advancing north.'

'And how many shields does he have?' asked Widukind.

'I am told he has a total of fifteen thousand with his host,' said Alwin. 'In all fairness, I must also tell you he has a second army of nine thousand that crossed the river Ems two days ago and is now north of Osnabrucke, and heading towards Verden from the west. Furthermore, there is a cavalry force of five thousand Black Cloaks, coming north from Thuringia. That force has been ordered to attack Orhum, burn it, and then to march on Verden from the east.'

# Chapter Twenty-seven

## Truly terrible news

They gathered in Jarl Brun's chambers, in a small annex to the main hall: Jarl Brun, of course, Widukind, Tor, Jarl Hessi, and a dozen Saxon commanders.

'The priest said Karolus meant to burn Orhum,' said Hessi, whose hall it was.

'Three Frankish armies are coming here to Verden,' said Jarl Brun, 'nearly *thirty thousand* spears. All of them converging here. How many warriors do we have – including all the recruits who have recently come in?'

'Two thousand, two and a half. Maybe as many as three – there hasn't been time to count all the new recruits yet,' said Widukind.

'When will your Westphalians get here. Three thousand more spears, you said,' Jarl Brun barked.

There was a long silence.

'Widukind?' said Brun, even more loudly. 'Where are your Westphalians?'

'They have been delayed,' said the Saxon Wolf. 'But that is not the point, we need to decide now...'

'You might not think it the point, Widukind, but they are threatening to burn my lands, and *my* hall at Orhum. That's the fucking point to me and my Eastphalians!'

'And what do you think they will do when they get here, Hessi?' snapped Jarl Brun. 'Verden is just as much at risk, if not more so, from vengeful Franks.'

'My friends,' said Widukind, 'I have a suggestion. It seems perfectly clear to me what we must do. We must all go back to our own lands, and scatter widely or perhaps disperse into the First Forest; go into hiding for a little while — I am going north to the Dane-Mark on urgent business with my patron King Siegfried. We know that Karolus cannot keep his gigantic armies in the field for long. He cannot hope to feed armies of that size for more than a month or two — thirty thousand men? Ridiculous! If we disperse, we give him no target; then Karolus will be forced to disband his *scarae*. Then, when the moment is right, we reform our ranks, summon all good Saxon men in from the forests and the fields — the Westphalians, too — and strike at a time and place of our choosing!'

'Forgive me, duke,' said Jarl Brun, with a honed-steel edge to his tone, 'but I do not agree with your... suggestion. It is far from clear what we must do. I believe you lost all of your family lands in Westphalia many years ago. Yes? And now it seems that even the Westphalian people do not wish to support you in your attempt to regain these ancestral lands. So *you* personally have nothing left to lose. Nothing. But I and my people cannot disperse — Verden's my home — and thirty thousand Franks are about to fall on it. I won't have a single pure-blood stallion or brood mare left. And Hessi here is about to have an army of Black Cloaks slaughtering his servants, raping his women and putting his hall and his grain barns to the torch.'

'We must all be prepared to make great sacrifices for the cause,' said Widukind. 'I lost my ancestral lands; that I believe was my greatest sacrifice——'

Jarl Brun rudely interrupted him: 'Hey, you've said nothing so far tonight, Tor, what's your counsel?'

Tor shrugged. 'I will be honest with you. I have had my fill of Saxony – and of Saxons. I am going north to the Dane-Mark to grieve with Bjarki's widow. I shall be leaving here in the morning. You should all do what you think best. It is no longer any affair of mine. This I do know – I know that my brother Bjarki was right: the Franks are too powerful to be beaten. Karolus can summon up too many spears for us *ever* to defeat him entirely. We might win a battle, we might capture one fortress, but the Christians will always triumph in the end.'

Widukind glared at her. 'Your heroic brother once said to me, Tor, that as long as one stout-hearted warrior of the North stands with his feet planted on his lands, ready to defend them against all, ready to die for them, then we are not defeated, and we will *never* be defeated. I believe in that idea with all my heart.'

'I loved my brother,' said Tor. 'I grieve for him and I hope that Odin has welcomed him to his Hall, but he did sometimes say some very stupid things.'

Then she turned and walked out of the chamber.

–

Tor left Oddvin and Captain Mogils in charge of the surviving Ymirsfjord warriors – the two hundred and fifty-six of them – and told them to pack up the camp and march north as soon as they could, but she herself set off at first light, with only Joralf, Sambor and Rask for company on the fifty-mile foot-journey to Treva, the hall on the island in the middle of the Elbe River, which was once home to the fallen Guthrum.

She reached the island fortress in five days, after taking the journey slowly, rising late, stopping to make camp in the early afternoon. She hunted when she saw game, and enjoyed the sensation of being among a few trusted people. The shoulder wound pained her but it seemed to be healing. When Tor entered Treva, she found news from the south had outstripped her: truly terrible news.

She sat with a female Nordalbian warrior whom she knew called Styggr at a table in Guthrum's hall and she told her what had occurred in Verden after her departure.

'Your Ymirsfjord people, Tor, all pulled out smartly the day after you left,' said Styggr, 'and a few hundred of Widukind's closest followers went into the First Forest to hide from the Franks. But the rest of the Hohenstein army stayed right there in Verden, and when the Frankish king's vast army came in sight, Jarl Brun and Jarl Hessi sent out gifts and envoys to greet him, with that odd Angelcynn priest arranging it all between the two sides.'

'How do you know all this?'

'I had a lover in Verden, a good man called Karl, who served Jarl Brun in his *hird*. When the rest of my Nordalbians came back here to Treva, I stayed a few days with him. We planned to be wed and he wanted me to meet his father.'

'Go on,' said Tor.

'All the talk was of surrender. Jarl Brun and Jarl Hessi told their people that they would submit to Karolus and seek his forgiveness, and ask his mercy. They said they had surrendered before and Karolus had treated them with decency and honour. He would surely do so again. So, when the King of the Franks came to Verden, they held a big ceremony in the Thing-Mound field – near where you were camping. It was a sight to see. Since I was not part of the surrender – Nordalbia must remain entirely independent of the Franks, the jarl's mother is insistent on that – I watched events from the branches of an oak tree in the hills north of that field, perched up there all day.

'Karolus arrived, surrounded by many of his noblemen and priests, and took up his station on the summit of the Thing-Mound, just as Jarl Brun did when he held his big assemblies there. The King of the Franks wore magnificent robes of scarlet and gold, and he wore an iron crown on his head that flashed with many precious jewels in the sunshine. The men of Brun and Hessi came slowly into the field. They had agreed to lay down their arms and also to be dressed as Christian penitents, in simple linen shirts, bareheaded and shoeless. Their hands were tied in front of them with rope, to symbolise their submission to Karolus.

'The whole field was surrounded by Karolus's troops, Black Cloaks, mostly, but also some of his Red Cloaks too. Many thousands of them – five thousand? I don't know – many more than were at the Hohenstein fight. Their cavalry were stationed behind all those infantry shields. An impressive display. Indeed, it was frightening just how many spears Karolus possessed.'

'How many Saxons submitted to the Franks at this ceremony?' asked Tor.

'It is difficult to say – four hundred, maybe five hundred Saxon warriors. All the warriors in Jarl Brun and Jarl Hessi's *hirds* – their personal followers, but none of the new recruits. My Karl was with them, in a penitent's shirt, his hands tied, just like all the rest...'

The Nordalbian woman stopped and began to weep. Tor put a hand on hers on the table. Tor said: 'Don't speak, if it is too hard. We can talk another day.'

'No,' sniffed Styggr, 'the tale must be told. For their memory, if nothing else.'

She wiped away her tears, lifted her chin and looked Tor in the eyes.

'The Franks executed them,' she said, 'every single one. They killed them all. They made them all kneel, then they chopped off their heads with their long Frankish swords. They had teams of Black Cloaks undertaking the bloody task, and those men soon became drenched in blood, and exhausted, so they brought in fresh gangs of Red Cloaks and the slaughter continued. They killed Jarl Brun first, and Karolus made a clever little speech saying that he forgave them their *sins*, and for making war on him, but Almighty God could not forgive them for their *crimes* against the Church. He said this was true mercy, the mercy of a quick death. Then he said the same thing to Jarl Hessi, who struggled quite a bit, and cursed the king very loudly, calling him a filthy liar and an oath-breaker. But it did not do any good – soon enough, his head was off too. And then they started on the ordinary *hird*-men, and on it went, on and on. And, all the while, Karolus watched and he had one of his clerks read from a scroll, reading aloud something called his Capitularies, which is a list of cruel new laws for Saxony, reminding all the people there of all the crimes that were now punishable by death, which seems to be most of them, so far as I could tell.

'The clerk read the Capitularies out, over and over again, while the Black Cloaks lopped off their heads. My man Karl was one of the last to be killed, and I watched them all until him – the field of the Thing-Mound became a lake of blood, the Red Cloaks splashing as they walked through it. But I stayed and watched my Karl die. He died well, without fear, without pleading for his life. I'm proud of him. After Karl, I'd had enough and I came down from my tree.'

Tor went round the table and embraced Styggr in her arms and they wept.

—

Four days later, around mid-morning, the *Fafnir* docked at Ribeshaven and, within the hour, her three other ships had joined her in the harbour. Tor told the Ymirsfjord warriors who packed the benches of all four vessels to wait for her in the port, and not to go into the town. She would only be gone a day or two, perhaps three, she said, then walked the two miles to Ribe, with only Sambor as a companion, the bald giant stumping along beside her and carrying her gear.

She went to the compound and sought out Edith. Her sister-in-law was sitting at the long table in the centre of the hall, and the moment Tor came in view, she stood and opened her arms. They embraced. Then, both already weeping, they sat side by side on the bench and Tor told her all she knew about Bjarki's final days and hours.

'He loved you so very much, sister,' said Tor, sniffling. 'And I swear that you and the children were in his thoughts right to the very end.'

'It is my fault,' said Edith, bursting into a fresh storm of tears. 'I am to blame. I sent him off to war when all he wanted was to remain in Ymirsfjord. I told him he must think of Lili and Hildar and keep Christians far away from us.'

'You must not blame yourself,' said Tor. 'I, too, pushed him to go to war. I said that he must not shirk the fight. I asked him if he wanted to live for ever.'

'He did not wish that,' said Edith. 'Nor to die in his bed a sick old man.'

'He was Fire Born,' said Tor. 'He was a true warrior. And if we had not persuaded him to fight in Saxony, the gods would have found another way to bring him to the battle. It was his fate. The hour of every man's doom is set, and none can escape it. And, by Odin's will, Bjarki Bloodhand died a good death in battle. No warrior could ask for a better one.'

At that moment, Hildar came toddling over to the women, a stumbling, stomping but determined gait, pursued by the maid tasked with minding him.

'Mumma, Mumma,' said the little boy. 'Want milk. Want my drinkie.'

'He can speak?' asked Tor in amazement. Edith smiled at her proudly.

The servant was hovering over the toddler, the horn of warmed milk in her hand. Hildar extended both his chubby arms to Edith, wanting to be picked up.

'Would you like to feed him?' said Edith.

Tor gaped at the other woman. Then she looked at Hildar. And, without a word, she reached down and picked him up, seating him on her leather-clad knee, and looking into his angelic face. 'Greetings, little man,' she said. 'Know who I am?'

Hildar put out a pudgy but surprisingly powerful hand and seized Tor's nose.

'Want milky,' he said forcefully. '*Milky!*'

'You had better give him this,' said Edith, taking the horn of warm goats' milk from the maid servant and handing it over to Tor.

Tor put the horn to Hildar's lips and cuddled his warm little body against her side as he eagerly drank. 'I have *so* much to learn,' she muttered to herself.

The next morning, once again with Sambor as a companion, Tor went into Ribe and found her way to the great hall. Once inside, she asked for the king and was told by Mundi the steward he was in his bed-chamber, but too ill to see visitors.

After a little persuasion, she was admitted to the chamber, accompanied by Mundi, and Tor was shocked to see the frailty of the king. He was as thin as a stick, and his face was a yellowish grey, with blue bags under his eyes. The room reeked of sickness: the smell of piss and the fusty breath of a dying man.

Siegfried was not alone.

The Duke of Saxony sat by his side, on a small stool, speaking to him in a murmuring tone. When Tor came in the room, he stopped and looked up at her.

'Tor! You must have heard about Verden,' said Widukind.

'I did,' she replied.

'I was telling Siegfried about the blood-soaked barbarity of the Franks – and of that monster Karolus – and explaining to him why he needs to lend me his Danish spearmen so that the Christians can still be resisted. Before it is too late. The war is not over – the slaughter at Verden must be avenged. The spears of the Dane-Mark will make Karolus answer for his crimes, let none doubt it.'

'Has the king declared you his heir yet?'

'What?' said Siegfried, rousing himself on his many pillows, sitting up a little. 'How does this woman know about that? I told you to keep it quiet, Widukind, till I was well enough to make the announcement in my court.'

At that moment Abbio the Crow came into the chamber. He was grasping a big steaming cup. 'I've prepared a possset, highnessss,' he said. 'To make you sssleep.'

He ignored Tor, passed her and came next to the bed, holding out the drink in both hands for the king to take. As Siegfried reached out his stick-like hands for the cup, Tor stepped in, swung her boot and kicked the cup clean out of Abbio's claws.

The big clay cup shattered against the wall of the chamber, staining it yellow.

'What are you playing at Tor?' snarled Widukind. 'How dare you behave like this before the king. Beg his pardon immediately, then get out of here. Abbio, apologies, could you kindly make up another posset for his highness?'

The Crow started to move towards the door, but Sambor blocked his path.

'You. Stay. Here,' he rumbled.

'What is going on, Tor?' said the king. He seemed confused, frightened, like a child. She could see drops of yellow liquid on his pale face. 'Why did you do that?'

'I have something to say to you – indeed, to all the people in this chamber,' Tor said. 'When I have said what I have to say, you may judge if what I did was right.'

She pulled a three-legged stool towards her with her boot, and delved into the leather pouch hanging from her belt. She pulled out the tiny wooden doll, the figure with the nails hammered into its head and chest, and the scrap of yellow silk cloth to indicate hair, and placed it on the stool, so that everyone could clearly see it.

Mundi the steward came a little closer and peered down at the object. He made a noise of disgust in his throat. 'I know what that is,' Mundi said. 'It is evil. A curse-charm. You must burn that thing, Tor. Don't touch it. Just burn it.'

'I found that hidden in the iron boss of Bjarki's shield after the battle at the Hohenstein in the Süntel Hills. It was placed there by Halfdan Siegfriedsson, your son, highness – whom I suspect was secretly a Christian. Some of my men say they saw him making the sign of the cross before the battle. He wanted to kill Bjarki, or drive him mad, which would have been the same thing since, if he had gone Galálar, I would have killed him myself, even though it would have broken my heart.'

'But why?' quavered the king. 'Why would Halfdan seek to kill Bjarki?'

'For the throne,' said Tor. 'Halfdan did not know, highness, that you had decided to make him heir. He was certain you would choose Bjarki over him.'

'But…' said the king.

'Halfdan had been trying to kill Bjarki, or send him mad, for some months before that,' said Tor. 'He was given a curse-charm, similar to this one here, and he placed it in the thatch above Bjarki and Edith's bed in our guest hall. It worked – it made Bjarki very sick. You saw its results, highness, at the reconciliation ceremony. But we found the curse-charm and we burned it. And so Halfdan was forced to find another powerful talisman. And he was supplied with one by the very same *seithr*-working person who had given him the first.'

'Are you sure about this, Tor? It seems most unlikely,' said Widukind.

Tor ignored him. 'The one who gave him the first curse-charm also gave him the second,' she said. 'That person also wished for Bjarki to die. For vengeance. That evil person wished to be revenged on Bjarki for a wrong my brother had done him. He hated him far more than Halfdan did. I believe they made a murderous pact between them. Halfdan would place the first curse-charm above Bjarki's bed, and the second in his shield boss. The other one would do all he could to help Halfdan to become King of the Dane-Mark.'

'This isss prepossterouss,' said Abbio. 'You can have no proof of thisss.'

'He is right, Tor,' said the king. 'You have no proof. You have found a *seithr* charm, a curse-charm, and perhaps it is true Halfdan placed it in Bjarki's shield. He was his shield-bearer, after all, and if he was honest and diligent he would have found the object and disposed of it. But poor Halfdan was killed in the battle. My son cannot explain, he cannot defend himself, nor can he bear witness against anyone else.'

'I may have proof,' said Tor. 'There is another man now, who seeks to be your heir.' And Tor looked directly at Widukind. 'And the king is sick. Again, he is sick. How many times have you been ill, highness, in recent months?'

The chamber froze. The silence was absolute.

'What are you saying, Tor?' said Widukind. His expression was only of mild concern. No sign of guilt. 'Perhaps we should speak of this in private. We should not trouble the king, who needs his rest, with this disturbing nonsense.'

'I think not,' said Tor. 'I will say my piece before the king, and before his steward as a witness. And I say this: your close friend and counsellor Abbio is a *seithr*-worker

– we all know it. I say he made the curse-charm that was put in the rafters above Bjarki's bed. He made the other charm, too, which was put into Bjarki's shield boss. He was in league with Halfdan to make the Frisian the heir to the Dane-Mark. He hated Bjarki for stealing Edith from him. But I think he would have killed Halfdan too, eventually. For his true aim was to make you, Widukind, King of the Danes. And to that end, he would work his evil magic against anyone to benefit his own lord. You ask for proof? I shall provide it.'

Tor pulled her razor-sharp seax from its sheath and walked over to the massive bed. King Siegfried cowered away from her and Mundi shouted out, 'No, Tor! Wait!'

But Tor was already digging in the dry reeds of the chamber's roof, cutting into the thatch and showering the king below with broken sticks, dust and old vegetation.

Tor paused for breath and said: 'If I am right, there will be a little figure of the king hidden up in here. And this curse-charm will have been placed here by Abbio.'

As she said these words, an object dropped from the thatch and fell on the bed.

Mundi stepped forwards and peered at it. It was a tiny wooden doll, almost the twin of the one Tor had placed in the stool, except it had a piece of white cloth to approximate its hair and the figure was striped with red and white paint.

'You,' said the king, pointing a skinny, shaking finger at Abbio the Crow. 'You are the one who put that accursed thing there! You did it, *seithr*-worker!'

# Chapter Twenty-eight

*The first sight of home*

Faster than Tor thought possible, Abbio turned and ran for the door. Sambor grabbed for him but the Crow ducked nimbly under his arms and he was out of the portal and into the hall beyond before debris had ceased falling on the bed.

'Mundi,' said the king, his ancient body given power by his rage, 'get after him now. Summon the guards to find him. Go!' He coughed feebly, but ploughed on. 'Search Ribe, seize him; bring him to me. I shall have the truth out of that foul sorcerer; I will have it cut from his body, if it costs him his life.'

The steward made a fast bow and ran out of the chamber.

Widukind had not moved. He was staring at the doll on the bed. 'I can't believe it,' he said. 'I can't believe Abbio would do such a terrible thing without my knowing.'

'I can't believe that either,' said Tor. 'I think you knew about this, duke. It may even have been your own scheme to start with. You wanted the throne.'

'Tor! How can you say that, after all we have been to each other? After all the love we have shared over the years, all the times we lay side by side...'

'What has that to do with it? We fucked. It doesn't make you innocent.'

'Tor, help me up,' said Siegfried, plucking feebly at his bedding. 'Summon the servants to bring hot water and clothes.' He had a new strength in his voice. 'And I want that thing burnt. You do it, Tor. Watch it burn with your own eyes.'

He pointed a shaking finger at the curse-charm still lying on the blankets.

'As you command, highness,' said Tor.

'I have been abed far too long,' the king said. He looked over at Widukind, an angry gleam in his faded eye. 'I believe I'll rise from my bed and sit on my throne today – and perhaps sit there for a little longer, too.'

They searched Ribe high and low, every house and hut, every inn and ale-house, every forge and forester's lodge, and combed the countryside around the town just as thoroughly, discovering the slumped hut deep in the marshes south of Ribe where Abbio had woven his spells and created his curse-charms.

Siegfried, who seemed to have a new-found vitality now that the foul little doll had been burned, along with the doll from the shield boss, ordered the sorcerer's hut in the marsh be pulled apart and scattered, since it was too damp to burn. Yet there was no sign of Abbio. Folk whispered that he had flown away into the night on his crow wings, using his powerful *seithr* to make his escape.

Widukind, meanwhile, had been kept under armed guard in a storeroom in Ribe and, after three days, when it became clear that the Crow would not be captured, Siegfried summoned Widukind to hear what he had to say for himself.

'I am innocent, highness,' said the Saxon Wolf, smiling confidently. 'I knew nothing of Abbio's plans. I accept he may have been the one to try to harm you with magic. But I had nothing to do with this crime. I am blameless.'

He was standing in the hall, his hands tied with rope, and looking clear-eyed up at the old king in his throne on the dais, flanked by Tor and Mundi.

'Abbio is your creature,' said the king, suddenly sounding very tired. 'He has been in your service many years. He acted maliciously, and treasonably, to hasten my death and ensure that you, his master, would ascend to the throne of the Dane-Mark. How could you know *nothing* about this plot against me?'

'I did not know because Abbio did not tell me. He must have known that I would never countenance such a foul action, so terrible a crime… Tor will attest to my good character. I've been a faithful servant to you, highness. All I have ever tried to do is serve you, and your realm – and the good people of Saxony.'

'The only one you have ever served is yourself,' spat Tor. 'You hoped to rid Saxony of the Franks only so that you could regain your own lands and become the lord of Westphalia once more. And you are prepared to shed the blood or any man or woman in pursuit of that end. You cajoled and manipulated my brother to fight in your wars, and many others like him. And, to my shame, you persuaded me to aid you in that endeavour. And now, when so many of those good folks who believed your lies are dead on the battlefield, you come crawling back to Siegfried, begging for more Danish spears.

'I think you would do *anything*, Widukind, no matter how foul, no matter how wicked, to help achieve your personal ends. I think you would happily betray each and every principle you claim to hold dear. You would kill your friends, your family, your lovers, sacrifice any number of honest folk, even a whole nation, solely for your own advancement. I think that the Westphalians knew that – your people, the ones who know you best. They did not come to your banner with their three thousand spears, they did not come when you called because they recognised your true character. They knew you would carelessly sacrifice their lives to achieve your personal betterment. And, wisely, they chose not to lay down their lives for you and your dreams of glory.

'You ask me to attest to your character, duke – to say you are a faithful servant to King Siegfried? I will not say that. I believe you are a greedy tick affixed to the hide of the North, sucking the blood of its people and growing fat. Were you ever to become King of the Danes, I have no doubt you would embroil this land in war with the Franks, blithely spending the lives of good, honest Danish folk, and any others you might persuade to join you, all in the name of ambition. I find you despicable.'

'You find *me* despicable? Who are you, you ill-tempered Svealand slattern, to call me that? A woman who pretends to be a warrior, a freak, a joke, laughed at behind your back all across the North. You came to me begging for love, oiling into my bed like the pathetic, lonely trull you are. You are nothing. I am a man of high birth and illustrious lineage – my noble ancestors once ruled unchallenged from Frisia to the First Forest. Yes, I do desire to regain my patrimony, of course I would be the lord of Westphalia again. What man of honour would not? And you have the temerity to sneer, after all I have done—'

'Enough,' said the king. 'I have heard enough from you this day, duke.' The old king's sallow face was flushed pink with anger. 'I will not have folk shouting at each other in my presence. I will have decorum. I have heard enough from you both to make a decision. This is my judgement on the matter.'

He paused, breathing heavily. Mundi leaned and whispered in his ear.

'No, no, I do not need to rest, Mundi. I need to resolve this matter – now!'

Siegfried took a few more laboured, wheezing breaths, then finally he said: 'Widukind of Westphalia, so-called Duke of Saxony, this is my judgement: I cannot prove beyond doubt that you were complicit in the attempt to poison me with *seithr*. However, you admit that your servant Abbio was responsible for this grave crime against my person, and you clearly would have been the beneficiary, had Abbio's attempt to extinguish my life been successful. It is my ruling that you are therefore responsible to some degree for his actions. Even if you did not know what your man was attempting to do – which I doubt – you must still accept a part of the blame that falls on him. Therefore, I banish you from the Dane-Mark. You will be escorted to the Dane-Work and released at the border unharmed. However, you are not to set foot within the borders of my kingdom ever again. On pain of death. If you are ever found in the Dane-Mark again, I swear on my throne that I will have you immediately executed.'

'But, highness,' said Widukind; his confidence seemed to have crumbled, and his voice had taken on an ugly whining tone, 'where shall I go to? How shall I live?' He looked distraught, even appalled by King Siegfried's judgement.

'That is not my affair,' said the king. 'Go wherever you will; wherever the gods guide your feet. I care not. Guards, remove the prisoner from my sight.'

'Go to Saxony,' said Tor, 'go to the homeland you claim to love so dearly. But never come near me again. The next time I set eyes on you, I shall kill you.'

They set sail for Ymirsfjord the next day, with Edith and her children, as well as Bjarki's shield-bearer Erik. Tor had spoken bluntly to the boy. 'You are Bjarki's son,' she said. 'He lives on in you. Therefore you are my kin, and all my life I shall ward and watch over you and do whatever I can to help you, wherever you may be. But I think, for now, you should come to live in Ymirsfjord with us... mainly because your spear technique is appalling and it needs a great deal of work or it will bring shame on the family. And, as for your sword skills, atrocious is too kind a word for them!' And she grinned, and punched his arm.

Tor, Erik, Oddvin and Sambor travelled in the *Fafnir*, and the rest of the *vikingir* sailed in the other three ships, helmed respectively by Captain Mogils, Rask and Jorlaf. The weather remained wonderfully fair, not a single cloud in the sky, and the seas were soft and benign. They made good time, and in three days, at dusk, they were rounding the cape and turning the *Fafnir* into the fjord, with the settlement a twinkle of lights some miles to the east, when the Great Horn boomed out on the headland to tell all the folk who had stayed behind at Ymirsfjord that Torfinna Hildarsdottir was returning to her home at last.

She stood in the prow of the *Fafnir*, with her right arm curled loosely around the dragon's head, as the soft night fell on the high cliffs on either side, and the ship surged up the fjord towards the village, simply savouring the first glimpse of her home. Her left hand rested gently on her lower belly. She could feel nothing yet, her body had not begun to swell, but Edith had told her that she could not expect much change in the first three months. Yet she knew beyond doubt that *he* was in there. Her child. Her monthly blood had not come in its season but, more than that, it was a certainty in her heart, in her very bones. A kind of glowing warmth in her core. She knew.

Widukind's seed had found purchase in her belly.

She thought of the last time she had been with him, on the eve of the battle, with Bjarki sick and sleeping in his bed, and she recognised that although she had known, even then, what kind of man Widukind was – how self-serving and how shallow, and how ruthlessly he spent the lives of others – she had still lain with him in lust, and taken his essence into her womb.

Should she be troubled by that? By the taint of his seed?

No. No, she should not. Bad fathers do not make bad children. Her own father had been a monster and she and Bjarki had grown up decent and kind.

Bjarki. How she missed her foolish, brave, long-suffering brother. She would ask Edith to make a blood sacrifice in the little temple in Ymirsfjord – not a living person – Bjarki would have hated that – just a chicken or a goat, something for Odin, something to persuade the All-Father to greet her brother with a hero's welcome in his Hall of the Slain. And while her brother was feasting and fighting in Odin's realm until the very end of time and the great battle of Ragnarok, Tor would remain at Ymirsfjord, caring for her brother's widow and his children, looking out for Edith and Lili, Hildar and Erik, and perhaps in a few months' time, her own child, too.

And one day, if the gods were kind, years from now, she would join her brother, her beloved oaf, at the feast of heroes and take her place beside him once more.

–

Bjarki was walking. He was walking in a beautiful meadow with a babbling stream running down the middle and thick woodland in either rising flank. He thought he was somewhere in the First Forest, for this place looked familiar to his eyes. He felt calm and happy, content to be moving, all his limbs working well, his body fully healed.

He was striding along at a fine pace, full of youth and strength, a kindly sun shining on him, not too hot, pleasantly warm, and a breeze wafting the smell of wildflowers into his nostrils. Wood anemone, thrift, columbine and kingcup. He looked left and saw a great red stag in the fringes of the woodland, a beautiful creature, with spreading horns and huge liquid eyes. It snorted as it saw him, ducking its head up and down as if nodding to him, a greeting or acknowledgement, then it turned and galloped away, disappearing into the trees.

He was feeling an ease of spirit, a comfortableness, he had not felt in many years. He strode on down the meadow-valley. The springy turf under his boots, the gentle wind on his cheek, the feeling of progress as he walked. It was a kind of bliss, he realised. A perfect hour, in a perfect day.

Ahead of him he saw a hall, a very fine hall, built on a raised mound above the rest of the green valley, a timber-built place but enormously long and many storeys high.

The gable ends were decorated with the skulls of bears and boars and wolves, gleaming with black and red paint. The tiles of the roof were made from gold and silver and dazzled in the evening sunshine. It looked like the home of a mighty king, a great lord of men, and Bjarki, who was beginning to feel a little tired, wondered if he might be welcomed in this palace, allowed to spend the night, whether his name would be known by the master of the house.

As he drew closer, he saw a door in the front of the building was open, and he could see the glow of firelight inside, hear the sounds of merriment coming from within. There was something beside the open door. A large, dark object.

Bjarki quickened his stride, eager to reach this grand house before nightfall, and he saw that the dark object by the door was, in fact, a bear – a huge she-bear, black as midnight, but with fiery eyes, sitting on her haunches and patiently watching him approach. The she-bear was very old, Bjarki could see now. White hair at the muzzle.

'I greet you, Mochta, Mother of Bears,' said Bjarki stopping short of the door.

'I greet you too, man-child,' said the Bear. 'I have been waiting for you.'

'Why? Why were you waiting for me?'

'So that we might go into the Hall together, as is only fitting and right.'

'I do not understand,' said Bjarki. 'Where am I? Whose fine hall is this?'

'I told you once before, man-child. We are joined inseparably. We will be together, you and I, for ever – for we are both one and the same being. Our twin spirits are fused into one entity. Man and bear, bear and man:

*berserkr*. And I believe you know very well whose hall this is.'

'Where is Garm?' said Bjarki. 'Where is your beloved child, Mochta?'

'My child is with your child. He would remain in the Middle-Realm.'

'Am I dead, then? Are you dead, too?'

'We are where we are. Let us go into the feast together, man-child.'

'Why are you doing this, Mochta? Did you accept death for my sake?'

'As I said: we are one, you and I. Besides… I am told there will be fighting.'

# Epilogue

*Christmas, AD 785 – three years later*

The Archbishop of Saxony opened the door of the private chapel off the nave of the great church of St Mary at Attingny, in the heart of the territory of Austrasia in the Kingdom of the Franks and slipped inside. He waited respectfully by the door for the tall, sumptuously dressed man with red-gold hair and a great beak of a nose, who was kneeling at the altar, to finish his devotions.

When the praying man finally looked round at him, the archbishop said: 'All is prepared for the ceremony, highness, all that is required is your presence.'

Karolus Magnus got slowly to his feet, and went over to the archbishop, who was also his chaplain and chancellor, putting a friendly hand on his arm. 'Are we doing the right thing today, Alwin? I sometimes wonder. It would have been much simpler to have given the order to have their damned Saxon heads cut off the day they came crawling in to us, like we did to the treacherous pagans at Verden.'

'No, sire. I gave them my solemn word, my sacred vow, that they would not be harmed. I would not wish to break it, even for you. You've said yourself, many times, that every man deserves one chance at redemption but no man…'

'No man should be granted two,' said Karolus. 'Yes, I used to say that.'

'And you are right to say it, highness. This is a very different situation to that in Verden three years ago. Jarl Brun and Jarl Hessi and their rebellious Saxon rabble had submitted to you once before, as you will surely remember, and they had *already* been given their one chance at redemption, their one chance to become good and true Christians. Yet they rejected Christ, rejected their vows and rebelled again. They began burning our churches and slaughtering our folk. You said to me then that they should be denied a second chance, despite my pleading, and you were quite right. But with these two, the ones in the church who now await your presence, it is quite different. These two men have never submitted before. They are not oath-breakers. They should be given their one chance, like any other soul on Earth. If they rebel, if they revert to their evil pagan ways, we will have no mercy on them – neither will God.'

'You are wise, my friend, beyond your years,' said Karolus. 'Do you also think it right and fair that we make this Saxon fellow Count of Westphalia, the title he specifically demanded?'

'I think he would not be here today without that reward,' said Archbishop Alwin. 'He has longed all his life to regain his family lands. More than anything else. He told me so himself, once, some years ago, in the Dane-Mark. Do not fear, highness, I am certain we are making the right choices this day. The new Count of Westphalia will surely govern his Saxon lands in your name, and according to your good Christian laws and decrees and, God willing, we shall have peace in Saxony at last. That is what I have worked for, and prayed for, all these many years. That the ancient homeland of my people will know peace and the love of Jesus Christ, and that all Christians in that country shall thrive and prosper, and live lives of humility and faith in the worship of Almighty God.'

'Amen. Then let us perform this most holy of ceremonies, Alwin,' said Karolus, 'and make a Christian lamb out of the man who was the Saxon Wolf.'

The two men went out of the chapel together and into the body of the church. A choir of monks was chanting psalms, and there were a dozen Frankish nobles and priests standing by the beautifully painted walls. Karolus and his new archbishop, the man once known as Father Alwin, walked towards the rear of the church where two figures were kneeling humbly in plain linen shifts beside the stone font. Both men were very thin, worn down by much travel and trouble, by years running and hiding from the vengeance of their many enemies.

When the haunting singing had stopped, Archbishop Alwin smiled at the two men and said: 'Do you, Theodoric, son of Theodoric, known as Widukind, Count of Westphalia, promise to renounce the Devil and all his evil works?'

Widukind replied, 'I do renounce the Devil and all his evil works.'

Then the archbishop said: 'And do you Abbio, servant and companion of Theodoric, son of Theodoric, also renounce the Devil and all his evil works?'

Abbio said: 'I do renouncccce the Devil and all his evil workssss.'

'Then with his highness, Karolus, King of Francia, standing duty as your godfather, and in the presence of these good monks and this congregation in the House of God, I shall now baptise you into the Faith of Our Lord Jesus Christ.'

# Historical Note

## Widukind

Widukind of Westphalia is a historical character. And while I have made him out to be a vain, self-serving, even treacherous villain in this novel, a man who is happy to sacrifice his friends and compatriots to advance his own interests, I think the real man was probably rather a heroic individual, and certainly he remains something of a folk hero in Germany today, a similar figure in stature to our own Robin Hood.

Time and again, Widukind raised the Saxons in rebellion against the Franks, defending their pagan way of life against more powerful and far better organised invaders, who sought to convert his people to Christianity at the point of the sword.

He was a Saxon aristocrat, probably called Theodoric, and the name Widukind, clearly a *nom de guerre*, means 'Child of the Woods', which is a kenning for wolf. This is why he is referred to as the Saxon Wolf in this and previous novels. His nickname probably came about because he made good military use of the thick forests of homeland, in which wolves and bears still abounded. His tactics were those common in asymmetrical warfare: ambushes, hit-and-run raids and, most of the time, a strict avoidance of full-pitched battle (the victory at the Süntel Hills was a rare exception). As well as possessing many military virtues, he must have been extremely charismatic: he persuaded his people to fight and die for his cause, when it must have seemed doomed, again and again, so I have imagined him as a great orator, a Winston Churchill, if you like, a dazzling public speaker.

In truth, I had to imagine a great deal about Widukind, because historical facts about him are scant. He appears a few times in the *Royal Frankish Annals* (*RFA*), one of the few historical sources for the period, as a leader of the rebel Saxons and one who for many years refused to submit to Charlemagne (Karolus in these novels). Jarls Brun and Hessi, incidentally, are also named in the *RFA* as leaders of the Saxon rebels from, respectively, Angria and Eastphalia, and they both submitted to the Franks a decade before the Saxon Wolf. Widukind, we are told, often sought refuge with King Sigfrid (Siegfried) of the Dane-Mark, who was his staunch ally. Indeed, it seems Widukind was constantly popping in and out of the Dane-Mark. His *modus operandi* was to go south into Saxony, raise a rebellion, attack Frankish fortresses, slaughter the occupying troops, cause havoc then, when things got too hot for him, flee back into the Dane-Mark, safely beyond the reach of Charlemagne's vengeance.

I believe Widukind fully deserves his place in the global pantheon of outlaw heroes. However, his life as a wanted man and hero-on-the-run came to an ignominious end in AD 785, when he finally surrendered to Charlemagne and was baptised a Christian at the church in Attigny – a town now in north-east France – along with his most loyal follower Abbo or Abbi (Abbio in my novels). I should admit here that there is no evidence that Abbio was a creepy sorcerer who wielded *seithr*, although the north European pagans did practise 'magic' routinely, and preserved skulls from the Viking era have been found with the teeth filed into points.

Perhaps strangely, it was Widukind's conversion to Christianity that made me decide to depict him as a villain. When writing historical fiction, you are obliged to follow the history whenever possible and, since we know Widukind was baptised at Christmas in AD 785, I felt I had to work this truth into my story. But I had a problem. In my fiction, Widukind is advocating heroic resistance to the Franks one day, and historically, the next day, he is submitting meekly to baptism. How could I explain this *volte-face*? I tried to imagine what the Saxon Wolf would desire most of all in his heart of hearts – apart from the liberation of his homeland, of course, which did not happen. I decided the Saxon Wolf would probably want what any deposed aristocrat desperately wants – the full restoration of his lands and titles.

Since it was Charlemagne's policy to reward the Saxon rebel lords who submitted to him by appointing them as his regional counts (*comes*) and restoring them to their fiefs under his authority, the ending I came up with seemed entirely reasonable. There is even a suggestion in a biography of Saint Ludger, a missionary to the Saxons, that Widukind was appointed to a high administrative role in Saxony after his conversion, which helped persuade me to shape the ending as I did.

I also suspect that Widukind fought the Franks all those years partly out of a desire to regain his 'rightful' aristocratic place in the world. He tried to liberate Saxony from them many, many times – and completely failed. So, at his wits' end, he agreed to convert to the faith of his enemies to achieve that long-held ambition.

The Saxon victory in the Süntel Hills, near the Hohenstein, about eight miles north of modern-day Hamelin, was Widukind's greatest triumph. Indeed, it was the only major victory the Saxons enjoyed over their far more powerful enemies in more than thirty years of warfare. The site of the battle, chosen with great care by Widukind, is as I have described it – a long spur of high land with steep, almost impassible slopes to the north, south and west. At the western end is the Hohenstein rock formation, now a local beauty spot. The only possible avenue of attack was from the east through the thick forest, which made the perfect cover for an ambush. Widukind relied on the arrogance and over-confidence of Adalgis, Charlemagne's chamberlain and the commander of his heavy cavalry. Also present were two other cavalry commanders, Gallo, the Count of the Stables, and Worad, the Count of the Palace. (Bishop Livinus is an invented character based, like Father Alwin, on the many English missionaries who came over to Francia and tried to convert the pagan Saxons to the True Faith.)

Widukind lured the Frankish heavy cavalry into an unsupported attack on his formed infantry. He deliberately brought his men out of the makeshift fortress they had constructed near the Hohenstein to tempt the fool-hardy *cabellarii* under Adalgis into attacking him. Adalgis was killed, as was Gallo – and Worad only saved himself by fleeing the battlefield. The *RFA* says this: 'The loss to the Franks was greater than numbers alone, however, for two of the legates, Adalgis and Gallo, four counts and as many as twenty other men of distinction and nobility were killed, as well as others who were in their followings and chose to die at their sides rather than survive them.'

It should be noted that the *Royal Frankish Annals* were written by Christian monks and Charlemagne was their patron, so they can hardly be considered impartial. What is clear though from the *RFA* entry, is that the defeat of thousands of elite, highly trained Frankish heavy cavalry troops by a small ragtag army of rebel infantry was a serious humiliation for Charlemagne. And the description of loyal Frankish followers nobly dying beside their commanders is, I think, an early attempt by the *RFA* at spinning some very bad news indeed.

### The massacre at Verden

It is very difficult to say how many people took part in a historical battle or event. Actually, it is extremely hard to establish numbers of people who participate in mass actions even in the twenty-first century. In my journalist days, I remember reporting on a large pro-Taliban demonstration in Peshawar, north-west Pakistan, in late 2000, just after the 9/11 terrorist attack on the Twin Towers. I ran alongside the huge crowds of Afghans and Pakistanis trying to get comments and arrange impromptu interviews with their leaders. Afterwards I conferred with fellow foreign correspondents, and we tried to estimate exactly how many people had taken part in that day's demo. Our guesses ranged from two to ten thousand; one French guy suggested fifty thousand.

The point is, it is very difficult to tell. The *RFA* says that at Verden, after the surrender of large numbers of rebel Saxons to Charlemagne, 4,500 Saxon warriors were summarily beheaded as a warning to the others:

> '...the Lord King Charles rushed to the place
> with all the Franks that he could gather on short

> notice and advanced to where the Aller flows into
> the Weser [i.e., at Verden]. Then all the Saxons
> came together again, submitted to the authority of
> the Lord King, and surrendered the evildoers who
> were chiefly responsible for this revolt to be put to
> death – four thousand and five hundred of them.
> This sentence was carried out. Widukind was not
> among them since he had fled to Nordmannia [the
> Dane-Mark]. When he had finished this business,
> the Lord King returned to Francia.'

The problem is, I don't believe it. I don't believe that more than four thousand Saxon warriors would allow themselves to be meekly beheaded like that. And think of the sheer, hard, physical labour involved in all that slaughter. Since the *RFA*, penned by Frankish monks, is our only source on the massacre at Verden in AD 782, I don't think we have to accept the numbers involved as gospel (yes, pun intended).

Janet L. Nelson, author of the magisterial biography of Charlemagne, *King and Emperor*, writes, '…the figure of 4,500 is suspiciously large, and its tidiness increases suspicion. It could well have resulted from a scribe mistakenly (or through deliberate inflation) adding a zero.' Clearly a terrible massacre took place at Verden, but I suspect only a few hundred people, perhaps about 450, were actually beheaded. Enough to send a strong message to anyone in Saxony who was tempted in future to defy Frankish hegemony. And the message was received in Saxony, loud and clear, because a period of relative peace followed this barbaric act of royal retribution.

The Grand Assembly was not the unique event that I have suggested it to be. Frankish kings held these kinds of mass assemblies, sometimes called a Marchfeld, almost every year. They were originally held in March – hence the name – but later on they took place in May, which is when my Grand Assembly took place at Lippspringe (at the 'source of the River Lippe', says the *RFA*). All the king's important vassals from across his empire were duly summoned to a chosen place and a great deal of military, legal, religious and administrative business was transacted over several days, perhaps even extending into weeks. I imagine it as a cross between a parliament, a music festival and a military tattoo, held just before the campaigning season began.

Foreign delegations were invited to these great assemblies from the nations surrounding the Frankish lands, with both allies and potential enemies attending, and their ambassadors enjoying a golden opportunity to speak personally with the king. For example, at the assembly in AD 782, a delegation from the Avar Khaganate (in what is now Hungary) was received by Charlemagne. Since he was then making plans to invade their lands, it seems likely that they were trying to prevent this from happening. There was also a delegation at Lippspringe from the Dane-Mark, which was headed by a man called Halfdan, which means 'half-Dane'. This is all we know about this historical character – that he headed the Danish delegation to the Grand Assembly in Lippspringe – and after that he disappears from history. But he must have been a high-ranking member of the Danish court, and a relative of King Sigfrid seems likely. His illegitimate son and heir seemed plausible to me.

The rebellion led by Widukind in AD 782 was most likely sparked by the announcement by Charlemagne at Lippspringe of the raft of new laws – known as Capitularies, from the Latin title of the document *Capitulatio de partibus Saxoniae* or the 'Ordinances concerning Saxony' – pertaining to his newly conquered territory. And they were every bit as draconian as I have described in this novel. Indeed, I took some of them word for (translated) word and put them into Karolus's mouth. For example, 'If any one of the race of the Saxons hereafter concealed among them shall have wished to hide himself unbaptised, and shall have scorned to come to baptism and shall have wished to remain a pagan, let him be punished by death'.

From then on, to eat meat during Lent, to make an offering at a pagan shrine, to cremate your dead, to damage a church or injure a missionary, monk or priest in Saxony was punishable by death. Charlemagne had, in effect, made being a practising pagan a capital offence. Some historians also suggest that it may have been an attempt at suppressing local identity – a way of turning bad Saxons into good Franks.

No wonder the Saxons rebelled, despite the overwhelming odds against them. And although this rebellion ultimately failed, and the punishment at Verden was severe, the pagans were not discouraged for good. The Saxon wars, which began in 772, continued smouldering away until 804. Indeed, smaller Saxon rebellions against their Frankish overlords continued even after the death of Charlemagne in 814.

However, Bjarki and Tor will play no further part in them. I have hugely enjoyed writing about my two fictional heroes over these past five Fire Born novels; they now feel like real people to me. Almost like members of my family. But enough is enough, and it is time to turn the page on this chapter of my writing career and move on to the many other projects that now clamour for my attention. I hope you have enjoyed reading about their blood-soaked adventures as much as I have writing them. And may the Bear guard you, dear reader, wherever your journey takes you next.

# Acknowledgements

For those who want to read more about this fascinating period of history, I thoroughly recommend Janet L. Nelson's superb biography of Charlemagne, *King and Emperor*. It was my guide to some of the trickier political aspects of Frankish society, as well as giving me a greater understanding of the long wars between the Christian Franks and their pagan Saxon neighbours. But, for the granular details of the Battle of the Süntel Hills, I made extensive use of David Nicolle's excellent and very accessible book, *The Conquest of Saxony AD 782–785*, which is an Osprey publication, beautifully illustrated by Graham Turner, and filled with many explanatory maps and diagrams.

I would like to take this opportunity to thank my agent Ian Drury of Sheil Land Associates for his wisdom and guidance over the years, and for introducing me to the excellent team at Canelo, who have published all five of my Fire Born novels. Craig Lye, my brilliant editor, has been a joy to work with over the years. He is forensic in his analysis of any novel's weak points, but also appreciative of my efforts, while being firm in his views. I look forward very much to continuing to work with him on other projects.

Lastly, I would like to thank my lovely wife, Mary, who dextrously keeps all the household/business plates spinning in the air, which allows me the privilege of being able to ignore all that background noise and spend all my days contentedly writing.

Angus Donald
Tonbridge, June 2024